About Richard Cohen's previous work:

On *Domestic Tranqulity*:

"*Domestic Tranquility* is a beautiful first novel—built on observations so minutely and constantly intelligent that one feels as intellectually engaged by it as emotionally seized." —Sheila Weller, *The New York Time Book Review*

"A deliberative, painstaking, yet warmly empathic first novel which explores the artifices of domestic tranquility and the fearfulisolation, hostility, and anguished love beneath." —*Kirkus Reviews*

"*Domestic Tranquility* is a devastatingly convincing anatomy of a family.... Richard Cohen reaches deeply into the hearts of his three characters, illumninating with clarity the foibles, flaws, darksides, and resilience of us all." —Gail Tansill Lambert, *Best Sellers*

"Cohen is a good chronicler of everyday life. He has the gift of showing the hilarious and the horrible in our mundane activities. In a gentle yet powerful way, he gets inside a small, important moment and unfolds the meaning of that moment for all to see.... He writes about loving and caring and hurting with wisdom and wit to belie his years." —Mary Hart Murray, *The Fort Worth Star-Telegram*

On *Say You Want Me*:

"It is to Mr. Cohen's credit that he steers clear of a predictable conclusion....[He] is skillful at detailing the nuances of the bond between Brendan and his son." —*The New York Time Book Review*

"[This is a] poignantly imagined, perfectly realized novel of two-career family life in the 1980's....The book explodes in beauty and pain when things that must change mix and ignite with the things that can't....I started reading it one night and read straight through until 4 a.m." —Jack Miles, *The Los Angeles Times*

"Cohen is a writer as intuitive as he is stylish....Cohen also has an uncanny ear for the ways in which men and women try, withvarying degrees of success, to talk to one another." —*Chicago Tribune*

"A dazzling new novel....Couldn't be more up-to-the-moment." —*New Woman*

"What is amazing about Richard Cohen's handling of a marriage on the downslide, a new love affair, and the complexities of parenthood is that his voice always rings true, without fail.... He's a spectacular writer, a distinctive voice to be heard." —Ruth Pollack Coughlin, *The Detroit News*

Pronoun Music

stories

Pronoun Music

s t o r i e s

Richard Cohen

Cover Art: Painting by Dan Ramirez, *Song/Song: Red's Spark*
Design & Composition by Shannon Gentry

Printed in the United States of America

Library of Congress Catalog Card Number: 00101773
Cohen, Richard
Pronoun Music / Richard Cohen
ISBN: 0-929355-03-3

Published by Pleasure Boat Studio
8630 Wardwell Road
Bainbridge Island • WA 98110-1589
Tel/Fax: 888.810.5308
E-mail: pleasboat@aol.com
URL: http://www.pbstudio.com

First Printing

Some of the stories in this book have appeared in
DoubleTake, Michigan Quarterly Review,
Beloit Fiction Journal, and *Passages North*

for Susan, Eric, & Nick

Contents

Theme from a Summer Place

On an August night some thirty-five or forty years ago, the outskirts of New York City lay ambivalently awaiting annihilation. Missiles in Siberia were aimed directly at them—at them, who never even went into the city to shop anymore! The missiles were governed by crude Russian systems that were almost guaranteed to go haywire, to mistake a flock of geese for an American attack or simply to let loose at the command of a loony, embittered general who had drunk too much vodka. The outer boroughs, the suburbs, and the scrubby hills and dairy towns that were called "the country" tossed their blankets and sweated their sheets in anticipation of their demon lover. They had seen *On the Beach,* where a star-studded cast huddled in the last uncontaminated corner of Australia to beg another week or two from the fallout winds. They could scare themselves bolt upright at will by remembering the ending of *Fail-Safe,* a montage of New York scenes—perhaps even one's own neighborhood—where people play stickball and people carry groceries and pigeons flap skyward, and then the screen whites out, the bomb has fallen, and none of the ballplayers or grocery carriers or pigeons even knows that they have been instantaneously vaporized.

Cheryl Sadowsky, who hated her name and could hardly wait to change it to Ariel or Ariadne or something, had just scared herself bolt upright like that. She sat listening for the drone of MIG bombers coming in low across the drab grandeur of Canadian forests toward this obscure little bungalow colony in the Catskills. The steel frame of her cot quivered under her. She was a hundred and four miles north of the city, and she had read that you were in danger within a hundred miles. The first twenty miles, say all of Manhattan and the Bronx, were of course ground zero, they'd be obliterated in the first explosion, and the suburbs, up to fifty miles away, in the firestorm immediately afterward. It was the next ring, the outer suburbs and the lingering old-fashioned little towns, that would be most unfairly treated: they would die retching, hair falling out and skin blotched purple, within weeks. But could you really be safe at a hundred and four miles? She'd doubted it ever since this morning, when she'd first glimpsed the saggy screens and mossy walls of the cabins and caught the scent from the dining hall of meatballs braised with garlic and paprika.

Her parents, a brittle and arthritic pair, had picked their way down the gravel hill to the rental office without offering each other an arm, her father fuming pedantically, "If you don't want to stay here, we'll go." And her mother, "Go where? Who's going to have a vacancy on a Friday afternoon—a chicken coop?" And, as they'd been doing for at least as long as she'd known them, they ended up having planned themselves into a misery they couldn't back out of.

They were still at it tonight. Above the crickets, on the warm breeze that carried a Petula Clark song from the casino, she heard it:

"It's exactly like I've always said, one drink and you start getting hostile."

"Drop dead," her father told her mother. "Leave me alone."

Everyone at this colony is hearing this, Cheryl thought. Wafting through their open windows on our first night here, like the clarinet in "Stranger on the Shore." Tomorrow at breakfast I'll know what's behind the nods, the smiles. Just like at all the other summer places we haven't visited a second time.

Strap-heeled sandals slapped wooden stairs. "Ow, these goddamn mosquitoes...."

"Will you lower your voice?"

"I will not lower my voice after the way you were speaking to me—"

"How?" her father said. "Speaking to you how? Not angelically like you speak to me?"

"—in front of a casino full of people we're going to be spending the next two weeks with—"

"Yes, which you might keep in mind."

"—And *you* can drop dead too, with your sarcastic interruptions, you haven't let me express a complete thought—"

"Then we can both drop dead."

"That's the one thing we agree on. Why don't you drive us off a bridge like you threatened to yesterday? Why don't they drop the bomb, at least? Why doesn't the bomb fall tonight, it would be less painful, I swear, than being called an idiot in front of a casino full of people I've just met."

What about me, Cheryl thought, do you want the bomb to fall on me too? Well, but I can escape. This far north, we'd have at least half an hour's warning, maybe an hour. I'll take the car keys from his pants pocket and head for the Adirondacks, learning to drive as I go. Should I give them a ride with me? Please, don't let me be so sentimental that I take them with me.

"Look at you," her mother was saying. "The man who was born the same day as Kennedy. Why didn't you *die* the same day as Kennedy? Why did they kill him and not you?"

"Because I'm not worth killing."

Should she shout at them: Quiet down, don't you know you have a thirteen-year-old daughter trying to sleep? But with practiced timing, they stopped short of the brink, short of involving her—short of hearing her. Somehow they remembered how to creak open the screen door and shuffle to their shared bedroom. Somehow they never forgot how to march through the days as required. From sheer stubbornness they stopped answering each other, and from sheer fatigue began to snore.

Next morning, her mother was sitting at the formica table in the dining alcove doing nothing: no cards, no magazine, just her perpetual look of suspecting she'd been been left behind. She was a small, gaunt, olive-skinned woman with cracked lips and a wrinkled forehead, who wore the absence of makeup like a badge of honesty, of life's realities that you could do nothing about. Anxiously she ran stiff, short fingers through long, wavy, unpinned chestnut hair that had often been called beautiful, her best feature; and intermittently she stopped and glared in distaste at the tented-out strands, as if wondering when they would fail her. She had a repertoire of sour, grim, angry, and resentful expressions which she brought out unprovoked for the smallest occasions—ordering at a restaurant, paying a cashier—and of which she was certainly unaware, for if she had been aware of them, she would have been ashamed. When she noticed Cheryl watching, she dropped the hair from her fingers as if she'd done something wrong and didn't know how to explain it.

"Your father's trying out the pool. If you go down there, give him his cigarette lighter, he forgot it. To give him such a pleasure I'm not going down there myself."

Why did she assume that the first thing Cheryl longed to do when she woke up in the morning was see her father? She acted as if Cheryl was on her father's side, even though Cheryl kept telling her it wasn't so. She tried not to take any side, ever. But whenever she tried to tell her that, her mother took it as an attack.

As Cheryl started for the screen door, her mother pointed an instructing finger. "Listen to me. I know you don't want to hear it, but I'm your mother and I'm telling you, if the time ever comes when you want to get married, don't do it because when he was away you missed him. How do you feel when he's *there,* that's the important thing. Don't let someone talk you into thinking you love each other. And don't be too impressed if he's nice at first. After a few months it's a whole different story."

"Okay," she said, and hurried down the porch steps.

It took her several moments to feel shaken by her mother's lecture, and the feeling only lasted a second as she went on to explore the day. She strolled uphill through the resort, checking the facilities, ascertaining her coordinates. A pretty summer day—check. Cottages strung in a semicircle around a rocky, unmown common—check. Tennis court up here, swimming pool audible downslope—check. Main buildings—office, rec room—check. Dirt path leading probably to a woods or a pond—no time to check that.

No time to check it, because walking downhill toward her from his own parents' cottage was the being whom she had already come to think of, since last night, as That Boy. She and That Boy had stared at each other all evening, not boldly but with horrified embarrassed powerlessness to stop, as he watched the Republican convention on television and she, at the other end of the room, beat the adults at Scrabble. Now they were staring at each other as they approached—no, they dropped their eyes—no, they stared again—well, which was it to be? He was widening his path, but then, just as he was about to skirt around her, he turned and looked at her, not quite as if to ask, Who are you and what are you doing here? No, that commonplace and fumbling inquiry was shoved aside by something urgent—was her blouse on inside out? He gawked at her, bugeyed, in a way that seemed weirdly to have nothing to do with her. He was black-haired, tall, ascetically skinny, but wide-boned and knobby-wristed, his face a long, thin triangle that ended in incongruously puffy lips and a pointy chin. In his silence, he seemed to hold back till the last possible moment some trembling secret; he seemed about to burst with some atrocious boyish pride. And then, hoarse-voiced from the overgrown adam's apple, it came out:

"I give you Barry Morris Goldwater, ladies and gentlemen, the next President of the United States!"

"Oh?"

He blinked his bulging eyes. He wasn't handsome or cute but he had clear skin, no braces on his teeth, and a well-trained glossy haircut, although big ears. His fat lips gave him a kind of pouting formality, but his consonants splatted forth negligently like smudged horn notes.

"I'm one of the few people our age who realizes the historic importance of it," he said, and held his hand out to be shook. "I'm Gary Grabell," he said, accenting the second syllable and, somehow, implying unmistakably that it was a name to remember.

"Cheryl Sadowsky," she slipped in parenthetically.

"Think that's a good name for a senator or a cabinet member?" he asked, obviously referring to his own name. "I'm one of the most active volunteers at the Republican Club of Mt. Vernon. Sometimes they let me use the microphone in the sound truck—when we go around reminding people to vote?—because I sound like an adult. Have you been following the convention?"

"Why should I, it's just the Republicans. I mean, I'm sorry, I don't mean—."

"That's all right, you're just echoing your parents' political views."

Like too many of the things people said, this made Cheryl wonder about herself. Not that she was wrong to be a Democrat, but wasn't there some truth in what he said about *why* she was? But how could she ever manage to find a position of her own, a life without copying? Weren't all the positions already filled?

"I'm a conservative," Gary bragged, "because I'm an independent thinker. I believe in rational thinking. People are so irrational. Like, look how everyone's making a fuss about what he said about extremism. 'Extremism in the defense of liberty is no vice, and moderation in the pursuit of justice is no virtue.' That's *true!* And people are acting like it was fascist or something. Freedom and justice are the most important things. We have to fight to keep from losing them. Everyone knows that, but when he says it, people act like he's going to bomb Moscow or something."

"Just Hanoi."

"Right," he glared. "They're the enemy, and they *will* be bombed." He seemed to be waiting for a reaction. "Well? You're probably a socialist and you'd rather have America bombed than Vietnam."

Her first impulse was to laugh in his face, but then it occurred to her: This kid is going to grow up someday and actually be one of our leaders. The weirdness of the thought led her to take a tactful step downhill.

"Where are you going?" he said, and laughed, "Gotta go to a Party meeting?"

It peeved her to be called something she wasn't, but she accepted it because she knew she needed practice at boy-girl conversations. "How's the pool here?" she asked. "You feel like going swimming, maybe later?"

That led to normal subjects like, Where do you live, and What are the kids like there, and Have you ever been at this resort before?

"My little sister's at camp," Cheryl said, "but I went to that camp last year, I didn't like it. I don't do well in groups," she suddenly found herself confessing. (She had dreamed of someone to whom she could confess herself, confess everything. Was he the one?) "I mean, I do very well in school, but I like doing things on my own, so I'm going on vacation with my parents."

There was something about that last part that wasn't consistent, she knew. And she didn't know what to do about it.

"I'm kind of quiet too," Gary said, and when she looked at him, he added, "I *used* to be. I'm learning how not to be, at the Republican Club. Hey, did your school let you out early when Kennedy was killed? Ours did."

"No, they made us stay till three and they didn't announce it or anything. Our ratfink principal thought we were too delicate to hear the news."

Gary had flinched at her use of current slang, which she had only thrown in to try to sound cool. Mistakes, she was always making mistakes!

Gary said, "Don't get me wrong, I'm a Republican, but I was very sad too."

"Thanks. That's okay," she said, as if someone had consoled her for a death in the family. And she went into the ritual recitation of whereabouts: "It was a Friday, it was sunny, and I walked home instead of taking the bus, because I was going to visit my grandparents. And on the way I kept thinking, *There's something strange going on,* even though I couldn't tell what it was. There weren't enough people on the streets; there wasn't enough noise." She shook herself as if waking from a nightmare. "I was thinking, *I'll get to my grandparents' and it'll turn out there was nothing strange.* But I got there and turned on the TV...."

"Yeah." He was nodding over and over.

"It was like being in an episode of *The Twilight Zone,* where you walk along the street and nothing *looks* different, but you find out Martians have landed or you're on a planet where everyone is deformed."

"In fact," Gary said, picking up another thread entirely, "I was still a liberal last November twenty-two. I've changed a lot since then."

It was her turn to nod understandingly. "Yeah."

"Hey, *Twilight Zone*'s on tonight. Want to watch it? It'll just be a rerun, but.... "

"I probably haven't seen it anyway," she rushed. "Yeah, yeah, we'll watch *Twilight Zone,* great. Yeah, great, well, see you tonight...."

And having made an arrangement, they had to flee till the time for its fulfillment. Was it a date? Was this all that esoteric mystery boiled down to, cramming yourselves into a broken-springed, scratchy couch in front of a TV whose picture wobbled like an aquarium, your thighs neither too far from nor close to his?

A ping-pong ball echoed from the far end of the big pine-paneled room. Moths flew around the yellow overhead bulbs, which were netted with heavy wire just like in her old elementary school. From the newer, carpeted addition next door, where adults played cards or mah-jongg, you heard now and then a bursting laugh, sounding like it had been stored up for a long time. This was the night, regardless of her having dreaded and anticipated and planned and replanned it all day.

The *Twilight Zone* episode was one of the handful she'd seen, but she liked it anyway. It was the one about a little lost colony of Earthlings who'd crashed years before on an uncharted rock, and were waiting for the chance that a passing spaceship might rescue them. An old man, the actor James Whitmore, kept the young people's spirits up by telling them stories of home. "The Earth is green, Joey," he told the boy who followed worshipfully at his side. He told of meadows and mountains, of cities and harbors and stores and family reunions, of two dozen flavors of ice cream and a library full of books.... And after the commercial, a ship does find them, and the marooned ones go aboard—all except the old man. Panicking, he refuses to leave his asteroid home: "It's a trick, don't believe them, you'll get aboard and they'll sell you into slavery." They try to force him on, but he runs and hides in the rocky caves of his thin-aired hills. Finally the ship has to go—there's something about a deadline, one of these TV plot devices, the rescue craft has only so many minutes to rejoin its mother ship or what-have-you—and the old man, from his hill cave, looks up to watch the bottom of the craft rise into the atmosphere above him. And he sees his folly but it's too late, like words of hate that can't be unsaid, missiles that can't be called back. Why did he do it? Was he afraid of the reality he'd told stories about, or did he just want to be begged a little more, the one who'd held the colony together all those years? But the ship has lifted off and it's not going to make a separate trip for him. He runs out: "Wait, come back, take me with you!" He collapses on the alien ground; the camera viewpoint recedes above him. Looking smaller and smaller, really marooned now, he begins to talk to himself: "The Earth is green, Joey...."

"Oh, God," Cheryl said, to think of someone wanting something for so long that when it came, he ran from it. "How terrible."

"Yeah, isn't that a great one?" Gary said. And excitedy he began telling her or quizzing her about all his other favorite episodes— Have you seen this one? Have you seen that one?—and from there he went on to other television series, you couldn't stop at *The Twilight Zone* but had to compare it to *Alfred Hitchcock Presents* and compare that to *The Defenders* and on and on.... Each time he mentioned a new show, his leg pressed closer to hers and he glanced up to see if anyone was watching. Then he switched to rock groups and put his arm around her. When he mentioned the Beatles, his hand rested lightly on her shoulder. Advancing to the Dave Clark Five, he let his hand slip a little further down. The Zombies, the Kinks—his almost touchless finger tingled her collarbone to life. Conservatism, she began to think, must be some stage of hipness beyond where everyone else was. He knew all the groups—even knew, from reading British fan magazines which he got at a special Manhattan shop known only to him, about English groups that hadn't reached America yet but were waiting to, as if they were in line at the airport with their baggage. The Who (his finger strolled down her sternum), Them (between her breasts), the Pretty Things....

He jerked his head up as the screen door slammed and clattered. The ping-pong players on the other side of the room had finally left. His nose brushed the top of her ear. He murmured suavely in a James Bond accent, "Now it's our turn to play...."

They were tongue-kissing: she had a boy and was actually doing this with him. He knew the protocols, when to start and how fast to flick and how to vary his mouth movements in and out, side to side, in order to maintain a high level of interest. Except that he pressed too hard for comfort and a couple of times his teeth nipped her lip and she had to murmur through shreds of tenderness, "Ow, don't bite me."

She wished she could take over and tell him exactly what her body was telling her it wanted, but she told herself that wouldn't be cool. The cool way was to let the boy do whatever *he* wanted till he reached some invisible line you'd drawn on your body—but where was that line, for her? She'd never thought highly of all those conversations among her friends about *Would you let him do this?* and *Would you let him do that?* She'd lingered at the margins, throwing in a wry comment about how she didn't expect it to happen in this century. And now the test was here and she felt unprepared.

His fingers slid beneath her bra cup, and the main thing she felt wasn't the electricity of awakened skin, which was pleasant but after all mild, nor was it a feeling of doing anything improper or excessive, not at all. It was more a matter of trying to guess whether *he* was enjoying it enough: would he be satisfied by what he found there? Did she measure up to what he was used to—and how much was he used to, anyway?

He must have felt that he had paid enough attention to one breast, then to the other, and then to switching back and forth. The rules had been agreed upon, the terms had been drafted. A pause, and they came to a silent decision—not *made* the decision but came to it, as if they had been traveling toward where it already stood waiting for them—a shared decision that she would let him take her somewhere. Bumping hips, they walked out of the rec room, around behind the building, through a short trail in the woods to the baseball field.

Gary sat her down beside him in the moonshadow of the chain-link backstop. They helped each other down to grass level. He rubbed the whole length of her, and took her hand and showed her where to rub him.

Then he got very active and started moaning. She wanted to kiss more, but apparently that was a retarded, mawkish thing to want: he broke away from her mouth and fastened his teeth on her shoulder, gripping her arms tight and kicking spastically, with a clattering of bones and keys and coins and a belt unbuckling and sliding to his knees, a ballpoint pen falling from his pants pocket, until he knocked against her thighs and cried out in ecstasy, "Congressman William E. Miller of New York, the next Vice-President of the United States!"

He dropped onto her with all his weight. Like a tambourine, his clattering subsided, and his shoe tips, scraping a groove into the dirt, slowed like a roulette wheel. He fell away from her, onto his back, to whine a sigh at the Catskill stars.

She was trying to imagine what might be the appropriate thing to say, when he interrupted her thoughts.

"Oh, God, I'm all wet. I'm sorry, I made a mistake. Please don't tell anyone—"

"What's the matter, were they too flat for you?" she asked, glancing down at her chest.

"No, no, it's nothing about you. You're fine—it's gauche to overemphasize breasts—it's just, look—I shouldn't be doing this with anyone but Elissa. My girlfriend at home."

"Oh."

He sat up and pulled a handkerchief from his pocket and began swabbing inside his pants. "Elissa and I told each other we wouldn't be seeing anyone else this summer. And morality is important to me," he added vehemently, as if she'd accused him otherwise. "Conservatism isn't just politics, it's values we should live by. I believe in love; I don't believe in free love."

"Oh, is that your campaign slogan?" Buttoning her blouse in the dark, she looked up just in time for a glimpse of him desperately wiping his underwear as he stood and ran away. "I hope she finds out," she called after him, but soft enough to sound muddled in his ears.

She stayed behind, thinking, *Well, here I am.* On a deserted ballfield at night, the kind of place that would have felt alien to her even in the daytime. So didn't this seem like the perfect moment to be rescued? Yes, an unlit rural ballfield would be the place extraterrestrials would choose to land, descending from the Big Dipper to tell people to stop their madness. They would choose her as their go-between to the governments of Earth, because teenagers were the only ones who really understood things, and because of all teenagers she was the least corrupted without being unusably innocent. The saucer would spin downward, flattening the grass, churning up a whirlwind that would whip her oily hair into her eyes, and when the slender, beautiful bipeds tripped down the ramp on long, elastic limbs, she would give them a quick survey course on human history and then be off to Washington where she'd preach into a bank of microphones, "Destroy all nuclear weapons or you will be destroyed…."

She had told herself not to cry, but such warnings were only encouragements. Countless times in her life she'd wished she were in a place where she could cry safely, and now here she was: that was Gary's gift to her. She cried for all those other times and all their different reasons; all the things that would have seemed to have nothing to do with him, now had. And if she modulated her voice, weeping demurely rather than sobbing and choking and ending up with a stuffed nose, did that mean she was becoming mature?

She rinsed her eyes in the bathroom sink before entering the beige-carpeted game room. The bright little gathering spot smelled of floor wax and kibitzers' breath: exhalations of Lifesaver mints, of Canadian Club and soda, of meat sandwiches and sponge cake, and cries of, "Gin!" "She's cheating!" "Let me see that hand, you." "Look at this hand, is this gin or what?" The bookshelves were lined with Herman Wouk and Leon Uris, Fletcher Knebel and Allen Drury, John Gunther and Theodore H. White; from the maple cabinet of a stereo speaker came an orchestra of strings playing a song everybody knew but forgot the title of; and though it was the instrumental version, Cheryl knew some of the lyrics because she'd bought the sheet music for flute lessons. Something about a place where two people could share all their hopes and dreams....

By the wall stood Gary, behind a little octagonal table where a bejewelled, horse-faced brunette who must be his mother had stopped in the midst of throwing down a card to glance at Cheryl. His black eyebrows twitched; his mouth moved like a mouth that wants to open. A scene played itself out in both their minds at once—"Hi." "Hi." "How are you?" "Fine. How are you?"—but it didn't even come to that. Gary continued sneering at the way his elders were playing their hands. Cheryl turned away and, with an idle sway that she feared was hopelessly unseductive, flipped through a paperback of *Two for the Seesaw*.

Suddenly she realized her parents were in the room. They were seated opposite each other at another octagonal card table in another part of the room, and her mother was scowling furiously. If you're smart you'll go in the other direction, Cheryl scolded herself in almost a maternal tone; but she went toward them, drawn there, she didn't know why.

"That's what you want to throw down?" her mother was saying.

"Yes," her father said, "do you have any objections?"

"No, I'm just asking, that's all."

"You've never 'just asked' anything in your life."

Stung by his thrust, Cheryl's mother paused—that was her great weakness—to consider that it might be true. This allowed Cheryl to step in and ask what they were playing, and how the game was going—a little distraction to defuse the quarrel....

But it all fell apart when her father chose that moment to clean his teeth. This was what his wife abhorred above everything else about him. He sucked air noisily through partly opened lips in order to loosen a fiber of potted beef brisket from between his canine and bicuspid. It sounded as if some little homunculus inside his mouth was cleaning the teeth with a water syringe. But the fiber of steer mucle was tough, and held out against the storm. Air screaked again and again through Cheryl's father's mouth as her mother's face went through contrortions of loathing and revulsion.

Cheryl's mother smacked her fan of cards onto the table.

"What is it now?" Cheryl's father asked, knowing perfectly well.

"Must you?"

"Must I what?" he said, as if raising the bet.

"It's your turn," Cheryl suggested with faint hope to the woman sitting between them, who simply thumbed through her cards with a flustered air and did nothing.

"Don't you have any sense of etiquette...?" Cheryl's mother began.

Cheryl's father gave a victorious screak as the meat fiber broke free. He spat drily sidewards, took a drag on a Pall Mall, and blew smoke through nose and mouth. "I'm not interested in etiquette, I'm interested in true courtesy, something no one in your family has ever heard of."

"Courtesy, what do you know about courtesy with that foul mouth of yours...."

"Consider the foulness of your own mouth, not every sup-posed little hygienic *faux pas* that anybody else may commit...."

"'*Consider the....*'" Cheryl's mother mimicked in a woman's false bass. "Listen to him, he's using his biblical intonations, the man is delusional, he thinks he's a Hebrew prophet."

"I *can* prophesy that no good will come of this mockery—"

"Yes, yes, oh great one, lecture us about righteousness, you righteous fucking prick—"

Right in the game room, in front of their two tablemates and the kibitzers wandering among tables and the other foursomes at other tables—in this strategically chosen and tacitly agreed-on site, they were starting to let loose with profanities. Cheryl had to do something. But there was never anything. She'd tried it all. One of the first lessons she had ever learned was that you can't change anything. Apparently all these adults peeking from behind their cards knew it too. Maybe at least you can change your own surroundings....

"I'm going," she announced, as much to the strangers as to her parents. "Let me know when you can communicate like civilized people."

"Ach, another country heard from!" her mother said.

"This one should be a professional mediator," her father said contemptuously.

She rushed out, knocking past the corners of furniture. Heading for the door, she noted Gary still standing behind his earringed mother. You could have been my boyfriend tonight, you could have been the one who had the right to save me from this, she thought. For the duration of a footstep, she imagined he would spring forward and accompany her, protect her on their way out the door, enclose her in the arm of morality; but that was just politics. He stood as if behind glass, and bug-eyed watched her leave. If he was trying to transmit sympathy or understanding through the bobbings of his adam's apple or something, it was wasted.

The heavy thump of her father's bare feet approached her bedroom door. She clapped the pillow over her head, but when he started talking she threw it to the ground in order to answer him.

That grumpy, parsing, scrupulously blame-assigning voice which sounded tender only when it was apologizing. "Honey, I'm sorry you had to hear all that tonight."

"Sorry you said it, or just sorry I heard it? Are you sorry the whole place had to hear it too?"

Now *she* was sorry she'd said *that*. It was the kind of pickily cruel retort her mother would make.

"I'm sorry about many things, Cheryl. About almost everything, if the truth be known."

No, she didn't want to know....

"Why don't you just get divorced? You don't have to stay together for us, we've told you that. We *want* you to get a divorce. We can't stand it. It's been all our lives and we can't take it much longer. Do you remember the time Denise and I hid in the bathtub? I took her with me into the tub and huddled over her to protect her. How old was I, five, and Denise was two? And you pounded the door because you needed your blood pressure pills and I opened it up because I was afraid you'd break the door down? Do you know, last week, before we left for the country, I was going to bed with a knife under my pillow because I thought you'd try to kill us?"

"No, honey, I didn't know that," and to Cheryl's horror he had begun to sniffle. This was so unfair; what did he want her to do, hug him and tell him it was all right? At least there was no fear of her mother coming to join him. This was maybe the second time she'd seen her father weep, but never her mother, that was something Cheryl and her mother were both proud of, her mother never ever cried.

"Cheryl angel"—she cringed at the word. Her mother always scoffed when he called Cheryl *sweetie* or *honey*, those "phony" endearments he never called her by. "I hope someday you'll forgive us for exposing you to so much strife and acrimony in your life." *Strife* and *acrimony*: the vocabulary list of an attendance officer for the Yonkers public schools, a burnt-out classroom teacher. "I wish I could explain everything to you, but as mature as you are there are some things no thirteen-year-old can really comprehend about marriage."

"I don't want to. I don't want to comprehend it."

"Good, in a way." He made an unassuming little show of snuffing back his last sniffles, and stood heavily off the mattress, the cheap bedsprings squeaking. "You'll comprehend it soon enough. Or maybe you'll be luckier if you don't, who knows." He was starting to back away. "I know very little about it myself, despite considerable experience."

"Yeah."

"Maybe you're mother's right, maybe I am delusional. Maybe she's right about everything."

He was waiting for her to reassure him—No, Dad, you're both

right exactly fifty percent of the time—but she was tired of doing that. Worst of all, she couldn't disprove the suspicion, which rang in her mind in her mother's voice, that he'd come in here just to win points, to seem more noble than his wife, to get his daughter on his side.

His bare feet slogged away. She could visualize the fungus-yellow pearl of his toenails. His cigarette breath hung stale in the air, and she remembered, after the physical sensation faded, the smell of the sweat under his nylon watchband. She put the pillow back on her head.

But it turned into one of those nights when she couldn't sleep. They happened maybe once a week, sometimes more. It was hard to say why; they didn't necessarily happen on nights of conflict, though this time it did. They seemed to go through a cycle, pressure building up until, even if her parents had ignored each other or been content with idle teasing, she had to stay awake and awake and awake, as if she had an assignment to work on and couldn't sleep till she completed it. Different ends of her body took turns itching, and then there was the effort of not scratching, then the question of how much to cover herself: the sheet was too thin and the blanket too thick, and switching every few minutes became a downward spiral.

It must have been after three when she finally got to sleep, and before sunrise, sounds woke her. People stirring—maybe an intruder? Not in the kitchen or on the porch. The Russians are coming, the Russians are coming....

She tottered through the bungalow, grabbing onto things as the darkness drained from them: the rocking chair rocked ghost-gray under her hand, the doorjamb drew itself in pencil-colored light. Sound came into focus along with sight: the noises were definitely coming from her parents' room. She went to listen at their door. Arguing this early? No, it was bodies, not voices. Hitting? They'd never done that, as far as she knew.

Oh, how stupid she was. Now she recognized the sound, without having ever heard it before. That regular plunging, those rhythmic grunts.

She wanted to run, but running would have told them she was there.

At home, her bedroom was at the other end of the apartment

from theirs. But even sleeping right next door, she never expected to hear *this*.. Hadn't sex ended for them years ago? She had assumed an invisible divider down the middle of the bed—*Don't cross this line!* Wouldn't that be the only possible way for them to keep living together? Because they hated each other. The surest thing she knew in this world was that her parents hated each other.

Did she hear, did she really hear her mother moan from behind the door, from underneath her father, "I told you where, can't you remember?"

Cheryl imagined herself busting in on them and yelling: What are you doing? Why are you doing this, don't you know how to act?

You'll do this too, her parents tell her, *and who knows with whom and where and why....*

With Gary Grabell, the next President of the United States, ladies and gentlemen.... How would you like that *in thirty years?*

She tried to imagine making love with someone she had cursed, belittled, ridiculed, wished dead. It was impossible. It was nauseating. Her parents were not human.

An airplane droned overhead. She used it as cover to tiptoe back to her room. She lay face down on the shaky cot and pulled the covers all the way over her head.

When she awakens it will be late afternoon, or maybe she'll have slept through a whole day and night and it will be the following morning—yes, that's what it'll be. And in her sleep, the thing she's been expecting all her life will have occurred. The world has been extinguished. The details aren't as she foresaw them, of course; predictions are never fulfilled perfectly. But detail itself, all details, have been leveled over night.

She arises and hears an uncanny silence. She rushes through the cabin into the master bedroom, and this time no parents are there. They aren't anywhere. The entire human population has evaporated except for her. She runs outside and the other cabins are all empty too—no, wait, there *are* no other cabins anymore. The single remaining evidence of human craft is her family's paneled bungalow in the middle of an endless forest.

A neutron bomb would have killed them all and left the buildings intact, but this is something weirder. The civilization of Earth been wiped out by aliens, except that she's been kept alive as a specimen. Or has she been transported to a different world entirely: is this an asteroid that's been fitted out with trees and streams to make her feel at home while she's poked and examined? Or has an irregularity in spacetime sent her back into prehistory, to before there was a New York State, the time of the Iroquois or even earlier?

Guiltily, she realizes that she hardly cares which it is.

She heads down the former car path, which is now a thin dirt trail. Walking downhill, past the clearing where the cabins used to be, she's flooded by shock and remorse: *I'll never see Denise again, I'll never see my friends again.* But it passes quickly, she's so busy learning to survive.

Cheryl learns best when she's left alone.

She plots her course downstream, and follows a brook to a stream to a little river to a big river that looks much like the upper Hudson used to—although she can't tell for certain, she never saw the upper Hudson without buildings on the shore. On the cliffs above the shining river, she turns south. It's like walking on a relief map, the green contours familiar but no human landmarks.

Her explorations are unhurried. Each day she must find something nonpoisonous to eat and someplace flat or hollow to sleep, and there's no reason not to linger at any pond or hill that nourishes her. Years, that's what it'll take to get back to where the city was. What used to be a hundred and four miles is seen now as the landscape of a lifetime. What would have been 1965, 1966, 1967, 1968, 1969—she'll never have to live through those. Unknown upheavals—who knows what chaos?—nuclear attack on Hanoi? civil war turning America into a dictatorship?—will settle instead into a pulse of seasons, one year no different from the next except that winter is a little harsher or milder. Ripening, toughening, she won't have to worry about who is looking at her and what they think, or what they say behind her back.

Then, exactly when she's ready, when she's wondering if a whole lifespan like this can be bearable, she'll hear a deep voice singing in the woods (at first she'll think it's a hallucination), or see a footprint. There will be a boy—a man—and he'll have been spared too, and for the same reason: because Something thought them worthy.

I'm Ariadne, she'll say, and he'll answer, *I'm Julian, I'm Derek,*

I'm Nigel—the name will be a lovely one and somehow British.

At the sight of him, she'll remember music for the first time since the catastrophe. Violins: a song about a place, and the secret of the place is that it can be *anywhere* where two people share their hopes and dreams.

Together they'll open a path south beside the widening river, and they'll stand atop the palisade, the tumbled columns of seamed black rock, and view the slender, leaf-green, deer-trod, unhurt island. By that time, they might even have a baby. As soon as they can build a raft, they'll cross. On the island, they'll find a few more people, a few imaginative souls who have have walked here to see what was left and whether there was anyone else.

At the southern tip of the island they'll start building again, but not the way it once was. They'll build it the way it should always have been. It will be the only city in the world, because, being perfect, it won't need to be attempted elsewhere. Children who don't know any other kind of life will splash in its bays and dive for its salmon and hand-feed its birds. No one will ever make fun of these children for some blemish that would hardly be noticed if people didn't want to make fun of it—or some blemish they don't even have at all. The people who would have harmed these children will not be there. It would amaze these children that you could be called the wrong name so often that finally you answered to it. And there will not be multiple definitions of words such as *parent, husband, wife, friend.* Every word will be the name of one thing, and it will always be only that thing; if it starts turning into something else, it will have to get a new name. And anyone who lies will have to know that they are lying.

It will be that way, it just has to. Because please, somebody, anybody.... Anything else and she just doesn't know how she'll get through.

Cousin Gemma

I have worked hard over the years at building a satisfactory relationship with my mother. As an only daughter, this is especially important. My brothers are nice guys, "sweet" men, to use a word you often hear nowadays, but there are some things women can only talk about with other women. I don't mean necessarily sex, bodily functions, and the rest of it, but just things of the emotional fabric, the core of a person's perceptions. When I say "satisfactory," by the way, I mean that she and I will never be best friends, but as a person to talk to and depend on, we can manage that. As she approaches her eighties, this is what she needs and, given the limitations of what she can realistically be expected to learn in the way of new attitudes at her age, what we can hope for.

So when she said, in the midst of decaf, "You don't know your cousin Gemma," I did not bother to remind her that I had met Cousin Gemma once or twice as a child and that I have a very good memory for people. I knew that while she would go over some familiar ground, telling stories I had already heard before about this elusive, wealthy (in my mother's eyes) relative—besides boring me with complaints about everything from her childhood poverty to her dental hygienist's tone of voice—I, being skillful at asking the right question (partly thanks to her, I suppose), would be able to glean some tidbits which might very well give me a further clue in solving the mystery I have devoted so much time to: Why has my mother's life been so hopeless and joyless, such a waste of potential, in fact so utterly dreary and futile and colorless and uninspired as to make even casual contact with her demoralizing, despite the fact that she has a quick mind, a vivid spirit, physical health, and four loving children?

"Remember, this was 1940," she launched in, ignoring the fact that since there had been no prelude to the tale, there was nothing for me to remember. "I was a nineteen-year-old college girl just off the D train, what did I know? But young as I was, I was helping support my family. My father, that shmuck, didn't exactly go out of his way to find work. He used the Depression as a reason to goof off with his friends in the society, that club they had of men who'd all emigrated from the same town in Rumania. My mother, of course, cared about everyone in the world except her younger daughter. She would be upstairs giving—giving to people, that was how she made anyone who didn't know her think she was wonderful. Sending soup to the tubercular on the fourth floor, who drove me crazy all night with her coughing—and me she'd tell, 'Carla, make dinner. Carla, go to the store and get ten pounds of potatoes.' From the time I was this high, from six years old, she was sending me to carry heavy things back and forth all the time. No wonder I barely grew to five feet. The neighbors all loved my mother. A lot they knew."

"Yes? What?" I said, hoping to hear a morsel of remembered abuse or neglect, but Mom was protective of me when it came to such melodrama; I would have to feel my way toward it gradually.

"So that's the background in a nutshell. We're just making ends meet in the Bronx, and Cousin Gemma is growing up a rich girl up in Westchester."

I smirked. "A rich girl? You showed me once the house they lived in." (*You showed me once!* Talking to her, her speech patterns start entering my voice.)

"Yeah, so?" she said. "People had smaller houses then. A two-family frame house in Yonkers was a palace. To us they were rich, her father a doctor—"

"A doctor with no patients."

"That's exactly my point," she said with characteristic illogic, "that's what I'm trying to *tell* you. People forget that 1940 was one of the worst years of the Depression even though it came at the end. Excuse me, it was 1939, just around Christmas now that I recall. Out of the clear blue one day, the phone rings, and it's Cousin Walter—"

"The doctor."

"Gemma's father. Some doctor. When we were kids, my mother took my brother and sister and I to see him because she couldn't get us to go to sleep. This genius prescribes phenobarbitol. So every night for a year, can you believe it, she lined us up all in a row (in the bedroom we shared till I was fifteen, do you believe that?), and gave us a barbiturate to make us sleep. Listen, Roz, I could tell you things…"

"Okay, so he calls up." I urge her back on track. "Why?"

She sighed. "Why? He's a relative, why shouldn't he call? My mother's first cousin, and in our family we were always very close, a cousin was like a brother or sister; a brother or sister was like I don't know what."

"Like yourself," I suggested.

"God forbid. So he asks to talk to me. Not my mother or father. Me, who he knows from a hole in the wall. We've seen each other, you know, now and then, but the man never even invited my family to visit his in Westchester, we were too low-class for that privilege. So he gets me on the phone, how am I, am I in college, am I working, he heard I was working part-time in addition to going to school. Of course I can tell he doesn't really care how I am. Right away he asks me: Can I lend him two hundred dollars to help pay Gemma's tuition?"

"What?"

"I'm not kidding."

"Mother, that doesn't make sense."

"Of course not. There was a lot back then that didn't make sense. A doctor with a daughter going to Georgetown University, while I have to struggle to find a nickel every morning to take the train down to Hunter College, and he asks me for a loan. But a lot of doctors had a hard time in the Depression. Him especially, if he was getting what he deserved. People tried to avoid doctors, they couldn't afford to pay. My father paid Cousin Walter for treating me for scarlet fever (treatment!, that's a laugh, they put you to bed and took your temperature and prayed they didn't get infected themselves) by sewing new curtains for his house. (Me he kept promising new curtains but never made any.) Walter had very little income coming in but a position to keep up, including storing my cousin in a fancy private college hundreds of miles away. Come the winter term, he saw he wasn't going to be able to cover her tuition by himself. So what's he supposed to do, ship her home and make her go to Hunter?"

"Yes."

"Actually, she couldn't have gone to Hunter for free, not being a New York City resident. But anyway. Back then, people borrowed from relatives, not like today when your relatives won't even call you, like my sister never calls me, that narcissist. You think *I'm* self-absorbed? If you would talk to my sister you'd see self-absorbed."

"Well, that's why I don't," I said (while she was still muttering to herself, *"Mein shvester,* that nut.") "Not if I can help it. But back up, Mom. Focus on Walter trying to borrow money. Why you?"

"Who should he borrow from, my father? That's a laugh. Look, what did I tell you before? I was working. I had a job twenty hours a week doing stock and inventory in a Hebrew bookstore on Tremont Avenue."

"A Hebrew bookstore, this is getting more and more bizarre."

"What, you think I don't know about Judaism? I'm as Jewish as the next person, I assure you."

"Yes, I'm aware of that."

"Just because my father never once set foot in *shul?* He equally despised the Catholics, he would cross the street rather than walk past a church. He would spit on the ground if he saw a nun coming."

"That's good news, I'm glad he was egalitarian."

"But anyway, where was I, you got me so confused I don't remember what I was going to say next. But, yes, come the new year I was going to go to Washington myself to work on the census. That was a good job, believe me, and my mother, she might not have paid me a moment's attention when I needed it, but she made sure everybody else knew anything important her kids did."

"Important!"

"Go ahead, laugh, but it's one of the few federal government functions that is specifically mandated by the Constitution, that every ten years—"

"Yes, yes, yes, so you told Walter to fuck off."

"No." She glared through her chagrin.

"You lent him the money?"

"What else should I have done?"

In essence, I just laughed. What else should she have done? That was the recurring question of my mother's life, one of them I should say. It wasn't a rhetorical question. She really didn't know the answers to things, and wished someone would have told her. She hadn't dared to refuse her rich, older, male relative's request, so rationalizing with the ideology of *We-do-for-each-other,* she gave him two hundred dollars she'd been saving for emergencies that were much more likely to happen to her own parents.

"Needless to say," I pointed out to her, "he only called you after he got turned down by several relatives and friends he was closer to."

The expression this produced on her face was worth several minutes of listening to her digressions. She had never thought of this before, in sixty years. In contrast, I have always understood things *before* experiencing them. From early childhood, I understood that whatever else of a serious nature might be going on with my mother, I was entitled to as much comic relief as I could get from the situation.

"You think I was the third, the fourth…?" She let her musing drop, like a little girl who finally sees that it's better not to try to figure out why she wasn't invited to the party. This is a woman, bear in mind, whom, when she turned seventy, I gave her a child's birthday card that said, "Now you are 7!" and merely added a zero after the numeral. Everyone including herself agreed that it was the most appropriate conceivable card for her.

"You'll tell your brothers all about this and cast me in the most ridiculous light," she said. "I know that, you think I don't? You and those beloved brothers of yours that no man can live up to?"

"Cut it out, Carla."

"But who cares, I've got other things to worry about." (What she had to worry about is beyond me. She was in good health and all her bills paid up.) "I'll tell you the rest of the story just because

I'm your mother. The following month, I moved down to Washington, and as a nice gesture for the loan Cousin Walter invited me to stay with his daughter till I found my own apartment. Actually it took a little longer than I expected. Washington was filling up with young people then, even though the war hadn't started yet. Because the census, you know, hired people from all over—"

"Yes, the all-important census!"

"Oh, *sha* already. What I want to say, if you don't get me so *ferchottered* that I can't remember, is…" And she paused as if wondering to herself. "What a strange person she was."

"Yes, what?" I was afraid she was going to leave it at that. It wouldn't have been unlike her.

"The first evening, she greeted me very nicely and took me out to dinner."

"Remarkable!"

"But then at dinner, *noch,* she barely spoke. As if she was making clear that we had nothing to talk about—she, the great sophisticate, and her poor cousin, the lowly *nebbish* from the Bronx. And do you believe, for the next three weeks, while I was sleeping on her sofa and looking for an apartment, she never did anything with me again. Never socialized, never ate a meal at the same time as me, never suggested, 'Carla, let's go to a movie,' nothing? As if I was nothing more than a boarder, and she had to live with the inconvenience."

"Well," I said, somewhat let down if that was the high point of her oral history. And I continued my lifelong tutoring of her: "People are like that, they don't always show gratitude…"

"No, no." She jabbed my arm with her finger. When I was a child and she did that, I always imagined that she was giving me shots. Shots of what? "I know about ingratitude. I'm talking about something else. This is what I'm telling you: would you believe that the next time I saw her was at least five years later?"

"Yes, I would."

"It was when I got her wedding invitation. But listen to this, she asked me to be her maid of honor, in a very nice personal note—she had beautiful handwriting, they taught her at that fancy private school in Westchester she went to. In this beautiful cursive, with a fountain pen, she asks, I'm her closest relative her age, she's missed me so much and wished we saw each other more often, I'm the one person in the world she most trusts to be at her side on this occasion."

"Was she crazy?"

"That's what *I* was thinking!" Mom exclaimed over this coincidence in our interpretations. "I'm thinking to myself, what am I getting into here? Do I even want to go to her wedding, much less serve as her maid of honor, a second cousin I hardly know."

Of course, in her family a second cousin was like a first cousin…. But if I'd checked her on every inconsistency, it would have sent her spinning down more sidetracks than she already was.

"She probably asked five other women before you and they all turned her down," I said.

"You know, you think you're so smart! How do you know what people did or didn't do in 1945, 46, whenever it was? Were you there?"

"All right, you were the first person she asked."

"You burn me up sometimes, you and those brothers of yours."

"What? They're not even here. And you're lucky they're not, or they'd be laughing hysterically. I'm the one who treats you best. You don't realize it. You pretend to discipline them, but when they're around you let them take advantage of you. You act like they're the lords of the house, and then you say *I* worship them."

"All right, all right. If I had known what it was going to be like to have four such smart, verbal kids who never let you get away with the slightest *faux pas,* the smallest slip of the tongue…"

If she had known, she wouldn't have had the fourth child. She wouldn't have insisted to Dad that they make a last attempt at a girl after having three boys. Four was too much in 1960; no one was having that many kids in our socioeconomic sphere. I wouldn't have been here to bother her. To delay her reentry into the workplace by another two years.

"So tell me about the maid of honor business," I said wearily.

"It was crazy! I go there, to my cousin's house—"

"The palace."

"Yes, I mean no, what are you talking about, a nice house in the suburbs, that's all. 'Palace!' Listen to her."

"You trotted up in your carriage—"

"I took the New Haven Railroad, dragging my bags with me, and if you don't shut up I'm not going to tell you what happened."

I covered my mouth with my hand.

"So I *arrived*," she continued with a hint of vengeful grandeur, "a lovely house in one of the oldest neighborhoods in Yonkers, overlooking the river. I still remember those white shutters, and a lawn—big!—and the first few guests, it was morning, playing badminton outside in their long dresses."

"Long dresses, for an afternoon affair?"

"So your relatives overdressed back then, can I help it? So me, the nothing from the Bronx in my tweed skirt, I rang the bell and nobody answered. Okay, so maybe they're busy making preparations. I open the door for myself, it looks like a wedding without people: flowers all over, a wedding cake on the table, but no Cousin Gemma, no Cousin Walter or his wife Hettie. I go upstairs—*nu*, I hear some noise from the bathroom. All of a sudden the bathroom door opens, Hettie comes out with tears all over her mascara. Next is Cousin Walter: he's trying to pull Gemma out of the bathroom, but she's kicking at his ankles, and Hettie is pulling his arm from the other direction, saying, 'Leave her be!' So Gemma gets away from his grip and runs back into the bathroom, locks the door behind her. Walter is pounding and threatening, but Hettie stops him, he didn't know I was watching. Walter and Hettie look at me like they don't know me from third base.

"'What's the matter with you, I'm Carla,' I say.

"As soon as we get who I am squared away, Hettie all of a sudden throws her arms around me and kisses me like I'm their savior. It seems that Gemma doesn't want to get married after all."

"Good for her," I said.

"And what do you know about it? Did you know the groom, did you know Gemma, with those loony parents of hers? Who could blame her for wanting to get married just to get out of the house?"

"But she *didn't* want to get married."

"That's what I'm trying to tell you. She did and she didn't. She'd been going out with this guy since high school, the only boyfriend she ever had, so she woke up on the morning of her wedding and decided she didn't have enough experience of life. Is that the feeling you trust, or the other one?"

"Well, what was the groom like? Did she love him, was he worth marrying?"

"Who knows? He was an ordinary shmo, I suppose, what difference does it make? I never heard anything terrible about him, he worked in the garment industry. He showed up later and knocked politely on the bathroom door and tried to persuade her to come out."

"What an asshole."

"Asshole? For being polite?"

"Yes, actually. For trying to seduce her, i.e. coerce her and deprive her of agency in the most important decision of her life…"

"Oh, you and that feminism of yours, that's your point of view on everything nowadays."

"Please, Mother, I know some real feminists, next to them you can't call me a feminist. I'm telling you what everyone knows…"

"Yes, and we were backward then, don't you think I know that, how ignorant we were? What we were supposed to do, get in our time machines and ask you and your friends for advice? I'm telling you, Walter and Hettie were so at a loss they were asking *me* for help. They gave me a chair to sit on and everything. They let me alone in front of the bathroom door, at the top of the stairs, and I tried to get through to Gemma."

"And were you trying to get Gemma to marry him?" I said suspiciously.

"Of course, what do you want? I was their guest, they had given me a responsibility, the whole afternoon depended on me."

"Gemma's whole *life* depended on you."

And I remembered times Mom had urged me to reconcile with some guy I'd stopped dating, or to break up with someone I thought I liked. Although I would never call myself weak-willed or overly susceptible, I've always felt I should at least listen to the opinions of intelligent people and those who love me (and despite everything, Mom is both). Not to mention the fifth commandment. At times, my decision had been congruent with her advice. Had she influenced me? What decision would I have made otherwise? I felt queasy.

"Finally the judge arrives, it's fifteen minutes before the ceremony's supposed to start, and nobody knows what to do," Mom said. "Walter and Hettie were actually going to give up, tell the guests, Sorry, go home. Walter decides, Give it one more chance. He knocks on the bathroom door: 'Are you coming out?' From behind the door, Gemma says, 'Let me speak to Carla.' So she unlocks the bathroom partway, just enough for me to slip through the opening, and you know how skinny I was back then, people used to say I was like a concentration camp inmate. Maybe she opened the door six inches. Gemma knew what she was doing—Cousin Walter could never have gotten through the door with that gut of his. Anyway, would you believe Gemma and I sat in the bathroom together for half an hour?"

"Doing what?"

"Doing what? Talking, what else? About experiences we'd had dating various types of men, our hopes for the future, the usual mishmosh. I was gaining her confidence, see? I was showing her I understood her worries and fears. Don't look at me like that, I did *not* try to persuade her one way or the other! In fact I made a point of saying, 'Do what you want, so what if they all have to go home, they'll have something to talk about.' If I'd tried to persuade her, would she have listened? No, we just talked about this and that. I could see she was becoming thoughtful, and I let her make up her own mind just like I always did later with you kids. Maybe that's *why* I became a mother—it doesn't bother me if people show their immature side."

I had the feeling she was waiting for a response from me, but on purpose I stared sternly, like a journalist giving an interviewee enough time to reveal more indiscretions.

She shrugged. "So finally Gemma stands up. She looked—I don't want to say she looked awful, but I had to help her rinse her face off and reapply some makeup. And just before she opened the bathroom door to go downstairs, she gave me a wonderful hug and said, 'You're the only person I want with me today. You're the only person who could have gotten me through it.' I have to tell you, I was so pleased, it meant so much to me to be appreciated once in a blue moon."

"So you led her to the slaughter," I reproved.

"What are you talking about? You should live so long, a slaughter! It was a beautiful wedding. People have always opened up to me, that's what I'm trying to say. No matter what you and your wacky brothers may think, all my life strangers have sensed in me something empathic that understands. Here was my cousin, who I hardly knew from Hyim Yossel, but she instantly felt *simpatico* with me—that's an expression we used to use, it means—"

"Yes, mother, I know what it means." Meanwhile I was taking rapid but exhaustive mental notes so I could recount this in three separate brother-sister telephone conversations. My brothers largely depend on me for news about our parents; I'm the family clearinghouse. In return they give me psychological, financial, and legal counsel respectively. (As far as *quid pro quos*, they would not have been interested in the university press books that I market.) "So because Cousin Gemma had a character disorder she was excessively dependent on you to the point of ruining her life."

"Stop putting words words in my mouth. If you must know, Gemma and what's-his-name, the husband, had a fairly successful marriage. At least they never got divorced. Do you have any idea what it meant in those days to have a husband who made a decent living? No, you don't, so don't try one of your funny answers. She had a couple of kids, a girl and a boy, one's a movie executive now, and the other—that other one of hers, what's the use of talking? I don't think you've ever met Gemma or her kids. You would have been too young to remember anyway. She met your brothers once or twice, but by the time you were born she pretty much stopped coming to family things, she had her own life, her own, shall we say, concerns."

"Pining away with regrets for her youth."

"Oh, stop. I get a card from her every year at Christmas time, and always with a personal note."

"'Dear Carla, I'll always be grateful to you for my enslavement....' And you send her a card in return, I assume?" I said, dreading the negative answer I was in fact about to get.

A sour face rejecting the hypocrisy of etiquette. "If I send cards, I send one to her. Some years it's just too much for me, I have too much on my mind to bother with that stuff."

The question of what, precisely, is on her mind is one that has preocccupied a generation of specialists: myself, my three siblings, our father, and an approximately equal number of psychologists and social workers. She makes sure we don't take too much time off from our relentless pursuit of the answer.

A few months after the above conversation, I was helping Mom try to find a retirement home, a process straight out of Freud's

Analysis Terminable and Interminable. The New Jersey winters had become increasingly hard for her, and I didn't like to think of her misspending her last years in glum loneliness and isolation. (What else would she be capable of, you might ask? But I'm more hopeful, perhaps too hopeful; my therapist once teased that I should join the Optimists' Club.) With her deteriorating vision and the arthritis in her legs, driving had become ever more dangerous (I sometimes stayed awake nights worrying that she would end the life of some child-pedestrian), and when she walked, she was likely to fall, even on her own street and with the support of a four-pronged aluminum cane, which she was loath to use anyway. Mom had been a vibrant talker when she was young, but year by year she seemed more obsessed with her minor ailments and her perfectly routine biological glitches, so that we'd have to wait longer and longer for the good stuff, winnowing it out of more and more dross. At a family gathering she would find a way to divert any conversation into the all-important matter of how many times she'd gotten up to pee in the middle of the night, or whether she ought risk drinking tea so soon after fruit juice. When we tactfully hinted that she ought to be thankful not to have any major illnesses at almost eighty, she chided us for our lack of sympathy.

She was spending more time under self-imposed house arrest. She would skip her weekly reading group if she caught a slight cold. If income taxes were due or a certificate of deposit needed to be renewed, she would begin pestering us about it weeks in advance, brooding over it instead of reading a book or at least watching one of her favorite shows. The pettiness of her anxieties seemed in itself like a point of vindication for her: *See, this is how shitty life is, that I have to worry about nothing.* At one point she'd had friends in her neighborhood, but some had died and the others, she found reasons not to like anymore. This one was still married, disgusting my mother by paying attention to a husband; that one was so actively single that my mother couldn't keep up; this one came from a "wealthy background" and made her feel patronized; that one lacked a college education and didn't appreciate the Impressionists, much less the Abstract Expressionists. Positive joy, if that word can be used about any spark in Carla Soyfer's neurochemistry, surged up every time she found a reason not to associate with someone. Meanwhile she would report to us the minute details of her contacts with bank officers, medical specialists, and store clerks, as if they were combats and seductions, charged with interpersonal drama.

Rejecting retirement communities became a game for her like rejecting acquaintances. This one was too Southern, this one was too cold in the winter; this one was in too big a city, this one was too remote from conveniences. Finally I thought I found one that was perfect: Horizon View, an apartment complex for seniors on the Maryland shore. Close enough for each of her children to visit once a month, let's say, and close to Washington, D.C., a city she'd waxed nostalgic about, without ever revisiting, since the fateful year of the 1940 census.

I sent for a brochure, and set it down triumphantly in front of her. After a few preliminary minutes of claiming she couldn't read such small print, and searching for her eyeglasses in numerous bureau drawers, she could no longer delay looking at it. Behind bifocals, she squinched her eyes into the narrow leer of the eternally wary customer. She muttered the name of the community to herself, and with a gasp of horror, let the brochure fall.

"Are you kidding, I can't go there," she said.

"Why?"

"I can't," she repeated as if it was too obvious.

I almost expected her, at that point, to give up her stalling and dare all on a show of perfect honesty: to admit she didn't want to go there because it sounded too good, and to rely on my understanding to accept this. Instead, she said:

"Don't you know? I can't go there; *she's* living there."

"She? Who?"

"Who else? Gemma."

I'd been standing over her shoulder at the dinner table, pointing things out, an unflappable guide, but now I just thudded down into a chair, it was too much.

"Gemma's living at this place? That makes it even better!"

She wouldn't see it. She wouldn't confess. She was like a little child who's so determined to oppose her parents' will that she even refuses ice cream. But Mom can usually be persuaded to give up one of her ludicrous resistances if you talk to her, bully her with insistent logic—both because she's smart enough to be ashamed of holding a position once it's been proven to be feeble, and because dragging herself through an activity she'd hoped to avoid fits in with her philosophy of defeatism and provides many longed-for opportunities to complain. In a nutshell, she let me drive her to Maryland.

The retirement community was heaven, I won't even describe it. Its own private beach, a superb dining room with fine glassware and china, a caring, committed, experienced staff, a lively population with just enough Jews (but not too many), and a jitney service to nearby shopping and to cultural events in Washington and Baltimore. I had called Cousin Gemma beforehand, and we knocked on the door of her apartment, on which was hung a sheaf of dried Indian corn, with kernels of muted russet and violet, its husk a spray of soothing taupe.

Well, Gemma turned out to be very accurately the way Mom had depicted her, except for what you would never have guessed: that she was an exceptionally warm, likable person. Hearing about her, and then meeting her, was like hearing a report about a foreign country from some disgruntled vacationer—the prices are outrageous, the people hate Americans, everybody gets sick—and then going there yourself and having the time of your life. The disgruntled one could have had it, too, if only she'd approached things a little differently.

Gemma was a fairly tall woman (perhaps what my mother objected to), about five seven, with dyed and set auburn hair (reminding me of all the aspersions Mom had cast at women who "spend all their time in the beauty parlor"). She wore a simple, belted, beige, knit dress, gold teardrop earrings, and bone-color shoes with medium heels. She kissed us both, briefly and and with a ready warmth that quickly subsided into shy cordiality. On the way to the coffee table, she took my hand and said, "I'm so excited to see you!" to me as much as to Mom. It made me feel good. I was not raised among people who knew how to make a guest feel good.

Then the reminiscing. I hadn't realized how many memories Mom and Gemma had in common, considering how little time they'd spent together. Apparently they shared all kinds of cousins and aunts and uncles, and for that matter in-laws and friends, who had served as lifelong conduits of relatedness, an unbroken wireless service that worked wherever the receivers were. And I felt like a crucial audience for these tales of quirks from the immigrant generation, of long-dead relatives who until then had existed for me only as funny half-Yiddish names. There was Beatie Bialystok (as a kid I'd heard the name as "Beady"), who had married her first cousin and given birth to a genius who killed himself; Molly der Greener, so called because all her life she retained the overawed, gullible, shrinking attitude of a greenhorn just off the boat; and Bessie der Blinder, a cataract case, whose specter Mom had accosted me with whenever I had put handprints on our walls ("Who are you, Bessie der Blinder, that you have to feel the wall when you walk?"). They even recalled stories of ancestors from the old country, whom they themselves had only heard about: a great-grandfather who used to ride bareback across the Dniester River, a great-grandmother who rolled strudel dough so thin you could see your hand through it. Mom did more of the talking, Gemma gaily introducing the next name on the list and then letting Mom take over with the fully annotated biography. Gemma listening with delighted embarrassment, as if she feared her ancestors would overhear. Mom, conversely, dismissed each new name: "Who, him? That guy?" She had to show her distaste for coarse gossip—which immediately gave way, *shoyn fahrtig,* to free associations and uncorked grudges.

I felt like I was watching some awards show on TV, seeing two ancient actresses, rival goddesses of the forties, totter toward each other in their furs and pasty makeup to embrace in a way that only they two could understand.

Gemma refilled our coffees. Time came to share more recent news. First was Mom's turn to brag about her four kids: a therapist, a lawyer, a broker, a publishing executive. It pleased me tremendously when Gemma said that she always kept an eye out in bookstores for works published by the press I work for. I didn't happen to see any such volumes on her shelves, but keeping an eye out was good enough. Then, of course, Gemma's great success story, her daughter the movie producer, responsible or co-responsible for two atrocious hits and one respectable flop. The son, the younger child, was a struggling writer and illustrator of "graphic novels"—comic books for grownups, with provokingly gritty settings.

"He's still doing that?" Mom said. "How old is he?"

He was thirty-seven, Gemma told us nicely, and he believed that the graphic novel was the art form of the future.

"Well, maybe," Mom said, "although I would never have called that kind of stuff art."

Gemma tightened a forebearing smile.

"I mean, art is art," Mom explained. "Maybe they have some other name for what he does."

"Well, I'm not saying I understand his work completely," Gemma said, "but it has its own audience and they're quite ready for it." She leaned forward to check the levels of our coffee cups. Actually, of my coffee cup—Mom's she just gave a perfunctory glance.

"That's what I'm saying," Mom protested. "One person's art is another person's I-don't-know-what. If people like it, so let him do it. He makes a living?"

Was she aware she had insulted her hostess? If I knew, it would answer a lot about her for me. Whatever her motive, she kept muttering about this son of Gemma's she didn't even know, less audibly but somehow more insistently, as if there was something she just had to say further despite the stark absence of any new content: some opportunity not for clarification but for masochistic persistence—or even some perverse kind of apology, repeating her offensive remarks until they seemed so hopelessly foolish and pathetic they could be forgiven.

"Well, who knows," she said, and veered into a report on the craziness of contemporary art as if to assure Gemma that her son was not alone. This allowed Gemma to change the subject to the cultural attractions of the retirement home: classes in everything from tai chi to lowfat cooking; weekly piano singalongs of Hit Parade numbers; monthly van excursions to such remote outposts as the National Gallery and the Smithsonian.

"But let me tell you something, Carla, they bring in all these wonderful activities and who signs up? Two or three people. I don't even bother with it myself anymore, all their amenities. I can hardly function after five p.m., because I get up so early. I'm up before the sun every morning, I have my pot of coffee, and I'm downstairs when the delivery boy comes with the paper. That's my morning— the paper, and I'm taking an exercise class on TV. At lunch I talk to whoever I'm sitting with, but then we scatter, and dinner I don't need, I have only so much interest in who's going to be whose partner for bridge. Anyway, they're saying nowadays that longevity comes from reduced caloric intake. If you want to find me, the best time's at lunch."

"Lunch? I don't eat a big lunch," Mom said, almost to herself.

"You know," Gemma warned, dabbing her lips with a cloth napkin, "the people here, they're very nice, they'll say hello in the hall, they'll introduce their grandchildren, but don't let that fool you. Do you think any of them has ever invited me into her apartment for a cup of coffee? If you come here looking to make real friends, forget it."

What? Were they snobs, anti-Semites, reactionaries, recluses? No, Carla assured us, they were like people everywhere. They were wrapped up in themselves, they had cliques, they preferred their families to the strangers with whom they'd been thrown together by chance and economics. They spent a good deal of time in their apartments watching TV.

"And let's face it, as one grows older one finds that one's tolerance becomes limited."

"Tolerance?" Mom asked.

"Yes. Don't you find that? Tolerance for anything—other people, new situations, or late hours, or having to adjust to someone else's tastes."

Mom glanced at me in confusion, almost in fright. She wanted me to say something to save her.

"At our age we all have to learn to conserve our energy," Gemma said. "And making adjustments takes energy. Unless maybe you're different." She stood, went to the phone, and dialed the assistant director of resident services to get us a tour of the facility.

Did Gemma know that the few, normal reservations she'd expressed about Horizon View were enough to—as my mother might phrase it—put the kibosh on the whole deal?

"Well, Carla," she said when the assistant director knocked at the door, "I can't tell you how delightful it's been to see you again." The two old women hugged lightly and parted. "And *you!*" Gemma said, turning to embrace me. "So good-looking, and such nice clothes, a grown woman, Carla, can you believe it?"

"What are you talking about, I have grandchildren who are almost grown," Mom agreed.

"You," Carla said to me, "I want to stay in touch with. Call me on the phone, and—"

"I'll be here a lot to visit Mom."

"Of course, I know that. Make it visiting me, too. Have you ever had a friend who's this much older than you—not a mother, an aunt, but a friend?"

In a burst of affection I offered to drive Gemma to any of the artistic or medical destinations where I'd be chauffeuring my mother.

"God bless children," Gemma said as we hugged. "They can teach their parents."

We pressed cheek to cheek with a tender strength that came from deep within Gemma, I felt, as if from beneath her creamy skin and brittle bones she was sending a message, trying and trying to overcome her life. The bride hiding herself in the bathroom, relying on a distant cousin as a confidante…the lonely coed retreating behind social superiority…playing peekaboo inside an elderly widow who seemed fatigued from overrefinement. She was one of those people for whom, you get the feeling, happiness or unhappiness is irrelevant: they've traded both away for a certain look. I wished I'd known her before.

Mom moved into Horizon View, basically because I forced her—I practically put the pen into her hand so she would sign the application form. The months before the move were torture. She would have been anxious about any sudden change, but Gemma's warnings sent her into tremors. I got the brunt of it, it goes without saying. My brothers made frequent assertions that they would do their part and take her off my hands for a while—a night at the theater, whatever—and to give them credit, they did show up once in a while, but in the end, not unexpectedly, it was always me who had to face the serious issues. And calm her down, understandingly but firmly, through a million anxiety attacks. Several times she was on the point of cancelling her application, but I cleverly appealed to her reluctance to lose the deposit.

She tried to call Gemma a few times but always got her answering machine. Mom's calls weren't returned. I had thought of sending Gemma a thank-you note for showing us her apartment, but it happened to be a busy season for me, backed up with all kinds of commitments both personal and professional, and by the time I would have had a free moment to buy a card and jot down something nice, it was so long after the event that it would have seemed gauche. On the day Mom's moving van pulled into the retirement community, we did find a very lovely bouquet of local wildflowers waiting at the doorstep in a wicker basket with a warm "Welcome" note specifying that Gemma hoped to see us soon, implicitly atoning for not returning the calls. But Mom was preoccupied with getting set up, and felt uneasy inviting anyone to her apartment before all the shipping boxes were out of the way. Plus, Mom is a night person, and by the time she got around to thinking about calling Gemma it would be almost dinnertime and she'd stop herself: "What am I doing, she'll be asleep, if I wake her she'll hold it against me; if she's like me she wakes up five times a night anyway to go to the bathroom…."

Finally they got in touch, through sheer exhaustion of excuses. Mom suggested that they stroll down to the dock and watch the migrating waterfowl—but suddenly Gemma, who had scorned organized activities, now had all kinds of conflicts on her schedule. A hearing-loss seminar tomorrow, a discussion entitled "Let's Talk Leakage" the day after, and the day after that she'd need to rest from all the previous exertion. Then on the weekend her son was picking her up to go to the city for some shopping…. They'd better arrange something soon or the migrating season would be over; so okay, both Mom and Gemma pencilled in the following Friday for their ornithological observations….

Here it turns gruesome. The next week came, and every day, Mom called me to vent her predictions about how disastrous the waterfowl expedition would be; the Thursday came, and in the middle of the night Gemma woke up as if from a nightmare and discovered she had lost the use of her left arm and leg. A stroke. She could still speak, and her thought processes were unaffected, but the limitation on her mobility was so great and unaccustomed, at this late stage of life, that she needed to move to the Assisted Living wing for her own safety and comfort. That was at the other end of Horizon View, nearly a quarter-mile walk, and for Mom, who had recently converted from a cane to a walker, it was an unimaginable trek. To reserve the institution's van would have cost a ten-dollar minimum, just as if she were visiting a friend in Silver Spring or Bethesda. Mom was one of the poorer residents of Horizon View (yet not poor enough for government assistance). Besides, we learned that residents in Independent Living did not customarily visit friends who had transferred to Assisted Living, unless they were spouses, and not as often as you'd think even in that case. Illness and injury were so commonplace in a retirement community that if you paid a visit to everyone who succumbed to something, you'd have no time for those last little fulfillments you planned to squeeze into your own life. You merely sent a card and were grateful it hadn't happened to you.

While Gemma was in Assisted Living, Carla was becoming adjusted to her new life, getting acquainted with interesting people. A former minister and his wife became her steady lunch companions; a widowered, retired doctor gave her a teapot as a housewarming gift and invited himself to Mom's for tea; both the book discussion group and the travel discussion group actively recruited her, eager for the participation of any newcomer who was, at seventy-nine, four years younger than the average at this place and mentally completely unimpaired.

Mom mentioned Gemma frequently. She had turned her longlost cousin into an improbable goal to be striven for with dimming hope, a treat to be earned if they were both good—good patients, with good genes. Just as she had always acted as if the ordinary pleasures of life—a trip to Israel, a dress not marked down—were rewards reserved for others.

"When Gemma's well enough to leave that room of hers...If I can ever manage to walk that far without falling.... Look, maybe next time you can drive me to her, to that place there, even if it seems ridiculous to drive so short a way...."

I assured her it wasn't ridiculous, I would drive her any distance long or short if she asked. She just hadn't asked up to that point, except for indirect hints which on principle I refused to reply to, since I wanted to train her to express her needs forthrightly. I would drive her the two blocks to Assisted Living at my next visit.

But when I next visited, Gemma was no longer there; she had been moved to a nursing home. My mother wrote a reminder to herself to get the address of the nursing home, but by the time she got it, Gemma was dead. She had had two more strokes in quick succession, within a week of moving in.

I drove Mom to the funeral, which was held in the Baltimore suburb where Gemma had lived for many years before Horizon View. We sat on the side aisle, near the front, and listened to

Gemma's survivors tell who they thought she was. We, of course, didn't think we had anything to go up and say. We listened with the eagerness of learning. Mom put her hand on my forearm. Every time she heard some new bit of past history about Gemma, or some relative's little glimpse into Gemma's soul, her fingers would clutch at my skin, her nails biting into me as she whispered loud enough to annoy the neighboring rows, "I never knew that about her!" "*Oy Gutt,* did you hear that!" "It just goes to show you!" As I felt the pinching at my forearm and tried unsuccessfully to ignore the kvetchy exclamations in my ear, I couldn't help feeling that the right sentiments were within her, but that through some kind of self-denying magic they were all coming out—had always come out—wrong.

Mom still lives at Horizon View. She could be popular there if she knew how. She still goes to the travel discussion group, but what she mostly seems to learn there is how privileged the early lives of some of her fellow residents were: this one grew up as the child of an ambassador in South America, that one learned how to ski in the Rockies during the Depression.... Mom returns from those discussions with an inverse sense of wonder: she marvels not at how many interesting places there are in the world, but at how little she has lived compared to others. As far as the book discussion group goes, she's so upset at having to use a magnifying glass to read the smaller typefaces—something a good quarter of the other members also use—that she dropped out right after the retired doctor, pursuing her, joined it.

There are many places in the building and on the grounds where she prefers not to go because they remind her of Gemma. There's an exercise room at the end of the second-floor hallway, but she's never gone there: to do so, she would have to pass Gemma's old apartment. A group of women once invited her to join their regular lunch table, but she steered clear when she learned that they were asking her to fill Gemma's seat; and now she makes sure not to take her lunch at the same time those women do. If I drive her to a certain shoe store, for example (her bunion requiring extra room), she'll say with a start, "I think this is the one Gemma mentioned on the phone when I asked her," and she'll rush out of the area's most well-stocked collection of therapeutic footwear, unable to find anything comfortable to wear. If it's a hot day and I suggest a dip in the Horizon View pool, she'll put on a sour face: "I was never much of a swimmer. My cousin Gemma used to swim, she learned as a very young child."

What really drives me crazy is when she implies that if Gemma were only alive they'd be spending all their time together in an idyll of cousinly understanding, and she would be content. "I thought when I first came here I was going to…" has become a big expression of hers. She thought that when she first got there she was going to see movies; she thought that when she first got there she was going to take a French course. Now these activities are barred to her because Gemma isn't there to share them, just as the shoe store and the pool are spoiled for her because Gemma's ghost *does* share them. Reading the weekly activity sheet posted in the mail room, she clucks her tongue and says, "They're showing another musical; Gemma told me they're always showing musicals at this place."

She constantly lets the world know how gray life is for her without Gemma; but never, as far as I know, does she look back and say, "Fifty years ago we could have made it different."

I have to try so hard just to keep from screaming at her: *And if Gemma was here would you be going to the musical? If Gemma was here wouldn't you be avoiding her too, for some reason? Now you need Gemma to do things with? She's your buddy? What about the whole rest of your life when you hardly saw each other?*

One time, I really let her have it. I hardly remember what started it. Oh, that's right, come to think of it, she was moaning about how difficult it was, supposedly, for her to make friends there. Repeating almost word for word the warning Gemma had given us, except that when my mother said it, she made it sound immeasurably more dire. So I dutifully replied, "Well, what about that friend from the book group, and what about the doctor who had a crush on you," and she: "What friend? What crush? What are you talking about?"

I just lost it, I'm sorry. I began to shriek. "I can't stand it! I've been hearing this all my life! You are the most negative person I have ever met, and you made me this way too! What is it, what will satisfy you—death? Well, you're almost there. You're at the end of your fucking life and what are you doing? You're saying exactly the same things you said thirty years ago about how you can't do this and you can't do that. Nothing has changed. It isn't old age. It's you, it's the way you always were, and it's always been a crock of shit, there's only one thing you've ever been right about: that your life has been a waste, that you did not live. So in five years or ten years, when you die, it won't be any different; what you have now is death, and you spread it everywhere around you, you inflicted it on me from the moment I was born."

I said that to my mother, and I said a lot more, and she sat there, a small old lady in a dining chair, shriveling under it, as if under one of those beauty-parlor hair dryers she always bragged about never experiencing. I told her about conversations my brothers and I had had about her—painful truths that should never have been repeated. I told her how I dreaded her phone calls, and what I'd rather be doing when I was visiting her. I told her the names my childhood friends had called her. I told her I sometimes wondered whether I'd have been better off if she'd died in childbirth—that one wasn't even true, I thought of it as I said it.

I felt myself sailing into some realm of uncontrol, some high gray space, some stratosphere, like a balloon that only a giant could grab. I was screaming wild things and thinking, *Mommy stop me. Bring me back.*

But I guess I've always had to bring myself back. That skill, I learned early. When I get like this, there's usually some moment when I glimpse something in the recipient's eye, a fear, plus my feeling that if I were in their place I would hate me. At the last minute, I burst, like a boil, of my own infection. Crying. Not crying, not anymore. Just coughing and then trying to be still.

I felt as if I'd physically beaten her. As I settled down, I had little twitches in my arms as if I were swinging at her. She looks so frail lately, I often think, *Someday she's going to fall and break her hip….*

Just before I ran out of the room, she said, "Don't worry, this is nothing new for me either."

I can foresee that in her last years I'll have to spend a good deal of time with her which will not necessarily be pleasant. I want to be there for her, but to be effective I have to avoid being sucked in. I have to strike a balance. I have to learn to realize that there's a limit to how much you're going to re-educate an almost-eighty-year-old. I'm not going to succeed in making her a different person; I can only try to find little avenues of comparatively good feeling for her to walk down, as opposed to her usual main thoroughfares of anxiety, depression, et cetera.

I take her to a nice seafood place for crab cakes, or, if she feels up to walking, to a historical restoration where they show how Marylanders lived in the 1700s. If she starts talking plaintively en route about how Gemma would have liked it or how Gemma once mentioned this destination, I interpret it as a diagnostic sign she's tired and/or hungry. We sit somewhere, I buy her a Coke or a fruit juice. To her whines about Gemma I don't respond, except with at most a nod or an "uh-huh." After all, I lost a friend in Gemma too.

I have to learn—even if I have to force myself—to keep a distance. Once in a while no doubt I will have to say, "I can't make it this weekend, Mom, I'm going to a friend's." Even if I'm not going to a friend's. I may have to lie diplomatically, as an alternative to screaming and running away. Because what she has is catching.

On the Flight Path

I *came as soon as I could* would sound false, even though it was true, so he said the same thing in slightly different words; but the tightening of his mouth as he hesitated had the same damning effect as if he were apologizing for a lie, when he really had rushed down here. Anyway, his father's eyes didn't flash disbelief or irony, or forgiveness either; what was Jack expecting, magnanimity from the terminally ill? Bernard hadn't noticed how often or seldom Jack visited. Nor did he quip, "Just tell me you're not a ghostly apparition," as he had one night when Jack had appeared in his doorway, luggageless, after a thousand-mile escape from his latest love or job. (With an inherited sense of economy, he always fled both at once.) Bernard the wry, weary, cocktail-lounge wit, glad to welcome his failures home in the middle of the night, was a personality that had fallen away as uselessly as any other. (But I'm not a failure, Jack often counseled himself. I have succeeded at improvising a varied life, surviving challenges both objective and self-imposed, and reclaiming my joy.)

What the wizened swinger with white saliva spots on his chin brought out, staring through the same space he had stared through before Jack stepped in to fill it, were two dehydrated, confident syllables:

"I'm dead."

It made Jack feel unsteady, as if the room lights were dimmer-switching up and down. *My father, speaking, is dead, therefore I, speaking…must I be, too?*

All he could do was let it pass. "You're going to get better."

"I'm dead," Bernard repeated with strength summoned from the grave, warding off the phantoms who preyed on the living. And looking at him, Jack was guiltily tempted to grant the point. The old man's skull, dented, hollowed by loss of hair and weight, fluorescent shadows filling the bony contours, made him think of hills and valleys on an eroded planet.

He'd been hiding that reaction since he walked in, and the effort made him sentimental. Before he knew it, Jack was actually—a detail he would later proudly describe to his sisters—kneeling at his father's bedside, seizing his mottled, swollen-jointed hand in both hands hard enough to hurt it—go ahead and hurt a little, better than this deadness—and kissing the old man on the white-haired shoulder bared by the slippage of an untied hospital gown. Then he stood, fealty accomplished (and in case anyone should walk in), and tied the strings into a nice bow behind Bernard's neck, and gripped the withered neck muscles whose slackness scared him, and he held the hand again, more loosely.

"Dad, you're alive. Whether it's one year, two years, five years, even ten." The last couple of figures were sheer fantasy. "Be alive till the last instant, be completely alive up to the very last moment."

With an anxious whimper, with no energy except to mark himself off as taboo, the old man pulled his hand away from Jack's, just as he had pulled the intravenous tubes out of his veins in the middle of the night.

"I feel like I'm dying," Bernard insisted, and Jack hoped the switch from *I am* to *I feel like* was a sign of improvement. "I"—the very word made Bernard stammer hopelessly, lose his train of thought, then speak in a different way, in a faltering voice muffled by time-echoes. "Tell them I'll get there when I get there, I can't do this kind of work by an ironclad schedule. They think"—he mentioned some names Jack didn't know—"they think I'm a machine they put a nickel in and out comes copy: a speech, a brochure, an ad. Do I ever miss a deadline? Not a reasonable one. They're the ones who give me things late, with their meetings upon meetings. Then it's rush-rush-rush, get this done by yesterday."

"Dad."

Bernard blinked, and pushed the flats of his hands down on the mattress to try to shift his weight upright—a gesture that worked in a nonphysical sense, bringing him back. Jack pressed the button on the control handset to tilt the head of the bed, upward, and carefully lifted his father a few inches by the armpits. Resettled in the present, Bernard stared opaquely at the wall, where the cheerful blue of its lower half met the clean, professional white of the upper. He slumped until Jack feared he'd fall face down; but Bernard held that round-shouldered posture at an angle, held steady by who knew what. His lips moved and dribbled. The rest of him was quite still.

"Dad, you know where you are and what happened, right? You're in the hospital. You had one lung taken out. And some lymph glands. But lots of people live with one lung, and what are lymph glands? You've got plenty of them."

This diagnosis seemed not to impress Bernard. He licked his lips, unsuccessfully trying to draw back some saliva. He was absorbed in a point somewhere beyond the foot of the bed. Jack, beside him, looked in the same direction but could see only that it was the barest spot in the room.

Jack turned away and try to busy himself with things that wouldn't hurt. He picked up the cellophane-sealed box of chocolates on the wheeled dining counter. He looked at the digital displays on the monitor in the corner, the numbers and graph lines varying ceaselessly within limits that might, for all he knew, be reassuring. A couple of get-well cards on the bulletin board: a comically forlorn rabbit with an icebag on his head and a bursting thermometer in his mouth; a golden sunrise spreading rays through embossed italic script. Not enough cards! And not enough flowers, just one large vase and two little ones. He'd thought of Bernard as a man who knew many people, and whom many cared about.

And these—who put these here? Photographs of his sisters and himself. Childhood photos, adult photos—perhaps Bernard didn't distinguish between them anymore. Mandy with her husband and child, Jocelyn with a bygone boyfriend. The three of them waist-deep in an upstate lake when they were kids, standing splash-distance from each other, bone-skinny, and squinting with jokey, sunblinded impatience at the photographer. It might as well have been quicksand, Jack found himself thinking, and was so surprised, he feared it must be true. Turning water into quicksand: that was—used to be—the story of his life, wasn't it? So he erased it, which was the right thing to do with one's self-applied labels, and substituted: I was so proud when I finally learned to swim; and remember dancing with them in the casino to Sinatra's "Ring-a-Ding-Ding"?

"Dad." He sat on the edge of the bed, then got up immediately. "Is it okay if I sit here? It isn't uncomfortable?" Sat down again. "This is a very serious situation you're in, I don't want to minimize it. It's as serious as anything gets. But that's exactly why you can't despair, understand?"

"Tell her to meet me at that Italian place, what's it called, by Sheridan Square. Tiny, narrow place, cramped—white tablecloths—specials on the blackboard." Bernard inhaled louder than he was talking; with his eyes savoringly shut he looked more animated than with them open. Jack, eavesdropping on his father's past, didn't want to jar him awake. "She can bring her portfolio, what do I care, I'll look at her pictures. Because we first met at the Village Vanguard, she thinks I'm some kind of artiste." Eyes closed, he gave an intimate, snuffling laugh, like a man appreciating a wine cork under his nose. "Artsy women. I always get into trouble with them."

Jack pictured his father in his open-at-the-rear hospital gown, with unshaven face, knobby feet, and intavenous hookup, shuffling to his Village assignation at the rate of one quarter-mile per hour. He turned the thought into a fond little chuckle, tenderly taking his father's wrist.

"You've had great times, Dad. That's what I'm saying: now you have to meet this with all the life you have. Seventy-three years of it. You may be feeling weak now, but you have seventy-three years of strength still inside you, and you have to gather all that up and turn it into, into armor. All those cigarettes—there were good times when you smoked them, right? Women? Nights? Days in the city, in the country? Throw the cigarettes away, but remember all those people and those places and *that's* why you have to live these next years, to remember them and make them mean something. I know what it's like to despair on life—not that I'm comparing my situation with yours—but I know you can say Fuck You to despair and, no matter how late it is, start living again like you were just born."

And his father said, "Why are you bothering me with this? I don't even know you."

It was so like his parents, pushing him further down with each remark. But he'd been through enough treatment, far enough away, to get up again.

"Okay, Dad. Fair enough. I know what you're saying. I haven't been here much, but I'm here now. And I'll stay. There's nothing I have to go back west for right now, but that's neither here nor there. What I'm saying is"—he paused and gathered it inside him before he could let it out. "The girls have talked to the doctor, that very nice woman doctor, remember?, and I've discussed it with them and I met the doctor this morning on my way in, and the thing is to decide what can bring you out of this so you can face this crisis. And what we think is—we're all pretty much agreed— that you're very much depressed and have to be brought out of it. There are medications, but they could take weeks to start working. Really the fastest, most reliable treatment for a deep depression is electroshock. It has a bad reputation."

Bernard had begun to shake his head.

"But that's based on old images," Jack continued, "movies from the fifties with people screaming as they're strapped down...."

A crumb of breakfast dropped from Bernard's chin whiskers. The bubble in the corner of his mouth popped.

"Today they do it much better, they control the dosages and everything, and they give you a relaxant beforehand, it doesn't hurt. I've never had it myself, but I've had medications, I'm in favor of whatever works. With the shock, the only side effect usually is some short-term memory loss...."

"No, no," Bernard said, "stop telling me all this. Don't tell me how bad it is. All this negative stuff."

"What do you mean?"

Bernard shook his head at the interruption. "I told them, all right, anything, I'll put myself in the electric chair, anything to stop this." He sounded like he was about to weep from anger. "You're trying to convince me, but it's like putting roadblocks in my path. That's all people do here. Explaining, persuading, re-explaining.... Crap! I'm waiting. When are they going to do it?"

"Then did they explain about the memory loss? You won't remember the shock. You might not even remember the operation."

"I don't need those memories." He strained forward in bed, elbows buckling. "I need to use the bathroom. I can't walk to the bathroom." The bright cubicle with its steel fixtures was six feet away, through an open door within the room. Bernard lifted one hand off the mattress, reaching, and Jack rushed forward so the hand could land on his back. Carry his father to the toilet? Surreptitiously he gave a little upward movement to test the old man's weight—judged by mere poundage, it would have been easy enough.

Jack reached across the bed and pressed the button to call the nurse. "Mr. Redlich has to go to the bathroom, he needs assistance, please, right away...." And he held his father upright, arms around him, as they waited for help.

He's always needed a woman in his life, Jack thought, and now he needs one to prop him up while he pees. The image fascinated him like something repulsive, and to drive it out he snooped into the patients' rooms, to see who had visitors and who didn't, and how many flowers and balloons and what kinds of monitor hookups and IVs they had. The hallway smelled intoxicatingly of betadine and steamed meat; near the elevators stood a wheeled metal cart loaded with used meal trays; and in a doorway, a man younger than Jack, with a harrowed stare in a fallen face the color of a used gown, angrily gripped the left side of his body to keep it from sinking against the arm of his wheelchair. Jack liked the atmosphere of hospitals. Healers are healed. He had never been part of anything with the esprits de corps of a hospital staff; therapy groups, the nearest he'd come, were stitched gapingly together by fantasy and grievance. Would it have saved him if he had? If he were a doctor—maybe a cardiologist or a neurologist—he could very well imagine feeling that the hospital was his true home. He'd have a wife and children; they'd feel slighted sometimes, but they'd be proud of him and they'd never want for anything materially—

including existence, which in reality he couldn't afford for them.

But might-have-beens, like maybe-somedays and shoulds, were traitors to watch out for. His goal was to experience the present moment, and he went at it with solemn joy and considerable success. Already he could scarcely remember the city he had arrived from. Of course, he *could* remember it with a few seconds' effort: this wasn't amnesia, it was a setting-aright. He could almost hear her voice, the woman who was the place: "Did you stop loving me because I have to work on Saturdays? Did it not fit into your schedule? Were you jealous of my teenage son, or was it just that I'm old enough to have one?" Himself thinking she might be right on particular points, but overriding every other signal was the irresistible urge to run. And his well-turned, in fact prepared reply: "I'd rather be alone for the rest of my life than ever have another conversation like this." Phrases floated, colored reminiscently at the edge of her Nevada desert, a lipstick twilight after the sun had dropped below the horizon. Arguments became slogans—another danger, he must avoid living by the verbal formulas of a fumbled past. What remained clear and steady in his mind was how beautiful she had made herself for the meeting at which they knew they would agree to part. She had become a pinup of someone he would never meet.

Was it this mental poster of her—the knowledge that he hadn't lost it in moving—that sent a warm happiness through him? A heat-shiver of recovery started between his shoulders and climbed his head from back to front. Whenever that happened, what he hoped was to stand still and feel it fully, cherish it, for a half-minute which he could live on for at least a week.

In a passion he felt himself borne to the window at the end of the hall, and he blossomed gratefully within one of those eternal moments that opened his heart in fits. Under the spell of a surge of fluoxetine in his blood, he intuited a universal rhythm of sickness and health: a pregnant mother clutched her jumping belly; an aide hoisted a cobweb-haired, tallow-faced concave figure from car to wheelchair; a man in a gray suit stood slumped against the white brick of the hospital, covering his eyes with his hand. All merely the elegant improvising of an infinite mind.

And he thought, Dad is going to die in a year or two. I'm sad, but it's such a rich, accepting sadness, a sadness that thrills at the beauty of life. I'll probably feel this way even when *I'm* dying.

Where did my torment go? It used to *be* me. It went to some other land, leaving me here in a cleansed place where grave illnesses are no cause for distress and mortality is a poetic touch. (But I can't reduce my dosage or I'll plunge into, first, flat staleness, and then unbearable pain.) I'd probably feel this way in a concentration camp if they fed me enough pills. Am I shallow, am I deficient? Those questions are only lingering symptoms. The truth is, everything is as it should be.

Before, I thought the only thing wrong with me was that I thought something was wrong with me. Now I think the only thing wrong with me is that I think nothing is wrong with me.

Bernard, with a cloudy, cheerful expression, leaned over to observe the gray linoleum pass underneath his wheelchair, like a ferry passenger yearning toward the foamy wake. At his shaven temples clung stray, transparent curls of congealed adhesive; around his head hung an acetone scent like nail polish remover. In his room, Jack, Mandy, and Jocelyn waited; he gave a sideways twitch of his chin that said to the nurse pushing him: See my welcoming committee.

It took so long for the nurse to position his father in bed, Jack was forced to interject encouragements like, "Easy does it," "Getting mobile," "That's the way." The old man sighed with a weak dilution of sensual pleasure (the starched white sheet, the fat foam pillow, the warm quiet room); the onlookers' feet shifted in relief. Mandy and Jocelyn both had the family moonface and broad, freckled nose, but Jocelyn, the younger, was taller and had turned her hair blonde and wore coordinated outfits, while Mandy's thick-soled sneakers, chosen to compensate for her lack of height, only emphasized it, and she apparently had two pairs of blue jeans and four or five faded, milk-stained blouses to her name. The sisters talked to each other on the phone three times a day, and sent important news to Jack eventually, after decisions had been made. That was the way all three preferred it.

"My three nemeses in fine form," Bernard said. "Well, that was an experience—I think."

To help explain what still buzzed inside his head, he lifted one hand, fingers curled almost into an O, and turned it this way and that to examine it, grasping, in its loop, with palsied delicacy, some fragile, ancient jewel. "It was like I was standing in a big empty field at night, and a star came down and touched me on the head and showed me everything—all the answers. Then it zoomed back and I forgot it all." He turned with a minimal, energy-saving motion to the nurse, with whom he acted immediately familiar, since she was the current incarnation of the woman who took care of him: a lineage traceable through lovers and wives to his mother, whose favorite he always refused to believe he was. "Something tells me that if I tried to get to the bathroom on my own, I wouldn't make it."

"Something tells me you're right," said the nurse, a small, sallow woman with acne scars, large hands, brown lips, large irreverent hazel eyes.

"See?" he said, looking among his children. "Someone who talks my language." And he made a groping motion, less than a slap at the air: a vestigial pat in the direction of her hand.

He propped himself up, as well as he could, with contented readiness to be assisted. As he shuffled with slow, fractional steps within the enclosure of the nurse's arm, the back of his gown swaying in an unconscious parody of friskiness, Jack and his sisters shared looks that were nearly angry, nearly blaming: He's at it again, flirting with everyone in sight, why is he like that, whose fault is it, why don't you do something, what can we do?

"Lucy" (his second wife) "once told me," Jocelyn said, "how he once told her the secret of getting what you want: 'Act helpless.' That was advice from an adult American male."

"She told you things like that?" Mandy said, and Jocelyn shrugged.

"He doesn't have to *act* it anymore," Jack said, and as always, he felt that neither of them was listening to him.

They all listened, however, to Bernard's urination, a sound so vivid they could practically see it through the wall, and the flush and the almost inaudible shuffling and the spray of the water faucet. Then there was a curious moment of nothing at all, when even the still-pouring water seemed to have gone silent. Then came his scream.

They were running toward the bathroom door when he cried, "What happened? Who did this? What happened to me?"

He was staring at his face in the mirror, his fingertips tracing his cheek as if he had never seen that face before.

"What? What?" they asked him, and he wouldn't answer: if his children needed an explanation of his shock, that meant they weren't surprised by what surprised him, which meant they they were in on it....

"Mr. Redlich," the nurse said kindly, cupping her hand under his elbow. "Come away from the mirror."

"No, no!" He pointed at the face. "Who is that?"

"It's you."

"No. That's not."

She looked at the girls, her irreverence processed into a faintly irritable compassion.

"I'm not that old," he said.

"Come away from the mirror." She nodded at Jack, who felt a resentful pleased flutter: she'd finally noticed him. He hurried forward and helped her tug Bernard passively out of sight of himself. When he was back in bed, panting wet-eyed, every place a memory of a mirror, the nurse said with polite quietness, but not too quiet for Bernard to hear, "I've seen this happen. He doesn't remember the cancer. Because of the shock—it took away his memory."

Jack said, "He doesn't remember—?"

Mandy said, bitterly flattening a question into a statement: "So he doesn't remember how much he's aged."

And Jocelyn, in awe, storing the anecdote to tell friends: "He's aged ten years in the past one."

"It's possible he lost a whole year, that happens."

Jack knelt and took his father's hand. "Dad, do you know you've been sick?"

"I *feel* sick. Sure, I know I'm in the hospital, but—" And he made a gesture Jack would sometimes, in the future, practice privately in the dark when he wanted to remember his father: he pointed at his own face with all ten hooked fingers, an arthritic spasm of disbelief, a demonstration of what he feared to utter—a heroically controlled, Jack realized, panic.

So they began to explain it, as carefully and considerately as they knew how, and when one explainer caught a sibling's eye, the new explainer took over so that the explanation didn't flag, didn't leave any spaces in which Bernard could cry out or refute. He sat in bed, pressed back like an astronaut by the hand of gravity, and nodded at the wall like someone hearing a farfetched tale he'd been asked to take seriously but was giving them time to make convincing.

Finally they had told the whole thing, and he had to believe it because there was no more. They watched the flexing of his eyebrows, the pulses of his temples, the dilation and contraction of his pupils, the partial separating and reclosing of his lips, for signs of his inner state.

"I'm older than I thought," he said, and that, Jack thought, was better than either *I'm dead* or *I'm dying*. "If only I remembered how I got this way." He licked a spot on his lips that was already damp. "How old am I?"

"Seventy-three." Jack spoke for the group.

"That's what I thought." He tried to bargain: "I look eighty."

No one spoke for the group.

The nurse stepped back against the wall, Bernard's chart on her chest, and listened skillfully, her smile a trained polygon that urged them onto their own resources.

And whether Bernard felt obliged to accede to rational explanations, or merely gave up, he was more tractable by lunchtime. The looseness in his limbs when his children adjusted his posture or raised him to gum a spoonful of cherry gelatin, the cooperation of his floppy, sacklike muscles being moved this way or that, became almost playful, his demeanor that of an adult tolerating a children's game. His tongue flicked at a morsel of cheesecake, which dropped to the hollow of his chin; he made several attempts to whisk it with his fingers before Jack blew the crumb onto the bedsheet, almost fearing the gust would knock his father down. He wiped Bernard's chin clean with a moistened pinkie.

"I should thank you for the excellent valet service," Bernard said, clearing a frog out of his throat, "but I don't—I don't feel—"

"That's all right," Jack said, brushing the crumb to the floor before sitting.

Bernard was still not looking at them when he spoke to them, or, the first terror having been lulled, expressing curiosity about his situation.

"Is there anything you want, Dad?" Mandy asked tiredly.

"I'd like to be thirty-six. That was a great age."

He must have forgotten that I'm thirty-six, Jack thought, for his father hadn't given him a wink or smile.

"I'd like that too," Mandy said. "I mean, can we get you some fruit, or a sandwich or something?"

"After my next shock treatment," Bernard said, "I think maybe I'll want a pastrami on rye with mustard."

"We can get one for you now."

Jocelyn was looking at her older sister as if she admired, but didn't quite understand, someone's getting involved in a conversation with a confused hospital patient. She turned to gaze out the window and stroke the heating vents in the sill.

Jack was thinking, I'm wasting being thirty-six. It was a great age for him, why isn't it a great age for me? No, it *is* a great age for me, it *is*.

"A sandwich, I'm not electrified enough for that joy," Bernard said. "Wait till after my next treatment."

Wait till after: that was the family motto, wasn't it? If you wanted to have fun, wait till after you did your homework; if you wanted to play ball, wait till after you cleaned your room; if you wanted to spend money, wait till after you paid your taxes; if you wanted to live, wait till after you checked off every inconsequential item on your list of burdens; if you wanted to love, wait till after you hurt a hundred people worth loving. If you wanted to eat a pastrami sandwich, wait till after you had gotten cancer and had a lung removed and shrunk to two-thirds your former size and had thousands of volts passed through your brain. This is a wonderful moment, Jack thought, a moment of learning. I'm learning how to unstick myself. I can thaw everything that's frozen in my life by asking, what is it that I'm putting off now, what is this moment's *wait till after?* And refuse to wait—put nothing off—not one more second's diffidence.

Wait till after we leave this room.

"What I'd like to do," Bernard said, "after this chest thing is over with"—stage four lung cancer, "this chest thing"!—"and these electric...*storms*...I'd like to start my own shop. A little business for businesses, nothing too ambitious at this stage, maybe me and a receptionist. What people don't realize is, if you know how to handle the English language nowadays, you're always in demand. I can't go out and locate a vacant office in this condition." He indicated his hospital gown. "Maybe Jocelyn can do that for me." And Mandy flashed Jack a wry headshake: Jocelyn's the one he asks!

Bernard, visualizing his plan, pressed his fingers to the sides of his nose and closed his eyes. "Maybe some place west of the public library, they've still got some rentals there that aren't too much. I'll be a development house for business writing; set up a network of freelancers; maybe even get into the design end...."

"After all your treatments," Jack said quietly, and gave his sisters a look, and wriggled his nose uncomfortably to try to rid his voice of its perennial tone of asking their approval.

When they left the room—for after his venture into the future Bernard had begun to grow testy, and demanded to know why people were keeping him from getting his sleep—Jocelyn said, in a distant, wishing, tone, and having smiled at a passing doctor, "He'll feel better."

"From now on," Mandy said, "he might be the only one who does."

Six months later, Jack and Bernard sat on a wooden pier beside a rocky breakwater at the southern shore of Queens, watching a black sunspot grow, curve away from the orange sun, and descend toward them in the form of a painful silver glare: a trans-Atlantic jet drawing streamers of white vapor. The house where Jack had spent his boyhood summers was in an urban beach community that had been middle class Jewish, then working class Catholic; now it was starting to be talked about among sophisticated young families who, having been priced out of Manhattan, were training themselves to think that dwelling under an international flight path was as desirable as traveling upon one. Bernard was one of the few who had stayed to see all the changes: "What's next? Fashion models posing by the ice cream cart? They've already got cappucino at the refreshment stand." Too often for Jack's comfort—believing it, or worse, teasing him?—the old guy mused aloud about living to see the next stage in the neighborhood's evolution.

Jack sat in a white deck chair, and Bernard sat in a wheelchair with an aluminum pole from whose hook hung an oxygen canister, carrying life through plastic tubing into his nostrils. Jack made a sun visor of his hand, and looked up at the shining tail of the jumbo jet passing above his head: so low, he could see the bolted sections of the fuselage, and so big, it seemed impossible that air could hold it. For a second the whole pier was in shadow, and Jack felt as if a miracle were suspended overhead. "Sabena—Belgium," he said.

"Could be coming from Athens or Madrid; they're big there."

And the two of them inhaled with the rapture of the thought, *Athens, Madrid.*

"Get me Marian Swedro on the phone, would you?" Bernard said suddenly.

"Marian Swedro?" Jack glanced down at the cordless handset that lay on the dock, in place of a third sunbather, between their chairs.

"I'm working on her. Just get her for me, will you? What's her number, eight six something?"

"How the hell would I know?" Propelled by fond gripes, Jack rummaged for his father's address book under the chair, and punched telephone buttons. "Hello, will you hold for Bernard Redlich?" he asked the woman on the line, and the answer was gushingly affirmative. The spectacle of Bernard grappling with the handset and struggling to hold it to his ear made Jack wonder what kind of woman would yearn for a call from this oxygen-sniffing *alte kocker.* And of all things he'd ever expected to wonder about his father, he'd never expected to wonder that.

"Hey there, when can you come over?" Bernard asked into the phone, in the manner of some junior edxecutive during the Kennedy era coaxing a sevcretary to his Manhattan pad. But the last syllables were consumed by the roar from another skyborne furnance. "Wait, wait…."

KLM from Frankfurt.

"When?" Bernard shouted in the aftermath. "I know you can't drive. Tell your daughter to drive you here. She and my son can sit on the beach and talk about their inheritances." Jack made a face, but it was a playing-along protest, and anyway Bernard was bent so intimately toward the phone that Jack only existed for him as a fictitious chaperone. "I'll have some tandoori chicken delivered. We'll drink enough chardonnay to give our doctors a heart attack."

The date having been successfully made, he passed the phone back to Jack with an insouciant laxness that almost made it fall. The conversation had rejuvenated Bernard by making him blush; his skin looked not just pinker, but smoother. "Met her in the hallway of the convalescent home. She has some kind of degenerative muscular disease and emphysema. Only a year younger than me, but a very with-it chick. Did I ever tell you," he went on by way of natural transition, "how I almost became co-owner of a famous Creole restaurant in New Orleans? I was down there with a public relations convention. This was, what, sixty-two, sixty-three? I had split up with your mother a couple of years before. I'm at this table with five other guys, drinking Sazeracs, and there's a woman standing on the balcony, watching us. Staring at me. She's also drinking a Sazerac, incidentally. After ten minutes or so, I head for the men's room, which lo-and-behold happens to be on the balcony. We look at each other. She's wearing a white mink stole, a champagne blonde Peggy Lee wig, dark glasses. 'Come here,' she says. She opens a door with a key—it's her office. She's the owner, the daughter of umpteen generations of late owners. We talk for five minutes, if that long—who I am, what I'm in town for, when I have to be back. Then she says"—Bernard lifted a forefinger, and Jack knew the finger would have wagged coquettishly if it had not trembled, and the voice would have softened to velvet in imitation of the woman if it had not faltered on phlegm—"'I promise you, if you stay, it'll be worth your while both financially and otherwise.' Bam. Like that. Women used to do things like that to me."

"I know." Jack remembered his father, and owned black-and-white photographs of a young man with a razor haircut, in suit and tie or in fishing gear, who looked like a stronger Montgomery Clift. Let's see, I was living with Mom and the girls—was I three, did he leave us that young? A scene from some long-gone Hanukkah arose—a distressed young brunette distributing small gifts to three unworldly chimnney sweep types—it was soft-edged now, a soundless, sky-blue dream.

"But I had to go for the laugh," Bernard said. "I move in close like I'm going to kiss her. I whisper, 'Yeah, and if I'm here three weeks, you'll be the co-owner of Redlich's Creole Kosher Deli.'" They both shook their heads at a lifetime of passed-up chances. "That was a big mistake, maybe. And why did I say no? Partly because she was older. Partly because she had asked me. I always had to be the one to ask." And they sighed at the loveliness of old follies. "This is beautiful here," Bernard said.

"Yes."

"A vista where you can see things land. Maybe I'll hold a salon on the dock. Able-bodied people can come if they're my children; anyone else is invited if they're as beat as I am." He made a sharp, long, wheezing sound, as if he were still smoking. "You know, I feel so good it worries me? It started a couple of days after the last treatment. I'm like a kite. I'm up here but my worries are down there. From overhead it's a nice pattern. Drifting in the breeze. Sometimes I think, I'd like to get just one more shock treatment; the string would break; the kite would be free.... "

"I feel like my problems are in another land," Jack agreed. "I'm in exile from them. I used to dwell in them; now I'm somewhere else, and I couldn't get to them if I tried."

Bernard reached for Jack, but he wasn't very good anymore at stretching his arm out full-length: he gave a love-swipe to the arm of Jack's chair instead. "Ever think you should have married the little TV producer, what's her name, Helen?"

"Helene." Jack looked at the horizon. He wanted to be a clear sky, with a firm horizon. He strove for simplification, and on this subject the most painless simplification was, "Half the time. Half the time I think it."

"I see her name sometimes on the credits on the news. I always thought it was a mistake for you to leave her. She was a challenge, I'll grant you. But a vivacious girl, and also stable—a rare combination. And to look at her was a tonic to the system."

Jack burst out laughing. "Good thing you didn't wait till it was too late to tell me." He got some valuable practice, then, in controlling anger and indignation. *What were you going to do, write it into your will?* As it did so often, the conversation with his father became imaginary. He could bet, though, that Bernard had spoken on the subject to the girls: *He should marry her, why doesn't he marry her?* They would have analyzed his life, arrived at pragmatic solutions—and then kept him in the dark. Why, because he was distant, touchy, easily offended? No, those were only the rationalizations. The real problem was that he was only a male. You could be proud of a son (some sons, some other sons), you could be ashamed of a son, you could turn your son into you or into the opposite of you, but you couldn't confide in a son, you couldn't relax with a son. If you wanted to confide in someone, you needed females.

"The hell with it," Jack said. And he remembered (but, "Regret is a total waste of time," one of his favorite self-help books said) another woman, the recent one: "Is it because I don't like wine with dinner?" she'd begged. "Is it because I complained about your snoring?" How harsh she'd been that last week or two—every plea a scolding—how she'd hurt him by asking for things he couldn't give....

"You pissed her away, that's par for the course," Bernard said, and he only knew about one of them. He paused to take in oxygen. Then Jack heard a momentarily unidentifiable noise that seemed to come from his father's mouth and the nasal tubing at the same time. At first he thought his father was scoffing at him—not an unprecedented phenomenon—but it was more like a single surprised cough, a bark, too loud for this solitude. God, no, a coronary, a seizure?

The old man was shaking his head from side to side like a child being tickled. He was smiling ecstatically with his head tilted up, his eyes closed, tears streaming, beading up and spilling along his cheek-tubes.

"Even the might-have-beens are precious," he said, slurping inward. His head was moving as if he were trying to track a bee in flight, but he was looking at something within, blinking wetly as if he'd gone underwater and resurfaced. "You think it could be worth it—the cancer, everything—to feel like this?"

Jack, who had never seen his father cry, was filled with admiration not, as in the past, for his charm or his combative energy, but for this new feat. He took Bernard's hand, something he had to think about less carefully than he used to, and they sat there in the sweetness, in the pleasant weightlessness of not having any answers. The sun was warm on their skin. A shining path stretched from the sun to their dock. Air France or Alitalia or Iberia crossed the top of a purpling cloud, leaving for a mirage-city: Paris, Rome, Madrid, Barcelona.

"I'll stay here with you," Jack said.

"Well, that's worth it too. That's worth it most." And he grimaced at the world around him as if someone had added too much sugar to a daiquiri. "Why'd they have to make it so damn sweet?" he protested. "Why'd they have to make it so sweet?"

Jack imagined an electric shock tingling his father's jawbone, the way a too-sweet taste makes your teeth ache; and an answer came, belatedly as always, but this answer redeemed all delays: if you could feel this way for even one second, the last second of your life, it made everything beforehand worthwhile. Like sometimes when you take a hallucinogen, it seemed to Jack that every misstep he'd ever taken had cleared the trail to this perfection; every erotic or commercial gaffe had been a rehearsal for this rapture. He had stayed in too many bad places and abandoned too many good ones, but it could culminate in bliss.

They had infinity before them in the next few months. He sensed exactly how his father felt: one sunset lasts forever, a series of sunsets is the wealth of worlds. No need to rush the next decision; there was endless time. Like a boy copying the way a man walks or coughs or puts on his wristwatch, he thought: Me too, I'll spend eternity on this dock. Work will come, women will come, the world will come to me, wave after wave, the blur and glint of the horizon always forming the same shimmer. He was confident enough to sit and do nothing. It had taken him decades to achieve.

We will be here forever, in the magnificent roar of airplanes. Through his father's feeble hand, Jack could feel what it would be like to die. It was an ecstasy worth living for. Jack almost wished— no, did he really, or was this a trace of what he would have thought in the old days, something suppressed now by the medication?— but in either case it was no reason to be upset, a shake of the neural kaleidoscope, a benign interior entertainment—he wished he didn't have to go through the intervening forty years.

Putting Up Signs

Trying to become a great man and ending up a good man instead—was that his fate, Nels Goldstrom wondered as he stapled his daughter's photocopied face to telephone poles throughout the downtown area of Madison, Wisconsin? The poster's boldface headline asked, HAVE YOU SEEN KORIN? The caption explained that this sixteen-year-old white female, five feet nine inches tall and weighing one hundred twenty pounds, with sandy hair and hazel eyes, formerly frequented State Street and the Capitol steps; you might have seen her at the Loft, or Ella's, or the concession stand at James Madison Park. Below the Goldstroms' phone number was the announcement of a reward for information leading to Korin's whereabouts, serious replies only.

"Seen her yesterday," came a voice from behind, at shoulder level. A little snotnose with a struggling goatee, a red knit wool cap with white stars, and a second shirt instead of a jacket.

"Told us, tell you piss off," his buddy said—even shorter, with no facial hair and no cap, and tightly folded arms substituting for outerwear. It was late March, a thaw was in sight.

Said the third wastrel, an anorexic girl standing on the hood of a parked Range Rover, wearing a man's gray gabardine overcoat

at shin length, eyebrow and lip rings, and third-eye tattoo (tempo-
rary, Goldstrom hoped), "If she wanted you to know where she
was, she'd tell you."

Goldstrom, who could have carried all three in his arms from
here to the police station without major risk to his sacroiliac, rushed
up to her with strides just short of threatening. "Did she say where
she was going?"

"I don't know who the fuck you're talking about," said the
girl, and raised the toe of her boot in a way which, although apparently innocent, reminded him that she could kick straight into his
windpipe. "You'll just have to find another girl-toy, won't you?"

Disgusted, he took his sheaf of posters to the next block and
squeezed extra staples out of his gun to fasten his wishes more se-
curely. Those three specimens of at-risk youth assumed they knew
his daughter better than he did, though they'd never met her;
through tribal affiliation, she was one of them, while he was an
interchangeable enemy. But their parting challenge was empty: he
was not one of those abusers, those monster fathers. If he had
founded western society, it would never in thousands of years have
included, even among its deviations, parent-child incest, rape, sod-
omy, or any practice that linked sex and pain in any way. His neighbors, who may have formed the same ugly speculations, didn't know
that about him. He couldn't blame them. Who knows what might
be in the heart of a blond farmhorse of a man, a former student
radical turned tenured economist, padded stiff as an insulated attic
by years of lunch-hour weightlifting at the university gym and beer
after work? Sometimes he felt like wearing a nametag labeled, "Safe."

The doubts from his own household had the virtue of being
constant. His twin sons hunkered down with their homework when
he returned from crusading for their older sister. They were embarrassed by his exposing the family problems on the kiosks of
their city. Too bad. His wife Karen, plainer source of their daughter's
hipper name, stood up from the rocking chair and crossed his path
with a bittersweet smile of omniscience, on her way to check the
preheating of the oven.

He remembered when he was a grad student in Berkeley, driving up the winding faculty hills where the charming, terraced, redwood houses were wind-chimed and xeriscaped and security-
alarmed, and he'd say out loud, "These houses are the reward for

couples who don't have the nerve to get divorced." And Karen would reply, "When we go to these faculty dinners and the wife welcomes us at the door, I always feel like she's saying, 'Let me give you a tour of my cage.'" Their agreements, in those days, were not acquiescences, and their disagreements sounded like adventurous harmony.

But now they owned such a house, in not quite so picturesque or well-boutiqued a town, and it was absolutely taboo to tell Karen that she had become one of those wives.

She waited till dinner to ask, "Did you put up a lot of posters today?"

"Yep. Still have some left over, though." He took a big forkful of zucchini-and-four-cheese casserole. Closing his eyes to let the herbal flavors of his own garden fill his being, he heard in his mind Korin mocking, Korin who hadn't eaten with them even when she still lived here, Korin who (unless it was one of her insolent playmates) had strewn the garden with seeds whose young stalks he had snatched up and composted before they could be positively identified as illegal.

"I used marjoram in this," Karen pointed out. She was a tall, athletic woman of forty-five with a voice, not of velvet, but of warm, durable Polartec. Not inflexibly opposed to personal adornment, she wore turquoise Zuni bracelets whose stones brightened the hope for peace in her makeupless blue eyes; her long, loose, white hair shone from herbal conditioner, and her smile-lines were scrubbed with rainwater-scented soap. A good companion for canoeing lifevested around the shallows of Lake Mendota, or berrying at pick-your-own farms whose owners' Norwegian or German names were painted proudly on clean, blue silos, or playing two-on-two basketball with a pair of self-involved boy twins while your scornful daughter sketched the uninhabited end of the yard, or tutoring Nels Goldstrom on the fundamentals of human relationships, for which he was often grateful. "Think it needs more?" she asked.

"They say marjoram should be used sparingly, don't they?"

"But with zucchini...."

Goldstrom pushed back slightly in his chair and released a long sigh, the kind you give when you are full and satisfied enough to stand and go, although he was neither of those things and had no intention of leaving the table. He had been groaning aloud a lot lately, and like someone with a nervous tic who pretends he is simply brushing back his hair, he tried to make it look like something more acceptable.

"Do you have a lecture to write tonight?" she asked him, which gave him the opportunity to inform her that she had guessed wrong.

"Do you write out those lectures word for word or what?" asked Isaac, the older of the twins by six minutes.

"He isn't good at speaking without notes," said Jake, the twin with better posture and shorter hair, and when Goldstrom looked at him, said, "Hello? That's what you told me yourself."

Goldstrom gave him the no-nonsense stare which had, year by year, less and less effect on students in Econ 101, but which at least still caused his sons to resume eating. The boy—Jake, it was Jake, he sometimes still had trouble with who was who—was wearing a black No Fear sweatshirt, while Isaac's green fatigue top said, USMC Guantanamo Grenada Beirut Semper Fi. They had, it seemed to Goldstrom, been preparing since toddlerhood for their attack against him, laying down plans, through eyebrow liftings and derisive snorts, for some sudden, ultimate assault.

Squinting over a forkful of casserole, he asked his wife, "Hear anything from Mr. Meinke?" That was the detective.

"He's still pursuing all possible leads," Karen said, lowering her head to serve everyone another spoonful of quinoa pilaf. "He'll call as soon as he knows anything."

"He'll never call," Jake cracked, and the twins went into stereophonic hilarity, their voices unsettlingly deeper, it seemed to Goldstrom, with each sophomoric burst. In a rational world, wouldn't they sound more childish with each sophomoric burst? Apparently that wasn't the way things worked.

"Mr. Meinke," Isaac shook with laughter, hunching lower at the sheer ludicrousness of the name.

"Straighten your shoulders," Goldstrom said. "Oh, never mind, don't straighten your shoulders."

Karen gave him a side glance, assuring him she was not going to join in their offspring's mockery no matter how much he deserved it.

"Are you skipping dessert tonight?" she asked, tempting him to eat dessert. Losing with either choice, he regained half a point by answering with silence, passing the baking dish without taking any. He watched enviously as the three of them chomped down their kiwi-blueberry crisp with orange-mango sorbet.

"I better patch that back screen before mosquito season starts," he mused aloud. No one answered, he hadn't expected them to.

"Boys, did you get started on your research for the Native American Heroes paper?" Karen asked.

Mouths crammed with tropical fruit filling, they grunted indignantly at being supervised. Isaac and Jake, although not especially fond of each other, tried to be placed in the same classes whenever possible; they made no bones about the fact that this enabled them each to do only half the work and let the other copy that half. Goldstrom had once hesitantly brought this up with their history teacher, but the guy hadn't seen any ethical problem—it was a clever, efficient way to allocate resources in a cooperative learning situation.

It was not this fruit dessert, but another fruit dessert a week or so later, which was interrupted by the telephone's ring. Overriding Karen's settle-down glance, Goldstrom dashed shamelessly to the wall phone. The caller-ID readout showed a number with a 907 area code. He didn't recognize that. It made his voice tremble as if he were facing a packed lecture hall without notes.

"Hello?"

The caller's voice was so much, so exactly, what he'd hoped, that it took him a couple of seconds to believe it. He hadn't heard it in five months, since he'd slipped her a hundred-dollar bill while she was insisting on living in her friend's van at Picnic Point: since before she'd traveled south (he assumed) for the winter. So much, so exactly the voice he remembered, the voice he felt guilty for not keeping in his mind sixteen waking hours a day, the voice of the one who should be here, who should most be here, that it took him extra time before he felt hurt at what she said.

Rotelike, as if she'd memorized it so as to reduce conversation time, she proceeded in the annoyed, declaiming tone that always seemed to be aimed past her parents, above them, to some audience of pals urging her on from a corner of the ceiling. A tone he no longer understood why he used to object to: it was hers, it was right.

"I'm okay, I'm not in any trouble, I'm not coming back, I don't want you looking for me, I know you think you love me, if you keep trying to find me I'll keep going where you can't. Stop looking, stop worrying—stop everything, just live your own lives. I'm hanging up."

And she hung up.

907 was Alaska, he found out a few minutes later. That didn't mean she was in Alaska; her last call had read Singapore. As Mr. Meinke had explained, she'd probably met some hacker who knew how to patch the phone call through any random intermediary number, making it untraceable without special equipment. Mr. Meinke had sent inquiries to a Singapore investigative agency, along with a fax of Korin's picture and description, and seemed satisfied when nothing came of it. Of course, Goldstrom had been ready to jump on the next plane to Asia, but the forces of moderation had dissuaded him from that.

The one letter they'd received from her had been postmarked Grand Central Station in New York, with no return address, and the message had been inside an unmarked inner envelope that might have originated anywhere. Korin had never had a credit card, so there were no purchase records to trace, and an electronic search of her Social Security number had turned up no employment or tax history or bank account. "Bet she's establishing another identity for herself," Meinke had said with a note of admiration. "Not too hard for a sixteen-year-old, and there are books now that tell them how. What I'd do is, steal some kid's school ID, some kid with a common name—Joan Smith, Jenny Brown. Substitute her own picture, use that to get a library card and that to get a new Social Security card. Then she's home free. Could get a copy of the other kid's birth certificate just by saying she'd lost it, and with all that other stuff, a passport."

A passport. Korin in Morocco, smoking hashish on a beach; Korin in Nepal, hedonistically ruining an ancient culture.... Meinke's eyes had unfocused for a moment and Goldstrom could swear he knew what the detective was thinking: If I wanted to establish a new identity, what would I call myself, where would I go, and why don't I?

It was terrible living under a prohibition, no longer writing pleas in the Personals ads, not collaring unknown teenagers on the street and demanding to know if they knew her. This was the way Karen had wished to conduct the search from the beginning: dignified, don't make a spectacle—that would only repel Korin—don't pressure her into fleeing further, but rely instead on the slow, patient progress which Mr. Meinke periodically implied, without definitely stating, he was making. And preserve the home toward the day of Korin's return. Keep the same juniper-scented fire in the brick fireplace, the same photographs of Mexican villagers on the walls, the same rose-petal potpourri in the master bathroom and dried-apple-and-clove potpourri in the guest bath, the same Bach piano suites on the CD player. A total reversal from the past two decades, when Karen had optimistically persevered in changing and replacing every piece of decor, in her quiet quest for the perfect outer expression of her innerness. Now, she wanted every day to be the same, as if no matter how late her daughter finally returned, no time would have passed. The idea seemed to be that the gathered aura, the reiterated powerful image of her waiting kin, would transmit itself to Korin wherever she was hiding, and overcome her attempt to forget, and wrench her homeward.

Goldstrom wondered: If this was what Korin needed to run away from, why would keeping it intact draw her back? But this was a matter on which he knew his understanding was severely limited. He didn't even understand what had made Korin go away, what last-straw incident had put into motion the lifelong threat she'd first made at age five when she'd packed her crayons into a doll's suitcase and said, "What's a good place to be an artist? I'm running away there." They'd never done anything harsher than ground her for a month. Oh, Karen and Korin had yelled at each other just about every day, mother reminding daughter of something that would improve daughter—and daughter snapping back with sarcasm to show she was already, in her own mind, better than her mother—and mother scolding, and scolding for making her scold. It had hurt Goldstrom's ears, but the two of them had seemed like they were nicely settled into the habit and could have continued till the girl was twenty-one, or longer. She'd had cause for the usual complaints, but surely not to leave the whole thing behind. But didn't that somehow make it more admirable, if she obeyed the inmost call before desperation forced her to?

"Going for your late-night decaf?" Karen asked. She had guessed his intention before he'd intended it, and not for the first time. Okay, decaf was a good idea. As he pulled up his gum-soled boots, he thought, I'll drive around too, check the posters.

Would she guess he was doing that?

He took the old Volkswagen beetle, the second-and-a-half car, so called because this holdover from their past was used only for short trips that weren't worth the wear and tear on the Volvo or the Toyota. Spring snow showered pinkish-gold off the round hood as he pushed in low gear through furrows in the slush. The roads improved once he got off their obscure side street; and he drove through the snug, provincial city as if its streets were a graphic display of his life's errors.

He drove almost randomly, the scent of his exhaust overpowering the woodsmoke in the clean midwestern air, and at neighborhood bars and strip malls, at state office buildings and railroad crossings, he could read the history of his misguided attempt to lead a family. Sometimes it was in a private code only he could read: a traffic light where he and Karen had argued about which house to buy; a breakfast place where they had eaten in spiteful silence—but sometimes it was revealed to all in the face of his daughter in grainy black and white. The poster was untouched in the little health-food store where he or Karen shopped twice a week, but it had been taken down from the supermarket bulletin board, and it had been ripped, except for one corner, from the side of a phone booth on University Avenue. On a telephone pole on the grungy east side, it had been stapled over with other posters—for a political concert, a lesbian chiropractor, a motorcycle gang's benefit volleyball tournament.... He tore them off it as if tearing an aggressive man off her body.

Parking, he walked hatless in the wet snow, wiping his eyebrows with his jacket sleeve. He remembered every place where he'd posted his sign. Here was one where someone had drawn eyeglasses and a mustache on her! Here was one with a speech balloon coming from her lips, and vulgar suggestions emerging! And one with an anarchist symbol, and one with her face brutally crossed out, and one scrawled in the margin with a handwritten message, completely unrelated: "Dave, we waited for you here Sunday 11p you weren't here we went to the Cardinal. Us." And some were left clean and legible; and some were streaked and blurred with melted snow; and some were gone without a trace.

In the university bookstore, where he ducked inside to get

dry, he found three copies of his textbook, *Economics and Reality*, the same three copies that were always there. He touched their spines for luck, but what kind of luck was it? Even his colleagues didn't assign the book; he himself no longer had the heart to include it on his syllabus. It had promised to buy him a new house, and maybe a rental in Tuscany too—and it might have given him the leisure to be a better as well as a more well-known person, wasn't that possible? But a Harvard professor, who had condescended to him at professional conferences in all the major American tourist cities, had published a textbook the same year, and that had become the nationwide standard.

And here was something—here was something, he realized as he drove again, that he hadn't noticed in a long time. He parked at a converted schoolhouse on a hill above the frozen lake. Behind that tall window, curtained and lit, was once the bedroom of someone who had wanted him to follow her to Key West and play the stock market for a living. Evgenia. He remembered a stinging midwinter day when he'd tried to talk her out of spending her last savings on a ruffled bedspread and throw pillows. "I can sell them tomorrow if I have to," she'd said, "but tonight I need to be warm." And they'd made love under a weightless pile of new goose down, on a night too cold to open the chimney flue, and the next day she'd won an arts grant for her postmodern needlepoint. So much for economic theory. The cloth of fate was spun to fit her measurements.

If he'd gone to Key West with her, he'd be well up into the millions by now, just from leaning over in his beach chair to check the stock listings over morning coffee. And he'd wanted to go. Not just to Key West—anywhere he'd gone with her would have been Key West, would have been Atlantis, would have been Perelandra. That was ten years ago. Evgenia. Lucky she hadn't had a common name, the kind he'd be seeing wherever he looked. He'd heard she was on some smaller, more exclusive island now, linked to a real estate developer. Ten years ago he couldn't possibly have left, he had three children. He had four-year-old twins and a six-year-old girl. He had a six-year-old girl who counted on him to be there.

The old blue Volkswagen gargled its way home from the converted schoolhouse this slushy night, the same route it had taken on a dry, shivering night ten years earlier, when he'd told Evgenia that he was a responsible father and husband before anything else, and that she herself would surely lose faith in him if she saw him abandoning those to whom he'd made vows.

"No, Nels, I'm losing faith in you now," she'd said in the tone of sorrowful caress that he'd fallen in love with; an unfair remark, he thought, coming at a time when he was being so noble. And he'd gone home and undressed silently in the dark bedroom where Karen was waiting awake, and he wept in her armpit, and all she'd asked, lying face up and encircling him with a noncommital arm was, "Is that the end, then?" From that night, Goldstrom dated his existence as a man who put family and duty before all else, shouldering at least half of every load and never claiming credit, in the hope that someday Karen would finally give that to him on her own.

Nights since then, she trusted him enough not to wait up. The morning after his drive, he picked up the sheaf of extra posters from atop the bureau and began illicitly planning where to hang Korin's picture. It had snowed again before sunrise, a spring dumping of heavy, wet, gray grains that, when you scooped them up with one hand, adhered in a readymade, rough-edged snowball. The sky was brilliant, though, and the sorry snow shone. Neighbors were shoveling their walks, lifting away the bootprints of kids who'd passed on their way to the bus stop; and when Goldstrom, in shirt and vest and gloves, hefted his shovel out front, he noticed something odd, some pattern of glint and shadow, on the domed roof of the Volkswagen. He walked over.

A finger, or maybe a stick, had written in the snow on the roof of the little car. Capital letters, messy handwriting: "STOP LOOKING FOR HER."

He looked all around, as if the person who'd done it might still be there, as if he could tell who it was among the path-shovelers and the schoolgoing vandals. He wiped the hood with his forearm, and shook the burning wet cold off his shirt sleeve, spattering his pants. Only then did he wonder whether he ought to have shown the message to Karen. Well, he could tell her about it. But he wouldn't, for he visualized doing so and not knowing what kind of tone or introductory words to use.

The glistening day was like a spotlight aimed at him.

He put the sheaf of extra posters into the glove compartment.

And for the next six months, he drove around in the old bug, and opened the compartment regularly to look at Korin's face. He hoped that she would somehow know—her local spies would tell her—that he was obeying instructions and letting her live her own life. He didn't really like to share her with anyone else, anyway.

"Did you see this bill from Mr. Meinke?" Jake challenged him one afternoon in September.

"When *you* pay the bills, you can open them," he said, one of his paternal formulas.

"I didn't open it, I read the number through the envelope."

With amiable exasperation, Goldstrom snatched the envelope away from his son and tore it open. He read heavily, "One hundred...ninety-eight dollars...and sixty-one cents. Old trick, being precise so you'll think they're honest."

"Do you think he's cheating us?" said Karen, blocked in her exit by males crowding the vestibule.

"I don't know, maybe I can hire a detective to find out if my detective is cheating. He sure doesn't leave out any items, though. 'Automobile, one hundred forty-two miles, ten cents per mile.' Maybe he got a lead she turned up in Beloit."

"I've been thinking we should talk about that," Karen said.

"Lose the guy," Isaac said, slouching through the narrow space between them in order to join the circle, and popping a peanut-butter-and-chocolate bar.

"We've been spending hundreds of dollars a month on this for almost a year," Karen said.

"You want to stop looking for—" Goldstrom began, ready to fight.

"I don't want to stop looking, I want to think about our strategies."

"Hiring Meinke was how you wanted to do it."

"We have to adapt our strategies to the changing circumstances. If he had achieved any results, I wouldn't care how much we spent on him. But he's achieved no results, and we haven't bought a new sofa or rented a cabin up north...."

"So what's your strategy?"

"Trust her," Karen said simply, clasping her palms together. "Trust that she is living in a way she has chosen, and that it's not hurting her—not any more than living here would hurt her—and that when she's ready, she'll come back to us. She has told us herself that this is the way to get her back."

Goldstrom was shaken. "You want to give her up."

Karen smiled sadly. "I want to have her *as she wants to be.*"

Goldstrom pushed out of the vestibule, where the day's junk mail littered the welcome mat, and sat down at the foot of the staircase, needing a rest. He scanned again the itemized bill. It seemed the closest he could come to direct communication with his lost daughter. Telephone expenses...informants' fees...miscellaneous office...was it all just a penance he was paying, a show he was putting on to convince himself of something?

"She's almost seventeen," Isaac pointed out, chewing the candy bar. "If you keep doing this for another year, she'll be eighteen and then she can do whatever she wants."

Jake sneered. "You can still look for someone who's over eighteen. It's not like they're trying to kidnap her back here. They just want to find out where she is and what she's doing. So they can help her."

"Yeah, like Korin really wants their help."

"Wouldn't *you* like *Korin's* help?" Goldstrom asked his sons, and they went mute, glancing at each other. He added quietly, "I sometimes would."

With an instigating look at his twin, Jake said, "You want her to help us run away?"

"You know what he's saying," Isaac said.

"She could have used *our* help," Jake said, "if you want to know. We could have told her how to get through school. Even if we're two years younger. I mean, we don't like school any more than she did. No one does. Very few people. Most people just don't make as big a deal out of it."

"Yeah, you just have to know how to get through it," Isaac said. "Then you graduate and we're going to open up our law partnership and we can do whatever we want."

His future law partner added, "And if Korin's ever in jail and needs a lawyer, she'll come to us."

"Or if she gets busted for drugs."

"Hey, don't say that," Jake said. Turning apologetically to his mother, he said, "Korin has friends who take drugs, but she doesn't take much drugs."

"She doesn't take *many* drugs," Isaac corrected.

"I'm not saying she doesn't take *many* drugs. I don't know how many separate kinds of drugs she takes, do I?"

"But 'doesn't take much drugs' is grammatically incorrect."

"But 'doesn't take many drugs' is ambiguous, in fact it means totally what you don't want to say. Like you're saying she doesn't take many different pharmaceutical compounds?"

"Well, she doesn't."

"But what if she took *much* of just *one* drug?"

"It's still grammatically incorrect to say, 'She doesn't take much drugs.'"

"Yeah, but it's colloquial, and Mr. Botstein says it's sometimes okay to use the colloquial usage rather than correct grammar. What would you say? 'She doesn't take drugs in large quantities'?"

"Boys, please," Karen tried to say.

"She doesn't ingest large amounts of drugs," Isaac suggested.

"She isn't a major drug user," Jake supplied.

"If she uses drugs at all—which I'm not saying she does—she uses them lightly."

"Lightly? What are you trying to say?" Jake interrogated. "That she uses them light-heartedly?"

"Get away from me, will you? Mom, he's using aggressive body language, he's crowding my intimate zone."

"Yeah, well, I'm going to bust you in your intimate zone."

They were beginning to grapple, rattling the etched glass door of the vestibule.

From behind the visor of his arms, Goldstrom said, "Have these arguments when you're law partners. Bill them to your clients."

"This guy is too dumb to be my partner," Jake said. "I got the brains, fool," he jeered at Isaac. "I got the brains when Mom's egg split."

"Yo, chump, we're genetically identical."

"I need to get to rehearsal," Karen said. She was in a lesbian glee club although she was not a lesbian. "I still haven't memorized any of Vaughan Williams' carols."

"So you guys think we should fire Mr. Meinke?" Goldstrom asked, desperate enough to use his sons as oracles. "Jake, you're the one who's closer to Korin...."

"No, I am," Isaac said, apparently announcing their most recent revision of history. "And I say, as I've said before in this campaign, fellow Americans, lose the dick."

When Jake had recovered from hysterically congratulating his brother for that one, he said, "I think Korin deserves another month or two."

"They don't have deeply-felt opinions," Karen reminded Nels. "One just takes whatever side the other takes."

Goldstrom stood up from the staircase, sighing as if over an end-of-term grading book. "Gonna take a look at the furnace. Almost heating season, have to turn on the pilot light soon." He shuffled toward the basement door, knees aching in a way they never used to.

A later season, another year. Nels sits in his downstairs study, turning the pages of a scrapbook. Karen lights a lavender-scented candle to calm her nerves as she rechecks a recipe for pork roast with red wine and bay leaf. Just as the smell of the roast has permeated the house for the past hour, a jittery, avoidant silence has done so for the past forty-eight hours or more. Isaac and Jake have separately made sure to be away, the former practicing guitars with a group of buddies, the latter feeling the breast of his first girlfriend. From front to back of the scrapbook, evolution proceeds: an off-center snapshot of a gap-toothed, friz-haired girl too excited about life to realize that she wasn't pretty enough to grin with a balloon in front of her face; then a posed assembly of rows of reluctant children in bright-colored windbreakers, with skinny, squinty Korin squeezed pathetically between bigger kids; and finally a brief series of clippings from an alternative weekly newspaper: "Korin, please call Mom, Dad, or your brothers. We love you and miss you"; "K. We don't want to interfere in your life. We only want to know that you're okay. Please contact by any means you desire. If you need money we will send it discreetly per any instructions from you. Do not hesitate to ask"; "To our dear daughter, when will you forgive us whatever you must forgive us for? Please do not leave us in this limbo"; "Leave me alone. I know you think you love me. Your disrespect for my wishes does not show love. Wherever you chase me I can outrun you." That last ad, unsigned, might have been placed by many different people, as Karen had pointed out; but he had put it in the scrapbook over her objections. Recently Mr. Meinke called, asking if they'd heard anything from her—acting friendly, liked he personally cared, but he was only trying to scare up business. Today is Korin's eighteenth birthday.

"When we were her age, we met," Karen says, having walked in without his noticing.

"And we're still here."

"Still here." She sits on the arm of the easy chair to look at the scrapbook. Laughs low at a memory; touches the rim of a discolored polaroid. Goldstrom looks at her hand: the turquoise and silver ring, the swollen, tan knuckles, the oval nails with white calcium deposits which improved nutrition has not eliminated. She is wearing rumpled jeans and a loose-fitting gray smock, and she smells of chamomile and jasmine. He thinks, as he often does, that if he could at this very moment cry in front of her and tell her why, it would be a new world.

"What if she came back?" he says, to bring the subject around to the more admissible grief.

"I don't know. I can't even think that far."

"Maybe we'd get on her nerves just like before."

"There's a cheerful thought."

"What do you mean?"

"I don't mean anything."

He doesn't want another argument about who was being more sarcastic than who, so he lets it drop and turns the page of the scrapbook. "Look," Karen points over his shoulder, "camping at Whitefish Bay, remember, in our three-person tent with her little sleeping bag between us?"

And there is something in this he doesn't like. He never knew she has such glowing memories of Whitefish Bay, for one thing: she complained about the cramped tent when they were there, and since the twins were born they've never gotten around to camping again. He tries on principle not to object to people's preferences, the glitches in their taste or inconsistencies in their memory or logic, but God knows sometimes it rushes over him. Isn't there something pointed in her nostalgic recollection? Of course she'll claim that there isn't, that he's just being oversensitive. (It's curious how she calls him oversensitive, except when she acts as if he were a wooden post.) The fact that she mentioned fondly their camping trip to Whitefish Bay is absolutely nothing for him to get upset about. But that's exactly what's upsetting: she hides her reproaches where you can't see them.

It's this frustration that spurs his courage on. "You know, sometimes I think—I know you love our home, our life, it's very important to you." He has her full attention now. He swallows, moistens his throat. "Sometimes I get the feeling that you love us because we're here, because"—he deliberately phrases it in positive terms—"you love whatever you've been entrusted with. You're a loving person, so you love me. Because I'm who's here. Not because I'm me."

She considers her response, then gives a bleak laugh. "You're flattering me, Nels. Some people think that's the ideal, to love what's been given you. I'm not that perfect."

Now, what does that mean, he wonders? She still loves me for myself a little bit, though she'd rather love me impersonally for being the random soul she happens to live with? Or she can't bring herself to love me even though she feels it's her duty? And who are these "some people" who give her her ideals?

He imagines Karen sitting in a circle of weaving women, chanting reverently as they tread their looms, telling in counterpoint about the sacredness of the earth and the faults of men.

His faults are a constant grief to him and a cause of the disasters of Evgenia and Korin. His consciousness of them, he believes, is his redeeming quality; but although he can't remember his wife openly mentioning them recently, he thinks it unfair that she goes around looking like she knows what they are.

Sometimes he thinks she doesn't really know what they are. But sometimes he thinks she knows better than he does.

"So it's your ideal," he begins, knowing he doesn't have the fortitude to carry the fight through, "not to love me for myself?"

The phone rings before she can answer. Conversation stops; he darts over. They've been expecting a call on this day.

"Hello?" No one answers, but it isn't a hangup call, nor is it a relaying delay, the sign of a telemarketer using a speed-dial. The line is open, no static, no buzz, no breathing. A long, dark, echoless tunnel. "Hello?" he repeats. The caller ID reads a 512 number, but where is it really coming from?

Karen and Nels trade glances as if searching for a place to

chip at. She comes close to the phone, breath of herb tea on his shoulder. Fearing that she is about to say something either antagonistic or treacly, he preempts: "Korin? Is that you?" He wishes Karen would take over. He remembers to say, "Happy birthday."

The silence, on her day of adulthood, is all the reply Korin needs to give. Her parents conjure the words to fill it, in the black noiselessness which must extend long, longer, for all the variations of what she means.

"I'll go to the other phone," Karen says under her breath, and as she runs out of the study, the caller hangs up.

This time, Goldstrom has the presence of mind to dial *69, reaching the phone from which the call came. A woman's harried voice answers in a rapid Asian language; a dish crashes in the background; a background voice calls out, the woman talks over it. Then there is the beep: just a particularly chaotic answering machine. Goldstrom hates the things, and trying to leave a message for someone who is probably unknown to the recipient, he is speechless. He keeps the phone to his ear, straining toward the inaudible hiss of the running tape as if it were a memento.

A few weeks later, they are at a Chinese restaurant in a strip mall and the twins are arguing about what to order.

"Pork with cashews," Jake demands.

Isaac says, "No way, I'm allergic to cashews."

"You are not allergic to cashews," Jake insists. "I'm not, and we're genetically identical."

"How do you know all allergies are genetic? Don't you know about the theory of neural selection?" Isaac says.

To which Jake says, "Select my ass. You can't be allergic to anything I'm not allergic to, you dildo."

"I don't like that language," Goldstrom says.

"Well, it's the only one we speak."

Karen corrects the boys by modeling serenity.

Goldstrom stares vacantly past the wallpaper, a design of gold cranes flying over mountains, streams, pagodas. In the bottom of his empty teacup there is an ideogram in gold leaf; it probably means Harmony or Good Fortune or Merging with the Path or something like that. A clatter of plates behind his bent head; a rush of voices chewing off-key Asian consonants; he's sitting here with

Evgenia, holding hands and drinking Chinese beer. In fact, what if he'd met her before those snotty twins were born? Or even with Evgenia, with anyone, would some gravitational pull of character have caused him always to end up with snotty twin sons and a runaway teenage daughter, just as, no matter what golf course he plays, he always slices his drives?

He's placing a spicy prawn on Evgenia's tongue with his chopsticks…. No, he isn't. Karen is smiling at him as if trying to understand why he hasn't proven out better; and the phone is ringing at the cashier's counter, the phone is ringing….

"I'll get it," Goldstrom says, or more likely only thinks it, and standing, pushes through aisles of chairs toward the front of the restaurant, and next thing he knows, he is outside, looking up at the blank blue sky. Sun glares off the cars parked between the white lines in the lot; Goldstrom, on the pavement, is in the shade of the storefront. There is such a breadth of clean emptiness up there, it sways him back like a gust of wind, and jitters him as if he were one of the dancing points of light in his retinas. Only one little white tuft mars the blue, like the patch of superfluous hair he knows on his wife's thigh. He tilts his head further and tries to focus deeply on something, but there is so little to see, it is more like listening than looking. Close in his ear and miles far, the air hums with candid omniscience, like someone about to give him a piece of bad news. It's as if something is about to appear there. He waits for a white finger of jet-vapor to write on the high blue window; but no moment is the one in which that's going to be written: it's always going to be the next moment.

"Dad?"

He startles: is it a boy asking him to play baseball? No, that was many years ago. This is someone who once cared that he was a little bit better at baseball than his twin—and may still care. Goldstrom is alarmed to think of how much he prefers not to know about his sons; but don't they know everything about each other? Isn't that the way they want it?

This is Jake of the straighter shoulders and closer haircut. Goldstrom looks at him mildly, distantly, and says:

"You found me."

"Mom wants to know, are you coming back to the table to eat?"

"Do you want to know, too?"

Jake gives an odd look. "Sure."

But Goldstrom feels that he can have no honest answer to this question. He feels as if he is traveling the circumference of the earth and must not be stopped. All he wants to do is breathe the sky. His lungs sound in his own ears as loud as those of a suited astronaut. He has walked way out in the blackness; only a slender line tethers him to home.

"Could you," he begins, "could you let me stay out here, do you think? Go back in; you can all eat without me; I'll be out here waiting for you when you're done."

But he should know—his daughter knew it as a child—that of all the requests he might have made of life, that one will never be granted.

Good with Girls

Maya claimed to be a naturally occurring form of trans
sexual, like one of those weird insects you read about
that's male as a larva and female as an adult. She'd been
a tomboy up till the age of twelve, then suddenly been frenzied by
this humiliating ambition to become a *femme fatale*. The baseball
glove got tossed onto the top shelf of a closet; the skateboard was
donated to a thrift shop; there was one summer when she wouldn't
even put on jeans and sneakers anymore, in case it reminded anyone of her old persona. On a friend's advice she began wearing
dark plum lipstick and a cream foundation (to fix her complexion), with very short black skirts, black leggings, and single-strap
shoes. She was over that bohemian-tyke phase by the time she met
Scott, but he liked hearing about it—about all her phases, frankly.

"You mean you're a man trapped in a woman's body?" he asked.

"No, I'm a woman trapped in a man's body." And she rolled her
eyes downward, with the comic dismay that was the quickest and
least resistible of her many sharp weapons, toward her small breasts,
straight flanks, strong limbs, and embarrassment of body hair.

Scott didn't mind any of that. He loved her because she was
the only girl in his school who would even think of describing

herself as "a woman trapped in a man's body," much less say so to a boy. At least she was the only one he knew. If there were others, it didn't matter, she was the one he'd met first. That was another thing about him: over the past semester he had decided that as soon as he found one woman, that was going to be it, he would be devoted to her for the rest of his life and earn her devotion to him. Through an exertion of simple loyalty, he intended to eliminate from his life the maddening problems that drained everyone else's time and energy. The most agitating aspect of existence would be resolved, settled, checked off on his list: he would never have to worry about asking for dates, dealing with rejection, extricating himself from relationships without hurting the other person, determining the health status of a new partner—the whole guidance-class curriculum, in short (which meant, too, that he could day-dream through an extra hour each week). Thus he would have a competitive edge in whatever he did as an adult. Sometimes he got so involved in fantasies about his ideally rational romantic future, while slouching through the halls of West High, banging lockers with his elbow, and trying not to smile (someone had once told him his smile was goofy), that it made him late for class.

Scott had recently become famous throughout the school as founding editor of that rebel tabloid, *The News For Parrots.* Published either monthly or bimonthly depending on his staff's other commitments (band practice, family vacations, studying for finals, etc.), it was handed out free on streetcorners near the school, and supported itself financially through ads for sandwich shops, used-CD stores, and orthodontists. An attempt had been made to prohibit distribution of the periodical, but the advertising director's mom was an attorney and had threatened the school district with big lawsuits on free-speech grounds; the school had given in, several teachers and administrators were made to look ridiculous for trying to suppress the creative efforts of youth, the paper's circulation had tripled, and Scott had been interviewed on two of the three local network-affiliated newscasts. Scott's dad had gone leaping around the living room, gloating, "This'll get him into Princeton!"

"I don't want to go to college," Scott confided to Maya. "I want to keep running the newspaper."

Maya thought the idea of skipping college in order to maintain a xeroxed eight-page handout was the stupidest thing she'd heard recently—which was quite an achievement, given that she hung out with sixteen-year-old boys. But she loved him for saying "the newspaper," not "*my* newspaper." And she knew that he would go to college, if not immediately after high school, then a year or two later. What she wanted was to mold him—not into any final or static shape; finality was anathema to her—but into someone who would keep reshaping, refining, his soul as he continued through his own independent life, in the tradition of her own miraculous transformation from boy into woman. She saw in Scott the capacity for limitless development—it was why she had accepted him despite reservations—but she also saw that he was in danger of being sidetracked by the bad influences (parents, teachers, nice midwestern buddies) for whom success meant the conversion of energy into matter: a young person's wild, imaginative indeterminacy into some massive, and above all quantifiable, payoff. His susceptibility to stabilizing influences was what had made Scott an urgent case.

"I'm currently infatuated with the idea of becoming a surgeon?" she offered speculatively. "Just for a while; then maybe I'll go into hospital administration, or run for public office, or write essays about biology and society. Actually, I think my destiny in life is to prune things? Cutting back plants to increase their bloom; cutting out unhealthy organs; making my prose more concise when I'm writing a composition. I also do it with my friends and relatives." And she felt the bloom in herself grow, like red petals unfolding inside her, as she created her identity in the act of stating it: "I like to prune people to make them flower."

That was the first sign of trouble between them, because he said, "I'm not going to be pruned." And slumped back in the wrought iron ice cream parlor chair, giving her his cute smirk—at a time like this! He slurped the dregs of his banana malt (two attributes of his that needed pruning: the malts and the slurping) and pulling his long legs in from around her chair legs, said, "My destiny is to interview the Walker twins."

"The people you choose to interview, I like don't fathom your criteria."

"I'm documenting our way of life. I'm waking people up to the strange varieties of forms around us."

"The Walker twins are like fucking psychos."

Standing, he gave her a love-tap on the top of her head with his spiral notebook; she bore with that sort of thing at present. "Can I interview you instead?" he asked.

"No way, if you think I'm interchangeable with the Walker Twins."

"My dad says that nothing is interchangeable, not even subatomic particles." Scott's dad was a theoretical physicist who, after receiving tenure, had become a successful mystic. Scott and Maya had once made out in front of the television while his dad, on the public station, explained that time and eternity were two aspects of one thing, like thunder and lightning, particle and wave, male and female. Scott's mom was the secretary in his dad's lab, as she had been before their marriage, although his dad, these days, was rarely in his lab. "You and the Walker twins are just the only three people in Madison I give a shit about."

He had a way, Maya reflected as they exited the mall, of leaving you uncertain whether to feel good or bad, but certain you should feel bad about the uncertainty.

The Walker twins' name wasn't Walker; it was something formerly Yugoslavian, containing more c's and j's and s's than was completely reasonable, some of them festooned with alien-looking accent marks and others, inexplicably, not. They were identical twins, however, and were called the Walkers because they spent literally all their available time walking.

"So is this like the typical day for you?" Scott asked, trying to keep up with their superhuman strides. The Walkers were only about five foot three, but most of that length must have been leg. Fatless and stringy from perpetual motion, they had shoulder-length brown hair that flapped with their gait like cowboys' saddle bags, and gappy brown goatees, and they walked either with a pronounced stoop or a pronounced backward lean, depending on the wind direction. Unlike many pairs of twins, they made no attempt to individuate themselves: they spoke in identical rapid mumbles, and always referred to themselves as "we." Even Scott, who had learned their first names for purposes of his article, could not remember which Walker was which, except that the one who walked on the right had a drooping right shoulder and the one who walked on the left had a drooping left shoulder.

"Is this like your usual breakfast?" he called after them, hurrying to catch up. The interview was taking place on foot, of course, and though Scott was healthily built, he recoiled from physical exercise as a matter of principle, and was beginning to breathe hard. His tape recorder was on in his pocket, but there was no chance it would pick up their words, especially when mumbled between mouthfuls of breakfast burrito. He would have to use his memory, traditionally not one of his stronger faculties. "So, like, do you take the same route every day or what?"

In fact they had taken a different route every day since the age of eighteen, a decade or so earlier. In their heads was a perfect scale map of Madison, Wisconsin, marked as if with superimposed laminated layers showing every walk they had ever taken; if they ever followed exactly a route they had used before, something terrible would happen: they would die, Scott gathered, or the universe would collapse into a teaspoon of superdense matter. (And as long as they kept finding novel routes, they would live forever?) They had begun this practice the day after high school graduation (West High—a connection to his audience!); whether they had planned it in discussion, or simply started doing it in unspoken harmony, Scott couldn't find out. At first continuing to live in their parents' house in University Heights, they now shared an apartment in a renovated warehouse downtown, with thirteen-foot ceilings and exposed air conditioning ducts in the bygone fashion of the 1980's. At eight o'clock each morning, they rode the elevator down with the other commuters in their building and set forth, eating a takeout breakfast, pausing in the bathroom at the state capitol or some other public edifice, grabbing lunch to go, returning to the apartment for a microwaved supper, and unwinding with a postprandial stroll: a comparatively leisurely trip, maybe ten miles instead of their daytime thirty.

"But what if it's like minus twenty outside with a minus sixty wind chill?"

He assumed the answer although he couldn't hear it: they walked every day no matter what, if there was ice on the sidewalks, if the tornado siren was sounding, if there were severe thunderstorms with golfball-sized hail and a probability of damage to power lines and trees. His follow-up question would have been, "Do you ever disagree about where to go?", but they had reached the capitol square, and with a spasmodic flapping of their inside arms, which jerked back before their hands met, the twins turned their heads this way and that, and…walked in separate directions!

One of them went east, the other went west. "What in the name of the dear sweet Lord above…?" Scott said, trying to seem on top of things through mock confusion. He strove to be a flexible person—wanted others to think of him as one, for starters—but there was something about the unexpected splitting of a unity—or maybe it wasn't that, maybe it was the drawing-away of something that had been close (this was a region of himself he wasn't well acquainted with yet) that knocked him almost out of control, like a child scared by a balloon popping. When everybody else is laughing, and you just want to climb into someone's lap.

"Which one should I follow?" he asked aloud, sort of to a passerby, and then said, "Fuck it, I've got enough for this session." He leaned against a storefront window—the campaign office of some aspiring alderperson—and caught his breath.

"They walk together till they hit one of their special landmarks," he explained to Maya, as if she needed explanations as much as he did, "then they split up, then they meet at their apartment for dinner. That way they cover more territory. At dinner they tell each other where they went. That's what their dinner conversation consists of. 'East on East Wash., south on Baldwin.' 'West on Monroe, south on Seminole.' I bet that's the only thing they ever communicate about."

Scott and Maya were the youngest couple in the coffeehouse he'd invited her to that evening; everybody else was either adults or college students. College students sat hunched over notebooks or laughed in groups about other college students; adults read the newspaper or wondered what to say to their companions. The tables were of blond wood, the walls decorated with Hopi kachina masks and a mural of dairy cows.

Maya lit a cigarette; Scott lifted his eyebrows but refrained from criticism. "You think I shouldn't smoke," she said.

"If it's so great, give me a cigarette."

"No, it wouldn't look right on you. It makes *me* look sleek; it would make *you* look seedy." Urbanely shifting gears, she said, "I hope you make sure this article of yours isn't exploitative."

"What?"

"My friend Scott in California says journalism is an exploitative profession."

"You have another friend Scott?" It was the most relevant response under the circumstances.

He relied on his innate powers of reason to control his unseemly outrage. Another friend Scott—and the other one was undoubtedly hipper than him, the inevitable result of having grown up in California. She had another friend with the same name as him, who was hipper than him, and whom she missed because, with enviable sophistication, he wasn't there. If you want a woman to quote you as an authority, he thought, be absent. He considered using that as the motto for the next issue of his paper.

"I'm not saying that all journalism is exploitative," she said, ignoring his question. "If anything, we need more nonexploitative journalists, and that's why I'm encouraging you."

"So that's what you're doing. Encouraging me."

"*Scott,*" she chided.

"*Maya.* Maybe I'll find another friend Maya."

She laughed. "Are you jealous?"

"No," he said, with as much indignation and as little veracity as if his parents had asked him, Have you and Maya slept together? "You have another friend Scott," he said flatly.

"He's in California. I haven't seen him since the summer. He's just a very nice, smart, cool guy who sails his own catamaran. He goes out with girls where he lives, I have no idea who."

"Cool," Scott echoed.

"Scott would never be jealous of you. Actually, I've told him a lot about you."

He waited for the bad news.

"He says you have potential for development," Maya said, "but you're still a boy and he's a man." She licked a flake of tobacco off her upper lip, and dropping her voice languorously, said, "He's eighteen."

"A cool age."

"You're departing from the main issue anyway. It does trouble me somewhat that you pick these weirdos to study. When I read about extreme characters—I don't mean in your newspaper, I mean published writing too—I always ask myself, Is the author trying to raise himself by lowering his or her subject?"

"I consider *The News For Parrots* published," he said.

"Oh, I didn't mean—!"

"But in short, I like the Walker Twins. You're the one who's been dissing them."

"I haven't 'dissed,' as you put it —"

"I like their apartment, too. You know," he sped up in the excitement of reporting facts, "the county pays their rent? The building's in this special development zone where the owners get all kinds of tax breaks and zoning variances for giving ten percent of the apartments to mental patients? If I could get an apartment like that for free, I might go crazy myself."

Maya made a disgusted sound.

"It's a joke," he clarified.

"As in most of your newspaper?"

He tensed in his seat. "What do you mean?"

"Well, I didn't want to bring this up at this point, but when I read your first issue, I felt, like, had you tried to make it too light on *purpose* or something? I thought it could have used an article on politics."

"It's a periodical for youth. I try to reach them on their own level."

"You think students in a great school like West aren't interested in anything serious?"

"Scott is interested in everything serious," he presumed. "Serious catamarans. Serious sixteen-year-olds."

In Maya's tomboy days, she might have knocked him on his ass for being snotty, but now, as a woman, she understood the power of keeping her voice modulated and her hands in her lap.

"Scott," she said, shaking her head in disappointment, "haven't you ever just done the very best you could?"

It was as if some male friend of his had sucker-punched him, or called him gay or something. No, it was worse. His male friends were like the Walker Twins, only more versatile: colorful diversions, kinetic figures he would never really want to pace himself to. She was the one to whom he *talked* about his male friends and the Walker Twins.

"I usually do the very best I can," he said. *Usually* instead of *always*, to impress her with his honesty, which was itself a sign of trying his best. He trusted her to get such subtleties. And, still trying his best, he tried to say more, but he couldn't, he wouldn't be able to control his voice or to make sure he only said things he meant. Instead, he resorted to looking down gruffly at a crushed napkin on the floor.

Maya summoned him back, extending her fingers above his on the tabletop as if to say that she would touch him if he would let her. "Hi," she said, as if she hadn't seen him in a long time.

"Warmest good wishes to you. So now do we have to discuss how to strengthen our relationship?"

That was something his parents did all the time; for him to do it with Maya was a horror beyond anticipation. He had never actually overheard his parents discussing their relationship—partly through his own discretion, partly through theirs—but it was something they often warned each other, in the direst tones, would soon, once again, need to happen. He had heard so much about it, and so little of it, that it had become a threatened disaster on the scale of the disappearance of fossil fuels, or of having to make your own living. He had *done his very best* to avoid it. His whole theory of romance, in fact, was to pick someone with whom you could avoid it.

"This is where people go to do it," Maya said, glancing at the roomful of little round tables where knees could rub, and people could twirl their dates' cup handles. In the murmur-fog of older voices around him, Scott tried to pick up fragments that might help—*You hurt me; go away; no, don't go*—but the only thing he could make out was a woman lecturing her tablemate: "What he's saying is that your methodology isn't suited to your sample size...."

"Have you been here before?" he asked Maya.

"Just with friends. Have you?"

"Just with my mom."

"Oh, that's sweet." She blew smoke upward from the corner of her mouth. "Is your mom looking for a lover? People often come here for that."

"I don't know." He hadn't even thought to ask his mom leading questions. What kind of a newsman was he? Troubled, he sucked the last of his mocha malt through his straw. Despite cautioning himself not to, he slurped the dregs. When he looked up, the careful lack of reaction in Maya's eyes stirred him to protest—not so much against her, but against the whole world's, as condensed within her, underestimate of him:

"I'm a real journalist. I work hard. I like truth. Just because I like to joke too—"

"'A real journalist?'" she repeated, with a flurried laugh, a brief contralto embellishment. "Where did that come from, what does it mean, what is it guarding against? It's good that you have so much self-esteem, if that's what it is. If not...."

"What?"

"Well, if it's not self-esteem—if it's the lack of self-esteem—I mean, some women might like that in a man: insecurity, dependence. I don't. I don't want you to think you should use that kind of—you know, male *trembliness*—as a way of charming me."

"Do we have to charm each other?" he asked, genuinely surprised.

Maya was distressed at her lack of emotional control. To get where she wanted in this world, she would have to learn to work with people better. More painful still was the thought that she might have hurt Scott's (this Scott's—the real Scott's, though she didn't know if she should tell him that) feelings. Thinking of herself as basically a small, unimportant person, she felt it as an appalling injustice—to her as well as to the injured party—when she suddenly, no doubt through lack of practice, found herself wielding the power to hurt someone. It made her want to run right out and do something wonderful to atone, like cooking dinner for her parents or winning a five-kilometer race or getting an A+ on a test.

By her standards, she had severely chastised him. Oddly, he had gotten the point—he'd acted severely chastised, even though, for him, in other contexts, anything short of yelling and cursing scarcely registered. After he'd walked her home from the coffeehouse, they'd exchanged a cold kiss, more a communication of lipchill than a token of affection, and skulked apart. Now she worried that it might be her responsibility to call him and apologize. Yet if she apologized, it might be a relinquishment of her power to improve him. (Still more cruelly, he might act as if he didn't know what she had to apologize for. She could visualize his dumb schoolboy shrug already.) Apologize, don't apologize, apologize, don't apologize.... The inner debate was so upsetting, she dropped it altogether, forgoing apology by default. She must remember, in all situations, to choose the calmer gesture. And she had to do something about this habit of vacillating, too. It seemed a compulsion with her, as soon as she felt Impulse A, to stop short before acting on Impulse A and give equal time to whether she ought to act on Impulse B instead. Indecision put its arm around her in the seductive guise of openmindedness, but by the time she finished considering Impulse B, the opportunity to act on Impulse A was often past. For instance, she might feel an impulse to say something really nice to Scott, and just forming the compliment in her head would make her happy, but then she'd wonder whether it would make her seem weak; and even if she decided it wouldn't, their conversation would have moved past the point where her compliment would have been appropriate (and she'd had the happiness of thinking it, anyway). She had a whole stock of sweet things she had long wanted to say to him, that she'd never said. Was vacillation a trait she'd developed recently, since becoming a woman, or had it been lifelong? Sometimes it felt like one, sometimes the other.

"I think I blew it with Scott," she told her friend Patrick as they waited for the lights to go down in the movie theater they always went to when they had sorrows to share. "This is the trouble with me: I give advice to others but I won't take my own advice."

"What advice do you give yourself?" Patrick was reliable for therapeutic, neutral questions and for measured expressions of support that reflected in a more positive light whatever she had last said. He was the most levelheaded person she knew, having been on Tegritol for bipolar disorder since eighth grade.

As always, though, even his most innocuous questions made her uncomfortable, and she switched tracks. "Scott's my current project. I don't want to get less than an A. What I want to do with my life," she said, raising her voice slightly, with a happy shiver at reinventing herself on the spot, "is cross paths with as many different people and experiences as possible. Not to prune them or anything, but just to meet and see which direction we send each other in. Like every person is like a squiggly line making its way through the universe? Each new thing you do is another squiggle. And then at the end you look at how many squiggles you have and what kind of pattern they make, and then—"

"You die," Patrick said comfortingly.

"Right. Well, I want to intersect lots of other squiggles, and I want to affect their path so they squiggle off in interesting directions. Then they'll intersect other squiggles interestingly, and so on, and in that way, little personal encounters can change the world. Or do you think I'm an idiot?"

"I like the way you squiggle," Patrick said.

The theater lights darkened. "I would hate myself if my effect on Scott was to make him, like, spiral around himself like a snail instead of outward." The screen lit up, bluish; gleeful boxes of candy danced across it, hand in hand with merry cups of soda and jovial buckets of popcorn, and in tune to extremely loud music, thanked moviegoers for making this theater their entertainment choice, and requested their courteous silence.

"Sometimes I think he's too *true* for me?" she explained. A preview, approved for audiences of all ages, was beginning. *Shh!* went a Wisconsinite in the row behind her. "I mean, he's fanatically devoted to facts and journalism and things like that; he'll probably become like a TV anchorperson someday." Maya shoved her hand between Patrick's thighs to extract a handful of popcorn from the waxed cardboard container he held there.

It was the kind of movie she and Patrick were always fooled into going to: the kind that thrills you while you're seeing it, but evaporates from consciousness the moment you leave. Afterwards, when they traipsed, approximately side by side, into the neon lobby of the cineplex, it was lucky that Patrick wasn't making one of his ridiculous attempts at physical contact, because who should be lounging in the doorway of the video game room, blowing bubbles through a straw into a forty-eight-ounce Pepsi cup, but Scott, waiting for a different movie, a later show. Maya felt her face automatically start to go into a big, warm smile, but then she thought he would be affronted, and she stopped herself and made herself look serious. She walked toward him across the rubbery blue carpet. Game machines pinged scores; a soda machine whizzed; an usher moved a velvet rope.

Scott didn't look at Patrick, who had stopped behind, and neither did Maya.

"Hi," she said. "How are you?"

"Good. How are you?"

"Good." Then, tugged backward by an invisible string, she returned to Patrick with trotting sidesteps, smiling regretfully, called back by an over-full schedule. "Have to go somewhere, seeya later, call me, though, okay?"

She wasn't sure if he'd said okay or not.

"I feel so guilty," she told Patrick as they stood waiting for the bus. "I haven't seen him in days."

Two weeks later, stepping over the pile of his parents' junk mail on the welcome mat in the foyer, Scott noticed an envelope addressed to him in peacock blue ink in big, clumsy script. He tucked it under his shirt although no one was nearby, and went upstairs three stairs at a time to read it behind the locked door of his room.

> Dear Scott,
> I'm perplexed. I'm getting the awful feeling that you're trying to send me a message by not communicating with me. You haven't called. Whereas we used to bump into each other in the hall between third and fourth periods on Mondays, Wednesdays, and Fridays, perhaps you've now chosen a different route. I've stood in front of the bio lab and waited for you to walk by, but you didn't. I hope you're not trying to punish me. I didn't think you were the punishing type. I can understand if our interactions recently have left some misunderstanding, but that comes from not talking about it. If you're confused, check with a partner! Not having the moment between third and fourth periods to look forward to is ruining my school day, as if it wasn't a shambles already! Do you still like me? I like you.
> Love,
> Me

Scott's left thumb began to twitch, with quick double and triple beats like the tapping of Morse code—a code he did not know. He refolded the paper and rapped it against his cupped hand until the thumb settled down.

The punishing kind! She didn't understand anything about him. How could anyone believe he wanted to punish her? *He* was the one who was suffering from their separation. She would just say anything that came into her head to hurt him. ("You'll just say anything that comes into your head to hurt me." "Scott, I'm sorry

I hurt you, I love you, please forgive me….") The slippery candor of her letter must be a move in a game that women played with men. But it was a game he didn't want to play, or even learn. Even if he accepted the necessity of learning it, he felt that the achievement was years beyond him. A terrible idea flashed through him, that this was what maturation amounted to: when you were thirteen or fourteen, you looked forward to simple milestones like being old enough to drive, but when you were fifteen, sixteen, seventeen, you looked forward to *this*….

If only he weren't so great at recognizing duties, then he wouldn't answer her. Anyway, didn't he also have a duty not to knuckle under to coercion? He hadn't caved in when the authorities tried to suppress his paper; was he now supposed to go crawling back to some girl? Okay, he could go back to her, but he had to be tough about it. ("Did you have sex with this other Scott?" "Sex? Really, you can be so childish!") Okay, toughness would probably not work.

How could he even know how to answer her until he had consulted her about it?

It was that thought—that sniveling, insidious thought—which sent him to his bed. He flung himself face-down onto the mattress, then, flipping over like some kind of thrashing salmon, slammed the back of his head against the headboard to produce a truly satisfying ache.

He was grateful Maya did not know he was crying. The other Scott never cried. The shame of crying made him cry more forcefully, though it also made him stop sooner.

He heard the front door open and shut. There was the usual muttering and shuffling of parents coming in, grunting as they bent to pick up the mail (he really should have picked theirs up for them and placed it on the table), and heaving their briefcases to the hardwood floor. Scott waited till it subsided; then he slid across the hall to his bathroom and rinsed his eyes in cool water for such a long time, his parents might have become suspicious. Back in his room, he listened to a couple of CD's, then checked his eyes by pen-flashlight. Still telltale red. At best, his parents would worry he was on drugs; worse yet, they might understand him completely.

He lay in bed in the dark and tried to think of ideas for newspaper interviews, but having wept, it was as if he had become an empty-headed infant. The only thing he could imagine wanting was to talk to Maya again. And he knew he was imagining it as being more pleasant than it would be.

When his blinking eyes, in the darkness, felt dry, he sneaked to the bathroom and rinsed them again. They were passable: an especially snoopy parent (which his tried to appear to be, but weren't) might notice a little pinkness around the lids, as if he were getting a cold, but that was all. He went downstairs. Surprisingly, the foyer was dark, and his parents were neither to be found sitting at the dinner table sampling their latest discovery from an independent Wisconsin brewery, nor in the kitchen cutting up vegetables and gibbering about which coworkers annoyed them. In fact, the whole first floor was unlit. Scott opened the door to the basement and leaned his ear into empty space: there was no sound of television news, no keyboard-tapping, no modem-beeping. This was unlike them; they were usually so dependable, he didn't have to keep an eye on them.

Finally he located his dad stretched out in the redwood chaise on the deck, staring up into the overhanging maple, which was orange on one side and green on the other, like a raver's hair. Scott opened and shut the sliding door carefully so as to seem reluctant to disturb his dad's cogitations.

His dad, who wore a green baseball cap with the logo "100% Hemp," looked at him with the lingering smile of one who had recently viewed foliage. "Hey, chum, what's up?" his dad said—his way of sounding hip, evidently, by being sincere and ironic about the same thing at the same time. Scott's dad squeezed himself into half of the chaise and patted the empty half, inviting him to stretch alongside if he wished; but Scott did not.

"Hello, Father," Scott countered. "I've been planning my next issue."

"Admirably industrious. You know, I've been sitting here looking at this tree? It's amazing. There are possibly hundreds of thousands of leaves on this tree, and every one has an individual pattern of coloration—both the pattern, and the hues themselves, which have zillions of shadings. Not to mention the branches and twigs with their individual bends and twists and angles, and the bark with countless bumps and irregularities. Language could not possibly name all those variations. On this one tree, there is literally too much complexity for human language to describe. Only by looking wordlessly, not letting language arise, can we fully experience this tree. One tree. Then multiply that by the number of objects and events in the universe. Some people think language is the only thing that exists, but in fact—and I tell you this because you deserve to be the first to hear it, my boy—language is what *separates* us from the ground of existence. It's a net we put above the ground to keep us from falling. We have to fall through the net to have a real life—the only real things are down there."

"Good job, Dad." Scott glanced at the backyard: the tire swing hanging from the oak, its black rubber lip full of rainwater; the disused sandbox, its mound of sand pocked with rain and cat urine; the purple asters and long, seeded stalks of grasses, amid which a torn-laced softball and at least one shuttlecock, he knew, lay invisible. "Is Mom around?"

"My wife Roberta? I saw her recently; she must be in the house somewhere."

"Thanks." He patted his dad on the shoulder before leaving him to his thoughts. "Keep up the good work; we're counting on you." And he rushed inside before his dad could transmit any more wisdom.

He didn't find his mom at first, but some subliminal signal—a fading scent? a muted hum?—drew him to the second family room, where the door was ajar. He peeked through to see if she was there, and opened it just wide enough to stand in. She was reclining on the sofa's throw pillows, with one hand shielding her eyes from the light of the reading lamp, and writing urgently in her journal; and from this, Scott knew that his parents had had a pretty big fight. They had finished discussing how to strengthen their relationship and were recovering; or else they were preparing themselves to discuss it, by gathering all the ammunition they could.

So that was what his dad's bullshit was all about.

"Hi, Mom, we having dinner?"

"Oh, hi, sweetheart." And the glow on her face when she looked up at him was embarrassing as usual: he could never feel he'd done enough to earn it. "We're just having pickups tonight: just microwave yourself something—don't just eat ice cream, though, okay?"

"Okay."

His mom wore blue jeans and sheer stockings, and the clash

between those garments struck him as poignantly naive. Her feet were as long as Maya's, but narrower, except for that stupid-looking bony wedge that protruded alongside the ball and made her always complain that she hated shoes. Discovering himself dwelling on this topic, Scott shuddered his mind blank and looked at the framed photographs of Jerusalem and Belfast on the wall.

"You can have ice cream after you eat something with protein in it," she added.

"That's an affirm." And, though it brought him treacherously close to breaking a personal rule—the one forbidding him to express curiosity about his parents' shenanigans—he asked, "Did you eat yet? Do you want me to fix you something?"

"No, honey, you're sweet to offer. I just want to finish my entry." Tapping the notebook of handmade paper with her fine-point pen, she smiled as if to assert that she wrote in her journal daily, whatever her mood.

"Okay, Mom." On his way out, he reset the door ajar with precisely as small a gap as he'd found it. He went to the kitchen, opened the freezer, pulled out an opened half-gallon of rocky road, got a serving spoon from the utensil drawer, and went up to his room, intending to remind himself later to microwave something with protein. There was nothing wrong with reversing the assigned order of courses, he reasoned: the nutritional total would remain the same. But he needed quick energy right away, to think.

Maya's letter was still on his desk; it had not magically disappeared.

Can't you answer a simple letter? Heading, salutation, body, closing....

Yeah, he told the voices of teachers and parents, *but I want to make sure I don't say anything you would say.*

Soon he would find out first-hand what people said to each other when they discussed their relationship. He would learn how to figure out whether someone still loved you or not, and how to decide whether to break up with them or stay with them, and how to get them to understand what you had said and what you hadn't. It was stuff you had to learn, like you had to learn geometry. But best of all was not to have answered yet. Best of all was to sit on your rumpled bed eating ice cream from a half-gallon tub with an oversize spoon....

He was already starting to push phone buttons as he considered this. (Fortunately or not, he always prodded himself when he knew it was time to act.) "Is Maya there?"

"Yes, she is." The inevitable irritation of having to go through adult doorkeepers. He visualized Maya's parents asking her about him—or, just as annoyingly, not asking.

At least this gave him an extra minute. And in that minute (actually more, since she liked to be late), a solution came to him: she wanted to be charmed, and so she would be. Charm came upon him from nowhere, because his woman wanted it. He was uplifted by a wave; he was in a flow zone; he even knew when to clear his throat right before she came to the phone.

"Hello?"

"Hello, this is *The News For Parrots,* we were wondering whether you would answer a couple of questions for us tonight?"

He could hear her controlling a laugh. "Yes, what are they?"

"Could you explain recent occurrences observed between you and Patrick?"

"Patrick? He's just the kindly manic-depressive I go to movies with. Why?"

"I'll ask the questions, if you don't mind. Secondly, would you want to attend a showing of a fine film with one of our editors, like, this weekend?"

"Yes, I would."

"May we quote you on that?"

"Please do," she said in her smoky, Virginia-Woolf-goes-to-the-cineplex voice. "I love to be quoted."

"Thank you, that's all. And thanks for participating in our survey."

He switched the phone off. And that was all he had to do! Was this the way his parents discussed their relationship? No, it couldn't be; they wouldn't act so miserable if they knew how to do this. He'd hardly had to say anything to her. He hadn't had to give anything away: hadn't had to explain or justify, infer or negotiate or comprehend. He was good with girls, that was the surprise. If he'd known, he could have been a lot happier over the past couple of years. It was like faking your way through an essay test: much more of a triumph than if you really knew the material.

What Makes You You

The sight of both his parents in the same room was like the sight of a comet or a mirage; Emilio didn't know whether to gape in joy or hide in dread from this untrustworthy wonder. It was he who had caused it: they only got together to talk about him. When Ms. Pereira, his mother, appeared in the classroom doorway, his nervous cough acted up. He had felt it starting in his throat as soon as he heard her steps coming from the Chatter Box, the private domain where she helped students learn to say *s* instead of *th* or stop saying "uh, uh" between words.

Mr. Rosner, Emilio's father, turned with a flurry of paper-shuffling. "I'm so glad you could drop by."

She smiled as if he had committed a dysfluency. "Otherwise you'd have to hold the conference with yourself."

"I'd have to ask myself, 'How is my son doing, Mr. Rosner?' Then turn my head the other way: 'Just fine, Mr. Rosner, a welcome addition to the class.'"

They couldn't even say hello anymore without adding some extra, adult meaning, which they made a game out of. It was quite an improvement over yelling, which they no longer had to do since they were separated. And every time Mr. Rosner saw Ms. Pereira, he seemed to stop for a split-second to see how she'd changed, as if she were a student who had graduated and returned for a visit.

The three of them sat at a little round table spread with Emilio's folders, and the adults smiled about sitting in child-sized chairs, their knees sticking up and aimed away from each other.

"The long-awaited conference!" Mr. Rosner said, and cleared his throat when no one said anything. "Having Em in my class is a pretty brave experiment for all of us. A decision that took real courage for you, Em. Just remember, if an experiment doesn't work out exactly the way the scientist expects, that doesn't mean it's a failure."

Emilio looked at the photographs of diverse harvest festivals on the bulletin board. Pumpkins and gourds, costumed dancers, beribboned booths, sky-climbing bonfires. Where were they; how could he get there?

"Are you with us?" Mr. Rosner called him back. "Just one small, minor, teeny clerical matter before we start: in future conferences, Em, will you want an old-fashioned report card with a lot of checks and numbers for eight zillion categories? Or a written evaluation where you can really explore my personal responses to your class work?"

"Report card," Emilio said.

The teachers looked at each other.

"Well, let's think about it," Mr. Rosner said.

"Why do you say a report card?" Ms. Pereira asked.

Emilio felt hopeless already. He waited as long as he could before shrugging. Shrugging safely between them, at a pumpkin.

"A report card gives you a lot of exact grades, supposedly," Mr. Rosner said. "But how exact are they, really? Did some supercomputer make them up? No, I did, a human being. And to tell you the truth, I don't know how I can translate another human being—you—into a list of numbers. I have a picture of you in my mind. It's a pretty clear picture and a very positive one, but if I have to take that picture and reduce it into statistics—"

"All right, evaluation," Emilio said.

"—and fit it into a chart, a printout of seventy-five-odd categories—"

"Can you just see Daddy sitting up all evening making checks in seventy-five little boxes?" Ms. Pereira said.

"I'd rather have the evaluation," Emilio said desperately, and Mr. Rosner made a check mark in his grading book next to "Evaluation."

"Okay, solved that one!" Mr. Rosner said. "Now let's talk about substance, 'cause substance is what I really like to get down into. Em, what do you think about the year so far?"

Emilio, though he could not say anything, hoped his squirming told his parents that he meant it in a friendly spirit.

"Emilio," Ms. Pereira said.

He laughed. Nothing funny had been said, of course, but weren't his parents always grinning and laughing about things that weren't funny?

"Let's start with Speech," Mr. Rosner said. "How are you liking the Chatter Box?"

"I like it."

"What do you and…your mom…do there?"

"Talk." He smiled at his mother. She had dark red hair, almost brown but more interesting, and always wore dangly earrings.

"What do you talk about?" Mr. Rosner waited. "What did you talk about last Tuesday, do you remember?"

It's a secret, Emilio thought. Mr. Rosner looked frustrated.

"Emilio's making excellent progress," Ms. Pereira said. "He's learning to project his voice so others can hear him. Also to breathe at the natural places so he doesn't have to repeat words and syllables. I'm trying not to treat him specially, so we'll probably finish in a month or two. But I wish I could keep him forever."

"The temptation of the Chatter Box: everybody wants to stay there forever." Mr. Rosner frowned down at his class list, then turned the frown into a purse-mouthed funny face. "Okay, Emilio, how about the regular subjects: Superreading, Adventures in Culture, How to Build a Solar System, Sometimes I Feel, and It Figures?"

Emilio hid a smile. He was ashamed to tell anyone, but he liked them all.

"Emilio?"

Shrug. "They're okay, I guess."

Mr. Rosner sighed. "Okay you guess. And Physical Development—gym? Mr. Devaney writes"—Mr. Rosner pulled out the pink copy of the gym teacher's report—"'Polite, responsible, but needs more self-confidence. Sits out half the activities….'"

There was more but Emilio didn't listen. He recognized the style from first, second, and third grades. He didn't mind the criticisms but was surprised at being called polite. He'd have to correct that.

"Emilio," his father said, breaking into a daydream about stealing the gym teacher's whistle, "we love you. Your parents may not love each other anymore"—and it was odd how he stammered his next words, as if he needed some time in the Chatter Box—"but they'll always love you. We thought long and hard before we decided to try out this experiment of having you in my class. But we felt—and I think you felt too—that it was our best alternative after the troubles you had last year. You've been very quiet this year, but that's better than calling people names like you did last year and almost getting suspended. Yes?" he said, which was the way he always finished a speech when he wasn't sure you were listening. But he always covered for you by talking more. "Well, we know some things to work on this year if you want to. Participating—that's the big one. Say yes to opportunities! For instance. In Free Time, when someone asks you to brainstorm their terrarium project with them, you don't have to think about whether it's the thing you want to do most in the whole world. It's better than sitting by yourself doing nothing, isn't it? Emilio, it hurts me to see you not answering like this, whether it's in a conference or every day in class. You make me feel like I'm giving you the third degree. It hurts my feelings. Don't you agree that if there's a new project in the classroom that you haven't tried before, you don't have to refuse to do it just because it might not be your favorite thing?"

"I guess so," Emilio said, and grasping that upbeat note, Mr. Rosner drew up a contract for the coming quarter. He wrote, "Goal: To participate in new activities and say Yes! to opportunities" and had Emilio sign all three of his names. They were like the three doors in a television game show; as he wrote each one, he imagined himself choosing it: I'll take Name Number Two.... And let's see what's behind there....

"Well, that was a productive conference!" Mr. Rosner said, and Emilio found that he didn't have to choose at all, just leave the room clean for the next contestant.

Afterward, he sat in the Chatter Box while his mother wrote

evaluations of some of her students. He flipped through a book on nocturnal animals, imagining himself as an owl, a panther, a mole. What if the Chatter Box were an underground burrow on a palm-shaded island, where he and his mother hid all day, only emerging in the moony, tropical night? Safe from the sun they would huddle in an endless speech session, talking strange lands into being. For instance, a place of cold winters where children rode yellow buses to overheated, old, brick schools. Impossible, they would say—no one would agree to live there.

"Meow," he said to the panther in the book, forgetting he would be overheard.

His mother smiled, and he blushed. "Want to borrow it?" she asked.

He shook his head.

Then, from the way she paused, he could tell she was about to ask him a different kind of question.

It was, "Did you think your father was too negative?"

Was this a Chatter Box session, or merely a conversation occurring in the Chatter Box? He gambled on the latter, so that instead of talking fluently he could mumble, "I don't know," acting absorbed in the book. He knew she saw through him.

Suddenly she lunged out of her chair and was hugging his neck. It seemed improper within the school building. He grinned.

"We'll go to that new Thai restaurant for dinner, I read a good review of it," she said. "I know it's hard, Emilio. You're quiet because you have so much to think about. I have things to think about too. Sometimes I wish I was a kid so I could not-answer questions. Adults have to ask the questions; that's not always so easy. You know, your father's a great teacher. Here you are in a public school and you're getting more innovative, nontraditional approaches, more individual attention than most private schools."

"I don't want individual attention."

"But you deserve the most of anybody!"

Kneeling, she pressed his shoulder to keep her balance. She looked up at him so beautifully, it made him wonder what he would do if she ever got old. He might have to run away.

"Does he say nice things about me?" she asked. "Or nasty ones?"

Heaven was a place where nothing was ever evaluated.

Dan Devaney, the gym teacher, lived with a black-belt wife and four heart-healthy children and a bounding dalmation in a house with an oak tree growing through its deck, and a tree house overhead in the oak tree, and a basement made sacred to sports. Skis and hockey sticks leaned in the corners, bicycles hung from the walls, barbells lay crossed like legs, there was even a boxing ring with red ropes and padded corners and a bell you hit with a mallet. Emilio flicked it with his fingernail, smiling at the shy ringing. The dog having been locked in a bedroom, there seemed nothing to fear.

"Why don't you and Eddie throw the football around?" Mr. Devaney said. Eddie was his youngest son, two years older than Emilio, a big, curly-haired kid who looked mopey and awkward just standing there, but fierce and well-coordinated as soon as he had a ball in his hands.

"We'd rather shoot baskets," Eddie said, including Emilio without having acknowledged him in any other way so far.

"This is quite a setup, Dan," Mr. Rosner said.

"Whatever," Mr. Devaney called out to Eddie. "Find something Emilio likes and do that." To Mr. Rosner he said, "It's a child-centered environment—and I'm the child. No, we have a lot of fun here."

Emilio would have liked simply to look at the photos on the wall. Four boys in hockey uniforms, lined up in order of height, pushing one another and laughing, the smallest one Eddie when he was Emilio's age. A blonde on skis, at the round top of a mountain, blowing clouds of breath at the photographer, was Mrs. Devaney with no lines on her face. And the centerpiece, a black and white picture of a teenager in boxing trunks, gloves at chin, his threatening eyes peeking out behind them.

"That's me at a hundred and five pounds," Mr. Devaney said. "You ever put the gloves on, Emilio?"

Emilio wished he didn't understand. Gloves like for winter?

"Emilio, want to box?" Eddie said, and Mr. Devaney said, "Good idea!" and Mr. Rosner said nothing.

Emilio looked at the rough pine staircase that led to the main floor. Eddie's mother was not coming down in the nick of time to offer them lunch or scold them for being masculine. He didn't like strange houses! And yet he wished he could explore here, for there must be all kinds of curiosities that he had never seen before—sporting goods he hadn't heard of, and pictures of people who had died, and dusty trophies a dog had chewed on. He wished he could hide under the staircase, screened by spider webs, and spy on how a different family lived. But only if they didn't hurt him!

Eddie had swept four boxing gloves off a shelf and onto the floor. Then he got two pieces of blood-red headgear that looked like catcher's masks without the protective bars. Before Emilio knew it, Mr. Devaney was lacing the gloves on the boys.

"Just a practice round or two, to see if you like it." Mr. Devaney winked at Emilio. "Eddie, just defend. Let Emilio throw the punches and you block."

"I don't want to," Emilio said. He looked at his father. Mr. Rosner mouthed the words, "Go ahead!" and pretended to swat an invisible punching-bag. Emilio tried to step toward his father, but Mr. Devaney tugged him back in order to tighten the laces.

"Eddie's well-trained in the sweet science," Mr. Devaney said. "I've taught all my kids to defend themselves. You do any of that with him, Allan?" he asked Mr. Rosner. "Any karate lessons? Great confidence-builder. There's a good karate school over by University…."

"I don't want to," Emilio said, as Mr. Devaney fit the headgear around his chin. It felt worse than being at the dentist. He saw himself standing there, his only chance lying in making them feel sorry for him.

Eddie, in headgear and gloves, looked as big as a man. The two fathers sat in folding chairs at ringside.

"We'll box two-minute rounds," Mr. Devaney said. Eddie climbed through the ropes into the ring and began hopping on his toes, bobbing back and forth, jabbing the air. "Emilio, get in there and do some warmup."

"I don't *want* to."

Mr. Devaney laughed. "Self-defense is something everybody needs to know. I give my kids a lot of choice in life, but there are things no one has any choice about. Some guy comes up behind you in an alley, he's not going to ask whether you really want to be mugged or not."

Mr. Rosner rubbed his hands on his knees. He wore the kind of expression that often led to an extra homework assignment. "Just give it a try, Em."

Emilio's legs felt so heavy and wobbly he could hardly lift them over the ropes. He wished he could run away; imagining it, he got to the center of the ring without stumbling. Although he stood rigid in one spot, he felt as if he were spinning, like a camera going through a three-hundred-and-sixty degree rotation, the photos and the fathers and the ropes all blurring until he might collapse from dizziness.

He kept his hands at his sides until Eddie, shaking his head, came over and lifted Emilio's gloves for him. "Stand like this." And he stood like that, but he swore not to move.

Mr. Devaney struck the bell loud—for a good five seconds, Emilio could hide within the echo. But Eddie began shuffling in midring, circling him.

"Move around," Eddie said impatiently. Just so Eddie wouldn't get angry, Emilio took a step to the side, a step back. He kept doing that. He tried to move enough not to get yelled at and to stay out of Eddie's range. The air was like syrup and time had stopped.

"One minute, and no punches thrown," Mr. Devaney said.

Mr. Rosner, sitting beside him, had his cheeks puffed out.

Upstairs, far away, a telephone rang. Someone would be talking, exchanging news—there was a world outside this basement. You don't have to be here, he told himself, but he didn't believe it.

"Thirty seconds," Mr. Devaney announced. "Go get him, Emilio."

"Hit me," Eddie said, and thumped himself in the chest. He stopped right in front of Emilio, hands dangling, making himself a target.

Emilio gave him a pleading glance, one he thought anyone could have understood.

"Hit me," Eddie said.

Just to stay on his good side, Emilio threw a left jab that didn't even reach Eddie's chest. Eddie brushed it away. "Again. For real this time."

Emilio repeated the jab, touching the chest lightly. Then he stepped a bit closer and hit a bit harder. Eddie flipped the punch away and jabbed Emilio's upper arm. It wasn't so bad. Emilio bobbed more, copying Eddie's style.

"Hard as you can," Eddie said, dancing.

But Emilio's arms were becoming sore. He wanted the round to end. Eddie hit him in the arms, trying to force him to punch. *He's not supposed to do this*, Emilio thought. *His father told him just to block me.*

He couldn't escape; Eddie was too fast, surrounding him. (His mother crying, "How did you get these bruises?" and taking off his shirt and castigating his father, who wouldn't know what to say.)

Maybe if I throw one more punch he'll be satisfied....

From the corner of his eye, Emilio saw Mr. Devaney pick up the mallet. At that last moment, Eddie punched Emilio in the gut, twice, three times, four. The punches shoved him this way and that like gusts from a hurricane. He staggered, the ropes scratching the back of his T-shirt. Each punch turned him in a different direction so he wasn't looking when the next punch came. He saw the corner post with its red padding; the saucer-shaped chandelier; a glimpse of his father's face; he felt punches to his side, his ribs, his cheekbone. While he imagined his father rushing in, shouting, *Stop this!*, a punch to his solar plexus doubled him over.

He waved his hands in front of his face so that Eddie wouldn't hit him anymore. And the echoing bell said, *Stop this, stop this!* as he stumbled about the ring, looking for a place where he could catch his breath. Eddie closed in and hit him in the chin of the headgear, in the stomach, the headgear again, the stomach again, as if it would repeat forever....

"Time!" Mr. Devaney shouted. Then the gloves and headgear were being pulled off him, with the laces still tied.

"When the bell rings, you *stop*," Mr. Devaney scolded Eddie.

"Dad, it was just one combination." Eddie swatted himself in the face with an open glove and lurched around the ring, rolling his eyes goofily. Emilio, hunched over, tried to laugh as he knew he ought to, but it turned into a cough.

"You're okay!" his father said, and turning to Mr. Devaney, said, "Well, I guess you overmatched him." But before an answer could come, Mr. Rosner peered closely at the photographs on the wall, hands in his pockets, knees jiggling. "Really neat stuff!"

Mr. Devaney took Emilio by the shoulders and straightened him upright, like prying open a jackknife, and stared into his eyes. Mr. Devaney looked worried, but he tousled Emilio's hair and gave

a serious, doctorlike smile. Emilio couldn't figure out whether he
had passed inspection or not.

Mr. Devaney tossed the equipment into a corner of the basement. And while Emilio was remembering the way Mr. Devaney
had looked at him, and imagining how Mr. Devaney might treat
him in gym from now on, and trying to figure out how he should
have fought, Mr. Devaney, Mr. Rosner, and Eddie started upstairs
for a snack.

"Not coming, champ?" Mr. Devaney said. "We'll save a sandwich for you."

Emilio didn't want to be called "champ" if he wasn't a champ.
He wanted to join the others but dreaded the way they would look
at him when his face poked to the top of the spiral staircase. They
would be disgusted at the sight of such a coward.

He paced in circles inside the boxing ring. Then he began to
bob and weave. He threw expert jabs and uppercuts. The opponent rushed at him but Emilio fought back bravely. The opponent
could attack from all directions at once, invisible, instantaneous,
but Emilio knew how to move and how to think. *That Emilio*, said
an announcer in the corner, *he knows how to fight*. Take that, take
that! Two quick jabs, look at that footwork!, Emilio is coming on
strong, the opponent is staggered, Emilio has this match under
control, he throws a right, a left, a combination, and in the last
glorious second an uppercut that knocks the opponent for a loop!

"I see you got in some trouble in third grade," said Fred, the school
psychologist, wigwagging his finger down a page in Emilio's file.

"I stopped."

"Oh, you stopped. Now you don't get in trouble anymore.
You don't bother the grownups and they don't bother you, is that
the deal?"

Emilio was amazed: Fred had guessed it exactly. But he didn't
seem angry. What was he after?

"They still bother me," Emilio said slyly, and Fred laughed.
He had a graying beard, a pencil tapping his lips, and a way of
acting casual while he was asking a question, then zooming in with
a stare while you answered.

"Tell me about the time with Ms. Jonas," Fred said in a spirit
of enjoyment.

Emilio fidgeted.... He bobbed, slipping the counselor's punch, and deflected the attack by stepping into it....

"It was recess, some kids were sliding down the snow on the hill in the schoolyard. I was watching them. And Ms. Jonas starts yelling at them, 'No sliding down the hill!' So I said, 'If they can't slide down they'll have to stay on top of the hill till spring.' She gave me this nasty look and said, 'I don't like smart kids.' So I said, 'Then why are you a teacher?'"

Fred twisted his mouth as if trying not to laugh.

"So she grabbed me by the coat"—Emilio grabbed himself by the back collar to demonstrate—"and took me to Tom, I mean Mr. Hughes, the principal. Mr. Hughes asked me how my parents were doing since the—since they got separated—and I asked him how his dog was doing. He has this beautiful golden retriever, Sweet Jane—"

"I know," Fred said.

"—and Mr. Hughes said to Ms. Jonas, 'You never answered his question. Why are you a teacher?' And he told Ms. Jonas to let kids slide down the hill from now on."

"Quite a victory for you," Fred said.

Emilio tried to figure out what kind of answer he was supposed to give. Would his file become worse if he said nothing, or if he said the wrong thing?

As if thinking of something on the spur of the moment, Fred asked, "How is it for you, having Dad and Mom as your teachers? It must be hard sometimes to figure out when they're being teachers and when they're being parents. All three of you having to walk that fine line."

Emilio allowed himself an interlude to think about the expression, "walk a fine line." It puzzled him. It made him imagine a beautiful, swirly line on a piece of paper, stomped on by someone's muddy footprint. He liked thinking this way, and he wished people would let him do it always.

He blurted, "Did you ever date my mom?"

"No, I'm married. Happily. I wouldn't—no, it wasn't me." And Fred scribbled rapidly in his pad, looking suddenly very busy.

Had he insulted Fred without knowing it? Emilio regretted having spoken so freely. And what if Fred was a friend of Ms. Jonas? Going to Ms. Jonas at lunch and saying, That Emilio Pereira Rosner is a little brat, let's make sure he gets put in a bad class next year.…

He had nearly stepped into a trap. He had been tricked into revealing himself, showing off, and showing off made people hate you. Conferences were a way of getting you in trouble even when you hadn't done anything wrong.

"Emilio?"

He had missed a question. Fred looked very understanding about it—but was writing it down.

"You know, I'm a very unusual teacher," Fred said. "I approve of daydreaming. I've found that some of the most interesting kids are the ones who daydream. I used to do it myself. I used to daydream about running away from school and going to a magic island where only my friends could come. Are your daydreams anything like that?"

But Emilio was on his guard; he wasn't going to give anything more away. From his repertoire of shrugs, he chose one that was like a wriggle, a bashful slinking into his chair.

"If you had a magic island, who would you invite?" Fred asked. "Who are your friends?"

No way was Emilio going to turn in his few friends, have them brought to an inquisition in Fred's office. His imaginative footwork eludes the lumbering guidance counselor.… Emilio is too fast, the opponent's too old.…

"Come on, Emilio, don't make me feel like I'm pulling teeth here. I'm trying to get to know who you are and what's bothering you—or what's making you happy. I want to know what makes you you."

The repetition made Emilio laugh a little, unwillingly. You, you, you, you.… The word they were always throwing at him, echoing like the chime of punches in his head, accusing him of being him. And what could he do but stand there in his body, his Emilio self, incapable of taking a single sidestep away?

He looked at the pencil wagging in Fred's fingers, getting ready to write.

Fred dropped the pencil when he saw Emilio glance at it. "I'm not asking so I can put it in a file, Emilio. I won't write anything down if you don't want me to, fair enough? Emilio, would you mind looking at me? I know your mom's been working with you on eye contact."

And Emilio throws a stinging right to the eye! He catches the larger adversary flatfooted—the eyes blacken and swell—and as in a video game, the guidance counselor shrinks with each blow that lands. He becomes transparent, his outline flickering, his expression comical with dismay. He's smaller than Emilio now; he has to stand on his chair and jump in order to see over the desk…. Don't worry, Fred, you'll be fullsize again for your next appointment….

When you win one bout, Emilio knew, there's just another, meaner fighter awaiting you at the ring of the bell.

He looked hard at the frustrated ex-heavyweight, who had so disastrously underestimated him. "Is it time for me to go to Environmental Ed. yet?"

When he was supposed to be in Environmental Ed., he went to the school library, where you could wander in and out, waste time, as long as you had some pretense of a project to do. Ms. Meyer, the librarian, a short woman with curly gray hair, insisted that you call her May, and if you danced on the oval rug or marked your height on the doorjamb, she praised you for discovering an original use for the library. Her room was furnished with sofas, a rocking chair, portraits of Crazy Horse and Red Cloud, and a human skeleton that some kids swore was real and others scorned as plastic. Emilio knew it was real—he had asked his father—but to his bewilderment, that hadn't settled the argument, only made it more complicated and nasty.

"Hi, hon," May said, "I was just getting some science fiction from my private stock, really neat classic stuff. Have you ever read *Twenty Thousand Leagues Under the Sea?*"

She plopped a stack of six books on his table and walked off, and Emilio knew she wouldn't so much as glance in his direction until he'd had time to examine all her selections undisturbed. But he also knew that even without looking, she knew what every child in her library was doing at every moment.

He stashed the books on the neighboring table. There too, May had set bait for children: she left books lying around unshelved, where anyone could lay hands on them. Emilio pretended to be a secret agent foiling May's plan by reshelving the books; but there were traps within traps: he couldn't take his eyes off the title of one book, printed in bold red block letters on a slim, white spine. The title was *Champions!* Emilio tried not to touch it, but that would have been like not trying to pull the sword out of the stone, or like shutting the curtains on an alien who landed in your backyard.

There was a boxer on the cover, sweat streaming over a flat nose and bruised cheek, his eyes calling you names. Midway through the book there were photos of boxers, black and white and Hispanic and Asian men, some of them huge and well-fed and soft-looking, some short and skinny and dwarfed by their baggy trunks; some captured at the instant a glove squashed their faces into confusion, some gloating over toppled rivals. Some looked old but simple, as if they had been left back many times; some looked young but old-fashioned, like the picture of Mr. Devaney on his basement wall. But those guys could kill Dan Devaney, they could knock him down with one hand and Mr. Rosner with the other....

May was walking toward him. He hid *Champions!* behind his back.

"Find any good Jules Verne or Ray Bradbury yet?"

"No."

"Must be something good if you don't want me to see it." She pretended to peek behind his back. And she sounded like she was going to say something else, but the library door opened and it was Ms. Pereira, with her interesting hair and dangling earrings, making the place, for a second, and much more than May's hand-picked furniture, seem not like school.

His mother gave him a surprised look. "Is this your library period?"

"Environmental, but she said I could look for something."

"Well, if you've found it, go back to class."

It was school after all.

Ms. Pereira and May, a tag team, stood conferring with their backs to him. Come on, come and get me! But while he dared them in his mind, he ducked out. Protecting the unchecked book against his chest, he slid out of the library, making sure not to go too fast so they wouldn't suspect anything.

He wasn't stealing it, he was taking it home. No one else could ever want that book as much as he. It was *his* book.

He went to the boys' bathroom and latched himself into a stall. Behind the pale green door, he peeled the catalogue sticker from the dust jacket, then tore off the flyleaf, which had the school's stamp on it, and wrote his name and address on the inside cover.

The door of the boys' bathroom bangs open, it's May Meyer smacking the stalls till she finds the one that's least echoey, the one where he's sitting…. No, that was just a scared daydream, for even if May guessed he had taken the book, she probably wouldn't accuse him directly; she'd ask Ms. Pereira to return it. If there's one thing Emilio knows, said a voice within him, it's daydreams!

Emilio felt sick in his stomach; as soon as he'd defaced the book, he wished he hadn't. He was always doing things and immediately regretting them: acting up, telling people off; whatever he really wanted to do, especially if he did it without thinking, he would feel bad about afterward. Now he couldn't return the book undetected even if he wanted to. So either he would keep it hidden forever, his prize an eternal secret, or his mother would find it and subject him to, *Emilio, where did this come from? Why did you do this? This is damage you can't undo. I really think you'll have to talk to Fred about this….*

He wished the boxer on the cover could tell him what to do. The sweaty, punch-dulled face seemed about to say something—perhaps not advice but a challenge, a champion's challenge for a child's own good. As classy a boxer as this, worthy of a book cover, he must be on your side, but how could you be sure?

Come on, kid, you afraid to fight? No one's going to come in and stop you. You can do anything you want and not get in trouble. What else do you want to do? Show me you can take *this*…. The book swung into Emilio's face, the fighter's forehead butting his. It slammed and slammed, and when his eyes watered at the sting, he hit himself again to scold them dry. It was like repeating a math problem till you understood it. The impact flashed and smarted, and for once he didn't know how to sidestep it; the hard binding caught him with the same move over and over, funny as a video game figure that always said the same thing in the same spot:

Emilio's afraid, Emilio's afraid….

He tore the dust jacket down the middle, slashing the boxer's paper forehead, between the puffy eyes and down the cheek like a scar. Then he ripped the cover into smaller and smaller pieces—quarters, eighths, sixteenths—fractions he was learning about in It Figures. The book had fallen to the floor, but Emilio was too busy to notice. He demolished the boxer, cut him into tiny squares, on this piece just an eye, on this piece a corner of swollen lip, and the slick bits of paper staggered to the gray tiles, and he peeled them off the sticky floor, flung them into the sink, and washed them away, out of school.

He picked the book up, blew the floor-dust off it. This is how you make something yours, he told himself. No one gives it to you, you take it. No one else can help you, give you, show you. They can't tell you anything and you can't tell them you've learned this. You have no teachers.

Possible Future Stepmother

What surprised Emilio was that they didn't spend the car trip telling him how much fun camping would be. These adults were too cool for that. Instead they conducted a strikingly mature conversation to which Emilio studiously listened. The key to talking like an adult, he decided, was that you were supposed to avoid at all costs responding directly to what the other person had said. For example:

Father's Date: "If she was going out with someone, that might make things easier for you."

Father: "'HONEY FOR SALE'—should I stop?"

Or:

Date: "There are some good books on how to deal with the children's reactions."

Father: "'WORSHIP THE LORD SLOW WE LOVE OUR CATS.' Now, I wonder how they want to punctuate that?"

Not only was this couple perfectly attuned in their sophisticated mode of discourse, they both instinctively shoved their seats so far back that he was left with no legroom. Therefore, he warned himelf to get used to the idea that Elissa—Ms. Li, the school audiologist—was his possible future stepmother.

His father was Mr. Rosner—Allan Rosner—his fourth grade teacher. Fourth grade was over, thank God, and had been declared a successful learning experience at the final parent-teacher conference, where Mr. Rosner was, of course, both parent and teacher. The camping trip was "a much-needed break for us all," in Mr. Rosner's words, and "a special birthday treat" in the words of Emilio's mother, Ms. Pereira, his speech teacher, who although treating herself to a couple of weeks on the coast of Portugal, had a legal right to make as many comments as his father. As always, Mr. Rosner had given Emilio a choice: in this case, birthday party or camping trip. Emilio, despite having no interest in the well-adapted species or food webs or prairie restorations Mr. Rosner would undoubtedly find on every innocent hiking path, had chosen the camping trip because his father had argued for a birthday party. Emilio dreaded the thought of inviting people, for they might not come. It wasn't that he didn't have friends—he had quite a few, they liked the way he talked back to teachers—but he was convinced that if he tested their friendships, he would fail. He didn't test well. ("You're smarter than these numbers show," his father had told him more than once, but to Emilio it seemed a logical impossibility, like saying that a car was going faster than its miles per hour.) And who would want to spend an afternoon at their teacher's house?

"We're almost there," his father assured him, though Emilio had scrupulously refrained from asking when they would get there. As a sign of maturity, he did not reply.

To make up for having had to look at the backs of their necks for five hours, he surged ahead of them on the trail to the campsite. They were hefting fullsize backpacks crammed with tenting and cooking equipment, food, propane canisters, first aid supplies, and a Scrabble set, while his responsibility was limited to a daypack containing a change of clothes. He trotted just far enough ahead so that they would think he couldn't hear their conversation, though he could.

"I know the guidebook said primitive," Ms. Li said, "but I didn't think it meant *that* primitive."

"I brought a shovel," Mr. Rosner said. He called forth to Emilio: "Pick us a good campsite!"

What was a good campsite? He rejected the first one on principle, although it looked okay. The second was virtually identical, the clearing perhaps a couple of feet closer to the lake. A stripped log lay on the ground as a bench; a charred iron grate covered an ash-filled hole; those were the only conveniences.

"This is it!" he said, and slammed his daypack to the ground like a football player celebrating a touchdown. He performed this display, though, only because there was as yet no audience present.

"Should have bought wood at that place at the intersection," Mr. Rosner said.

"Think you can swim in that water?" Ms. Li asked.

Emilio contributed his own non sequitur: "I think nobody's at any of the other campsites."

Stretching and sighing, the adults slipped their packs to the dark, damp ground. Ms. Li stood still, calm-looking, focusing steadily on the section of weed-rimmed Fancy Pond that showed beyond the clearing. Mr. Rosner paced the edge of the campsite, turning his head this way and that as if checking an auditorium for exits. The forest floor was sun-dappled rather than shaded, a weave of woods through which you could easily thread to the neighboring sites. One tall, straight tree stood in the open clearing, as skinny and solitary as Emilio, and as yellow-green as he felt sometimes when a parent shook him out of a dream to tell him it was morning and he had to go to school.

"Aspen," Mr. Rosner said, as if he had a label ready to stick onto it.

"I can't believe there isn't at least an outhouse around here somewhere," Ms. Li said.

Hands in the front pockets of her jeans, she strolled away down the muddy path to the gravel trail, looking for facilities. She was tall and bony and prone to plaid, and wore a black flattop haircut that she brushed up with stiff fingers when she was ruffled. Emilio was always glad when he was called down for his annual hearing test.

"She's not gonna find what she's looking for," Emilio's father said.

Emilio felt terribly sorry for her, as he imagined her stumbling around gripping her bladder and moaning.

"Well, let's get this tent up before she comes back," his father said.

The forest-green plastic tent had been advertised as exceptionally easy to put up, but when Mr. Rosner spread it on the
ground, he discovered he had questions. Which side of the orange
groundcloth went faceup, and how clean and dry did it have to be?
How many stakes were needed to secure the tent, and did they go
through both layers of the shelter or only one?

"She knows about this stuff, maybe we should wait for her,"
he said in a tone Emilio had often heard in the classroom: a tone of
frank admission that Mr. Rosner did not have all the answers.

But sometimes—especially given a time limit—you just have
to guess. "Well, we'll just do the best we can. If the tent collapses
on us in the middle of the night...."

It will be her fault, Emilio heard the unspoken end of the
sentence.

It would be safer to step back and watch his father complete
the setup than to offer help. But Mr. Rosner never gave up on a
child; he used words like rope, to pull Emilio back in. You could
always count on him to invent some innovative strategy in his work
with children, and this time—while Emilio, listening with alarm
and dismay, wished to burrow into the dirt or fly into a tree—Mr.
Rosner was being spontaneously confidential.

"Well, we've been through a lot this year, but the worst part is
over, I think, how 'bout you? Actually, Em, I'm—I'll tell you—
your mother and I had a lot of good times together, but I have to
put that behind me, and I want to seize this chance to begin a new
life. Almost to rejuvenate myself—do you know the word? It means
to make someone or something young again. Like, I used to go
camping when I was a kid? I want to start doing it again. Just for
the joy! For delight in plants and animals, in wood scents and the
calls of birds.... I hope you'll get to like it, too, but I know that the
things most worth learning can take the most time...."

Mr. Rosner paused ever so slightly—a response was called for—
Emilio gave a sort of understanding little grunt.

"We learn *people,* too, you know," Mr. Rosner said, as he
frowned and grimaced at parts of the tent support. "We don't just
meet someone the first time and decide we like them or we don't
like them—that's Hollywood nonsense. Elissa—at first sight she's
very pretty, but I feel I'm just learning what an extraordinary, unique
person she is."

She's nice, Emilio thought, and knew his father would have been glad if he had said it aloud.

He looked up and spotted a crow landing in turn on each of the trees that bordered the clearing, and cawing from each one. If this were a magic land, what would the crow be saying? *Get out of here, this is my forest. Get out or something terrible will happen to you.* Emilio sometimes believed that all the things of the world spoke in their own languages, which people couldn't understand. When he was younger, he used to think that he would grow up to be the one person who could understand those languages; but now, at eleven, he suspected that the best he could hope for was to know they were spoken. Most of what they said were warnings—but warnings of what, he didn't know.

"Well, this will do till she gets back," Mr. Rosner said, and at the very words, the lakeward side of the tent collapsed with a sound of wind-flapped fabric, as if it had puffed out its cheeks and waited till just the right moment to exhale. "Damn it," Mr. Rosner said. "Of course it doesn't come with directions, 'cause it's supposed to be so easy."

Mr. Rosner sat hunched on the stripped log and stared at the tent, his skinny knees banging against the rickety framework of his arms like a kid rapping on a classroom window, "Let me out!" His sandy curls and aquiline nose looked youthful, fragile. Emilio, to demonstrate sympathy, strolled over to the tent, picked up a handful of the clothlike material, and let it fall.

"How long has it been since she went?" Mr. Rosner asked, looking at his watch. "Half an hour?" He kicked his heel into the dirt until it made a wedge-shaped indentation, a potential fossil footprint. "Let *her* try her hand at it."

Mr. Rosner cupped his hands over his nose and mouth, and breathed audibly. Emilio wanted to ask, *Dad, what's the matter?* But he had never in his life done that.

Scenes came to Emilio's mind: his father sitting in a patio chair, having escaped outside after a fight with Emilio's mother, and breathing so loud, Emilio had turned around to look for monsters. His father searching the kitchen of his newly rented apartment and moaning because some perfectly ordinary utensil—the cutting board, the colander, the carrot peeler—had been left back home, that is, at Ms. Pereira's house. His father standing at the school bus station at three o'clock, watching Ms. Pereira chat with one of her students (her hand on the student's shoulder, her auburn hair and dangling earrings bright in autumn sunlight—she was glad to be back for a new school year and showed no signs of strain), and Emilio, at all such times, wishing he could ask his father questions and say things to make him feel better. But wishes don't always come true.

Wingflutter, twigfall: a bird, small and plump, with yellow breast and gray, quick-fanning wings, dove zigzag through the copse. Tracking it, Emilio saw someone stepping through from the campsite on the left. Ms. Li, crouching, her arms in front of her to shield her face from low branches, was returning. When she broke into the clearing, she looked happy.

"I met a couple across the way, but no one's next to us. We can make noise if we want."

Mr. Rosner looked as if she had taken a bathroom pass on a pretext and then skipped class the rest of the day. "Thanks for joining us. Where were you?"

She paced the circumference of the tent thoughtfully. Then, with an amiably derisive smile, she wiggled one of the aluminum stakes, which rose from the ground shedding clumps of mud. She drove it, hard, into a different spot, and walked around redoing all the stakes so that the sides of the tent would stay up.

"I see," Mr. Rosner said, bending for a closer view.

"Hey!" Ms. Li said as if just noticing Emilio. "Guess what I saw on the other side of the lake. A great blue heron! Did you see it?"

They hadn't seen it. She urged them down to the water: all three of them ran to the meager, mossy shore and stood on wet rocks and scanned with excellent effort the curve of the little lake, the spindletopped pines and peeling birches, but they had to agree that the hook-necked, slate-gray bird Ms. Li described had not waited for them. All at once, the landscape seemed empty. You could look for a moment and see a beautiful creature if you were Ms. Li, or you could look all day and miss it if you were Mr. Rosner and son. Emilio wanted to go home.

His father turned away. "I'm gonna drive back to that intersection and get some wood," he said in a pleasant enough—though a little scratchy—tone, and hurried off before anyone could say anything.

Ms. Li gave Emilio a smiling shrug.

"Tonight we'll see the stars through this," she said, reaching up to touch the transparent panel in the tent roof.

"It's fun sitting inside here in the daytime too," Emilio said.

"Oh, why's it fun?"

"I don't know." He hated that kind of question. All he had to do was risk a free remark about something he felt—forget to test every word before he spoke it—and an adult would try to find out what it meant and try to get him to join in finding out. He wasn't angry at her—she was nice, and she really couldn't be expected to understand someone his age. It put him on his guard, but he was used to that.

"You know," she said, "I haven't seen you very often, but I feel as if I know you well? It must be because your father talks about you so much. He's always bragging about you. Well, I mean, he's not obnoxious about it or anything, but he speaks often about things you and he do together, and how smart you are, and whenever you do something good in school. That was how I got to come on this trip—he was talking in the teachers' lounge about how he was going to take you camping, and I said it sounded nice, and things led to things. You're very well known in the teachers' lounge, you know. That's one of the things I like about him—how much he loves his son."

Why doesn't he tell *me*? Emilio had a vision of himself staggering around in amazement, clutching his churning stomach. Of course he gave no outward sign of this.

"Hey, can you do me a favor?" Ms. Li asked. "Can you rub my neck? It's all sore from that backpack."

Rub her neck? How did you rub someone's neck? He couldn't picture it, except like rubbing with sandpaper, and wouldn't that hurt?

"You don't have to do anything special," she said, with the smile of an adult talking to a child. She bent her head forward, away from him, and swept her hand over her head as if her hair were still long and had to be kept in place. Emilio looked at the smooth, olive-tawny knobs of her neck vertebrae and was almost afraid his touch would paralyze her. "I'd just like to get some of the kinks massaged out of these neck muscles. Go on, it's hard to do it wrong, I'll walk you through it. Mostly use your fingertips and thumbs."

He did, because it would be more embarrassing not to. He placed all ten fingertips on her smooth skin, and held them there for a few seconds getting used to it and trying to figure out what to do next. Then she began guiding him: telling him to concentrate on the parts just to the side of her spine rather than directly on it, and to rub in circles, working the muscle underneath without shifting his hands over her skin.

"Good, fine, that's great," she said. "Do you want to be a masseur when you grow up?"

"No," he said, telling himself that it was advisable to make conversation with the client.

"Well, at this point you've got the perfect size hands for this work. I ought to open a spa using kids as staff. What *do* you want to be when you grow up?"

"I don't know."

"Yes you do."

Another of those understanding adults. But he didn't mind this one. "A couple of years ago I used to want to be a principal."

She laughed out loud. "A principal? I guess with your background it makes sense. But God. Like Tom Hughes...."

"I don't anymore, but I wanted to because a principal bosses teachers."

"Aha!"

"Now I'm not sure, but I may want to be either a video game inventor or a doctor. An ear, nose, and throat doctor," he added, thinking of it on the spur of the moment.

"Good choices. So you never wanted to be an astronaut or a cowboy or that type of thing?"

"When I was younger."

She nodded, and it made the bones move pleasingly under his fingertips. Then she began bobbing her head slightly, up and down, left to right through its whole arc of mobility, and it felt so good, it was as if he were rotating his own head the same way, like he sometimes did when he stood on his mother's lawn after she was asleep and looked at the stars.

"This is great, it's relaxing me, it's doing worlds of good. You learned a new skill today, and you'll be able to use it the rest of your life."

He didn't see how. Requests to rub someone's neck must be highly infrequent.

"This is something for you to know, Emilio. People aren't one thing all around. They specialize, sort of. One person is very good for giving neck rubs, another might be very good at teaching. Or dating. Or living with. You have to find people who are good in the areas you're interested in."

I'm interested in living with, he decided.

In a notably relaxed voice, she said, "I'm afraid of tornadoes and hurricanes." And added, in the tone of someone taking a survey, "What are you afraid of?"

The question scared him. The only thing to do was to choose an adult way out: an irrelevant remark. "Did you really see a great blue heron?"

"Of course. Think I lie to kids?"

"No." He explored the valleys between her vertebrae, giving each a few seconds of deep, soft thumbwork. "I wish I saw it."

"Harder," she instructed. "You won't hurt me."

"It's getting cloudy," he said, proud of his cautious gratuitousness. The sky in the transparent panel of the tent roof, which had been clear and blue, was now gray and flocculent as if something had slid shut. He didn't want to be rubbing her neck anymore or answering her questions, not because he didn't, but because he didn't know how. He saw the first raindrop hit the plastic skylight and drip downwards, spreading into two smaller drops.

"Don't stop so soon!" she said, but he had already stepped back and put his hands at his sides.

It seemed eerily humid inside the tent, as if their breath were misting the atmosphere. He wanted to stay inside, but he couldn't, it would hurt him—he didn't understand how, but he must not expose his lack of understanding. He didn't believe it would hurt him, but he must take no chances. So he told himself that he wanted to see the rain.

Slouching out of the tent in a moody movie-star way, he almost bumped into his father. Mr. Rosner held in each hand a bundle of raw firewood wrapped in a polyethylene skin with a handle; elbows cocked, he squinted quizzically up at the sky. A raindrop fell on the bundle in his left hand, then on the one in his right.

"I wanted to be sure I bought an ample supply," he said, as if explaining his fate. He dropped the bundles to the ground, and more and more clear raindrops hit their plastic skin, and dark raindrops marked the sandy soil beside them.

The tent was lit by two flashlights standing bulb-down on the ground. Their reddish-yellow coronas, eclipsed suns, threw confusion into shadows and gave faces the features of intrigue. A steamy smell of curried black beans, braised vegetables, and tofu mixed with those of propane fuel and damp socks. There had been no campfire, of course, and Mr. Rosner's steaks remained—either going bad or becoming nicely aged, opinions varied—wrapped in their supermarket packages inside his copious backpack. Mr. Rosner kept apologizing: "I should have checked the forecast.... Emilio must be tired of playing cards by now...." (Emilio wasn't, but Mr. Rosner's saying so made him want to quit.) And launching edifications: "Well, it's good to know how to deal with the unforeseen.... We're thrown back on our own resources...."

But to Emilio, being in a tent in the rain was no different from being in school, or visiting your father on a winter day when it was too cold to go out.

Finally the percussive rainwork, which had thumped and stretched the skin of the tent all evening without relaxing those underneath, eased off, and Mr. Rosner gave Emilio permission to go outside. It was lovely out there. Emilio just breathed, that was all he wanted to do at first. He stood in the clearing and tried to avoid being hit by belated raindrops, and enjoyed it just as much when they hit him. He practiced karate kicks and strikes on the slippery wet aspen trunk, and delicate scraps of bark fell, and his knuckles got excitingly raw. He was defeating all the other green belts of his dojo for a trophy. He was ascending in rank, sparring every black belt in the dojo for his own treasured black belt.

The adults' voices came from the tent, and he couldn't help it, he listened hard as he could.

"I'm sorry, that's the way I am," Mr. Rosner was saying. "I sometimes have" (inaudible) "issues, okay?"

"But *I'm* not the issue."

"I didn't say you were."

"Maybe *she* is."

"I think I'm not ready to do this." Mr. Rosner's voice rose. "To have this kind of conversation. Just the other day I remember thinking I would rather be alone for the rest of my life than ever have this kind of conversation again."

"Hey, you know how to make your date feel good."

"I'm trying to get to the truth as a precondition for making us *both* feel good by whatever means are necessary."

"Why did you invite me?" Ms. Li asked suddenly, and Emilio felt scared.

"Why did you accept?" Mr. Rosner asked.

Ms. Li was silent. A droplet landed on Emilio's hair, spreading wetly without any rebound. Some animal ran through branches in the woods: Emilio liked how you couldn't tell which direction it came from.

"Still raining," Mr. Rosner complained.

"I didn't make it rain," Ms. Li said.

Emilio turned his back to the tent and began punching the tree again, in slow motion, to work on his form.

"…not a perfect person, okay?, and obviously wasn't a perfect partner for fourteen years," came his father's voice, and Emilio rushed back. He desperately wanted to learn about his father's imperfections—what they really were, not just what he could glean for himself. He hovered just far enough away so that his moonshadow wouldn't fall on the tent. The voices wavered as if from inside a radio. "…trying to become more patient with myself. I'm just hoping others can become more patient with me."

After a moment, in a calm voice Emilio strained to hear, Ms. Li said, "I'm afraid I'm going to reject you."

After that came whispers and murmurs that Emilio, though an expert on adult quarrels, couldn't decode. And legs shifting and plastic rustling and bags being bumped. He tried to open his ears as much as possible. Were they shoving their sleeping bags apart? Were they giving each other the silent treatment?

In the vacuum left by stifled voices there arose an undertone, louder than insects or wavelets but just as constant: the phrases no one had to say in order for him to hear: "Little jerk, you're always in the way." "Little nothing, no one wants you here." "Get out of here, run through the woods, get lost." Nowhere even to go.

He retreated to the edge of the clearing, under dripping trees and branch-webbed sky, as if he had been sent there on detention for something that wasn't his fault. He walked in circles the way you do when ordered to remain in a confined space. He kept trying to scrape the mud off the sides of one sneaker with the other, a task that was oddly comforting for being frustrating.

If only kids could tell adults what to do! It would be so simple, really, like a teacher giving seat assignments. You, Dad, sit over here and be quiet, and don't get upset about little things all the time. You, Elissa, sit right next to him and be nice....

There was a light above the far shore. Wait, was there one? Yes. It was over the trees. It rose and dipped like a wave. It was bright through the mist, its glow spreading for many yards, lighting up treetops and turning black leaves briefly green again. Then it went out.

As quietly as he could, Emilio walked down the little path to the shore, and looked, and thought. He tried to remember what had just happened, with complete accuracy and none of the logical fallacies Mr. Rosner had lectured about in Critical Thinking. He reminded himself not to jump at the first conclusion, but to analyze the available evidence and anticipate opposing viewpoints.

Okay, he thought, I've done that and I still believe what I saw.

He walked back and peeked into the tent. His father was sitting crosslegged at one end, looking downcast, and Elissa was at the other end, legs outstretched into the yielding tent wall, reading a book by flashlight.

"You're not gonna believe this, but I think I just saw a UFO?" Emilio said. "At the other side of the lake?"

"Were you at the other side of the lake?" his father asked in a tone that was both sharp and mild at the same time.

"I saw it from here."

Mr. Rosner went, "Hm, hm," and made pondering faces that morphed into faces of mature dismissal, but Ms. Li dashed through the doorway, wobbling the tent stakes, and into the open to look at the sky.

"Where did you see it?" she asked, as if a famous rock band had walked by and she was hurrying for a glimpse.

Emilio pointed with his chin: it would be too dark for her to see the gesture, but she might hear it in his voice. "Up there."

They looked together. "What was it like?" she asked.

"A light. I don't know."

In the absence of the mysterious light, the sky seemed darker than normal. One big, slow-moving cloud covered the moon. Even the scents of pond and vegetation seemed dark. Emilio felt that the world was full of everything but people. He and Ms. Li were the only human beings left after a global cataclysm. They would explore the woods together, and for food they would hike into town for canned goods left by the departed natives. The first couple of years, Ms. Li would guide and tutor him, and then, when he was able, he would begin fertilizing her eggs in order to repopulate the earth. He would cut her flattop with scissors from a deserted convenience store—or, if she preferred, she could grow her hair down to her waist. That would be nice. They were standing close enough for the air movements around their arms to mingle. It was wonderful to look at nothing next to someone.

Then his father blustered out of the tent, calling, "It was somebody's flashlight, that's all," in a voice to warn away any aliens in the vicinity. He joined the woman and child looking at the black-on-black line of treetops across the lake. "There's nothing there," he said.

"It was too big for a flashlight," Emilio said, "and it wasn't coming from the ground, it was just up there by itself."

"They make some pretty awesome flashlights these days, you know. Or pond gas—or it could have been somebody's fire, or a reflection of something, even far away. And let's not forget the obvious: an airplane or helicopter."

"It didn't make any noise, Dad. And it would have to be a reflection *of* something, and what? And I'm telling you, it wasn't like a fire or a flashlight or anything. It was just up there, it didn't come from anywhere on the ground, and it was round and big…."

"Those are good theories," Mr. Rosner said, as he often did in class. "I think you might be exaggerating a wee bit about its size and mobility, but let's assume you're right about its not being a flashlight or campfire or aircraft. The question is, then, what are the possibilities? Those aren't the only three things in the world that shine. Let's brainstorm."

In brainstorming, students were supposed to broach ideas as quickly as possible without censoring themselves or criticizing others; however, as so often happened in practice, the first seconds sagged with disconsolate silence. And in the silence, the light appeared again. It was the same light Emilio had seen. Beside him, Ms. Li inhaled with excitement.

Mr. Rosner said, "You gave an accurate description—good job!"

"It's a little higher this time," Emilio said for extra credit. "Higher above the trees. But basically the same." He looked at the profiles of the adults. They appeared oddly relaxed, drained of tension, their habitual muscle configurations overridden, like when you don't think anyone is observing you, or when you're asleep. "So what do you think it is?"

Mr. Rosner did a thinkaloud, like when he modeled analyzing a math problem or a short story. "Well, it may be any of the things we've speculated about, or it may be something we haven't thought of. In my opinion, it's of the earth, because statistically, in our neighborhood of the universe, most of the mysterious things are earthly rather than unearthly. If it was a flying saucer, why would they land here anyway? Because out in Virgo 23 they'd heard about Fancy Pond? Why don't we just say it's the presence of mystery and wonder in our lives? Which we should always welcome."

Welcome, Emilio thought, and it made him feel tender and safe—which made him suspect there weren't really aliens present, because if there were, he'd be terrified.

"I think they're trying to scare us," Ms. Li said.

A cold gust blew from somewhere, and Emilio imagined it was the draft from a spaceship, and he kept himself from shivering, so as not to give away his location. But Mr. Rosner gave an imprudent, convulsive wriggle and rubbed himself on the upper arms. If he'd been a friend of Emilio's, Emilio would have risked exposing them all to laugh, "Scaredy-cat!"

In their side-by-side privacies, they kept looking at the sky for five, ten minutes, but the light didn't return. As they walked back to the tent, there was a minor disagreement over how it had vanished: Emilio said it disappeared instantaneously like a light switch being turned off, Ms. Li thought it traveled away in at least two simultaneous directions, and Mr. Rosner insisted it dipped into the trees, although not all the way to the ground.

"Well," Ms. Li said, "northern Wisconsin is one of the UFO

hot spots of the world. People around here have been seeing things for decades. If they'd land anywhere, it *would* be here."

"You keep up with the subject?" Mr. Rosner asked sarcastically.

She walked into the tent ahead of them, and was in her sleeping bag without a sound by the time the others crept through the tent flap. In the light of weakening flashlight batteries, she undressed inside the bag, with a slithering of nylon, a shifting protrusion of elbows and knees, and a decisive final zip.

It was weird: somehow Emilio didn't completely believe that she believed in the sighting. And he didn't believe that his father didn't believe.

It was obvious what was going to happen. The aliens had parked in the lot a quarter-mile away, and, taking the mud path to the campsite, would peer into the tent and find him the only one awake. Kindly they would invite him to their world. He would accept on condition he could take his father and Ms. Li, but they would inform him, sorrowfully, that their ship only had room for him to bring one companion. Confronted with an awful dilemma, he would choose Ms. Li for the sake of the aliens' scientific knowledge: they would want to learn about both human sexes.

He must have spent more than an hour turning inside his sleeping bag, trying to find a comfortable position, looking up through the clear panel at the stars, and imagining everything, from being cooked in a supermicrowave by ten-foot-tall reptiles to being made President of Earth Youth and sitting on the right hand of the Chair of the Council for Galactic Peace.

Then he heard movements. They came from inches away—from inside the tent! He heard bodies moving, breaths sighing—whether sleeping or awake, he couldn't tell. Then one zipper opening—slowly this time—and then, he was sure, the other.

He listened in amazement. The unfathomable was occurring within arm's reach of him. An urge went through him to stand up and ask out loud, "Are you really doing what I think you're doing?" But they would have yelled at him—or worse, facilitated a frank and open discussion of sex, just like the ones he sat through in Family and Consumer Education (FACE) every Thursday after lunch.

He was shocked by how little sense of decorum vacationing

schoolteachers had. He pitied them for trusting him to be asleep. He was appalled that they might not even care.

Then the full horror of what was going to occur struck him. The aliens were going to walk into the campsite and Mr. Rosner and Ms. Li wouldn't be able to do anything about it, because they'd be locked together. (How long did it take lovers to uncouple? He might want to ask the question next term. It seemed to him it must be a complicated, delicate procedure that would take a long time.) Slick-skinned, dwarfish, tendril-limbed creatures with ghost complexions and Humpty Dumpty heads would slink in, grip him with fingers as light but unpryable as superalloys, and these two would be lying there going, "Ooh, aah," sweating and rolling while he was spirited beyond the solar system to spend his adolescence and adulthood in a zoo, in a force-field cage, alone. They would be seized with unbearable remorse, they would vow never to have sex again!

Sounds of feet and hands and lips; squishes and slides and light thuds. Emilio could visualize what was happening, because his mother (not so much his father) let him watch sophisticated movies as long as they discussed them afterwards. But despite the fact that he had seen it on the screen and heard about it in the classroom, he still couldn't believe it.

"This thing's too small," Ms. Li said. "It's not built for two."

"We could get on top of the bag," Mr. Rosner whispered. "Are you stopping?"

"I'm uncomfortable."

"Look, I'm sorry I've been nasty to you. I've been trying to upset you, I don't know why. You have to realize this is the first time since the breakup…. I feel like I don't know how to do anything."

"I'm not necessarily the best listener for that kind of self-examination or introspection or whatever you want to call it. I like men to be more stoical and unemotional."

"I wish I'd brought a bottle of Jack Daniels to make me more stoical."

"I wish there was more room in this tent. I had claustrophobia as a child."

"Maybe if we hadn't brought him along."

"No, he's the best part. I wish we could go on a moonlight

hike. Wake him up and march out of here and walk all night."

Emilio was opening and shutting his eyes while Ms. Li spoke about him. Eyes open, he was here in the tent trying to observe without being observed; eyes shut, he and Ms. Li were holding hands to help each other over slippery boulders on a midnight trail.

"Go by yourself," Mr. Rosner said. "Obviously neither of us is ready for a long-term situation."

"Don't tell me what I'm ready for. I wanted to like you."

A pause, then more of the wordless sounds, which, though not exactly loud, had a kind of projected and suppressed, stage-whisper quality. Mr. Rosner's voice in a questioning tone; Ms. Li's, dubious but open to agreement…a male laugh…a female shushing.…

"Well, I guess that was about a two-point-six on a scale of five," Mr. Rosner said later. "Sorry."

"If you apologize for one more thing, I'm gonna sleep outside. I don't think you have anything to apologize for, but if *you* do, why don't you just not do those things?"

"But that's all I do, don't you get it?" Mr. Rosner said in a high-pitched voice. "I do things so I'll have something to apologize for afterward. If I wasn't going to do that, I'd have to undo everything I've ever done in my life." And he lurched up out of the sleeping bag with a violent zipping sound, and stood bent-kneed, bumping his head against the transparent roof panel, and staggered in a running crouch through the narrow end of the tent. "What did I do?" he said, more to himself than to Ms. Li. "What did I do, why am I here, I wrecked my family, I hurt my son."

"I thought *she* did," Ms. Li said.

"Why am I not in my life anymore? I had a life and it's gone. Where is it?" Mr. Rosner half-sobbed, weaving in circles, calling to the sky.

Emilio realized he couldn't lie there any more without letting them know he was listening. In his deepest voice, he gave a soft, long groan, as if their discussion had just awakened him from a dream.

"Shh, he's up," Ms. Li said.

"Go to sleep, Em," his father said through the shaky wall. "I'm just looking for something in the dark."

Emilio tried not to move a muscle. By being still now, he hoped to convince the adults that he had slept through the whole encounter. Through the rooftop panel, he watched a tiny white light and strained to decide whether it was moving or not, but he couldn't tell; and he worked to make his movements as undetectable as that star's.

In the morning, everything looked clean. The downed log bench was slick from the rain, and the old charcoal in the fire circle looked like a mound of black smudges. Emilio scratched a white notch into a drop of hard pine sap; he could smell rainwater in the crevices of bark.

Ms. Li put her arm around him from behind. "I'm so glad that rain stopped, aren't you?" She was lugging her backpack by one strap, so its edge trailed in the wet dirt. It looked fully packed.

Mr. Rosner came out of the tent, setting his backpack carefully on its side, and began pulling out the aluminum posts.

"Are we leaving?" Emilio said, flustered because it was what he had formerly wished, but hadn't wished aloud.

"After a quick breakfast," his father said. The tent settled with a puffing hiss; there remained one or two bubble-shaped humps, which Mr. Rosner swatted flat.

"Aren't we going to hike and stuff?"

Mr. Rosner shook his head with woodsmanly regret. "Trails'll be nothing but mud, Em. If you really want to hike for miles in the mud, we'll try it"—he looked at Ms. Li, who did not acknowledge him—"but I don't think it would really add much to the quality of our experience."

"We've seen what we came to see," Ms. Li told Emilio.

Being visited by aliens or hiking in mud—which was more impossible? His father would probably say, "There are arguments on both sides." Emilio watched Mr. Rosner fold the green sheet into a fat, air-layered rectangle, then shake the orange ground cloth and whisk the twigs and leaves and mud off it. Emilio was glad his father hadn't called for volunteers.

I come from him, I come from him, Emilio thought, and it seemed as unbelievable as thinking, I come from one-celled creatures that traveled across space and landed in the ocean a billion years ago.

He was waiting to find out what the adults, this morning, thought about last night's light in the woods. But neither of them mentioned it. In fact, once Emilio took notice, he realized that his father and Ms. Li were hardly speaking to each other, except for the tersest exchanges:

"You want coffee?"

"I'm not hungry, thanks."

Their voices were steady and low. Ms. Li kept her eyes on inanimate objects: the blue flame of the propane stove; the tin mug. Mr. Rosner wandered and shifted, squatting in the wet sand—grunting—then getting up and pacing—sighing—and checking his bag to see if he'd packed everything—snorting.

"You know, Em," Mr. Rosner said, "this journey hasn't been a loss at all. We've gotten used to primitive camping, and we still have time to get back to Madison and see a movie. The two of us."

Mr. Rosner hadn't even mentioned the light in the woods for the purpose of debunking it. As if it had never happened. The most important event in your life, perhaps, and you weren't even supposed to refer to it! This was an adult habit that completely baffled Emilio; he had no hope of ever mastering it.

And this, he understood suddenly, was how extraterrestrials got away with visiting Earth undetected. They knew that people wouldn't talk about them. A flying saucer could follow Mr. Rosner's Volvo out of Fancy Pond and down the highway all the way to Madison and land on the dome of the state capitol and it wouldn't be in the news, and if Emilio asked his father about it, he would smile, "One important step toward maturity, Em, is learning to accept the limits of our understanding." It was if they had placed a sticker on the event—"Do Not Discuss"—and if they removed the sticker they would die.

All the way home, Emilio stole glances at the sky through the rear windshield; and he thought he could feel the distant presence of wise observers, though of course there was no sign of them. And he glanced at his father from behind and below, and—maybe it was the angle—the face looked new to him, as if Mr. Rosner had a clone who was substituting for him: gaunter, gray-skinned, but handsomer in his tiredness, and possessed by thoughts Emilio was almost as afraid of someday having, as of someday having no thoughts at all.

Stoical and unemotional. Stoical and unemotional. He would have to look up the first word in the dictionary (if he could figure out how to spell it without asking his father), but from its proximity to *unemotional* he could guess the general meaning. He looked at the top of Ms. Li's flattop above the neckrest and told himself, *You'll never get a girlfriend.*

"Worship the Lord. Slow, we love our cats," he said to himself, turning to read the sign from the opposite direction. "Worship the Lord slow, we love our cats."

His voice got fuzzier as the miles passed. His father hadn't said, "You didn't get much sleep last night," but Emilio virtually heard it, and before his head touched the perforated cushion of the car door, he had begun to dream. He saw a future stepmother. Her face was indistinct. Although she could hear and speak perfectly, she had chosen to communicate only by holding up signs: beautiful handpainted swirls, spiral-armed multicolored circles. He could read them—they were exclusively for him. They told him who to be. They told him how to become. They told him how to grow.

"Don't wake him," someone said, but the stopping of the car had tossed him forward—he dreamed he was a windblown tree—and with his eyes still closed he thought, *I'm awake anyway.*

They were in Madison, in front of Ms. Li's lakeside apartment complex. She turned around in the front seat and reached to touch his arm.

"See you at your next hearing test," she said.

And to Mr. Rosner she said, "Pop the trunk, will you, so I can get my backpack?"

Well, at least I'm good for giving massages, Emilio thought. And with no one watching, he gave what his mother often criticized as his "exaggerated smile," ferociously baretoothed, cartoonishly fixed, and directed, in this case, at an imaginary spectator who didn't need any legroom at all. Contrary to what his mother said, he wasn't trying to make fun of anyone; he really felt like smiling so much he was embarrassed.

He shut his eyes for the short drive home, to see again the many-faced sign-bearer whom an expert dreamer like himself could always call forth. Unlike real people, who vanished like flashes in a forest.

Delicate Destinies

T he envelope was so light—as if it held not my father's post-
humous collected works but their ashes. Twenty-eight ancient sheets of onionskin, browned and crinkled till they
deserved their name. Three short stories, written long before I was
born. His widow had sent them in a black envelope with a white
gummed label. Didn't she have any subtlety at all? I knew her grief
was real; was it unreal to her until she falsified it?

The stapled corners tore though I slipped them out of the
envelope as gently as I could. His manual typewriter had had a
good, dark ribbon, but the lines were uneven; the counters of the *e*
and *o* were filled with ink; the periods punched holes in the paper.
In the upper right corners of his title pages were exact word counts—
1,283; 2,965; 3,032—from my father who had sacrificed his life
to the withholding of words, especially those that were not words
of contempt, criticism, refutation. He had never even told me
enough about his stories for them to have become a family legend.
These were the titles: "Eyeglasses," "A Brother's Oath," and the
short one was "Descartes on the Subway." I despaired.

"Dear Seth," his widow Sylvie had written, "Sorry it's taken
me so long to get to this, but you know how hard it is for me to

look at anything relating to him. I have not been able to make a copy so would you please make one for yourself and return the originals to me and, Seth, should these stories tell you anything about him, and anything you find out, will you please share it with me?"

It was a weekday evening; I had no date and no work, and it was winter. I put on some Mendelssohn for warmth, and the green-shaded table lamp, dim as my parents' Bronx apartment. I made coffee and spread butter on a roll, and stared at my right hand, because if my father were spreading butter on a roll he would be using his left.

I began reading, wishing I could hide my eyes and read at the same time.

Oh, they weren't so bad. And I'm being too modest. He was a bright, bright man, he had gifts, and all three stories had prompted handwritten notes from the editors who'd rejected them. One of the notes, virtually an apology, urged my father to send more work. The editor was renowned for discovering new writers in the 1930's and 1940's. The magazines were famous. But my father with his analytical mind had cut through the niceties to the essence, to the rejection he had counted on. A glimmer of discouragement was all he'd needed. He concluded that he was talentless, his efforts doomed to futility. Rather than strive and suffer anymore, he gave up. I imagine him—it would be just like him—telling himself that it was their loss, not his; by spurning them he would show he saw through them.

How bright could he have been if he believed in himself?

"Eyeglasses" told an anecdote that had happened in real life to my uncle Joey; but in the story, my father made the protagonist seem like himself. Joey had quit school after sixth grade to work as a messenger boy for a bootlegger. A few years later, when he was "making good money" at a job he never explained to us, he took his mother—my grandmother, whom I never met—to the eye-glass counter of the five-and-dime store and bought her a pair of reading glasses. One sunrise, Joey came home blearily from work and found her in the kitchen, wearing the glasses, reading *Anna Karenina* in a language he hadn't known she could read—English. "Mama, what are you doing?" Joey cried out. The story, as both my father and Uncle Joey told it, ended with her shrugging in embarrassment, afraid she had done something wrong.

"A Brother's Oath" was about the famous but mysterious time when my father and Joey didn't speak to each other for three years although they slept in the same bed. My mother used to throw this scandal in his face when they had arguments. As a child, I struggled to visualize it: not speak? Not speak to your own brother? I couldn't imagine a normal human being doing what my father had done. Only once, I dared to ask him about it. I assumed that he would hit me, but he laughed with blunt evasiveness and said, "We were dumb kids, not like you." I could have beat my head against the wall trying to understand.

And his story didn't explain. And the editors felt the same bewilderment. "Well written but not realistic—how could they have not spoken?" said one of the notes. Apparently the editor hadn't spent much time on Elder Avenue.

My father had with unerring perversity chosen exactly the wrong literary influence for his personality and material. Those two stories were narrated with the terse, Hemingwayesque objectivity popular then, with its arrogant claims of iceberg-like concealment—and with the result that even a reader who was his son could not feel what the characters were feeling or why. You stupid bastard! I could see him in the curtained-off "sleeping area" he lived in till the war, crafting with scrupulous rigor the tight, constipated sentences of the Michigan fisherman. Shmuck! There are no trout in the Bronx River!

So my grandmother was merely a timid woman who sat before a window most of the day, clutching her stomach. My uncle was merely a loutish boy who, for unknowable reasons, maintained a destructive vow of silence. There were clear descriptions of a coal-heated apartment, though. And there was a passage about a teenager discovering literature in the Fordham Library, which I could feel.

I agreed with the editors. There was something missing from those stories, and I wanted to tell him, Keep trying, and open up a little….

But "Descartes on the Subway" was in a different vein. It was youthful work of a high caliber: an impressionistic, tentatively stream-of-consciousness description of a subway ride under the East River. The first-person narrator is an aspiring composer who, to the shake and clatter of the train, is working on a symphony in his head—one of those urban rhapsodies of the Thirties, with movements entitled "Orchard Street" and "Mulberry Street" and "Mott Street" and "Park Row." It was almost as good as Dos Passos except Dos Passos did it first. Every detail was vivid, the unraveling woven cane of the subway seats, the wet, yellow eyes of a straphanger who, the narrator imagines, may have suffered typhus as a child in the old country. The style was occasionally marred by an Anglicism, the result of my father's excessive reading: "There was nothing for it but to change at Borough Hall." And you didn't learn where the narrator was going or who was in his life. He didn't interact with anyone on the train. But you didn't miss the parts my father couldn't do. You didn't need verification of what the young composer imagined about his fellow passengers. You didn't even need to know how well the author understood his narrator's problems. You got the sense of a man who would never overcome himself but who would accomplish something in the attempt to do so. Stepping through the subway door, late for an undescribed rendezvous, the young man concludes: "I think, therefore I think I am."

The well-known editor wrote: "Really nice, thoughtful. I'd like to see something of yours that has more than one character in it."

I felt sick to my stomach. I knew how my father's magic would have closed the open door. I felt idiotic for taking heart at the encouragement now.

I could see my father opening the envelope fifty years earlier—knowing before he opened it that it said No—and it seemed as if I myself were doing it. And I saw myself, after reading the death sentence, shuffling speechlessly, prematurely old, behind the bedroom curtain where, if my brother was lying in his own axiomatic despair, I would sink beside him without giving a clue, and never tell anyone. Because to examine it would have been to reveal its folly. And I would decide to kill myself, but I would devise a slow, clever method. I would become smitten during wartime with a neighborhood girl I hardly knew, and seduce her with love letters quoting Marvell and Donne, and after she married me I would never say a kind word to her, and I would blame her for my disappointments. After she left me I would never admit I missed her, but I would drive alone to the special places we used to drive—to the clam shacks on City Island, to the Kensico Dam in Westchester, even to the boys' department of Alexander's in White Plains. And at seventy, I would keep the symptoms of cancer stoically unmentioned until I was past curing.

In the window I saw myself holding the fifty-year-old letter. Snow flurries were falling, and I held my hand up to the gap in the frame where the draft blew. We were having one of those stretches of Hudson Valley winter when it snows just a little almost every day, a daily reminder. In the dark glass, my face seemed illuminated by the light of my own eyes. Half the people in my family, male and female, have the same look: slight build, congenital pouches under the eyes, and thick brown hair that lasts a lifetime. When a new cousin or nephew or niece is born with the family look, I smile at the infant's photograph and wonder, "Is this the one who'll break the spell?"

I knew it would be fruitless to send my father's stories to magazines at this date. Apprentice efforts by an unknown dead man, their only value was as historical documents, and mainly for my own family. So I took them to a desktop publishing shop and had two hundred copies printed. I designed a nice plain cover and wrote a one-page introduction. I mailed them to everyone who had known my father. To close relatives, I delivered them by hand. Afterward, I had fifty copies left over for the attic.

One day Sylvie and I drove together to present a copy to Uncle Joey. He was in a nursing home suffering from the same form of cancer that had killed my father. Joey was in remission, a state my father had never reached, but the treatments had weakened him to the point where he couldn't take care of himself. The nursing home was convenient to my father's cemetery, but Joey couldn't travel the shortest distance. Sylvie and I stopped at the cemetery and placed a copy of my father's book on his grave.

"A lot of good that'll do him," she said, and scrunched up her square face till her eyelids looked like children's fists. She was a big, bulky woman who made her living sculpting bronzes for suburban department-store galleries. This was a woman who boasted that when a gynecologist had touched her in an improper way, she fastened her hand around his throat and pushed him, without much effort, across his office and into his door. She was an inch taller than me and probably outweighed me; and at the sight of her thick wrist rubbing exhibitionistic tears across her face, I felt uncomfortable for not being capable of them.

Sylvie was from a family my own family considered coarse. Her parents ran a clothing store under an elevated subway; they kept a kosher home although they did not believe in God; they belonged to a beach club where bald retirees and pillow-breasted widows played gin rummy by poolside. These things and more caused my mother to label them "those typical Jews." My family were not typical Jews. Exactly what we were was never explained to me.

I threw my arm around Sylvie's hulking shoulders and helped her to the car. I felt like a football manager consoling one of his players after a loss. Her prolonged faithfulness would have displeased my father, I thought—unless he saw that she was afraid of never finding another man. In that case, touched by his own powers of inference, he would have pitied her.

"You've read them, the stories?" she asked.

"I've read them."

"I can't. I'm afraid to look at them."

"I've read them a lot."

A crew was pulling the tarp off a fresh hole. A man in a baseball cap rode a power mower on a hilltop. Another screwed a green hose to a spigot.

"Then, Seth, will you do me a favor?" Sylvie said. "Tell me what you think of them, and would you please—would you please tell me he didn't have the talent? He shouldn't have kept writing, he was right to stop?"

I drove slowly to the cemetery gate, trying to read each carved name I passed.

My uncle Joey was the uncle I was most afraid of as a child. Not that he treated me badly; on the contrary, he visibly and unsuccessfully struggled to ask me questions that would relax me and let me show who I was. I, in turn, longed to join him in his strange world of saloons and dirty jokes, but I must have feared it would hurt me. There was a connection between us of unspoken, bashful fondness, a wish that we knew each other better, a shared perplexity at how to do it. If I were less frightened, I would have assured him that I was frightened of almost everything, not just of him.

We rarely visited Uncle Joey's apartment because it was on the other side of the Bronx and poorer than our place. My mother was reluctant to set foot there and my father to expose Joey to her reactions. I remember the first time I visited Joey—was I four, five?—and learned I had to climb stairs instead of taking a slow, squeaking elevator. The stairwells smelled of cabbage, beer, and cigars. When Aunt Margaret opened the door I gaped in awe, knowing that she was a Catholic, a completely different type of human being, but not actually seeing how. She was plump and fair-haired like my maternal grandmother and—I had not thought this possible—both quicker to embrace us and quicker to scream.

I always thought of Joey himself as more Irish than Jewish, although he had refused to convert at marriage. He didn't look like my father and me. With straight blond hair, twinkling blue eyes, round cheeks, and broad red nose—a face I later realized was pure peasant Polish—he spoke in a lilting tenor through a wide, tight-lipped smile. He was expert at mimicking priests and contrite drunkards, and had been known to accompany his wife to mass on Easter. He gave Aunt Margaret a weekly housekeeping allowance from his salary as a subway motorman; lifted weights in his spare time; went to bars on Friday nights and came home reeling and black-eyed and bloody-knuckled, bragging of what he had done to the mick who had called him a hebe. Joey was the only relative I ever heard talking about sex. Perhaps the last memory I will ever lose, of anything, will be of Uncle Joey wiping a wet ring from my mother's table with his handkerchief, saying about a distant cousin, "She'd sleep with a snake if somebody held it down."

I heard Joey's exploits whispered of by my titillated parents, and only put the facts together as an adult. He had had to fight off insults from non-Jews all through the Army and working life, for the simple reason that he preferred to hang around with them—unlike my father, who primly avoided rough company.

When he felt his younger brother needed shaping up, Joey barked practical familial wisdom mixed with scraps of public-library erudition. I was amazed that anyone dared speak to my father in that tone. I think it was partly Joey's way of filling uncomfortable silences, partly his revenge for my father's college education. My father served him back with cold, intellectual sarcasms, mocking, for example, Joey's competitive way of plowing through the most intimidating tomes. When Joey advised my father to ease up on me, my father said, "Oh, did you get that from *The Anatomy of Melancholy*?" I didn't know whether to be grateful to Joey for defending me, or to sneer with my father at the ain't-saying dropout.

"I wonder if he'll talk to us," Sylvie said as we walked through the lobby of the nursing home.

"Why, is he mad at us?"

"That's not the question."

On the cinderblock walls were crayon drawings by children in the local elementary school. The carpet was thin blue nub and bare furrow. The nursing home had been young when I was.

"Brothers are brothers," Sylvie said. "They're exactly alike, the two of them. Stress makes them clam up, that's all. Your father used to give me the silent treatment if I took the newspaper before he did. When he went into the hospital he wouldn't answer the doctor's questions unless I repeated them. Your uncle's going out of his mind with fear—why should he confide in anyone?"

I didn't remember my father giving me the silent treatment. I remembered him yelling at me. Did that mean he had loved me?

"When we were first going together," Sylvie said, "you know how I go upstate to the art fairs in the summer? Your father used to travel with me and sit in the corner of the booth, not say a word for hours, smiling. I used to worry about him—'Don't you want something to do? You want to take over selling for a while?' No, he said, he was fine. He just liked to sit and listen to me. Later, when he was sick, he told me it had been the happiest time of his life."

When we reached the third floor, all the patients' rooms were locked for lunchtime. We strolled; I snooped. On a patient's door was a photo of a boy on a tricycle, a grandson, who might visit here and, because his grandmother gave him a cookie and let him sit on her bed, take back a memory of happiness. Here was a wedding invitation from 1952, and here a laughing woman in a one-piece bathing suit was having her back anointed with suntan oil by the disembodied hands of someone who had been snipped from the photo.

And here was a door with no identifying marks except Joey's computer-printed name. It occurred to me that saying nothing might be the hardest thing on earth. There is residual communication in the plainness of a door, the impersonality of a printout. Eliminating every trace of information might require a purity of purpose, a discipline, that made literature seem frivolous by comparison. The doors decorated with mementos allowed me to see inside a little bit, with the faulty X-ray vision we all live by; but to block all vision, to withhold all signs, to erect a perfect shield—wasn't that somehow heroic?

"Did you ever hear the story," I said, "how my father and Joey, when they were teenagers, for three years—"

"Why they didn't speak to each other? It's very simple. Each was waiting for the other to speak."

I laughed. "I don't get it. Did they hate each other? What did they do if they wanted to rearrange the covers?"

"Each was waiting for the other to speak." She repeated her simple lesson. "Luckily, when your father did that to me, I was a person who speaks. 'What's the matter? What did I do wrong? Tell me.' And your father would tell me, a little bit, eventually. But with his brother, they could out-silent each other. Maybe they were both lying there for three years hoping the other one would ask him what was wrong."

At the end of the hall, I leaned my forehead against a wire-meshed window. In the parking lot was one bare, small maple, its trunk taped like a baseball bat.

"Joey idolized your father," Sylvie said. "Why do you think he's sick now? Your father's death threw him completely. The fact that his younger brother had died. Now they can't refuse to speak to each other anymore. Look," she pointed with her chin.

A troop of old people emerged from the elevator and made their way down the hall. Except for a man and a woman arguing, they seemed to be walking in meditation. They spaced themselves in a graded solitude without abandoning each other. Differences of velocity kept the mass expanding like the universe after the Big Bang. Some traveled in clusters of three or four, giving out isolated mutterings while the rubber tips of their canes and walkers clopped on the carpet. Some took tiny steps with supporting partners, keeping a constant distance from the rest. A hairless man groped the wall with one hand while his tripod cane prodded the floor as if testing thin ice; when the group slowed to gather its strength, someone called back a question to him, but he, slowing in unison with them, didn't answer, and the gap didn't close.

It took me several seconds to understand that one of these

white dwarfs was my powerful and scathing Uncle Joey.

Stooped, he shuffled in the middle of the crowd, in an untied ash-gray robe, a larger man gripping him by the elbow. Joey's hair was completely white, his skin almost equally pale. The laboring arms, the beer-filled gut, the impish, round cheeks, existed only as stretched skin. His friend helped him turn toward his room. Joey gave him the key to open the door. I had made eye contact with Joey for an instant; but as his door opened, he looked up as if noticing us for the first time.

"You're here?" he said.

It took him a long time to reach his bed. I stayed behind him, straining to keep to his pace. He swung his feet up with the grimacing concentration of someone finishing a long series of leg lifts.

He gestured for us to sit in the orange vinyl guest chairs or on the empty second bed. "I'm lucky, I got no roommate since two weeks ago."

Then he looked at me and, after a long pause, said, in a tone of enhanced recognition, "Seth." Perhaps, after first recognizing a face and a kinship, he had now reviewed his memories of me.

"How are you doing, Uncle Joey?"

"You didn't send me a card."

"I'm visiting you today."

A little taken aback by that, he glanced at Sylvie. "You?"

"Me? I'm all right, Joey, and you?"

"You're all right?" he said, incredulously.

I was afraid he was going to lapse into a final silence, the simple habit of greeting and inquiry having become too hard to remember. Sullenness might make him feel like a boy again. There seemed to be a deliberateness in the way he made his eyes glaze. When he looked out the window, it was evident he was not looking at anything but away from us.

Trying to get him to speak to me, I asked him how the staff was treating him; how often he saw the doctor; how my cousins were. The tremor in his scowl increased. I had always had trouble getting people to open up. He stared through his reflection and the clouds.

It was then that Sylvie proved her mettle. "Here, Joey, we brought you something," and from her big, man-bashing pocketbook she produced a pint of cheap scotch. She cracked off the bottlecap, and sat on the edge of Joey's bed to show him the label.

Lolling his head with moribund roguishness, he said, "She knows my brand, the minx."

He lifted his shrunken arm and pointed to the paper cups on the wash basin.

I'm not much of a drinker. In my parents' house we were afraid of alcohol, perhaps because it would lead to experiences like the one Joey, Sylvie, and I now had.

We toasted Joey's health in gargle-sized paper cups, and licked the spills off our thumbs. Sylvie gulped her drink quickly so she could help Joey get the liquid to his mouth without wasting it. Taking his first sip, he gave a grimace of surprise, as if discovering an undebilitated part of his body.

With the second drink, he became sociable and charming. And I learned something about my family: we weren't glum, taciturn people at all, but natural talkers who feared our strengths. Perhaps my father should have drunk more! I imagined him fueled by alcohol, with a gleam in his eye and secrets on his tongue, winning people over with the quips and disclosures that in reality he had used only for attack. And writing—becoming the kind of boozing, troublesome American writer about whom I could have written a proud memoir.

That hour in the nursing home, Joey told us stories from his motorman days: how he had had women in his control booth between stations; how his brakes had failed once and he had said over the loudspeaker, "Attention, passengers, our next stop will either be A Hundred and Twenty-Fifth Street or St. Luke's Emergency Room."

He told how my grandfather, in 1910, had hoped to emigrate to Germany, the nation the progressive, assimilated, scientific-minded Jews of that time admired most; but Germany had a military service requirement for male immigrants, and he had just come from seven years in the Russian army (where he had been made company clerk because he was the only enlisted man in the company who could read and write Russian), so he reluctantly chose America instead, and made my existence possible.

They were stories my father should have written. Maybe ones he had planned to write. Or ones Joey should have written.

The dying man made us laugh and love ourselves. The nursing home didn't seem alien anymore; a paper cup of whiskey didn't seem outrageous. Joey didn't laugh, but at least it seemed like our laughter meant something to him.

I asked for more stories. "What were my grandparents like? Joey, why didn't you ever go back to school?"

He let out a groan. He tipped his cup so he could look into the bottom, and the dregs spilled onto his gown. He held out the cup, his hand trembling. "Sylvie, could you get me some water?"

Since when did my Uncle Joey prefer water?

After helping him with the unobjectionable beverage, Sylvie signaled toward the door. "He's tired, we shouldn't wear him out. Joey, you want us to leave, say so. We can come back, it's no hardship to drive down."

It was startling how tired Joey looked once Sylvie said he did. His forehead was white and damp. He slumped in bed and struggled to raise the blanket to his chin.

I picked up the meager, paperbound book from the neighboring bed. "Uncle Joey, here's something I want you to have...."

I stood the book upright on his rib cage and wagged it with nervous ingratiation. We don't have to be solemn about this, I thought. We've drunk together, we've shared old times.

He looked at his brother's byline. "Ach. The stories...."

Effortfully he opened the volume and turned the pages. He felt the glossy, untouched leaves.

"Have you read them?" I asked.

"Have I read them?" He was silent for a long moment. "I was the only person he let read them. He was very shy about his ambitions. I tried to encourage him. I used to tell him, 'It looks good to me but I'm not objective. Get another opinion.' First he wouldn't send them anywhere. Then I told him, 'Look, you're putting a burden on me.' So he sent them some places...."

Some memory made him wave me away, and he let the volume fall onto his chest. It slid off him, onto the edge of the bed. He glanced at it and then ignored it.

Joey said, "He got crumbs of good wishes but nothing solid. They hemmed and hawed and said no. He tried to act like he didn't mind. I knew he was terribly upset. In our family the things that bother us most, we pretend we don't care about. I remember he said to me, 'I think I ought to stop.'"

I constructed my next question like a trap. "And what did you say?"

"He told me he thought about this story business all the time; it was like a craziness with him, it kept him up at night. Names of characters would swirl through his head, people he didn't know anything about, and he would try to figure out who they were and what they were doing. He was afraid, it got him so overexcited. He said anything that got him so overexcited was probably wrong."

"And what did you say?"

"What do you mean? I didn't tell him to stop or not stop. What did I know? I was a working man. I knew there were people who had to write, act, sing, no matter what, even if they were poor. Was he one of those? He didn't know, himself. I said—I forget the exact words, of course—something like, 'My opinion don't count. The people who count turned you down.' I said, 'If you do work no one's paying you for, you're braver than me.'"

"And you wouldn't want that." I turned and looked at Sylvie. If I had looked at Uncle Joey another second, I might have taken the weak, helpless, dismal, confused old man and pounded his head against the wall.

Sylvie was standing rigid with anger, like a handcuffed prisoner who wants to take a swing at the judge.

"They were very close," she said. Can a deadpan voice shake? Trying to close her coat rapidly, she had to repeat each button.

"My father looked up to him," I said.

"They could communicate without even speaking."

"So imagine how much weight a spoken opinion had."

"A single word might change his life." We looked at each other. She slung her pocketbook over her shoulder. "I'm glad you liked the whiskey," she told Joey. "Any time you want me to pour it down your throat...." Running out of the room, leaving me alone with Uncle Joey, she cried out, "Meet you by the car."

I sat on the orange vinyl chair in the corner, staring at Uncle Joey's bed, imagining it empty.

I wished he and my father had never broken their silence. I saw them living their lives as enemies: rising from the shared bed and finding the nerve to keep their bitter vow. Then the words of people he loved could not have tortured my father, and his own words would have been what he valued. I understood completely why they had stopped speaking to each other; that was no longer the enigmatic part. What was puzzling was why they had started again.

I shouldn't say anything to Joey that would enlighten him, wound him. I hesitated to risk even, "I'd better go," or, "Thanks for the stories, Joey." I shouldn't give him the benefit of catharsis. I should refuse to show him how angry I was. If he understood, and felt remorse, it would be his victory, for what good would that remorse do my father?

Once, deciding to stay aloof from a dispute between neighbors, my father had told me, "The world is better off without my wisdom. Or, if it's worse off, it's deservedly so." At the time, I thought he was joking.

I wished I could seal Joey in a room for the short remainder of his life, and never know whether he was worse off for it or better.

But looking at his shriveled face, his whiskey-wet lips, I felt my father's sentimentality come over me: the compassion for frailty and illusion that he had tried to mask as scorn. My father hated the thought of ever believing an illusion, and condescended to the rest of humanity, who always did.

If Joey had encouraged him, would he really have become a writer? Is destiny so delicate? And even if Joey was at fault, didn't I owe it to him that my father's sayings were coming back to me in bursts of grateful memory?

"No one deserves more punishment than the one we all get," my father had said.

I stood and grasped Uncle Joey's hand, though it scalded me. I touched my lips to his damp chalk forehead as if telling a child to be brave. I put my father's book in his hand and closed his fingers on the binding.

"That's your brother, don't hurt him," I said, and heard my father say the same words to me, thirty years before, when I had fought with my younger brother over a snatched baseball card or a mocking glance—indignities that used to enrage me so, I'd dread that I would kill him. I literally heard the sentence, as if my father were in the room. Then I rushed out. Uncle Joey and I never exchanged another word.

When I talked to Syvlie about this in the car, she accused me of being soft-hearted.

Refuge

When the subject came up, my mother wished it away. "We didn't lose anybody in the camps, our family was all in America by that time. Maybe some distant cousins, that's all." What she should have said—it took me thirty years to realize this—what she should have taught me was, "We lost six million brothers and sisters."

But I can't blame her for being in a time and place where one's deepest wish was to be mistaken for an average American. In my memory, our roan brick apartment building is bright red like tempera paint; a nursery silence enfolds the arguments and ambulances; and the black silhouette of the subway station, blocking the bottom of the afternoon sun, is both a protective membrane and an escape route. Running commando missions in the defoliated courtyards, we divided ourselves into Americans and Germans: if you were unpopular or had been captured in a previous round, you were condemned to be a German. The phrase *holocaust survivor* had not yet come into vogue; we called them refugees—sometimes "refs"—and spoke of them with the condescending sympathy, and the contempt for their mistakes, appropriate for greenhorns. When I held my mother's hand at the bakery or the butcher's, I might turn my glance from her merely freckled wrist to the fascinating wrist of the next customer, where a five-digit number was tattooed. I wondered if the tattooing had hurt. I wondered if they wished they could have the numbers removed. Were they ashamed of these markings when they went outside the Bronx? Or were they proud of belonging to an exclusive club? If you had a tattoo on your wrist, did it keep you from being able to enjoy Godzilla movies and chocolate egg creams and Mickey Mantle home runs, or did it make you enjoy them more? Sometimes I imagined that people with numbers on their wrists had been built in a factory.

My best friend Donny's parents had numbers on their wrists, and accents that caused me to keep asking, "What? What?" whenever they had me over for dinner. Esther was a beautiful, strong redhead with Slavic cheekbones, slanted brown Magyar eyes, and— what I didn't notice at the time—an orphan's desperate longing for, and inability to accept, luxurious stability. Lee was a barber, a tall, lanky, curly—and ditto the part about not noticing—temperamental, irresponsible, frustrated man who could barely speak English but who seemed to have instantly learned everything there was to know about getting along in America. At that age I never thought about what a beautiful woman and a barber would have had to do to stay alive in the camps. Or about what my parents knew about what they would have had to do. I loved them as any boy loves the friend's parents who treat him to sponge cake and invite him to sleep over. Who and what and how they were still able to love, I have no idea.

Donny and I often said that we knew everything about each other, that we were inseparable, blood brothers. We spent so much time in each other's apartments that our siblings hated the friendship. It was Donny's older brother who once warned me that the next time he saw me reading a book in his house he would beat me up. So naturally Donny and I plotted weeks in advance to be chauffeured together to the movie that had been previewing all season, *Tarzan's Greatest Adventure.*

"*I* should take them?" his father asked, on the morning of the festive day. "My vun day off?"

"Please, please, we have to see it the first show of the first day that it's playing, because—" Donny faltered.

"Because then everyone will know that we're the biggest Tarzan

fans, and we deserve to be, because we *are* the biggest Tarzan fans,"
I said, with a logic Donny visibly admired.

"Tarzan," Lee said derisively. How any mere human being
could fail to be awed by Tarzan was beyond me. But he held up his
hands as if surrendering. "Vhatever you say. Vhatever you vant."

The movie was playing in Parkchester, the middle-income
housing project a couple of miles southeast. An overcast July day,
gray as a photograph, and under the black marquee of the Loew's
American, hundreds of people cramming to get into the picture.
The line stretched to the left: boys and parents three and four
abreast, grimy elbows and seersucker shirts, clip-on suspenders,
cowboy ties. By local standards it was a patient crowd, shoving and
cursing only in fun: we knew the theater didn't sell out until the
line reached the Chinese laundry around the corner.

Just before the movie started, we heard a shout from behind
us. "Leib!"—that was the old, obsolete form of Donny's father's
name, which he didn't use in public anymore. And a man looking
very different from Donny's father—short, blond, red-faced,
stocky—but somehow very much the same, stepped out from the
rear of the line, the part that was in danger of not getting tickets,
and came up to us with the kind of nonchalant hurry that I had
sometimes seen in movie villains evading pursuit in crowded de-
pots. He pulled by the neck a boy our age with eyeglasses.

"*Nu? Vie geytz?*" Leib said, unsurprised, shaking hands as his
friend melted into line. Some people behind us muttered—"What
the hell, who does he think"—but Leib and his friend were already
absorbed in a conversation that seemed as if it had started long
ago. They spoke in Yiddish, that language of spits and throat-clear-
ings, the short friend's voice lower than Leib's high, puzzled questioning. They pushed us children forward for comparison, like prize
turnips.

On a hunch, I glanced at the short man's thick, red wrist as it
darted forward and back between the men's shirt fronts. When I
saw the five blue-green numbers, I felt like a detective who has
guessed the murderer.

Donny and I tugged each other toward a shoestore window
for the giggling fit which was our only response to the new boy.
His hair was not so much blond as colorless, his glasses were held
together with white tape, and he carried through life, like a Kick

Me sign, the unheard-of name Elie. We absolutely snubbed him.

Always plotting new escapades, we whispered a plan to slip through hundreds of legs and be the first into the theater, but the line had already begun to move and Leib took hold of us by the shirt collars. The place was oversold. The best seats we could find were three-quarters of the way back. Soon all the seats were taken; then the aisles began to fill with people. There were small children in parents' laps, there were pairs sharing single spaces. How were we to be able to hear Tarzan's bloodcurdling call?

Then we saw our way out. The walkway in front of the first row was only partly occupied—only a few were bold enough to risk their eyesight there.

"Daddy please please please please please, Papaleh can we huh huh huh huh?" Donny pulled his father's sleeve like a bell rope, not imitating any one particular cartoon character but cartoon characters in general. He could put me in hysterics.

One day that summer, we had explicitly divided our roles. I was the leader when it had to do with brains or running, and he was the leader in everything else. Donny and I were the same size— a matched pair of runts whose mothers sacrificed many an evening to take in waistbands—but he was a lot tougher. Donny could beat up the bigger boys who used to feast on me as I stood crying, wondering what they had against me. I supposed it was because Donny had experience fighting his older brother. Whenever I asked my parents about it, they shrugged as if with knowledge they didn't want to share. "Donny is Donny. Would you rather be Donny and have Donny's parents?" Which forced me to say no.

"All right, all right," Leib said, preoccupied, the short friend jabbing him in the shoulder. "*Gey.*" And switching to hard, rolling German—a language his knowledge of which Donny often bragged about—he ordered us to get moving. "*Raus, raus mit dier!*"

We stepped on feet, bounced off laps, scrambled into the aisle, over bodies, to the spacious front walkway where we stuck out our feet in unfulfilled hopes of tripping someone, as practice for careers of setting intricate jungle traps. How we managed to endure the movie without getting splitting headaches, I don't know; but we came away knowing that the twenty-foot-high Gordon Scott would be our mightiest lifelong inspiration. The movie was so great that we wanted to read every name of every crew member on the closing credits, but our view was blocked by hundreds of Bronxites competing to be first out of the theater. We stood on empty seats, and showed off our agility with repeated, swift escapes from the clutches of the collapsible seat bottoms. When there were just enough people in the aisle to make a good obstacle course, we raced back to Donny's father, planning to slink across the row, leap up, and surprise him.

But he wasn't there. An empty row of nubby, bud-red, folding seats—I've seen that motif in dreams more than once since then. As if anticipating those future dreams, I stared in an attempt to change what I saw. I knew I had to say something, and I knew it couldn't sound worried.

"Aha, I detect that he was going to us while we were going to him." So we ran to the front row again, this time using the other aisle so as to cover all possible trails. No Lee, and no Lee's friend with stupid-looking son.

Donny smacked himself on the forehead and began to talk like Jerry Lewis. "You mean when we were here, he was there, and when we were there, he was here, and the here and the there and the when and the where and the I don't know what, boy oh boy oh boy is this humiliating!"

Plan B was to wait for his father in the lobby. But if he was there, it was too crowded to find him, and when it cleared out, he had cleared out with everyone else. We ran back into the auditorium, where the ushers were sweeping up popcorn, and tried the rear exit, on the theory that Donny's father knew us well enough to try to catch us sneaking out. Then we ran around the block to the marquee, where the line for the next show was four deep. Lee wasn't pacing in front like any intelligent person, nor was he waiting in ambush at the ticket booth, and the attendant wouldn't let us past the turnstile though we reported our loss in our fastest Hanna-Barbera deliveries.

"Some guy was looking for you but he left," the attendant told us, patting his stiff black pompadour omnipotently.

We sat on the curb outside the theater, playing gutter soccer with a cigarette box.

"We could walk home," Donny said.

"We could call my house. We could call *your* house."

"I don't want to get him in trouble."

I wouldn't have cared about that, if my father had abandoned me.

It was inconceivable that a lost child's father would go home without him; perhaps even more inconceivable that he would leave behind a friend's child with whose safety he had been entrusted. Decent families didn't act that way, and since I knew Donny's was a decent family, I didn't know what to make of this at all. I was sure that if we waited long enough, Leib would show up, hugging us, burbling about all the places he'd searched and the people he'd asked and the anguish he'd felt. Apologizing.

The ticket-holders' line grew till it stretched around the block. Donny nodded to himself. "Come on, let's go."

"Go where?"

"Home."

"By ourselves?"

I felt nauseated and wobbly, the way I felt whenever I went for a checkup and the doctor said I needed a shot; the way I had felt a couple of years earlier when my mother left me at the schoolyard gate on the first day of kindergarten. It wasn't that I thought the shot would harm me or that I wouldn't like kindergarten; it was that I wanted to plead with the world, "Not yet! Just give me a little more time! I know I have to go through this, but tomorrow or next year, not today!" You want to plead with someone, and since you don't know who it is, you plead with anyone.

Donny smacked me on the arm to get me moving. There was the squeal of big wheels braking, and black exhaust in our faces. A bus lumbered past us, slowing to its stop at the end of the block. We ran toward the hiss of the opening door.

One foot on the rubber step, Donny asked the driver, "You go to Pelham Parkway?" I was astounded at his worldliness. I still didn't quite believe the driver would let us on. In my opinion he ought to bar our way with a fatherly arm: "Just how old are you boys, anyway? Only seven? You can't be riding a bus through the Bronx by yourselves." And he would call the police on his two-way radio, and they would drive us home in their patrol car and Lee would be disgraced and have to take us to the movies every single weekend as punishment....

But not only did he let us on, he gave us free transfers and showed us where to change for the Thirteen bus—and he trusted us to do it. It was the first time I ever dropped my own fifteen cents

into the fare box (with its churning like a metal stomach when it
digested the coins), the first time I ever lurched to my own seat
without a hand to grab onto. We rode under the black-girdered
bridge over the train yard, past the the power plant gate where men
in blue helmets straggled for the tavern—an institution unknown
in our neighborhood. Past St. Dominic's School, where kids much
tougher than us accepted a discipline we would never have stood
for. Swinging on the standees' pole from neighborhood to neighborhood, over streets where I would have been scared to walk, I
learned what Tarzan must have learned when he swung on his first
vine: it was easy. We jumped in our seats in this jungle bus, giving
loud calls and swatting each other while the adults sat drowsy as
lions. We pulled the cord just to hear it buzz, knowing no one
would be too annoyed, and laughed because there was nothing to
cry about.

By the time we exited at White Plains Road, I was too sophisticated to shout, "We did it!" Instead I said, "Wait! We can't go
home yet, we have to explore the area!"

We pounded our chests and gave blood-curdling yells, but I
yelled louder, because for once the suggestion had been mine and
Donny had approved it.

The bus stop was on busy White Plains Road, which we had
to cross by going upstairs into the elevated train station and down
the other side. In the great savannah of Bronx Park we ran behind
boulders to escape enemy tribes, treading around the shards of glass
so they wouldn't pierce our paws. The express train screamed in,
and in its fading we heard—I'll always think we heard—a real lion
roaring in the zoo a few blocks west. Then we were army lieuten-
ants escaping from a German prisoner of war camp. Crossing the
border after a narrow escape from honking cars, we blended into
the civilian populace, sidled through the aisles of the stationery
store, and strolled nonchalantly to Donny's safehouse with a shoplifted memo pad and eraser.

In the outer hall we gave our Tarzan yells again, but nobody
heard us so stopped pounding our chests and hit the door instead.

"Who are dese monsters?" It was Donny's mother, Esther.
"Vhere ver you de whole time?" She gave me the special wink which
somehow helped me understand her accent. Her red hair was set in
a stiff flip; she wore gold earrings inlaid with black cultured pearls,

and a blue shantung dress about whose price my mother had more than once wondered aloud. Those refugees, Mom had said, they really know how to live.

We rambled in, swinging our arms. The foyer smelt of roasting chicken, potatoes, paprika. "We escaped from the Nazis…."

"You're in enough trouble vitout dem. If Seth vasn't here—"

Donny clapped me on the back. "Thanks for being here, old pal old buddy old chum!"

Then Esther said something to him in Yiddish, from behind her back, and it was as if a different person had said it. Donny stiffened, ears red, eyes fleeing into their corners to seek a friend. A scalding language.

"It wasn't our fault," he protested. "That dodobird left without us."

It seemed to me that the *look* his mother gave him was in English—rational, empirical, unawed by power. But she spoke again in Yiddish, in words of coarse salt that furrowed her glossy red lips. Donny kept trying to answer in his mother's language—I didn't recognize even the beginning of anything he said—but she shushed him with pushing-down gestures, and motioned toward the bedroom door, where Lee was shuffling out.

"You left us!" Donny said. "You left two children in the theater by themselves and went home yourself, how could you do that!"

The man looked as if he'd slept for a month. He wore a dark purple bathrobe with a satin collar, and black socks you could see his skin through. There were pillow-wrinkles on one cheek, and the loose robe made him seem startlingly thin. He wandered among us as if there was something on the floor he had lost, nodding at the maroon carpet like a pigeon in a playground.

"Leave your father alone," Esther said. "He told me vat heppened. You ver running around, playing? Everyting is play for you; you don't know serious."

"Mom, you won't listen to me!" Anger and frustration bent him forward as if he were going to jump on her—to hit her? to hug her?—but it was impossible, under the circumstances, to do either, and he wrenched himself away to face the simpler opponent. "You never take my side, just this stupid ref's!"

He must have known what would happen. Screaming in his

father's grip, he disappeared into the bathroom. We could hear him begging, but there was something foregone and almost comical in it, as if they were suffering a ritual neither could alter. The toilet seat slammed: Lee would be sitting with Donny sprawled over his lap. Then came the first smack of the razor strop on Donny's backside.

"Mom, help!" Donny called out, but it reminded me of some character in a Disney movie who has fallen out of a raft and is swirling through rapids, battered by rocks, with no hope of rescue. And then there were no sounds except leather.

Esther rested a hand on my shoulder and tried to smile at me. "He's nasty to his father, yeah?" All the time the whipping was going on, she rubbed and patted my shoulder as if I were the one being hurt. I wished she were my mother—but not here. I wished she were my mother in some magical cave or Manhattan penthouse, someplace which, owing to simple lack of time, I had not yet discovered.

Donny's brother Sandy had rushed out of his bedroom to laugh at us all—it must have been a treat to witness a beating you weren't the recipient of. Sandy was a sunken-cheeked miniature of his father, except that Sandy made belligerent, hit-and-run eye contact.

"Oughta cry more, he'll stop sooner," was Sandy's professional advice.

Then the bathroom door opened and my hero was shoved out, stumbling but catching his balance. He had been crying quite enough though we hadn't heard a sound since that first outburst.

"Stupid ref," Donny muttered, and Sandy teased, "I'm telling him you said that," and Esther whispered, "Sha, sha." Lee came out of the bathroom with the razor strop slung back over his shoulder: a beautiful fat strip of saddle cowhide embossed with the maker's name.

I had heard about these floggings but never witnessed one before. Whenever I told my mother how much I liked Donny's family, she alluded mysteriously to the razor strop and advised me to be glad I was only spanked by hand. Now that I'd seen it, though, I wasn't as horrified as she might have thought. Donny was in pain but he hadn't been damaged. He had said the exact same defiant words after being walloped as before. I didn't like pain, but I loved knowledge, and Donny knew things I didn't.

I tried to imagine being hit with the strop and not succumbing, not showing fear. It seemed like a physical impossibility.

"Look at him," Sandy pointed at me, "standing there like a moron."

"In his family is different," Esther said. And she gave Donny a little push which even I could see wasn't a punishment. "Go lie down in your room for an hour; den is dinner. Lee, put det strop avay or the kids vill start svinging it. Seth, till dinner you can read a book."

Read a book was the most welcome invitation imaginable. And this time I had permission from the authorities; so when Sandy tried to yank the G volume of the *Golden Book Encyclopedia* from my hands, I held tight, as I knew Donny would if he wanted to read the encyclopedia, and said, "Let go, your mother told me to."

"*Luzz 'im,* " Esther scolded Sandy. "Leave him. Someday he'll learn how to talk vit people. Till den, leave him his books."

A strange comment, I thought, coming from someone who spoke with an accent.

Donny's hour of confinement was almost harder for me to take than for him. Halfway through, Sandy and I sneaked into the boys' bedroom. Donny was lying in bed, staring at the ceiling, with his arms folded across his chest. The look on his face was that of someone who is patiently planning a crime.

Sandy jumped on the bed and pinned Donny who didn't flinch. "He really gave it to you. You should have heard you: 'Please, please, oh, I'll do anything but just don't hit me....'"

"Shut up, liar."

"Yeah, what are you gonna do? I'll break your arms." Sandy pulled Donny's wrists till they were clamped at Donny's sides. He leaned close over his younger brother. But this wasn't going to be a fight: neither of them wanted to encounter their father again that evening.

"You should of seen what happened before," Sandy said. "When he came home and said you were lost? Know what I think really happened, he just got up and left without you. Talking to his friend so he forgot. But he tries to act like it's no big deal. Like it's okay because he looked for you a couple of minutes before he came home. So Mom slapped him."

"What!" I said. But it was worth hardly a glance from Sandy.

"Then he hit her, then she said she was going to leave him. She's holding the bread knife at his neck. So what does he do?" Sandy was laughing and slurping. "Goes and changes into his bathrobe and says he needs his rest. And if she wanted to, she should call the cops if you weren't back by dark. Too bad you didn't come in a little later."

Donny sneered, "Leave me alone," and kicked the hand that was tickling his foot, but failed to push Sandy off the bed. Then the door opened and Esther said, "Come eat, boys, dere's good soup."

The thing was, it wasn't good soup. And that bothered me. A romantic mother like Esther ought to be a good cook. Her menfolk acted as if she was, but my mother's cabbage soup was a million times better. My mother's cabbage soup was sweet-and-sour, deep orange-red from lots of tomato paste and lemon juice, with globules of chicken fat and shreds of beef brisket. Esther's cabbage soup was salty and tart, pink and paprika-specked and potato-cubed. I took a sip and didn't want to take any more.

Lee made a sharp comment—"*Ehr ess nischt?*" I understood it—"He isn't eating?"—because my parents also said it.

"He's not used to it, that's all," Esther said. "His mother makes Rumanian style, right?" she asked me. "My cabbage soup is Polish. Is two different ways of cooking, that's all. The Rumanians like sweet. Seth, you like cabbage soup sweet, yes?, but my family likes salty like I make. If you don't want it, you don't have to eat. You could try just a little."

I tried another sip or two for Esther's sake. But I couldn't help making a face, which embarrassed me. It embarrassed me even more that she laughed.

Everyone else was devouring theirs. Lee had finished all his soup before I had even decided not to eat mine. Donny and Sandy apparently had an ongoing race to see who finished each dish first. In the small, overlit cell of the dining room, I was the only one who lacked a normal appetite. My stomach was seesawing in dread. If cabbage soup was like this, what would dessert be? What would watching television be, what would visiting relatives be? (I reminded myself that Donny's family had no relatives.)

Esther said, "Maybe you'll like better my roast chicken."

That brat Sandy said, "Maybe you should cook a whole new meal for him, Mom."

And that's when I began to cry, like a baby. I wished I was instantly back home, not because I didn't like Donny's family but because I assumed they would no longer like me. I had a clear picture of myself: bright pink and puffy-cheeked in a way that contradicted my dark, narrow features, and helpless in a way that contradicted the fists I brought to my eyes—and this shameful mental picture fascinated me so much that staring at it prolonged my crying. One part of my brain told me to stop and another part told me I couldn't. I wanted to take another spoonful of soup but the warm liquid in my mouth was tears, choking me. I was the center of attention, something I didn't normally like, but I was too upset to let that stop me.

"*Vuss is duss?*" Lee asked nervously.

"Vat's the metter, darling?" Esther asked me. "Vat are you crying for, tell us. You vant to go home?"

I shook my head; and both the question and my answer made me cry more.

I couldn't have explained my crying if they had tried to beat the explanation out of me, and when I asked myself what was going on, it only triggered another squall. I supposed it had something to do with being left by Donny's father—but nothing bad had happened. Or with witnessing the beating—but I had heard about them before, and why should I make more of a fuss than the victim?

If someone had forced me to give a reason, I might have said it had something to do with the soup. I couldn't believe a mother could make a soup so salty and tart, and that a family could enjoy it. But that would have sounded silly. You don't break into tears because of the taste of a soup.

"What a crybaby," Sandy said. Donny was silent and grim. Esther stroked my hair and said soft things to me. But the reaction I remember most clearly is Lee's. It was as if he could no longer see me. His washed-out gray eyes circled the walls, looking for an escape route. Of the four reactions, his was the most like what I would have done.

To my amazement, my humiliating display didn't alter my status among them. A few minutes later, when Esther eased my soup bowl away and I did manage to stop weeping, there was no post-mortem discussion as there would have been in my family. Memory was worthless, food was everything: our utensils clicked in concentration over garlicky chicken. After ice cream—pistachio and strawberry, unfathomable flavors—we three boys left the table and played Go to the Head of the Class, and as always, Sandy cursed me for knowing too many answers.

When I got home, I would tell my parents' I'd had a good time. There was no reason to tell them of Lee's losing us or of the violence or my crying. They would have interrogated me and discussed psychology. They might have turned against Lee and Esther, possibly even prohibited me from visiting Donny's house anymore, and that would have been completely wrong in a way I couldn't have hoped to make them understand. My parents could see things from so many well-informed, subtle angles that you couldn't explain anything to them.

In the lobby of my building that night, the lighting seemed different on the black and gold floor tiles, and my steps echoed more heavily. And I expected that my family would seem different: that in contrast to Donny's parents, they would be unmasked as impossibly carefree people with tragically easy lives, who walked a fraction of an inch above the ground. It frustrated me, when I actually stepped into our apartment again, that they appeared exactly as before.

That day didn't change my outer life, the way I behaved, or who my friends were; but decades later, when some of our parents were dead and Donny and I were long-lost brothers with families on opposite coasts, it began to change me through thinking about it.

Uncle Wolfie

I once borrowed Uncle Wolfie's charisma for five minutes and it got me into bed with the girl I wanted. This was in college, about ten years ago. A little place in Greektown after a game at Tiger Stadium: roast lamb, stewed squid, tiny cups of mud-bottomed coffee. We fidget with our glasses of ouzo, both of us wondering whose place we're going to next if anywhere. I signal the waiter for the check and give him my credit card. A minute later from behind the cashier's counter comes the owner as if something's wrong. He's underlining my name on the card with his finger. He's short and heavy, with a black mustache and a white dinner jacket. I can't tell if he's angry or worried or what.

"Fox? Are you connected to Wolfie Fox?"

Surprised: "Yeah, he's my uncle."

Owner lifts his hands to the sky as if an incognito angel has visited his humble taverna and he almost missed it. "Why don't you tell me?" He tears up the bill and gives me back my credit card. "You don't pay here. You Wolfie's nephew, come here any time, we make it a cheap date for you, all right?" Winks at my plump brunette, who, under pressure, plays along with a smile. "Now go tell Wolfie how we treated you. Don't go yet. We got some more ouzo for you, free, and in between you try our special baklava."

And he throws a glance to the waiter like someone who has rolled away from an oncoming truck: startled, thankful, and a little pissed off like Why-didn't-anybody-warn-me?

The next time I saw Uncle Wolfie was at Hanukkah, which would have been a few months afterward. I told him about this, also how it had impressed my date, and he laughed as if he knew about that latter aspect of it in particular. And said, "That son of a bitch owes me ten thousand bucks, thinks he's gonna get away with it for a free meal?"

This clinched the answer to the question I'd been asking since childhood: "What does Uncle Wolfie do for a living?" My parents gave me various explanations depending on my age, but always within that same vague concept of getting money from people who could ill afford it in return for certain undefined services and general goodwill. Somehow people paid to keep Wolfie's continuing friendship, and it seemed like a very smooth way to make a living. Later it would be, *People give him money to invest for them*, although to think of him as a licensed broker was laughable—worked out of a bare office, no files, no business card, basically didn't look the part even to a twelve-year-old. *He helps people build things*—that one was justified by the fact that he visited construction sites and shot the breeze with contractors and foremen. And of course, *He owns some apartment buildings, he's a landlord.* I had proof of that with my own eyes: my father went to the inner city once a month to collect rents from Wolfie's tenants, an automatic pistol in his hand concealed by a sport coat over his arm.

My father was Wolfie's older brother, which must have gnawed at his gut from about age twenty onwards. Dad was not only older, he was bigger. It was just his slumped posture that made them both seem the same size. There was a strong family resemblance, the thick square face and straight dark early-graying hair, but my father wore rumpled polyester shirts and shapeless shoes and let the hair grow out of his ears; Wolfie wore only natural fabrics with slim lines, and went to a gym and a tanning salon and a barber—haircut every week—where he had all his outward animality snipped away. A werewolf with a trim.

My father worked for Wolfie off and on ever since quitting college in the early 1960s. Whether quitting college was Wolfie's suggestion or his own brilliant idea is something I don't know. But that's when the cycle began which lasted really the rest of Dad's life. He had almost as many jobs as there were years, and after each one predictably failed to live up to his hopes, he fell back on Wolfie's generosity. He sold tires, performed auto inspections, taught driving, dispatched taxis, sold tickets at the Silverdome, sold magazine subscriptions, sold nutritional supplements, sold chain-link fence, bought a cinnamon-roll franchise (with Wolfie's money), typed hospital records, and at various times went back to school to become an emergency medical technician, an air conditioner repairman, and a masseur. His most promising job was mailman, since that involved a pension, but he was so disappointed at being stuck sorting mail instead of delivering it that he languished as if he was an opera tenor who could only get work as a singing waiter.

Stints for Wolfie were more predictable: collecting money from one debtor or another and moving it down the line. Aside from the rents, there were times, I'm pretty sure (having put two and two together over the years, including stuff he told me before he died), when Dad sat all day in a luncheonette in Inkster writing numbers in a memo pad. And times when he traveled from city to city with a brown briefcase that felt sometimes empty (I hefted it while he was in the bathroom, but I didn't dare to open it) and sometimes full.

Something else my father may have done for Wolfie way back when, I'm not sure about. He might have "persuaded" people who were reluctant to pay. You wouldn't think so when he was a shlumpy middle-aged guy sitting in his den watching cooking shows on public TV, but Dad was very strong, especially for someone who never did a pushup or any other exercise in all the time I knew him. Every so often, he liked to show it in public. I remember once, I must have been seven or eight, when we lived on a suburban street in Southfield which turned out to be a shortcut to a new mall. Dad had been bitching for weeks about how fast the drivers went on our street. One day he must have just decided, *Okay, this is the one I'm going after.* Or maybe he'd had a bad day at the tire store. But I'm riding my bike up and down the asphalt, Dad watching, and this red Mercury with a broken muffler roared by, two young males sitting in front. Dad didn't pick an easy target. He ran after that car—the only other times I'd ever seen him run were when he hobbled after me during backyard games, acting old to let me beat him. Caught up to it at the corner stop light. Stormed down on them, knowing exactly how to do this thing, and shoved his arm through the driver's open window and closed it around his neck, and pulled the guy's startled head out the window. I had raced up on the bike to see it. And there's Dad squeezing this guy blue and growling at him, *"This is a residential street, the speed limit is twenty-five miles an hour."*

I doubt whether he could have beaten up Wolfie, who'd taken boxing lessons as a youngster, paid for by Dad's after-school earnings. The times I'd seen them pal around with their fists, it was Wolfie jabbing and feinting—"Hey, boy, catch this, how you gonna deal with this?"—around my father who stood sullenly like a parked car. Hands at his sides, playing dead on his feet, Dad seemed to gain weight on the spot.

Wolfie was the guy who gave me a ten dollar bill every time I saw him; the guy, who, when we played hide-the-matzoh after Passover dinner, slipped a twenty between the sheets of unleavened bread—my father, living in the past, still thought the prize should be a quarter. Wolfie was what my mother called "a fun guy, a real man of the world," and he gave me the skeeves. His gifts of money— I couldn't bring myself to spend them. I'd put a ten dollar bill on top of my bureau and forget about it, treat it like a wall picture or knicknack, something that had value for its appearance—and would still be complaining I needed a raise in my allowance—until my mother would notice it: "What is this? Money means nothing to this child, that's how good he has it." She'd float the ten over toward Dad, who'd stoically bend to pick it up off the floor and deposit it in my college fund.

"Look," she teased as he shoved the ten into his pocket any old way, "Look at your father, he doesn't want to know where the money's coming from."

"I know where. I know more than you. My sins are an open book. Everyone should be so honest."

And I'm going, "What, what?", because this was still at the point when I thought Uncle Wolfie was just a landlord. I didn't see what was shameful about collecting lawful rent. I see myself as a child always going around with "What, what?" on my lips, pleading for information, trying to figure out what world I was in and who ran it and what the right way to act was. Maybe because of my own attitude—maybe they picked up signals from me—adults seemed to enjoy telling me just a crucial bit less than would have really helped. I remember it as an era of being put off with, "I'll tell you later," and, "Mind your own business," and, "Who asked for your opinion?" I learned how to get by without ever being really sure of my footing. Even as an adult, going through so many different contexts in a row—the military, the university, jobs, cities, a marriage—it seems I've always stayed in a situation till just before I would have understood it. Not understanding till it's over, whereas a simple tip, a kindly offered piece of a glimpse of a portion, would have made life possible. One semester at Western Michigan I signed up for a course on Myths of the Frontier, which sounded to me like the ultimate in romantic escapes?—It wasn't till finals week that I realized the course wasn't about the heroes and villains of the Old West at all. It was a course about *scholarly interpretations* of the West: which theorists had debunked which other theorists' pet theories. The course bulletin hadn't described it, the professor hadn't defined it, and I hadn't caught on. I'm sitting in this seminar room week after week, doodling, waiting till they leave the preliminaries behind and get to Billy the Kid and Wild Bill Hickok. I had missed the whole course while sitting in it.

It surprises me when I realize that we probably only saw him—Uncle Wolfie—three or four times a year. It felt like he was always present. We talked about him like he was a TV star, or more precisely a baseball star because sides had to be taken, you had to root for him or not. And the teams were Mom and Wolfie against Dad. Which made me feel that Dad ought to choose me to even up his strength—but Dad was one of those guys who'd rather play all alone than sign up a weak hitter.

So here we are, for instance, that summer when our whole family worked in Wolfie's camp up by Lake Charlevoix, except for my younger sister who was a camper. I was a counselor in training (a CIT), Dad the assistant camp director, a position which I now think had been invented to tide him over a slack season. Mom, with the summer off as a school secretary, was the arts and crafts director: she spent her days teaching little girls how to make wildflower pressings, ceramic ashtrays, and keychains made out of those long strips of plastic that you weave together. Lanyards. Wolfie spent weekends at the camp, devoting the rest of his time to business in the city. His wife, Aunt Hani, was the office manager/bookkeeper/nurse, and their son, my cousin Adam, two years older than me, was a senior counselor. So the whole place was like one big Fox family gathering, except in cabins in the woods, and with a cast of extras, a couple hundred pubescent and prepubescent Jewish kids.

Adam was the camp's star athlete; he got a swimming scholarship to Michigan State and once was invited to the Olympic tryouts but failed a drug test. (He told his father he failed to make the team by a tenth of a second. I think if Wolfie ever found out that his son was smoking pot, he would have sent him to the emergency room with some busted ribs.) What I remember from that summer is Adam teaching me the butterfly stroke. What I've tried to forget is my father bringing along my next year's algebra textbook, taking me aside during free time to work on a page each day. "The smart kids get a head start during the summer; why shouldn't the mediocre ones?" Dad was very big on a work ethic for me, had me delivering newspapers and shoveling snow from age ten, was pressuring me despite my lack of any mathematical aptitude (although why do I believe *that?*) to become an accountant because, "It's a good field." In a way, I welcomed the times when he turned his attention to my sister Sara, despite the difference in the way he treated us.

Sara the A student, the gymnast (until her breasts weighed her down at age thirteen, and then she was the Drama Club president). When Sara finished her page of math problems, she asked Dad for brain teasers as extra enrichment. There was nothing quite like seeing the two of them try to outfox each other (so to speak) over one of those questions where you have to deduce the professions and relative ages of five people with names like Mr. White and Mrs. Gray and Ms. Green. Sara actually *has* become an accountant, as well as a trusts-and-estates lawyer. She calls Mom every day from her office and me once every few months, and for someone who makes half a million dollars a year and is the single parent of an adopted biracial child, she has kept a girlish pixieishness that lights men up when she walks through the cocktail lounge of an airport hotel. One time, I set a friend of mine up with her. Their first date—a glamorous meal, an innovative, upscale restaurant—is followed by a month of intense courtship during which they never see each other—they communicate entirely over the phone. I heard from the guy that ninety percent of it was her calling him up to cancel at the last minute, then calling him the next morning (or even the same night, if her first-choice date had fallen through) to reschedule. Then she started calling him to ask him for the most intimate kinds of personal advice as if they were old best friends: should she sleep with So-and-So (his rival), should she have plastic surgery, should she sleep with her plastic surgeon....

A month of this, Jason told me, and he felt like he'd been through several grueling years of marriage, including divorce and reconciliation, without setting eyes or hands on her. Finally she calls and tells him she can't take it anymore—*she* can't. Of *his* supposed unreliability and games. As a parting gift, so to speak, she tells him a decision she's made: this is going to be the last time she ever goes out with someone from one of the *lower professions*. Jason is a pharmacist.

Okay, so two years later, he's at the Henry Ford Museum with a friend, and meets up with her by chance. Waves hi. Sara rushes forward squealing and cooing. Throws her arm around...Jason's friend. Who, it turns out, had been her buddy during a sensitivity workshop. Jason she didn't look at. I assured him she honestly didn't remember him. He wasn't important enough for a revenge snub.

So while Dad and Sara were enjoying their algebra problems at Camp Wo-Ha-Ni (a name made up of Wolfie and Hani all smushed together—Wolfie's real name, Milton wouldn't have gone), I'd be smoking with Cousin Adam in the woods, or sitting guard outside Joey's bunk while he humped some female counselor while his kids were at archery or something. (A major coup for me at sixteen. I sometimes inherited his hand-me-downs: my first girlfriend was one of Joey's exes, and she was even a year older than me.) If Uncle Wolfie was in the vicinity, of course, these adventures could not take place. Instead, Wolfie might challenge Adam to swim the lake.

Wolfie was about five foot seven, with a big barrel of a ribcage that made his ass stick out for balance, and thick, black hair all over, and when he ran toward the water he pumped his knees belt-high, perpetually showing off the virtues of exercise. He had a loud, phlegmy laugh that let you know he was having a ball in life and he expected anyone who wanted to hang around him to have the same.

For him, the best time of all was when he was cheating somebody. He'd strip to his bathing suit faster than Adam and dive smack into the water before I gave the signal. It was too hard to argue with him so we both allowed him the head start. I'd be standing on the sand, timing them with Wolfie's stopwatch. When he came up, dripping, to learn his lap speed, he'd slap me on the back with his wet hand and bark something pseudo-encouraging like, "Barry my boy, what's happening, you just hear bad news? You had money on the other guy?" He tried to wind up people like a kid winding up toys. He went jovially around from one of his little soldiers to the next, and once a toy was going, he forgot about it until it wound down. Who was winding *him* up, I don't know and I don't want to know.

Get this, the one Wolfie wound up tightest was my mother. Sometimes you could see the wince in her eyes when she'd brushed close to him.

Every Friday night the camp held a dance. Wolfie loved dancing. Wolfie and Aunt Hani were always the first couple on the floor, cajoling all the shy campers to join in. They twirled a fantastic lindy to early-eighties rock, Wolfie spinning Hani with one hand and yelling: "Come on! Loosen up, kids! Don't let an old man put you to shame!" For the next song he'd pull some scared older girl onto the floor and swing around with her until she had to laugh because any other response would offend him. Then—I kept track of this, but only afterwards, in hindsight, so I can only half-swear it's true—invariably at the third song he'd dance with my mother. Often a slow song, come to think of it. They had a joking thing with each other—it lasted for decades. He often called her "darling" and "gorgeous" and "my girlfriend," which leads me to believe that in fact she wasn't. (If she was, they would have been careful to hide it.) Even though they had reached adulthood during the sexual revolution and everything, that sort of blanket label for a generation never really applies to most people. I think Mom is the kind of person who still thinks, "Well, he wasn't what I expected but I married him and I have to live with my mistakes." Not because she feels beaten down but because it makes her feel strong, like she can carry a lot. And in fact, after I was an adult Mom and Dad grew surprisingly tender to each other, trusting, familiar, like you're supposed to.

The last dance, she saved for Dad, who waggled his hands up and down without lifting his feet, a pathetic attempt to dance rock 'n roll. It was like he was saying, "See, children, we needn't be ashamed when we look foolish." Everything he did, he acted like it was a lesson. Should have been a schoolteacher, except that he wasn't well-educated enough.

Dad couldn't wait for the dance to be over. He hated being the object of a group's attention. (Although the percent of the crowd that was actually paying attention to him was minimal to nonexistent.) The dining room lights would come back on, the older boys would push the tables and chairs back onto the floor, and Wolfie would kiss Mom goodnight: "Thank you, sweetheart. The greatest dancer." Which was obviously untrue, Aunt Hani was on a whole higher level than Mom. Clap Dad on the back: "How's it going, kid? Ready to sign up for the rhumba marathon?" Dad wouldn't respond. At the time, he seemed too slow to keep up with Wolfie's repartee, but later I realized it was the smart way to react, and I have often used it myself in various situations.

One night after a dance, my mother and I were taking some fresh air outside the dining hall, under those fierce white stars of a cold Great Lakes summer. She was humming to herself. Her head was bopping from star to star as if she was tracing the constellations to the beat of a song. Although as far as I knew she wouldn't have recognized any constellations—at least no one never taught me any. The crazy thing about Mom and Dad was, she married him for his money: the money she thought he must have, when he was doing jobs for Wolfie as a young man and dropping large bills onto bar counters and driving a shiny Buick that was registered to I-don't-know-who. This is not to say she didn't love him, but she chose him out of two or three other possibilities who might have been equal at the time, and that misconception about his earning power might have been the crucial tip of the balance. While I was a child, she pioneered that whole thing about women working, being breadwinners, knocking themselves out for a little self-esteem. Did she sometimes wish she was Aunt Hani, whose job was to be a well-dressed wife? Maybe once in a while, a twinge, but the fact of the matter is, I think more highly of my mother than that. You can't help having a fantasy in contrast to your life.

She made sure no one else was stargazing within ten feet of us and then said quietly, "Your father really can't stand Wolfie."

It stunned me, that's how naive I was. Hate Uncle Wolfie? But they were brothers, and we saw them so often and had fun—because Wolfie churned out fun like an ice cream machine churning out blue moon or rocky road—and Dad agreed to whatever Wolfie told him, and Cousin Adam and Aunt Hani were nice, weren't they? This was years before the incident of the Greek restaurant; it was still when Wolfie, as far as I knew, was a real estate investor.

"Why can't he stand Uncle Wolfie?" I thought it must have been something about Wolfie's overly boisterous manner, the way he made a handshake seem like a war and couldn't just let you sit quietly.

"Never mind, I shouldn't have said anything," Mom said. "Open your mouth and you get in trouble, right? I still haven't learned."

She blew cigarette smoke up at the sky, a white trail of cosmic dust. Then, absentmindedly, she offered me the pack, and when I hesitated, she said, "What am I doing?" and hurried it back into her purse, and rushed off before I could ask her anything more.

That was the summer I stayed in Cousin Joey's college dorm for a week before my high school term started. Adam was already an East Lansing legend. He had this big motorcycle, a BMW (this was before Harley-Davidson got revived) with fringed black leather saddlebags, and he used to park it outside the dormitory cafeteria so that when he finished lunch, everybody would hear him roar away to swimming practice or to his next act of intercourse. One of his girlfriends at the time was this blind student, Megan, who was a star of the dorm in her own right. Adam was so cool, he could go out with the blind girl and no one would think, "He can't do any better." Megan was the kind who's so well-adjusted her clothes are always color coordinated; she even frosted blond streaks in her hair; she was like, "Hey, I'm not missing a thing." She didn't use a cane or a dog, she always had someone's arm to hold onto, and if she knew a route very well, like from her single room to the shared bathroom, she would walk down the middle of the hallway with absolutely no assistance. She was the dorm's tragic beauty and most boys were nervous about ever talking to her, although the fact is, oddly enough, she was only moderately good-looking if you examined her face carefully; it was the dark wraparound glasses and perfect grooming that gave her an aura, so that people would murmur behind her back, "Isn't it terrible, and she's so beautiful too!"

Megan would sit behind Adam on the motorcycle with her frosted hair blowing back, grinning like the queen of a realm whose extent she could scarcely imagine. Except that Adam would sometimes be with other girls, sometimes right in front of Megan's blank eyes. People watched, and nobody told her, just like sometimes you hear about a bunch of teenagers finding a dead body in the woods and not telling anyone. She found out all by herself, because she could tell the sound of Adam's BMW. There was a whole row of motorcycles parked under the café window, but his had its own special, brisk, loose, overpowering rumble, as if it was trying to pass every other vehicle on the road fom the moment it was first starting up. One time too often, she heard it revving outside the window when she had expected him to come sit down to lunch with her. So she gets up, walks confidently to the exit with her hand on the wall (she always sat near the front of the lunchroom in order to minimize obstacles), and outside to the motorcycle, where, just as she suspected, when she feels around to swing her leg over the rear seat, she touches the buttock of another attractive young woman.

Adam and the other girl had seen her coming the whole way but hadn't tried to escape—it was too fascinating to stay and learn how far Megan would get and whether she'd discover her rival. The other girl, when Megan's hand groped her, was delighted, like someone in hide-and-seek who's been in such a clever hiding place that she's relieved to be finally found. I don't think Adam minded losing Megan, who after all had built-in limitations. He could never lose the points he got for being the first one into her.

P.S.: Adam later became a veterinarian, a large-animal vet up in dairyland. He became famous for, whenever he castrated a calf or a colt, saving the testicles to dry, grinding them up into a powder which he'd mix into pancakes and bread. He'd serve it to his buddies, the local professionals—so they could all increase their net worth, no doubt. But I want to describe when my father picked me up at Adam's dorm after that week was over.

There was no elevator in the dorm, so Dad looked particularly shlumpy after hoisting himself up three flights to Adam's room—in brown suit pants and a yellow golf shirt. Adam sees a possible opportunity to tease: "Hey, Uncle Sid, how's your trigger finger doing lately? Been taking any more target practice?"

And Dad reacted with his most moralistic scowl. It wasn't exactly that he thought he was better than other people; it was that he knew he wasn't, and he was so disappointed—and going around like that was the only thing that might make him better than them. He would get these deep lines alongside his flared nostrils. His face was pulled tight and flat and red. So he says to his own nephew, "One more wisecrack out of you, sonny, and you'll find out about my trigger finger. No matter who's protecting you."

In the car going back to Southfield, I tried to ask him what was up, but he refused to talk about it. "Nothing, never mind. A tenant was giving us trouble about the rent."

"That's all? What did Adam mean about your trigger finger? Did you—?"

"I said that's *all*. Never mind. Leave me alone. It's nothing you need to know about."

"Well, *Adam* knows about it, why does *he*—"

"Hey, you. Listen." He let the car slip a little to the right, almost crossing the yellow shoulder line. "I said never mind. I mean what I say. Do you want me to pay for your college?"

It had been a long time since he'd had to threaten me about anything, and never something as important as my college education. I'd thought I was too old to be treated that way.

I didn't have to answer to answer.

He said, "Shut up about this subject and don't bring it up again. *Vershtay?*"

"I guess."

Was he genuinely warning me off, or was this just the kind of "No Entry" sign that dares you to enter anyway? (Would he have gotten something from talking to his son about this stuff? The answer is Yes when you imagine any two human beings; but when you think about yourself and him, it's a bit more complicated.) Double messages give me trouble. In fact, figuring out whether something is a double message or not gives me trouble. I usually figure it out accurately enough, long after I could have used the insight.

It was only quite recently, in fact, that I learned the details about my father and the pistol, and I learned it by chance: I happened to bump into Cousin Adam at the airport. Adam and I, the longer we haven't seen each other, the more affectionate we act when we do, so we were all hugs and grins in the middle of this huge chaotic terminal, and we stood against the wall for about an hour waiting for our planes. (Didn't go into a bar—neither of us is much of a drinker.) Finally, after exchanging news of how everybody was, I remembered I had a question I'd set aside ages ago. A question I'd forgotten I was waiting to ask. I asked it as if it was just another bit of family catching-up.

Hey, Adam, remember that time I stayed in your dorm..., and blah blah blah, and then I got to the point where I asked him, "...my father and the gun, what was that all about?"

He told me. My father had shot someone for Uncle Wolfie. Not killed—temporarily disabled, I believe. It was one of Wolfie's residential tenants, yes, but not an ordinary one; he was also into Wolfie for several thousand dollars, which he'd borrowed to pay a different loan shark, under the impression that he could stall Wolfie more easily. The debt alone would not have gotten him shot; getting them in deeper is the game, it's what you want to do, not something you want to avoid. (So that ultimately they're so in debt, and so terrified after one slapping-around, that they sign over their restaurant to you, or their house or whatever. Then their slate is clear and you leave them to their fate.) This was a special thing because Wolfie was tired of this guy, who never even paid a full month's rent on his apartment and had clearly demonstrated that he was less afraid of Wolfie than of whoever else he owed. I get the feeling part of it was because Wolfie was Jewish—the guy didn't think Wolfie would have the balls to really go after him. It was important to show this *shaygitze pupik* that such was not the case, that if you fuck with the Jews you will inevitably get fucked.

So Wolfie says to Sid, my Dad, "I want you to take care of this."

At first Dad tries to back out: "This isn't my kind of thing anymore, why don't you get one of your younger guys," and so forth.

So Wolfie: "It's not that big a deal, just rub his face on the floor, don't have to make him bite the curb." ("Biting the curb,

Dad learned that in Philadelphia when he was a kid," Adam told me. "Know what you do after you make someone bite the curb? You kick them in the back of the head.") Dad is still trying to get out of it, so finally Wolfie gives him the warning: "You like the security of working for me?"

Okay, so that's it, no further arguments there. Dad goes to the tenant—this is Sid Fox doing this! Says, "Give us the installment debt plus back rent." The tenant doesn't have it. Dad—I see him fastidiously removing the sport coat from his arm, showing the gun. Just showing the gun should do it, right? Possibly whipping the guy's face with it once or twice. But then, *in midztkaddrinnen,* as my parents used to say, in the middle of everything, what do you know, Wolfie shows up: Wolfie Fox, the older brother himself. He wants to see how Dad is handling it—it's a test on Dad.

But it backfires. Wolfie's presence enrages the tenant. It brings him to boiling point. Tenant gets in Wolfie's face, cursing, cursing his mother, the usual. (Dad's mother, too, of course.) Wolfie laughs, doesn't flinch. Then the guy either spits in Wolfie's face or shoves him—Adam wasn't sure which. But it's not advisable to do, either way.

Wolfie says coolly to my father, "Shoot him."

This stops my father cold.

But Wolfie: "I said shoot him." But then he eases up a little; he says to Dad: "Your choice which part." Like a customer asking his butcher for lamb chops: "Give me some nice ones."

Now, my father always had this attitude, which I don't know where he got it from, this air about him. As if he was saying to the world, all his life, *Well, if I can't earn a decent living, at least I can act like it's because I'm too pure.* No, I do know where he got it from. It's the part of him that could have been Wolfie, but got tricked into being Sid. So he stands there with his moral face on—but his moral face has no effect. This is Wolfie who he's keeping waiting—not the best strategy. So, because time is ticking, Dad points the gun downward and gets off a chip shot to the ankle or shin, somewhere around the foot.

The guy is moaning and bleeding. "Want to take another shot?" Wolfie asks, as if giving Dad another chance to win a pink teddy bear.

And Dad, trembling almost so he can't speak, says, "I should shoot *you,* you son of a bitch."

Wolfie laughs like it's Dad's first good idea ever. Dad storms out of the apartment.

"And do you realize," Adam laughed, "that after that time they always avoided each other?"

I was confused. "But at Passover…at Hanukkah…."

Those holiday gatherings where even though Dad was the host, Wolfie would be offering cordial instructions from his chair at the far corner: "Do us all a favor, skip what Rabbi Eliezer said. Everybody's getting hungry." Which would make Dad stubbornly make us go through the entire Haggadah before we ate. After dinner Mom and Wolfie would quietly set time aside for a private talk which, for all I knew, was as innocent as having to do with their kids' schools. Aunt Hani going up to Dad as if to balance the pairs—her hand on his shoulder with her tanned and braceleted arm—although it wasn't balance at all, she was Wolfie's delegate, she had no feelings for Dad. And Sara, Cousin Adam, and me sitting at three separate places at the table, like cars at a three-way stop.

"The families still saw each other," Adam told me, at the airport terminal wall, "but if you studied the situation, Wolfie and Sid sat at opposite ends of the table and rarely made eye contact. Not that your Dad stopped working for mine. He still went around for the rent and collected his little extra pay. The day he died, of the heat? What do you think he'd been doing? Walking around Detroit all day with his coat on his arm, ringing doorbells, until he had a heart attack."

I stared past my cousin, the way Dad taught me to focus on the horizon when you think you're going to be carsick. When I glanced back at my relative, he was still there, of course, but I kept turning my eyes to the ticket counter or the security gates until he had to go board his plane.

When I tell this lore to women, they have different reactions. The one at the Greek restaurant, as I said, got hot thinking about it. But that was back in college. Everyone is much tamer now. Last night, I was out with someone I really wanted to make an impression on, so I used all of it, more or less exactly like here. She just kind of looked at me and said, "All right, now can you tell me a story about yourself?"

I didn't know what to say.

Those Kooks

Having a detective for a father gave me surprisingly little cachet among my peers at P. S. 105, Bronx. First of all he wasn't a private eye, he was a police detective; and he was a sergeant, a singularly unromantic rank lacking any of the dash of a lieutenant or the grit of a street detective; and to top it off he wasn't in Homicide or even in Narcotics or Vice but in Larceny. No one in fourth grade even knew what larceny was, much less cared about stopping it. (We didn't know what narcotics or vice were, either, but we knew they were enticingly wicked.) Even my father didn't seem unduly keen on bringing larcenists to justice. He talked about the men he arrested—they were almost always men—not as culprits or villains or perpetrators of evil, but as poor shmucks, little *goniffs*, little *momsers* or *vonces* or *shmeggeggies*— very much the same vocabulary he used to describe me and my playmates. Once, when I asked him if it was fun to arrest robbers, he said, "It'd be more fun to arrest the City Council"—a remark that not only confused me about whether Dad and I were really on the same side, but thoroughly flustered my teacher when I reported it during a Social Studies lesson.

Sergeant Lou Soroker, when off-duty, was not to be found

slugging back bourbon from a half-drained bottle or combing his hair in hipster waves, but sitting in a white shirt and tie in his own living room, reading the sports page of the *Daily News*. His hours were a mystery. Because he liked the evening shift, I didn't see much of him on weeknights when other fathers were home with their families, but he was already up, fully clothed, in front of "that damn paper," as my mother called it, when I was getting ready for school in the morning, and he might still be sitting in the same nubby green armchair, after making a circuit of all the other seating in the apartment, when I returned at three o'clock. There were odd weekdays and sometimes an entire week when he didn't have to go in to the precinct at all. "I caught enough bad guys this month, they gave me a rest." At such times, I think we all felt that he was on *our* case, staking us out, pencilling notes about our suspicious behavior in the newspaper margin under cover of doing the crossword puzzle. Greeting me and my friends as we trooped in, dirty and bruised from playing off-the-curb, on our way to a bottlecap football tournament in my room, he lowered the paper to bark out a stiff, comradely, "How's it going, men?" Detectives did not sound like that. They sounded like, "You're going to Sing-Sing, Lazzari, and your goombah pals with you." They sounded like, "Let me buy you a drink, Dollface, and maybe you can light my cigarette." They did not sound like graying City College graduates who wondered aloud about when their sciatica would be bad enough for disability leave.

Alas, it was one of Lou's few pleasures in life to destroy the pleasure of others, and he did his best to deflate any glamorous images of his profession we might have had. (If he hadn't, maybe I'd be a detective today myself instead of a therapist — which is sort of the same thing but internal, isn't it.) Friday nights when my mother and I sat riveted in front of *77 Sunset Strip*, competing with Efrem Zimbalist, Jr. and Edd "Kookie" Byrnes to solve their cases (we usually won), my father would amble in front of the screen, biting a prune danish or slurping a bowl of schav in order to have the full mouth necessary for appropriate commentary about television. "Crap. Garbage. Divorced from reality." (How could you get a divorce from reality, I wondered?) "I'd like to see one of these twerps fill out a witness report." For Lou was a devotee of paperwork. He didn't deduce the names of criminals from hunches inspired by tenuous shreds of evidence; he read and initialed documents, he annotated transcripts of confessions, he evaluated the results of others' legwork. "Sergeant is a supervisory position," he huffed when I asked him if he'd been in any car chases lately; there was the same proud debunking note in his voice as when he complained about his back. And when I asked him if he thought our building super might be the thief who had stolen a stained glass window from the lobby (I think it was Abraham fleeing the fires of Sodom), he shook his head: "That was just some kid, some *khaleyrier's* prank. When there's a serious crime, we usually know who did it; what's hard is getting anyone to testify." So insistently prosaic, he must have spent a large part of his life pushing down the poetry in himself, inspiration by inspiration, like a beat cop shining his mystery-killing flashlight methodically into every alley; and he retained so much of the humdrum presence of his flatfoot days that when old folks in the neighborhood upbraided me for my boyish sins, they called me not "the detective's son" but "the cop's son."

It was my mother, Rochelle, who possessed a taste for danger, a sense of intrigue. Not much bigger than me and my friends, she was as loud as fireworks and twice as scary. She conducted interrogations: "Where were you? Why are you so late? What did you eat on the way home?" Or, if I brought a new friend: "What's your father do? Your mother? She works?" (That said in a tone of incredulity.) "Who does she leave you with? What, you come home to an empty apartment? You make your own snack? And you don't mind?" Followed by a triumphant, "I see!" And she twisted arms—literally, using the time-honored summer-camp torture, the Indian Burn, rubbing my wrist until the skin reddened, as a mode of discipline when I drove her crazy enough (a point I reached at first unwittingly, and then by deft estimation just to where she would threaten but not deliver, and then, when I was old enough—what the hell, over the line, laughing as she grimaced with the effort of trying to hurt me). She had an uncanny gift for finding out the secret sins of others. She knew instantly that the cartridge pen and peacock-blue ink I suddenly began using had been shoplifted from Penrod's Stationery. She knew that I had more homework than I admitted to. This clairvoyance worked on adults, too. "So, Artie, did your father ever apologize to your mother?" she asked my best friend one day as soon as he set foot on our threshold, and though she might as well have been talking Yiddish as far as I was concerned, Artie blushed. "So, Spencer," she confronted another friend, who hardly ever came around for fear of her, "your father blows his savings on a new Pontiac and crashes it right into a subway girder." She was five feet tall, wore high heels indoors and out, and tied her long, peasant-blonde hair in a thick braid that thumped against the small of her back, keeping the beat of her aggravation. I was her confidant from the earliest age, but as I get older the things that interest me most are not the things she confided to me but the things I gradually learn she didn't. Not the gangster who tossed her a silver dollar when she was an undersized child crawling down sewers on Fox Street or Jerome Avenue; not the grievances against her own mother—my angelic grandma!—for making her wash floors at age five; but the probability, which I understood embarrassingly late, that she was agonizingly lonely during the long, conscientious years of raising her only child; and the possibility, not once mentioned, because I have this dreadful feeling she never knew it herself—I inherited intuition from her, but not *this* intuition—that she and my father loved each other.

Well, there was never any external evidence. And, "Evidence, that's all that's important to him," she used to say. If he'd had the slightest consideration for her, he would move us to the suburbs, but—and this was what burned her up most—"The man won't leave the Bronx." He was a diehard native who still lived within the bounds of the Forty-Third Precinct. And he had good reasons to want to. It was a low-crime district, at least the part we lived in, where the tenements lined a green parkway down which, on weekends, horses clopped from rival riding academies (one offering Western saddle, one English) a couple of miles north.

"You want me to commute an hour each way every day just so you can live in Westchester?" he said.

"Who said Westchester? It could be New Jersey. Amalfitano lives in Fair Lawn, Curiale lives in Bergenfield." A couple of his squadroom buddies. "They don't make any more than you do."

"Bergenfield! Oh, to be in Bergenfield in spring!" And his wisecrack allowed me to laugh at her with impunity. "I'm a public servant of the City of New York and I have a rent-controlled five-room apartment."

My mother never got to live in Westchester, or even New Jersey. Her son was against her. "Please don't make us move to the suburbs, it's like television there!"

She knew exactly what I meant—it was she who had trained me to deride the "unreal" harmoniousness and "phony" civility of sitcom families—and given bitter pause, she herself doubted the beauty of her two-patio vision.

That summer, my parents, unprecedentedly, had someplace to go together. Every Tuesday afternoon they had no choice but to leave me alone—for one hour plus another hour's driving time.

"Are you going to see a psychiatrist?" I asked, jumping up with the excitement of my independence.

Rochelle said, "Don't be silly, what would we be going to a psychiatrist for?"

"Because you're crazy, ha ha," I said in my best Beatles put-on, which caused Lou to huff, "Don't call your mother names," even though they had called each other, and me, that word countless times. It was the favorite family epithet, applied carelessly to anything from a child's night terrors to a dime's rise in the price of chopped meat. In fact Rochelle soon admitted, like a game-show host who consoles a guest for just missing the right answer, that they were going to see a marriage counselor—not a psychiatrist but a social worker.

"We'll hire Melyssa next door to babysit for you."

"You want a mixed-up twelve-year-old taking care of me?"

That's how much in league with them I could be, against myself. Or was I just trying to earn points for high-mindedness, knowing I'd get what I wanted anyway?

Melyssa was the girl I didn't dare dream of as a girlfriend. She was an artist's daughter, and she was obviously planning to do some creative tinkering with her own life as soon as she could save up the money to run away. She was tall as most teenage girls and as skinny as most of them wished they were; her complexion was beeswax yellow, a metabolic quirk she flaunted like a deliberate statement; her stringy, sandy hair fell into her eyes and her mouth and over her blue denim workshirts, which the parkway sun shone through onto the triangles of her training bra; and there were triangles, too, at the hems of her jeans: the patches of flowered cloth her mother sewed there to make bellbottoms. This was in 1966, when The Mamas and The Papas, in floorlength paisley dresses or in goatees and Russian hats, were the weirdest freaks we had ever seen. Melyssa was past most teenagers in the neighborhood and she hadn't even gone through puberty yet. She did her homework behind the counter at her mother's picture-frame shop, a narrow, incense-scented place where, in addition to photos of sunsets and bridges, she offered psychedelic tarot decks, satirical greeting cards, and newspapers with surrealist puns for titles to anyone with the courage to enter. They had moved into our building quite recently, just before opening the shop: the nearness of the two rentals must have been why they chose our neighborhood, for unlike ninety percent of its residents, they were not Jewish, and unlike another nine percent, they did not *seem* Jewish, at least not in a way we recognized. They lived in the top corner apartment, 6L, while we Sorokers tended closer to the mainstream in 6K. In their bach-elor-sized one-bedroom, Melyssa had the bedroom; Andreya slept on a convertible sofa. The male on the premises was Andreya's boyfriend, a curly-bearded grad student in anthropology who loi-tered in their rooms all weekend—the only time cooking odors issued from their door;.

"He's not my father, I don't have a father," Melyssa said.

I tried to tell her that everyone has a father, because the sperm and the egg have to get together. (At age ten I still had the idea that they achieved this unlikely union in the stomach, as a result of kissing.)

"*I* don't have a father," she repeated with her mother's flip, collegiate sneer—an airy brusqueness implying innate superiority to the facts—and from that moment on it became my dream to talk that way. (Some of my patients have occasionally hinted that it bothers them.) It's from Melyssa that I date my lifelong fascination with slightly—I emphasize the *slightly*—older women.

"*Oy,* that Melyssa," Rochelle said, "I just hope her mother closes the door when she has her 'overnight guest.'"

Even today, whenever I enter a new friend's apartment it's like ex-ploring another planet. Invited into Melyssa's for the the first time after months of distant neighborliness, I was thrilled by every tchotchke on the shelves, every liberty taken from my own family's routines. They ate sandwiches for dinner! They kept a pitcher of iced tea in the fridge, and refilled it all year long! And their living room was not where people slumped, fatigued or fuming, in front of the TV, but where Melyssa's mother worked at easel and drafting table. On the walls, where, in any average apartment, you could assume, without even looking, the presence of off-tone reproductions of things painted by Frenchmen between 1870 and 1910, here instead were ugly, rough paintings you *had* to look at: jagged nudes outlined in angry charcoal, with translucent rectangles of color—medicinal pink, breath-mint green—stretched across their bodies like ineffectual blankets, leaving uncovered what the figures wanted covered. "This is Andreya's new work," Melyssa told me, as if she were not her mother's daughter, but her collector. Around her neck Melyssa wore, daringly and enchantingly, her pet ferret, Bosco—like a fur pelt, but one that scratched and nipped and had to be put immediately in his cage.

"Now let's have some deadly poison," she said, ushering me to the coffee table, which was made hospitable not with a cut-glass bowl of sourball candy, but with an open pack of Tareytons. She lit one and, after modeling the proper exhaling form, tipped the pack toward me. Given so little time to react, I couldn't possibly decide whether to turn myself into the kind of person who tried the cigarette or the kind of person who didn't—which was how I made decisions in those days. I stood dumbly until, from sheer need to break the silence, I asked:

"Your mother lets you smoke?"

"*She* started when *she* was twelve. She knows 'Do what I say, not what I do' is bullshit."

I repeated the expression to myself mentally, trying to figure out which was the preferable behavior. "So are you supposed to do what she says or what she does?"

She groaned. Then she led me to her bedroom and opened the drawer of a kidney-shaped vanity table littered with tubes of lipstick. "Let's make you up," she said

Though I remember yipping, "What! No!" I didn't put up much of a fuss, and once she got that first smear of coral on my lower lip, I sat quietly, messing up her strokes by breaking into smiles, quite happy to let her do whatever she wanted to me. The scents of coal-tar and flowers rising off my face were something I'd never experienced this close, not even when kissing my mother goodnight; the cold, sweetish paste on my lips, the granular cream on my cheeks were sensations I had never in my life expected to feel.

"You're getting pretty," Melyssa cooed, and I said, "Stop!" but not too seriously, and she reached for an eyebrow pencil to make some finishing touches. "Let's go to your house," she said, for we had permission to shift back and forth, "and see what makeup your mom's got."

"No!" I said, really unnerved now, not only at the thought of violating my mother's cosmetics, but of being seen during the two-yard dash from apartment to apartment.

"Yeah, your house is a drag anyway." And we were both too young to know she'd made a pun. "Okay, I know what."

"What?"

She didn't tell me, she showed me, taking me by the hand to the elevator. My eyes stung, sticky with mascara. I had hurriedly splashed some water on my face and wiped with a towel on the way out of her apartment. Dabbing at wet spots to try to make myself acceptable to my mother, I must have looked like a last-minute fingerpainting.

Melyssa pushed the chipped white button labeled "B," and the elevator gate shuddered shut. "Did you ever walk through the furnace?"

"Oh, no," I said, not to her but to anyone who might be near enough to save me.

"Come on," she said.

And she took me by the hand to an unmarked, dented, metal door opposite the basement laundry room. This was the door about which my parents always said, "You can't go in there, it's locked." It turned out not to be locked at all, just hard to push open, and at the moment, it seemed preferable to the laundry room with its gnashing of elderly washer-dryers, or the super's apartment, where an unseen German shepherd barked as if I was his last chance to grab a Soroker before the camp was liberated. I rammed the mystery door hard, to compensate for the mascara. As it opened, I stumbled forward into a rusty banister, the only thing that kept me from falling ten feet onto the floor below.

I had never known there was so much space under my own

building. We ran down the iron staircase into a cubical cavern about—well, who can say how big it really was, when I was small?—but it seemed so big the six-story house should have collapsed on it. We were in a sub-basement containing the furnace and the incinerator. One weak, bare bulb gleamed down onto a puddle on a clogged drain; thick steel pipes ran along the ceiling; I thought I heard water flowing somewhere. A burnt smell of cinders, not quite stagnant, wafted toward and away from my incongruously feminine scent. The place was neither cold nor hot nor a comfortable compromise, but both at once: damp, underground cave-cold and the heat of pilot lights with their intermittent flareups. On the floor around the well of the incinerator were popcorn-shaped brown kernels of metamorphosed garbage that had exploded out of the fire, or been kicked by the super.

A catwalk crossed the room in midair. It ended at a small door, like a coal chute, set into the far wall. To get to the chute, you had to walk the catwalk with the open incinerator on your left, and on the right the furnace, suppressed rage coming from its flame-slitted door.

"Walk," commanded Melyssa like a prison guard, although she was really freeing me. Holding tight to the rail, I shuffled the length of the iron catwalk. I stopped at the incinerator. The door had been left half-open. Looking in, I imagined my eyes melting like in the atomic blast we'd all been expecting all our lives. Mascaraed tears ran into my mouth. A crumpled New York *Post* spun inside the fire and flowered orange, flame-within-flame; an empty bottle of Passover wine toppled over from the force of heat; the legs of a broken chair keeled sideways. For some reason someone had even thrown out a brand-new baseball, the red stitching still unscuffed and the lettering still sharp and clean, with hands of blue fire flowing around it, rubbing it up. What would it be like to stick *my* hand in there, to breathe there? Staring at my destruction, I couldn't leave until Melyssa shoved me. "Move!"

She reached around me and unlatched the chute door. Stooping, I looked into a metal tube I couldn't see the end of.

"Okay, start going," she said.

I looked back at her as if to say, Don't you see the expression on my face?

"Start going!" she repeated, and gave me a smart whack on

the buttocks. I looked back—could I run away?—but strangely I trusted her. So I began to crawl. Once I had gone a few feet, I heard her boost herself up behind me.

The tunnel was chilly and smelled like rust. The scuffing of my knees echoed back from up ahead as if there was someone else there waiting. I decided that a slow, steady pace would seem most mature. Every so often I said something like, "Keep going?" or, "How much longer?" just to hear my own voice; and I liked the way she said, "Shut up."

My forehead bumped into the far door. "Ow."

"Find the handle?" she said.

I felt for it in the dark, opened it, and jumped onto the landing of an identical iron catwalk, in an identical bare-bulbed sub-basement. Was it Superman's Bizarro world; was it a parallel dimension in which my parents were dead…?

"It's the next block, see?" Melyssa said. She jumped down alongside me, and the metal stairs rattled. "Twin buildings. We just went from 2181 Barnes to 2181 Wallace. They used to have one super for the two of them, to be cheap—he had to crawl back and forth from one boiler room to another."

I laughed as I'd laughed the first time I'd ever been able not to cry from an injection. Nothing was menacing anymore—nothing, I imagined, would ever scare me again. I was already planning to dare my friends to crawl through: *Come, don't be a baby*, I'd tell them. I was ready to turn around and go right back through the tube like on a roller coaster that I'd mastered.

"No, we'll go by the street," she said.

I touched the makeup smear on my cheek. "But what if someone sees—"

"That's why you have to run fast."

So we did, and I did it laughing. Our strides shook the catwalk, and when a little round-shouldered old man struggled out of the laundry room with a cart of clean clothes, I stuck my tongue out at him—after all, I'd been expecting the same Gestapo who chased Steve McQueen in *The Great Escape*. We raced to open the elevator before he could catch up to us; as the door closed in his face, we hopped up and down to jeer at him through the chicken-wired porthole. Ascending, we heard, along with the hum of the pulley, his croaking, "Little bastards! Sons of bitches, I'll tell your mother!" Sinking to the floor laughing made for a nice inertial whoosh when the elevator stopped.

I almost hoped someone *would* see my makeup as we ran out of the building and around the corner to our home, and I don't know if anyone did or not. But when we got back to our hallway, my parents were there unlocking the apartment door, and I quickly smeared off as much more as I could. We banged into stout, sciatic Sergeant Soroker as if he were a base. He grunted, his keys shaking in his pockets.

"How was your first visit to the headshrinker?" I asked, with the joy of wanting to tell everybody everything.

The inevitable, "Mind your own business," came from both of them in slightly different words, harmonizing as spontaneously as John and Paul.

"I'll bet she didn't give you a snack," Rochelle said, right in front of Melyssa, who sulked over to her apartment door without waiting for her pay and without giving me any further notice. My mother took me into the kitchen and slammed a glass of milk down in front of me. "I don't know who's worse," she said, indicting, a grab-bag of neighboring suspects.

Lou and Rochelle accelerated their counseling schedule to twice a week, which gave me twice as much time with Melyssa. Not that they had been having a marital crisis or anything, only the same deliberate misunderstandings and shouted recriminations I woke up every day expecting to hear. Their counselor must have been especially at getting her clients in touch with their anger, because from the time they returned from that first session, the average decibel background in our apartment surpassed even its previous high plateau. Mom and Dad had received a broadcasting license.

Also a dredging license. The veteran crew of Lou and Rochelle Soroker went to work with a will, hauling up outrages and injustices from every layer of the past—not only what they had done to each other this week and this year and last year and twelve years before, but what their parents had done, which they now saw reflected in how they had let their spouses do the same thing; and how their former lovers would have loved them if only Lou and Rochelle had had the sense—which they could only have had if their parents hadn't done those things to them—to love back.

"If that bastard of a father of mine had ever once encouraged me to make something of myself," Rochelle said. "If my mother hadn't told me she wanted to abort me—but my father accidentally spilled the chemicals, and he took it as a sign I had to be born, that *noodnik*—maybe I'd have enough self-esteem today to tell you to go fuck yourself."

"But you just told him," I pointed out with the plummy moderation I had already, at that precocious age, achieved.

"Who asked you?" she said. "You're on your father's side now?"

"I'm not on anyone's side." I exchanged even-tempered glances with my father, who exasperatingly encouraged my neutrality. He fought off her attacks strongly enough—no problem there; what was so frustrating was that he wouldn't fight for possession of *me*.

"Where is *he* going?" my mother asked me as my father stood up from the table. "To read the newspaper as usual?"

He answered for himself. "I'm going to fuck myself like you told me to, you fucking foul-mouthed bitch." That was Lou's style: hard, blunt, concise, and viciously giving her an overdose of her own medicine. He was the only person in my acquaintance who didn't drop the *g* in *fucking,* and since I had never seen the word spelled in print, I believed this was one of his precinct-house mispronunciations.

Arguments like that one did not end in resolutions. They were merely set aside when wounded silence was followed by a change in subject, like whether they still had any appetite for dinner or whether the dry cleaner's was open after five. They weren't even arguments, in the sense that an argument attempts to establish the validity of an opinion by means of a coherent series of statements. Neither was trying to persuade the other of a thing; neither had the slightest gift for altering conditions or even imagining them alterable. These were just fits. The hate was always there, whether or not it was being voiced at a given moment, and whether it was being voiced in a scream or a sardonic mutter. Each was enraged at the other's refusal to be affectionate. I sometimes imagined that if one of them, just once, instead of being infuriated by the other's fury, had eased up and said, "I love you," they would be healed in one stroke: everything they had never said to each other would come surging out, all their need for each other would be revealed, their complementarity would become a positive, and though they might still yell now and again, they would know how to soothe themselves, perhaps by doing things I had never seen them do—kissing, snuggling, sharing a laugh. As Rochelle put it, "If the man had ever once brought me flowers, or a birthday present…." But since that was my mother's interpretation, it must have been wrong. Instead, if they had ever unwittingly let a phrase of love slip out, they would have overwhelmed it with curses the next minute: though their rage was about nothing, it had acquired a momentum stronger than anything.

Did I mention that this was when they started drinking? On their marriage counselor's advice? My parents ingested liquor with sniffs of trepidation. My mother approaching a bloody mary was like a housecat approaching the ocean. She'd had an alcoholic uncle somewhere down on Tremont Avenue back in the 1930s, so she was on tenterhooks lest she inherit the dread infirmity. Lou didn't drink because cops were reputed to drink, and he always tried to prove the world wrong in everything. Also, I only learned in adulthood, because he was one of those drinkers who could be sent into flaming orbit by two sips of a screwdriver. But in the summer of 1966 they resolutely took up the habit of a cocktail before dinner whether they enjoyed it or not, because their counselor, hearing about how anxious they were when they sat down to face an evening's skirmishes, suggested, "Why don't you take a drink to relax?" My mother pussyfooted around the subject for weeks—"Should we? I don't know"—until my father finally sucked in his gut, measured out precisely one jigger apiece, and snapped, "Le'khayim. I don't know what this is supposed to accomplish."

These, then, were the two debauchees whom I observed goading each other between sips, at the oilcloth-covered kitchen table overlooking backyard brickwork crisscrossed by the shadows of television antennas. Rochelle would merrily tease Lou—"Look at him, the man doesn't even know how to take a drink"—and banter would follow:

"Drop dead."

"*You* drop dead."

"We should both drop dead," said my father with his incorruptible sense of fairness.

"Well, you've got a gun. When are you going to use it?"

I turned my head from one to the other as if at a tennis match.

"I'll use it when I goddamn please," he said.

"I pray for the day."

That was the one religious sentiment I ever heard either of my parents express.

They were glumly doling out their evening highballs one summer twilight when Rochelle got wind of a rival pleasure.

"Do you smell something?" she asked sharply, and confronted the police about it. "I could swear I smell pot coming from next door," she told Lou.

"I don't want to know," he said, and opened the newspaper to the middle—the only man in New York who started the *Daily News* in the editorials. On the back cover, I read that the Mets' rookie pitcher had, astoundingly for that team, won another game.

"He doesn't want to know," Rochelle translated for me. "Well, what *do* you want to know?" she asked him. "Would you want to know if they were shooting heroin? Would you want to know if they were making bombs?"

In his own way, my father knew how to play to me, too. He drew out a white business card from his wallet and handed it to her. "Here's my card. If you wish to file a report, call me during my shift." He turned the pages to the stock quotations, although to my knowledge he didn't own stocks.

Rochelle was disgusted. "You think I don't know what pot smells like?"

"Smells are notoriously unreliable evidence."

"I'll go find something reliable," I offered.

"Wait, listen!" Rochelle said, scampering to put her ear to the bedroom wall. Frantically she waved me toward her. "They're at it again, come listen!"

Side by side, my mother and I kneeled on throw pillows, leaning across the scrolled walnut headboard in order to get the best listening post to learn what was going on between Melyssa and Andreya. She wanted to broaden my horizons, and to compare observations with me as well. And I loved that part.

"You old bitch!" I distinctly heard Melyssa scream.

"Get that thing away from me or I'll kill it!" Andreya shrieked.

"Then I'll kill *you!*"

"Well," Rochelle told Lou, "*now* are you prepared to do your job?"

He shrugged and rattled the newspaper. "A simple domestic dispute, it's not my area."

She turned from him, as if mercifully hiding her expression of loathing. "Quick, Genie, go next door and borrow an egg," she told me.

"An egg?" I said dubiously.

"An egg. What's wrong? I just decided to make meatballs for supper." She pushed me toward the foyer. "Look how he doesn't trust me. Go, just tell them your mother needs to borrow an egg, it won't embarrass you."

Why it wouldn't, I had no idea, but I trudged off to do my duty.

The screaming didn't stop while Andreya answered the door, it continued behind her, around her, like a frame, like the sweet, stinging, incenselike, somehow Asian aroma that also surrounded her. At that point in history, new experiences came toward you without your even seeking them, at regular, short intervals, and you'd check them off on a mental list to keep track of your progress up the ladder of evolution. This scent was something I'd been expecting, but not so soon, and the sudden advancement, like being placed in the accelerated class, made self-love swell and envelop everything around me.

Almost expecting it to make me high at the first sniff, I stood there with a goofy smile and tried to remember why I'd knocked. Also, Melyssa's mother was wearing an unbuttoned Hawaiian shirt with a black bra—no, it was not unbuttoned, it was torn open; by man, woman, girl, or ferret, I never learned.

Transfixed by her chest, it took me a moment to ask, "Can I play with Melyssa?" A pretext I found much more natural and believable than the egg story.

"Maybe you can tame her while you're at it." She shouted to the far end of the apartment: "Ferret Girl, get over here, someone actually wants to see you!"

Andreya was shortish and roundfaced, in thick glasses with clear pink frames that magnified the perennial owlish stare of a woman who had learned to expect rude visitors. The patient indifference with which she viewed me, like a speck on the horizon, made me increasingly aware that I didn't know where to look.

Sourly, Melyssa sloshed through the paint jars and half-drawn-on papers that littered the floor. She looked as if she had been painting, but she just happened to be wearing one of her mother's smock shirts. Whenever we met, I couldn't be sure whether Melyssa would condescend to greet me or not; this time she scrunched her nose in distaste and said to Andreya, "You want me to take care of him or something?"

"Does your mom want us to babysit?" Andreya asked me.

"I just thought I'd come over and play," I said with giveaway blandness.

Andreya scrutinized me. "So you're a peacemaker. I guess that's cool. You've got experience. You two go to Melyssa's room and—" suddenly she began to shout again, and though I was conditioned to assume that anyone shouting near me was shouting *at* me, it was obvious that her target was Melyssa. "Get that thing back in its cage or I'll drown it in the fucken bathtub!"

That thing was Bosco, who was swiveling around the room like a fur-coated, drunken skier, smacking his tail into chair legs and artworks, gathering dustballs in the process. Melyssa picked Bosco up with an as-if-sweet smile. Then she threw him at her mother's face. The ferret made no sound—ferrets rarely do—but clawed for purchase at Andreya's cheeks, and kept clawing while sliding down her neck.

Andreya screamed. She tore the animal off herself and kicked wildly at its belly, but did not, in the end, have the heart to drown it in the bathtub. I stood and watched this grown woman, an artist, sob as she pawed at her own face and neck and wiped the blood off onto her Hawiaiian shirt.

"Those kooks and their *meshuggass*," my mother said. "And that animal—what is it, a weasel?"

"A black-footed ferret," I said with my inherited sense of accuracy.

"Black-footed, no less! What's that, some kind of pedigree for vermin? A weasel, a ferret, what's the difference? They let it run through the halls like I wouldn't let a harmless puppy. If it doesn't have rabies we'll all be lucky. And that daughter! She'll be coming home with men soon, mark my words, to compete with her mother. Then—you want a prediction?" Why not, we did the same thing when we guessed the plots of television mysteries. "I'll bet you anything one of them comes home with a colored boyfriend. They all do it nowadays, to prove how hip they are."

She was referring to the flexible "they" who consisted of any and all females whose lives, in any respect, were more fortunately disposed than hers.

"Acting like sisters instead of mother and daughter, that's the kind of world we live in," she said. "Well, I'm glad I only have a son."

So I wouldn't come home with a colored boyfriend? So I wouldn't compete with my parents? And what did "only a son" mean? This was far from the only speech of my mother's whose multitracked innuendoes I've had to listen to over and over again in order to hear clearly. (As I tell my therapy clients, you can't rerecord your childhood, but you can remix it.) Anyway, there I sat, chewing a blueberry danish or a black-and-white cookie or some such treat, prudently correcting and qualifying Rochelle's slanders ("Melyssa doesn't bring men home"; "No, Bosco's nice!"), but eating them up too. I must have been a dream audience: big brown eyes as voracious as a ferret's, so dazzled by her performance that I was incapable of talking except for the occasional murmured protest addressed to the invisible self sitting beside me, my after-school self (for this was school all right), the one who could get up and walk out. She was laying out people's lives for me, and I didn't even have to leave the kitchen.

"You know that the word *assassin* comes from that stuff they were smoking, don't you? I've got news for you, your mother could have smoked pot any time she wanted when she was younger." Turning to Lou: "You're not the first man I ever went out with, if you recall. My first boyfriend was a labor organizer who lived in Greenwich Village. Three flights I had to walk up to his apartment, and believe me, the hallways were full of that stench. He would take me to parties with jazz musicians—*ach*, what's the use of talking?" This, like several other of her tag-lines, was a signal that more would follow; but I will summarize. Slapping her hand on the tabletop so her wedding rings clacked, she recited once again the piteous epic of her fall, from sought-after though hard-to-get Hunter College coed majoring in psychology, to wife of a pathologically unstriving civil-service form-filler who wouldn't even take the lieutenant's exam when all his friends were doing so. "It's no use, the man won't listen, that's the story of my life," she concluded. How she got there from a phantom aroma in the hall, I wasn't sure, except that she could get there from anywhere.

One thing that day, however, Lou and Rochelle agreed on: they would never again hire Melyssa as my babysitter. They had nothing against a little nonconformism, Rochelle claimed, but this was "going too far," it was "rebelling just to be different"— lacking, she implied, the high moral purpose of her own deviations from the average. Her clinical assessment: "It's crazy. Well, let them live the way they want, I could care less. Some people have better things to worry about."

Not only no more Melyssa, no more babysitters at all: my parents stopped going to the therapist; talking had made things go from bad to worse, they needed it like a hole in the head, what was the use? What had happened, I think, was that marriage counseling had brought them to the brink of divorce, and they were flooded with fear of change. They would have been indignant if anyone had suggested they were clinging to each other.

I hardly ever saw Melyssa anymore that summer. She struck puberty like an oil-well gusher, and didn't want a ten-year-old boy staring at her suddenly inflated chest or quizzing her about why she was in a bad mood on a particular day. When I knocked on her door and asked if she wanted to play, she smirked and shut it in my face with barely a "no." I spent the idle months sipping lime rickeys on luncheonette swivel chairs, and leaving without paying. I would browse for an hour in a store where the proprietor didn't know me, and as a point of honor, slip something I didn't need into my pocket: a bag of catnip from the pet shop, a packet of bunion pads from the pharmacy. I wondered why my parents didn't send me to camp or send us all to a Catskill hotel, and since it would be twenty years before I realized they couldn't afford it, that realization has no place in this story.

"I miss Bosco," I told my father as he made his eternal shuffle to the bathroom, and he grunted, "Who? Oh," and locked the door behind him.

It wasn't till September that we had an overture from them. It came in the form of an unstamped cream-colored envelope with a flowered border that slid under our door and spun into our foyer one evening.

"You are most cordially invited to the opening reception for a one-woman show of paintings," it said, and gave Andreya's full name and the address of the frame gallery she owned on White Plains Road, and the time on a Saturday evening two weeks from then.

"What is this?" my mother remarked, turning the invitation in her hand as if it were a message from outer space. "Only two weeks in advance they send it?" Her calendar was presumably chock full. "It doesn't tell how to dress — doesn't even give an R.S.V.P. number."

"Well, you can knock on their door and tell them we'll go," Lou said.

"We'll go? Since when? Lou Soroker at an art opening — you mean I've lived to see the day?"

"Am I invited?" I asked.

"Don't be in such a rush for disappointment," she advised me, using the occasion to impart one of her well-earned rules of life. She added ominously, "Who knows who these *meshuggeners* associate with?"

A background check must be performed. Sleuthing among the neighbors provided Rochelle with little new information, and frequent olfactory investigations unearthed no more suspicious aromas. Lou, working the files, reported that Andreya had no outstanding warrants nor any dossiers at Family Court or Bronx County Social Services. Further than that, he refused to go: "What do you want me to do, mobilize the FBI?"

So our acceptance was sent, and considering that we were only attending because "it beats sitting and listening to his phumpfing and farting at home," a remarkable amount of energy was expended on the details of dress. My mother went to Mr. Sandi and Mr. Billi's World of Beauty on Lydig Avenue, where the owners not only shellacked her hair into a wave but lent her "one of their heppest necklaces, it's hammered gold from Mexico, look" (sticking her upper torso out toward me), "they got it on vacation in Acapulco, I can just imagine what Sandi and Billi wear on the beach in Acapulco, *zukhen vey*."

I pointed out that the gold baubles hanging from the necklace had the shapes of squat, ugly, fat-nosed little men with scowling faces, who either gripped their own heads by way of their crotches in impossibly contorted positions, or held blunt instruments in their hands, or both.

"What's the matter with you, what are you calling ugly, these are gods, people used to worship them; look, feel, it's fourteen carat."

"People worshiped Rudy Vallee, and he was ugly," my father said from the other side of the bathroom door.

"Listen to him—Sergeant Soroker of the Antiques Squad! The man lives in the past, it's pathetic. Here we are, going to the opening of an avant-garde art exhibition and he's lost in the fog of his childhood."

And searching for fresh invective in the lee of her *bon mot*, we were off to the opening. I wore my brown tweed sport jacket with iridescent blue highlights, bought for seventeen dollars from Parkway Campus Clothiers for a cousin's bar mitzvah and never worn since, now that I was old enough to refuse to dress up on Jewish holidays. My father was in his detective outfit: a sharply pressed, shiny gray suit of no style or cut whatsoever, save the extra cloth for the bulge under his left armpit. I always felt that we were a sight when we walked down the avenue together, though in retrospect I see, on that crowded, hilly promenade of barber shops and kosher butchers, how every family whirled isolated in its own storm: a traffic of tornadoes, crisscrossing and veering. And each with its own weather-spotter, some studious, appalled little *schmendrick* like myself, fascinated by disaster. At times I ran ahead of my parents to get a look at them the way an outsider would see them; other times I was so demoralized by the them, I gave up resisting and let them suck me in.

Lydig Avenue descended to White Plains Road, under the black silhouette of the elevated subway. Frail couples, in overcoats as old as their marriages, inched out of the Greek diner and the Italian grill, fumbling with wallets and purses to keep their change from falling on the ground. Train brakes screamed overhead. With the whole width of the street to maneuver in, my parents remained side by side, in clawing distance. The wrinkles on the backs of their clothes seemed to inform on them cryptically. In my mind I heard acquaintances jeering, "Hey, where you going all dressed up?"— the more distant the acquaintance the better—but we didn't meet anyone we knew.

When we arrived in front of Andreya's shop, my mother crouched down outside the window, pressing her forehead to the gap between the paisley-bedspread curtains: "I can't see what's going on, it seems like they're trying to hide something."

I was already pushing the door open into a pulsation of electric blues, scented with wine, tobacco, and newly dry paint. Andreya stood behind the counter in a fur-trimmed day-glo shirt, as if to mock her shopkeeping self. Atop the glass display case was a tray of cocktail franks from Sonny's Delicatessen, with a shotglass full of ribboned toothpicks and a tub of mustard. I ran to the portable phonograph to see what was playing—*The Blues Project Live at the Café au Go-Go*—and only when I crossed the floor and didn't have to weave around anyone did it strike me that the place was empty.

Melyssa was sitting in the corner, one arm dramatically cocked in midair, not for a femme fatale effect but to let Bosco run up and down from her short sleeve to her bare skin. Andreya was behind the counter—I checked again, as if she might well have disappeared. That was it. My parents and I were the only guests.

"I didn't think we were so early," Rochelle stage-whispered. She examined the paintings with headshakes and grimaces that seemed to have been waiting confidently in the wings. "This isn't what they're doing now!" she objected. "I must say, from such far-out people I expected something more experimental. Today they're all doing Pop and Op and God knows what. This is more like what they were doing in the fifties, with all this figurative crap and this sexual *meshugass*." She gave me a significant glance, and answered my unasked, *What sexual meshugass?* "Never mind." She gave the paintings a second look: a second chance, as if at the last minute they might have repented and changed their style while our backs were turned. "No," she pronounced her verdict. "I keep up with the art world, I just read a big article about it in *Newsweek*, and this is not like what they showed there."

I would have expected Andreya either to be huddled in a corner by this point, crying and quivering, or to hurl herself at Rochelle with curses and counter-insults. That was what anyone raised by Lou and Rochelle Soroker would have expected. But Andreya did something the like of which I had never seen: she let the issue drop. Was Andreya the first adult I ever knew who had this reasonable, generous response in her repertoire? All I can say is, the first times I remember using it myself were after I knew her. Certainly this was the first time I can remember feeling sorry for an adult—which, given the adults I'd been around, does not speak well for me.

Andreya, acting as if she hadn't heard, came toward us smiling, her hands outstretched to grasp Lou and Rochelle's hands. "You came, you're so wonderful!"

My mother flashed me an eye-message: Did we make a mistake to come? Was everyone else smart enough to know you weren't supposed to accept her invitation?

"Sometimes I think this is the real reason to paint," Andreya said. "To get people together. I just want them to see the work and respond to it. They don't have to like it—they can hate it, that's okay. But I want them to respond and think and verbalize *their* meaning of the work, and it becomes part of the art, part of the conversation of art."

"Of course, what else?" Rochelle said suspiciously, stepping away. "I understand: you paint for people."

Even then, I could sense that she had gotten Andreya's meaning all backward by paraphrasing it. But Andreya did not retort, *No, you peasant, I don't "paint for people" in that vulgar way, I mean something lofty, even loftier than painting for myself alone....* In fact Andreya seemed quite pleased with my mother's level of understanding. That too was a whole new twist on being human. If my mother had ever told me she understood me, I would have hated it as an invasion of my privacy. Unlike art, she really did understand things about me.

I had to walk away to think about it, even though it wasn't well-formed enough in me yet to be called thought. I went over to the little folding chair where Melyssa was sitting. Bosco was currently wrapping his leash around the chair leg.

"Want to go through the furnace later?" I asked.

"'Want to go through the furnace later?'" she mimicked, falsetto, a deadly imitation of my childish idiocy even though it didn't sound much like my voice. In her own voice, which had become more undergraduate-suave than ever, she added, "If you can stop looking at my tits for two seconds, you can watch Bosco."

I hadn't been looking at her tits, but after she accused me of it, I did. They were not as large as I had anticipated—just a couple of anthill-size bumps—but they were bigger than when we'd played together, and the awkwardness of their size and shape—the shape of clumsy aspiration, not of comfortable achievement—was reason enough to resist her. She wore one of her mother's flowered miniskirts: it was too small for Melyssa, and the wrong style for her body and mind, and her lipstick (a novelty for her) was thickly smudged, and her hair was clean and perfectly sculpted to her shoulders and had nothing to do with her, like an older sister forced to supervise a younger. I see now that these all-too-visible facts had more to do with her belittling me than I myself had. At any rate, I had a high tolerance for insults. I petted Bosco and turned away.

Only a few minutes later, my mother was asking my father, "Well, are you ready to go?" A double-edged accusation that would blame him no matter which way he answered. And because she was right—I too was getting impatient—it sounded cruel.

The empty gallery was beginning to seem so forlorn, I didn't see why Andreya didn't just crouch behind the counter and weep. The cheap linoleum floor of the shop, without enough legs and feet to shade it, gleamed like yellow teeth. The cocktail franks were getting cold. The handful of us paced out isolated little figures, like ice skaters practicing.

I seem to remember that two other people came at some point, a gray-haired, woolly-clothed couple, tall and slender as Giacomettis, whom Andreya greeted effusively: "My mentor— mentors!—my professor and his wife. You made it all the way up here! I don't know what I'm going to do, do you think I should move downtown, what do you think, this is my new work, I don't know, I've been in isolation, solitary confinement, and nobody comes up to see me, I'm so glad you're here!" She hugged them forcibly, and they serenely pressed their cheeks to hers for a moment. I see the older couple as speaking little, and in murmurs, and as standing close together so that they took up less space than two people usually did.

And I seem to have a vision of them, this tall, overcoated, slightly hunched, self-contained couple, not saying much as she led them round the room by the arm. I see them gliding from painting to painting, giving each one twenty or thirty seconds, as if they had been there before—and then leaving. They had another party to go to, but they had decided to be late for that one, they said, in order to show their support for Andreya's work (which was beautifully hung, the professor's wife added).

I circled them like a thief sawing a hole in the floor, and when Andreya introduced me, they nodded instead of saying hello.

"I love them," she said after they'd gone. "They've helped me so much, they're people who really go out of their way."

Then she seemed to come just a little bit unhinged. She grabbed hold of Dad and hauled him to the counter, where she refilled his drink over his formal protestations.

"Lou, dance with me," she said.

"Oh, no you don't," Rochelle said under her breath, and aloud she said, "We've got to get this kid to bed some time tonight or he'll wake up with bags under his eyes as usual."

Did Lou turn slightly toward Rochelle, his scowl deepening in the direction of responsibility? He looked as if he was deciding which of two suspects to believe.

Andreya pressed forward, taking his hand in both of hers. "Lou, please, it's my first opening and it's just in my own gallery. I don't want everyone to leave when no one's even danced yet."

She lifted the folk-rock off the turntable and put on some old torch singer (Julie London reclining beckoningly on a mink sofa? Nancy Wilson packing a floor-length white gown to bursting?), and pulled Lou to the empty middle of the floor, and they moved together back and forth like two exhausted sea urchins at low tide.

And in a few minutes the tide began coming in....

And I saw why people dance.

I had once seen him and Mom trudge a minimal fox trot at a bar mitzvah, but watching him now it was clear that they had never danced at all. I was surprised Andreya knew these old, non-rock steps; it made her look older, but in a good way. They stayed for a second song and a third, and when it was a fast one with a Latin beat he smiled and said something to her, and she kicked one foot back and threw her head back, and spun away from him and returned.

"Circulate!" Andreya called to us, gaily and absurdly, in his arms, and Melyssa walked out of the strore.

"Here, Bosco," I crooned, stooping toward the floor and reaching out to the ferret, who was tied around the leg of a chair. He lunged for me, and I retreated.

"Enough's enough," my mother said. "Let's get the show on the road."

"All right, you want to leave?" I challenged her, in the same loathsome, abrupt bark my father would have used, and I stalked to the door.

Melyssa bumped into me on her way back inside. "Excuse me, O Great Hostess," she called out, "there's someone coming who I don't know if you want him here or not."

"Oh, shit, I'm not letting him in," Andreya said, and threw the door bolt shut from inside.

A high-pitched male voice said, "It's me."

With a grand gesture Melyssa reached out to open the lock, but the languid disdain of her movements gave Andreya time to wrench her away.

"Get away from there. Suddenly you want him for a father? Or what?" Andreya looked furiously at her daughter, who turned away with a laugh of pretended indifference.

From the street: "Hello? Let me in, please. I just want to speak to you, Andreya. I don't know of a single concrete reason for you not to let me in." He gave three calm, regular knocks on the door. "If you think I've ever hurt you, you're imagining things, and I'm not responsible.... If you don't let me in I'll use my key," he warned.

The lock turned, the door opened, but Andreya stopped it with her foot. One brown eye appeared in the opening: a post-cubist half of a face, with tobacco-yellowed saw-teeth, and fleshy lips cropped as if in a photograph: Andreya's boyfriend, or ex-boyfriend, the anthropology student.

"Andrushka, I'm your friend. You can't keep a friend outside like this. It makes me look bad, and I haven't done anything bad."

"You *are* bad, even if you haven't done anything yet."

"Andreya, we have a bond. We don't talk through barriers. We don't throw each other away." His tone was getting more and more reasonable, the way a father sounds until the moment he spanks you, or a teacher sounds so she has an excuse to give a punishment assignment.

"We've already talked," Andreya. "The talking part is over, this is the throwing part." She pressed against the door, but he kicked it and slammed it with his shoulder: it swung open.

"Andreya, listen to me—," he began, as if he was going to make a speech to a crowd. Then he went silent at the sight of the empty shop. A light of mirth crossed his face and disappeared, replaced by a light of pity. He went toward her with arms open, threatening a hug.

"Don't touch me," she said.

"How can you stop me from touching you?" he said in a tone of compassion.

As his arms wrapped around her, Andreya called out, "Lou!"

It sounded as if it meant something to her—as if it wasn't just a neighbor's name. Not like a spouse's name sounds, which carries all the things they've done together; not like a lover's name, which carries all the things they're in the thick of doing; but like a stranger's, which carries so much more, carries all the things they've never done.

My father had foolishly risked a third drink while Andreya's ex was trying to storm the shop. He swigged the second half of it in one gulp and smacked it down onto the counter. When he turned around to face the disturbance, his suit jacket was off, his shoulder holster right there over his white shirt, and his badge pinned, hastily but straightly, on the shirt pocket.

Then he was on the guy. He wrenched one of the graduate student's arms up behind the back, and squashed his forearm into the guy's windpipe. The student wriggled as he sank. When he had the guy kneeling, Lou pushed his knee into his back to complete the move—which, I hadn't realized till now, he had practiced hundreds of times in training seminars and refresher courses.

"Just don't move, sonny," Lou said. "So far you've got breaking and entering, assault, and resisting arrest. I wouldn't want to add assaulting an officer."

"If this isn't a panic," Rochelle said, "I don't know what."

I waited for Dad to make his stock reply, "Then you don't know what," but he was too involved in professional duty to notice her. I hoped he would handcuff the perpetrator, but that wasn't necessary either; he knew exactly how much of a psychological edge he had; all he needed to do was step back, and the grad student stayed there, on his knees, coughing, and trying to dry his tears solely through the power of facial muscles without lifting his hands from his sides.

"Are you all right?" Lou said to Andreya. "May I call someone to get that looked at?"

"Looked at?" she laughed. Then Lou touched a dark streak of blood on Andreya's neck. She let him. "Oh, no, no, the ferret did that this morning. *He* didn't touch me."

"He's also endangered the safety of two minors. Are you interested in pressing charges?"

From the floor, the ex began lecturing. "This is not a *case*, man," he said as he struggled to stand. "This is not about transgressing some local ordinance; this is about the deep structure of human interrelatedness.... "

"I just want him gone," Andreya said. "I don't want any contact with him."

Lou jerked his head from the ex to the door. "Scram," he said in a tone any TV detective would have been proud of, and I was too. He didn't need to watch the graduate student leave; he just assumed it; in fact the guy seemed to just assume himself out the door.

"Well, I wonder who's going to show up *next*," Andreya said, but of course, no one did. "He wanted me to go with him to the Sudan, to some Moslem village that he studies there. Can you imagine? He wanted me to go so I could learn about the women for him."

As always when someone said *Can you imagine?*, I tried to imagine it, and as always, I could imagine it in so many different ways that I couldn't tell if I was imagining it correctly. I envisioned Melyssa with sun-darkened skin, in a long, flowing, hooded robe....

She stuck her tongue out at me. "What are you looking at, you pipsqueak?"

I snickered as if joining her joke. I didn't even mind the insult: it was almost as if she was playing with me again. I probably would have minded if I'd realized that this was the last at-all-substantive communication we would ever have.

A few minutes later, I stood waiting on the sidewalk as my parents argued about whether or not to pick up a newspaper on the way home. The lights in the frame shop were still on, and I peeked in through a gap in the blinds. My first impulse was to call out to my mother in glee: *Look!* But then it occurred to me—and was this something else Andreya and Melyssa taught me?—I didn't have to tell my mother.

They were dancing together in the aisle of the display counter, Andreya and Melyssa, mother and teenager, heads on each other's shoulders, a ferret wrapping its leash around their ankles. They looked tired, propping each other up so that their party, maybe their only party for a long time, would not end too soon. And they looked unhappy enough, sure, but in a way I envied, not my parents' way.

Of course my father and Andreya did not have an affair. Our dwellings were paradoxically too close: neither offered a hideout from the other. There were kids around, and neighbors—it couldn't have remained a secret. And amid all the insults my mother ever cast at him, she never said a word about infidelity.

Besides, I know the suspect in question. I can't see him taking money from the family budget to rent a motel room, and I can't see him doing it in the darkness in Bronx Park or the Whitestone Drive-In. He would have had to arrest himself.

It was only by chance, several months later, when I walked past the frame shop, that I noticed it was empty and had a "To Let" sign in the widnow. Soon, painters came to freshen up the apartment next door before new tenants moved in. Andreya had had little enough furniture except for her easel and paintings; she must have moved out during the day while I was at school, and my mother had never mentioned it.

What did Melyssa do when she grew up, if in fact she grew up? It's easy to visualize the catastrophes, the self-destruction that could have happened to her in those years, and easy enough, too, to visualize the uplifting redemptions—love, religion, creativity, a meaningful career—but I'm holding out for more, for her. What I want to have happened to her is what she herself wanted, I think: I want her to have become a person like no other. My parting memory is of her dancing in a flowing robe on Sudan sands, a thing that, as far as I know, she never did.

And Andreya? My hunch is that she hated motherhood and longed desperately to escape from her ferret-handling jailer, but never could and therefore stayed sane and stable. I think that when Melyssa left home, as she must have done a few years afterward, it must have shaken Andreya, but I think it shook her into prospering conventionally. I see her doing her paintings in the finished basement of a suburban haven, and showing her work in malls, and telling stories of her bohemian youth to men on dates: the same story, reliably seductive, in restaurant after restaurant at the ever-expanding condominium frontier.

"And for her," my mother once sneered, "Lou Soroker took his gun out."

It was not literally true—he had only shown his holster— but that just added an extra twist to the remark.

Lou and Rochelle got divorced while I was working toward my master's degree in social work. She lives in Queens now, and he's still in the Bronx, a retired sergeant. Neither has remarried. Their two apartments, put together, would add up to about as much space as we had in Pelham Parkway.

I have forbidden my mother ever to discuss my father with me. I wish my father would talk about my mother a little, but he never does.

As for me, I have my practice, in this very nice professional building with a fountain out front and landscaped grounds. I treat the generalist's range of emotional problems: depression, anxiety, low self-esteem, marital and relationship difficulties, recovery— the old standbys. I'm the old-fashioned, deep kind of therapist—I warn my clients that from the outset. Brief therapies may make you feel better temporarily, and examining current behavior has its value in strengthening your defenses, but if you really want to change you have to go within, and that means into the past, as far as you can go and as long as you can stand. You have to see things you didn't want to see and hear things you wish you'd never heard. You have to look into the incinerator fire and marvel at what people throw away and what they keep. Sometimes it helps, I tell them. And sometimes it doesn't.

Dream Group Forming

D r. Jonathan Grove, the wellness practitioner, became afraid one morning at the sight of whiskers on his face. They were there again; they arose every night; there was no stopping them. Hair sprouted ceaselessly and pointlessly from human cheeks like grass from the earth. Rubbing his skin, he felt bedrock beneath. He was like the earth, a hard, blind thing giving forth life destined only to be mowed.

Then he imagined that the hairs on his face were not blades of grass, but tombstones rising from the ground. He was a cemetery filling with graves. Stone after stone, carved with the names of everyone he knew, would spring up on his cheeks, till the day when one of them would be carved with his own name.

He spread shaving cream over his cheeks, snow on the graveyard. But it didn't stop the grass from pushing upward.

He was afraid to shave it off in mid-vision.

With lather on his face and hot water running from the spigot, he pulled up the window curtain to take a look at the gingko tree, extracts of which were known to enhance intellectual function by dilating the blood vessels in the cerebral cortex. The eastern sun lit the tips of the fan-shaped leaves, their dark green hollows holding

shadow like bowls of distilled night. What made each leaf beautiful was how it shone with its own dread.

He forced the razor to his neck, scraping hard to get all the
nubs, and gave himself a cut on the jawline. Good! Cutting through
the mask to reach the flesh! Yet what was distressing was that on
most days, he shaved the mask without feeling the difference.

He pressed a wad of toilet paper to his jaw, and stroked all
around it with his free hand because, as has been determined in
numerous double-blind tests, there is a healing power in touch. He
still had some soft tissue over the bone; he was not worn down to
the skeleton.

"Would you rather be bone?" he asked his mirror self. "Would
you rather be glass?"

That gave him hope. If he'd been really bad he might have
believed he would rather be bone or glass.

Another troubling, early sign was that stray noises sounded
unlike themselves. The chirp of a bird in an ailanthus tree sounded
like the creak of a door. Maple seeds skittering along the sidewalk
sounded like the spinning of a bicycle wheel. A jet of water in a
neighbor's tub sounded like a telephone's ring, and sometimes like
a woman's voice calling, "Jonny, Jonny." Things had begun to reveal their undersides. The phenomena of nature were cards dealt
face-down, and sometimes you had to sneak a look to learn their
value.

He dressed in sweater-vest and tweed jacket, and checked the
answering machine in his consulting room, a partitioned area at
the front of his loft, a former zipper factory on the second story
above a discount showroom in the lamp district, on the Bowery
near Delancey. There were no messages. He flipped to today's page
of his desk calendar, already knowing it was blank till two o'clock.
He took up his post in the leather swivel chair, and brought his
fingertips to his lips, in the hope that by a harmonious alignment
of body with environment he could induce a state of synchronicity
that would give rise to an incoming telephone call. There was no
point in not placing faith in such measures even though they were
irrational. All one need do (the hypothesis thumped momentarily
through his mind like music from a passing car) was sit and wait,
and a patient would appear. Nor was there any receptionist to be
uncomfortable in front of anymore; he'd let her go a few months

back, when his referrals dried up after he'd taken a walk in the snow.

Though sitting quiescently is practiced by many cultures as a way to come face to face with the Self, Jonathan was not this morning in a frame of mind to concentrate on suchness. He swiveled, and drummed on his knees, and snapped up the copy of the *Village Voice* which he'd bought the night before. There on the back page was his classified ad:

> DREAM GROUP FORMING—Break free from the societal nightmare by nurturing your archetypal dreams. Learn to hear your self-guiding messages. We provide a safe birthing room for your new/old personality, your healing visions. Transpersonal, post-Jungian, multicultural, omni-gendered. Lower East Side location, affordable sliding scale, convenient evening sessions facililated by MD board-certified in psychiatry and family practice. Private consultations also available.

In fact an encouraging number of calls did come in, that day and all week, in sporadic clusters and singletons whose randomness composed itself into a spontaneous, elusive pattern. For a week he occupied himself happily offering details to the voices that asked him How much?, and When?, and Where?, and Do you take insurance? Next Wednesday evening, five people showed up in his living room. Jonathan sat crosslegged on the fringes of his Peruvian rug, finishing a preparatory breathing exercise and ignoring external stimuli. His five co-adventurers sat in the third-hand chairs he had bought from a coffeehouse that had gone bankrupt in the middle of the coffeehouse boom. The high-ceilinged loft was furnished with scattered islands of Danish Modern—a low sofa with a pole lamp, a pair of split-level teakwood end tables with zigzaggy table lamps—that might have decorated the set of some old *Playhouse 90* melodrama. On one wall was a lifesize poster of a matador killing a bull, captioned by a slogan in Spanish and a bottle of brandy. On the opposite wall, a tiny framed photograph of Lester Young playing saxophone sideways.

Jonathan reassured the fidgety participants with a transfixing gaze of nonattachment. Then he stood and told them what dreams were.

"We don't just dream at night. We're dreaming all the time, but so-called consciousness makes us unconscious of it. Daytime blocks it out like the sun blocking out the stars. The scientific evidence doesn't tell us this, of course. Brain-wave studies can't show that when we think we're awake, we're also still dreaming. But it's true. This morning you woke up and splashed water on your face and poured stimulants down your throat which effectively exiled you from the interesting half of your life. Within minutes you had completely forgotten your experiences—not 'dreams,' 'fantasies,' your *experiences*—of the night world. The alarm rang, the whip cracked over your head, your chains were locked in place before you knew what was happening to you. This is done to billions of people every day. This is a *political* crime. We are all internal exiles. We've been kidnaped from our homes. We're slaving for Pharaoh to build his pyramids, his tombs."

His closed his eyes and stood with head tipped back, palms extended outward, to show how at any point in so-called waking life one was free to enter the dreamtime.

"In this group we're not going to excavate and interpret—we don't commit that analytical sacrilege upon our own ancestral mind. Although what we do here *will* help us understand our dreams. What we do in this room is to *re-dream them*."

And he taught them how to do it. He explained that their goal was not to retell a dream like a story but to resume it like an experience. Narrating a dream aloud, they weren't to say, *I was in a house,* they were to say, *I'm in a house.* The purpose wasn't to realize that a house symbolized their mother's body—although if they spontaneously realized that, fine. The purpose was simply to go into the house again—rebuild it—and see what happened. Linger in the house, pace its rooms, inspect the pictures on the walls, remember its details. You notice a half-empty drink on the coffee table. Maybe there's a stale smell of smoke. How do you feel about being in the house? Are you happy, afraid, serene? Is it warm or chilly inside? Is someone hiding at the top of the stairs? And who are you who just entered: who is the dreamer? It doesn't matter if you make up the details at the point of narration, for the new details and those of last night come from the same place. Close your eyes when you retell a dream. If you want to stretch out on the floor, fine. If you want to, leap up and fight off monsters. If the sight of the house makes you scream, weep, tremble. Fine.

"I dreamed about a—excuse me," laughed a lanky woman with slightly buck teeth, "I mean, I'm on a ship, an ocean liner, and it's diving underwater and then it's becoming a whale."

"I'm diving too. I'm a whale—I dreamed I was a whale last night too," Jonathan said.

Now why did he say that? He hadn't dreamt he was a whale, not that he remembered. But he wasn't being dishonest. It came to life within him, this glad assertion of whaleness: his spout answers hers, the brow of her dream nudging the cetacean in his depths—perhaps even more meaningfully than if he'd genuinely dreamed of whales.

"I'm the whale and I'm watching the whale too," she said rhapsodically.

"I'm the whale," he incanted, "and I see another whale approaching on the distant horizon."

Suddenly she wavered downward like a heat shimmer in reverse, until she was stretched prone on the floor, and slithered forward like some flippered, flukey creature who has dared to try the land.

"The seas are drying," she moaned. She had some kind of half-outgrown hillbilly accent, and it gave her dream-chant the incongruity of the authentic. She wore blue jeans and a red plaid shirt, and had a braid of hair the color of wet straw, which was out of proportion to her thin, sharp-boned face, but in a memorable way.

"Whales need water," she called, as if ordering a Dr. Pepper and a pulled pork sandwich at a lunch counter. "Just 'cause I'm not a fish does that mean I don't need water?" And she began to sob.

Jonathan gave the others a glance of triumph. He refused to understand why they should look shocked or troubled or appalled.

He went to the kitchen, an open area in the far corner of the loft, and filled a glass with water. The slippery hardwood planks creaked under his bare feet. He knelt before her and brought the elixir—for if this wasn't a transmutation through alchemy, what was?—to her lips. She drank with thankful gasps. They hugged, gulping down oxygen in the unfamiliar atmosphere.

Brushing his pants off as he stood, Jonathan said, "Who else would like to recreate a dream this evening?" No one did. "Well, we're just about out of time anyway." And he wished them a good week, and they fled for the door. Except the lithe sea mammal, who swam up to him, shape-shifting into a woman at the last instant, and shook his hand in both of hers.

"I just want to thank you so much, this is going to be a wonderful experience. Another dream I had, I was going to this shaman? And he said to me, 'Lorna, now you must become a shaman too.' And I said, 'No, I don't have the right.' Now I know you're the one I dreamed about, and I believe you're going to make me a shaman too."

"Well, thanks," said Jonathan, and smiled, head up amid a swell of misgivings. She treaded toward the door, the straw-colored braid bobbing against the back of her red plaid shirt.

Next week, only two showed up for the group. In addition to the woman, who had introduced herself as Lorna Wineyard, there was Stan, a math professor whose wife, he explained, "…and, let's say, others—have told me—there's been a clustering of opinion recently—that I might benefit from a greater understanding of the emotional side of life."

"That's so brave!" Lorna said.

Jonathan professionally refrained from comment. "Well, would you like to start this session's dreams?" he challenged Stan.

Practically from the first syllable out of the poor mathematician's lips, Jonathan glazed over. He listened to the rain instead, to the healing drone of the torrent. The digital separateness of the drops blurred into a continuous analog tone that pulsed, if you listened long enough, pulsed like a sleeper's blood. Yet if you had ears to hear, you could pick out spikes in the pattern: a flinging against the window, a splattering on the lamppost. Was this what the struggle to become an individual amounted to: striving to be one of the few drops in the rainstorm whose fall was heard? Was it due to a raindrop's merit if it landed on a metal garbage can? Jonathan closed his eyes and reached out to the rain, and through visualization it massaged his skin.

"…I'm trying to order photocopies at the counter but the

clerk doesn't notice me...." Stan droned on in an embarrassed mumble.

Jonathan gave a loud, drawn-out groan. Startled, he shook himself open-eyed and made up a cover story: "Doesn't it make you want to complain out loud, when a sales clerk looks right past you?"

"He's giving me my change all in pennies," Stan went on. "You think the dream is telling me that I can change? Without getting my copies—without going through the duplication of day after day; without paying—without feeling that I have to suffer for each step forward?"

Lorna Wineyard, looking down with a well-informed smile, let the strap of her handbag fall from her shoulder. She opened the bag, an old bleach-spotted denim thing, and unzipped the little beaded Zuni purse she took from inside it, and stood up holding a penny to her breast. Her eyes shone. She walked up to Stan and, her arm uncurling outward in some totemic enactment of a flower meeting the sun, peeled open Stan's fingers, petal by petal, and placed the penny there.

"Here is your change," she said in exaltation.

Stan looked at the dark brown coin in his palm. Jonathan felt, in his own mouth, a taste of warm copper and sweat acids. Stan looked up at the knobs of Lorna's collarbone within her loose-necked shirt.

"Okay, let's take a break," Jonathan said, though it was well short of halfway through the session.

As expected, Stan, intoxicated with his initial success, ruined the rest of the hour by providing an enthusiastic flow of amateurishly analytical comments on the dreams served up by Lorna and Jonathan. When the session ended, Jonathan was depressed.

Stan approached to shake hands goodbye. "I had some reservations about your methodology, Dr. Grove, but if this gives me something to talk to my wife about, it's worth it for that alone."

Awkwardly Stan tried to slip his left arm into his damp raincoat sleeve while still using his right to shake hands. Jonathan, brushed by wet fabric, recoiled to the window and looked at the downpour falling through the street light.

Stan stepped up beside him to share the view and said innocently, "Would be a beautiful night if I didn't have to walk through it."

Jonathan found himself shrieking at the man. "You fucking moron, that's the kind of mind the City University of New York pays you to have? What do you know about a beautiful night or about walking through rain or snow or sleet or the pure sanctity of the northern lights? You think *numbers* are beautiful. People who think mathematics is beautiful know nothing about beauty. Who are you to tell us about the rain? The rain is not just wet, you know. The rain is never just wet."

And he was thinking, Am I too loud, and if I am, do I still care or not? Am I out of control yet, or still within the borders of control? If I can think this way, doesn't it mean I'm still in control; on the other hand, if thinking this way doesn't stop me from shrieking, doesn't it mean I'm out of control?

There was a last-second sweetness to it, like the moment before orgasm.

Stan had drained pale. He looked like a boy whose father has caught him trying on his mother's bra.

Lorna, having stopped on her way to the refrigerator, watched them with a glint of fascination, as if they were a nature documentary.

The following Wednesday, she alone showed up for the dream group.

They waited fifteen minutes, pretending someone else might show up. It was more a matter of hovering at a threshold. And then they crossed the threshold.

What dreams did they share that evening, and the Wednesday evenings afterward? Little point in recording them; Jonathan himself rarely kept track of the details. Frankly, his attention often wandered: he was too interested in looking at her, or in rehearsing his own dreams, to listen more than half the time to hers. What mattered was that in an upstairs loft on the Bowery, they inhabited a world of tigers and tempests, whispering fountains, soothsaying trees, naked salesclerks, Aztec priests, flying heads, and resurrected grandparents.

It was one of those stretches of New York weather when it rains every seven days, almost all season, like a declaration of a new sabbath. Every Wednesday night their flights through the solar system, their escapes from monsters, were reenacted to the drilling of a downpour on the sills. Jonathan had instituted the custom of serving a bottle of merlot at each session. He would light an aromatherapy candle, perhaps lavender or myrrh. Lorna Wineyard was the ex-wife of a dentist who paid her a generous maintenance. She arrived in dressier outfits for a couple of sessions, as if that was a way she had once learned of seducing men, and when Jonathan, quite deliberately, never complimented her on her outfits, she relapsed into bluejeans.

On the fourth or fifth Wednesday night, after the hour was up, healer and patient remained cross-legged on the floor, motionless except to turn to the rain in musing acknowledgment. The world was drenched but the dreamers were dry. Jonathan listened carefully: the rain would be saying something.

"Do you mind if I stay?" Lorna asked. "I'm afraid if I go back to my apartment it'll fall in on me."

So they took to dreaming side by side, on his double futon. The mattress lay on the floor, its scratchy green army-surplus blankets heaped slaglike after each night's quarrying. If he dug deep enough, Jonathan believed, they would uncover the one central dream which all others disguised. From then on, he and Lorna would always dream in unison, and every night it would be the one true dream.

Daytime was a dream of choking: he thrashed in a world where things refused enhancement. Obdurate and unhelpful, trees and buildings remained trees and buildings, and all birds sang one note.

His ad kept running in the paper, and once in a while, a new face showed up at the dream group, but since the introductory session was offered free, no new income came from those arrivals. They never reappeared for a second session. It would have been like intruding on a couple in bed.

"But you have regular office hours, too," Lorna encouraged. "What if when the holidays come around, more folks get sick and you get lots of new patients?"

"Who? The ones who throw a dart at the Yellow Pages and it hits my listing? I lost my admitting privileges at Beth Israel for making a scene with the chief of internal medicine. The other hospitals followed suit: administrators talk to each other, you know, they have a network, they blacklisted me, basically. All last year I was relying on referrals from friends. Then last year I went for a walk in the snow...."

Lorna looked puzzled. "You went for a walk in the snow and they stopped liking you?"

Jonathan cleared his throat. "It was up in New Hampshire, in the White Mountains. I was there skiing with—someone. Anyway, we had an argument, a terrible quarrel, you'll be glad to know."

"I'm not glad to know that, Jonathan."

He laughed. "Anyway, afterwards, I felt like I had to do something to tip myself either toward one side or the other, destruction or salvation. I want you to understand, I wasn't trying to commit suicide. I was putting mytself through an extreme test to see whether I could activate a powerful enough self-healing *chi*. I put on a robe and slippers and shuffled out of the inn at one in the morning and walked up a hiking trail in the snow and sat under a tree, some kind of pine or evergreen. And I sat in a meditative posture, although I wasn't actually meditating. And I decided, I'm just going to wait and see what happens. If I live, I'll be vastly strengthened, and if I die, then that was what was suitable."

Jonathan felt Lorna's hand cover his. He glanced down, ashamed to welcome her sympathy, but aroused by her sallow, thin fingers with their short, plain nails, their dry, prematurely wrinkled skin.

"I lived," he said, "but I wasn't strengthened. I sat there, at first freezing and shivering, then calm and strangely warm. Early symptoms of hypothermia, of course. I'd just started to drift off to sleep when a sheriff's deputy shone a flashlight in my eyes. They had a whole team of rescuers out to search for me—the sheriff's office and fire department, both. And it wasn't the woman I was with who called 911; she displayed no curiosity whatsoever as to why I'd left the room at one in the morning in my robe and slippers. The night clerk saw me wandering around downstairs and then saw my footprints when he went out for a smoke. He waited to call—he was uncertain, you know—but finally he called my room and when I wasn't there, called the emergency squad."

"Good thing he smoked, it saved your life."

"Yeah, so I was taken on a stretcher to their local hospital and then transferred down to NYU, where the staff were my colleagues, and I missed a couple of months of work, and when I got back on my feet, my referrals had dried up. Now I have to rely on whatever I can scratch up for myself."

With devout pity, which was sometimes all Jonathan thought he really needed, Lorna massaged the back of his hand with her thumb, stretching and smoothing the skin on its rack of metacarpal bones with an untrained concentration that was better than an expert stranger's touch.

"Why didn't someone do this for me last year?" he said. "Or thirty years ago?"

And the sweet self-display of his questions, as if overheard from outside, like the wail of an injured cat, made him suddenly moisten and, before he could debate whether to control it, overflow with coughing tears.

"Baby," she said, and wrapped his head in her arms.

The scents of knitted cotton and of hours-old antiperspirant and of woman's shaven skin rose to him with wondrous power. He let himself go all the way, sobbing, wetting the armcrook of her plum sweater, rubbing his nose back and forth to smell the dampened fabric. He could have laughed with joy at the sight of himself weeping freely. Yes, an upswing was overdue. He could count on the collective mind to send him some new patients soon, to help pay his bills, to keep hope alive a few months nearer to the time when he wouldn't have to keep hope alive anymore, when he could honorably claim to have seen his lifespan through.

In midwinter, Jonathan was sitting at his desk on a weekday morning, no patients in view and none expected, trying to estimate how long he could keep his practice open. Every time he tapped the numbers into his calculator, it gave him a different result. He didn't understand why civilization had not collapsed after the spread of this invention. Entries cleared themselves without his permission, or inscribed themselves in the memory without his willing it, perseverating on the screen through some silicate repetition-compulsion; correct sums, arrived at through the most tortuous retracings, faded when a cloud blocked the sun from reaching the photoelectric cell.

He burbled his lips with his fingers, a light moment in a performance of his life. "Not much left in the old portfolio. May have to give notice to the landlord before too long."

Lorna, looking over his shoulder (he commended himself on having the patience not to scream away this distraction), said, "Couldn't you rent a smaller office and sleep on the couch?"

Not screaming but laughing: "Don't you take me seriously? You see this calculator? Do you see these numbers? They're telling me the truth, something no human being has ever done." And he pounded his fists into the sides of his head, not knowing whether it was he or his delusion that was doing it, or whether there was a difference. If he hit himself often enough, would she cry for him? He shook the calculator in her face. "This incorruptible source of truth, this giver of precise answers…." He glanced at the digital display—it had reverted to zero. He threw the thing against the wall and, feeling how a sensitive electronic device would feel on being hurled into a wall, screamed with pain. The gray casing broke; a black gouge mark streaked the white wall. Jonathan sank to the floor, folded into his own arms.

Another hurdle that Lorna passed. She pulled him up and said, "Let me see," lifting her chin toward the folders of financial records.

She spent all that day figuring with a pencil and writing notes to herself on a steno pad. She sent Jonathan out for a restorative walk—just the fact that she trusted him that far was therapeutic. He stopped outside a pharmacy he knew, and wrote himself a prescription for four-milligram dilaudid tablets, often effective in staving off psychosis. And one for percocet with codeine, as a backup. He was admirably calm when he got home.

"You have enough capital to live for six months to two years," she said, "depending how you live and where."

"I do?" He was disappointed to be so solvent.

"Here's your strategy. You can survive in New York if I give up my apartment and help with the rent here. You're going to modernize your practice by getting back to basics. You'll still do all your wellness and psychiatry, but you have to do all the unglamorous little things too: runny noses, backaches, headaches, footaches, any ailment or infirmity that any human soul has within the greater metropolitan area, you will come to their aid and assistance on a walk-in basis. You, Dr. Jonathan Grove, are a pioneer in walk-in medicine, a brand-new field where people don't have to make appointments in advance and join some Big Brother health plan to exercise their right to the very best care. The problem is, though, why pioneer this brand-new field where rent's expensive, and there are already a million doctors? What you want to do is move to some other part of the country where nobody knows you. You start over again like Dr. Just-Out-of-Med-School-Wanting-to-Help-the-Poor. Someplace where there aren't enough doctors and most of the patients are on Medicare. East Tennessee-Kentucky's really pretty, prettier than the Catskills."

He looked down at his shoes and said very quietly, "You have to go with me."

"I'm going with you. I'm going every step." She sounded as if she had just maneuvered the captain of the football team into asking her to dance.

"Me in a cabin in the Smokies. I'll be fishing by the crick, shoes off, chawin' on my straw hat, and you'll ring the dinner bell to tell me that Mrs. McIntyre feels her time a-comin' on."

"I'll page you, sweetface, or call you on the cell phone. Everybody with a steady job's got one, so their wives can tell them what video to rent on the way home."

"Then I must get one too, so you can call me to emergency surgery while I'm off a-tendin' my still. And I'll page any durn revenuer who tries to hunt on my land, and when he's reaching into his car window for his cell phone I'll shoot him full o' buckshot."

"You're blending in already," she said, laughing at his accent. And she did a sprightly half-twirl, extending her arms like a fashion model displaying a blouse. "See, what you want to do, if you're crazy, is wear something so it doesn't show."

He learned that she set her alarm for six-thirty in the morning, on a principle of healthy living, although she didn't begin working till nine and didn't have to leave her room or get dressed to do so. She had a home-based job taking telephone orders for a consortium of less-well-known retail catalogues: surplus military equipment for domestic freedom fighters; hand-whittled toys and rocking chairs from Vermont's traditional craftspeople; individually designed dolls representing the eras of American history in a rainbow of ethnic hues and costumes; mail-order apparel for the shy transvestite; and much more, each catalogue with its own code number so that the militia member lusting for a twelve-inch Navy Seals underwater combat knife with serrated, super-light alloy blade and nonslip grip, for instance, wouldn't receive, by mistake, a slinky, shantung silk housedress with slit calves and plunging neckline, size extra-extra large, and red high-heel pumps, 14-EEEE. Lorna's phone rang all day, in the unpartitioned bedroom corner where she had set up her computer.

"First, could you tell me the catalogue number which you'll find in the upper right corner of your address label?"

Jonathan spent the mornings practicing reiki techniques, spreading his fingers over his facial pressure points as he looked in the mirror at the always startlingly scowl-lined, jowled, inscrutable middle-aged man who looked back.

"Now, sir, could you give me the page number of your first purchase?"

He made a thermosful of valerian tea each morning, a mild sedative that sometimes proved effective in reducing the stress of narcotic withdrawal, and by afternoon naptime he was faced with the question of whether to brew a second pot.

"We do have that item in stock, what quantity will that be?"

If there were no patients (a phrase he always strove to insert mentally before the day's malingering), he took it upon himself to help Lorna set up her new quarters: the bookcase and CD tower where she kept her discs of solace, tapes of encouragement, books with underlinings in many colors from many insight-harried nights, urging her to coax forth her inner voices, set out on daring paths, and prepare to receive miracles.

"It looks like we don't have the carbon-steel ninja sticks in stock right now, but I can back-order them for you if you'd like, and of course that does *not* get billed to your credit card until shipped."

He rehung her posters and samplers and plaques in his office and kitchen and bathroom, all of them bearing optimistic slogans that he felt obliged to try to live by. And he did, didn't he? That was the maddening part, he tried to live by every one.

"And shall I bill that to the Louisville address? I'm from Kentucky myself and I'm just trying so hard to get back home. My husband, he's a physician, a wellness specialist in Manhattan?, but we're looking for a rural practice he can buy, someplace where they really need the medical care and he can help out?"

My husband. What had she meant by that? Walking past her work corner with the air of someone who hadn't heard a thing, Jonathan incredulously replayed those two dreaded words as if to determine whether or not he had really heard them. Not wanting to interrupt while she was on the phone, he let the label go unchallenged; and that made it true, didn't it? They had never talked about getting married, but now they were; the caller, some horse-country paranoiac with a basement full of exotic weapons, his backyard glittering with pistol-blasted bourbon-bottle shards, was their witness.

How life grows heavier with a single word! He felt discontented, trapped, resentful, since that was the natural state of marriage.

Evenings were devoted to Lorna's researches into the state of rural health care. Logging on to public-health services and newsgroups, she obtained statistics for those American counties with the lowest ratios of physicians to population; discovering online trade magazines and professional journals, she pored over the classified ads in search of practices for sale. These she correlated with statistics for crime rate, cost of living, air and water quality, educational opportunities, and real estate values. On her little boombox tape deck, she played country songs—"Easy From Now On" was one she played over and over, in both Emmylou Harris' and Carlene Carter's recordings. Jonathan preferred Carlene's version: swinging blonde mane and rangy, fringed buckskin. Surely the hollows and peaks of Appalachia were dotted with divorcees aching to make his life easy; but he'd tip his hat, smiling, and tell them, "Thank you, ma'am, I've already got one."

But whenever Lorna hit upon a potential new location, there turned out to be something wrong with it. The community clinic outside Knoxville had recently been bombed. The storefront office in Pike County was in a high-crime area where drug deals were made in the convenience-store parking lot and motelkeepers stayed behind bulletproof glass.

"I thought we're just looking for some shitty old practice to buy," he said.

Yes, but it had to be the finest shitty old practice in fifty states, fully furnished with the memorabilia of a beloved old general practitioner's lifetime of service, right down to the well-worn porch rocker Jonathan could slide into as if he'd broken it in himself; cheap enough so that two or three patients a day would pay a live-lihood; bucolic enough so that it would be a pleasure to see no one at all. While Lorna occupied her spring and summer with the search, Jonathan didn't know how seriously to conduct his current prac-tice, how much to widen it, since he was going to pack up and quit soon anyway.

He ran a second ad; this one disclosed, in desperate essence, that he would accept any patient with any complaint, no matter how minor or demeaning, without inquiring into financial status. As a result he treated a homeless man for scabies: no payment, and Jonathan had to shell out for a preventative dose of Kwell for him-self and Lorna too. And there was the runny-nosed teenager (and, a few days later, his friends) with self-diagnosed back pain who knew exactly how many hits of exactly which synthetic opiates would help him. And the woman who claimed that a previous doctor had sewn live rats into her alimentary canal: at least she plunked down cash, and insisted on numerous examinations.

Almost the whole calendar was clear, but Wednesday evenings were kept free on purpose for the dream group. Jonathan didn't dream much anymore; the sessions consisted entirely of Lorna act-ing out, and of starting and finishing bottles of wine. Sometimes he toyed with the idea of writing a book on dream analysis. One night, after dream group, he got as far as creating a new document on his word processor and typing, "[Untitled Dream Book] by Jonathan Grove, M.D." Staring at the letters after his name, he felt a welling disgust. He could scarcely remember what "M.D." stood for anymore, or how the initials had gotten there. He went to bed with the somewhat pleasant expectation that he might not wake up.

But at two in the morning, he sat up in bed forcing himself not to scream. He had never had a pain like this in his life. Big waves breaking over him, drenching his forehead. Each wave started as a twinge in his intestines, but rapidly spread around his waist like a belt being squeezed tight and knotted in the small of his back. It squeezed till he could not take any more without crying aloud, and then it relaxed its grip and let him breathe. Pancreatitis, nephritis, drug withdrawal, abdominal migraine? He didn't know. And like a pain-echo, the thought flashed through him: he was *free* not to know.

"Lorna. Lorna." He murmured her name with each pain-wave, comforted by not being responded to: perhaps the oldest, most familiar sensation in his life.

He staggered to the office area at the other end of the loft, and turned on the desk lamp, and riffled spasmodically through his old textbooks on nephrology and endocrinology and oncology, but there was nothing—or there was everything. His pain could have been almost anything, but didn't fit any single diagnostic code—none that Western medicine could recognize, anyway. Even the psychiatric section didn't give him an answer.

Sitting on the edge of the bed, he palpated his lower back emphatically. And something brushed his arm, his cheek: it was the trailing fabric of a dream, breeze-stirred in the act of leaving, like the hem of a woman's nightgown. By straining to remember it, he forgot it, but he knew it had been life-asserting and reassuring, to warn against and fight off the pancreatic pain (he was guessing pancreatitis for the time being).

The dream was a symptom, he knew, and if he were consulting an acupuncturist, some wisely half-smiling, wrinkled, yellow-skinned, smoke-mustached sage, that uncorrupted healer would link the dream to the sensation of imminent recurrence in Jonathan's midsection, the empty expectancy not exactly in his kidneys but surrounding them, and would know exactly where to aim his drugless darts.

He felt so tired he needed to cry. Silently, so as not to wake his lover, he let himself weep and shake.

"It's passing, it's passing," he whispered, and with the pain, all knowledge seemed to pass from him too, in a great purging which, a few minutes afterward, he followed up with a resounding evacuation of his bowels. He felt the medical knowledge fly out of him like a dove flying in search of land. He tried to remember random facts—the bones of the hand, the stages of meiosis—and couldn't even begin. Giving himself a mental anatomy quiz from head to foot, he found no names, only the irritable feeling that he used to know them. What was the differential diagnosis for pediatric seizure disorders? What were the types and typical onset-ages of schizophrenia?

"It's all gone," he muttered as he paced the loft. "It's all over."
Then he shouted to wake Lorna: "It's all over, you can stop now!"

She stretched and moaned. "Last night I dreamed...."

"Who cares what you dreamed?" he said. Which part of him
had said it, he didn't know. A lurking jester-self, dashing out from
the shadows while his main self was distracted, had usurped his
speech center. Maybe she would think she had dreamed that, too.

Then he had a memory of—no, it was what he was actually doing
in the present—walking to the Delancey Street district office of
Social Security, on a day so smudged, so soured by its own inability
to rain, that the picturesque anachronisms of the Lower East Side
and their clashing postpunk embroiderings were merely transient
patterns of color and shape; and of waiting before a maze of glass
partitions, among people so shabby and rubbed-out they must have
much to teach him.

The case officer, Mr. Fetterman, was a bald man with red
curls on the temples of a bullet head, and eyeglasses with black
frames. Not much older than Jonathan, he wore the stunned and
smugly narcotized look of someone whose life had been saved by a
craze for conformity, and who, in the precious moments between
clients, might drum on his desktop to the remembered beat of old
heavy-metal tunes.

"What is this?" Fetterman said, holding Jonathan's application form away from himself. "What exactly are you asking us to
d   o   ?   "

"I'm applying for Supplemental Security Income," Jonathan heard
himself say, as if through an echo chamber on John Lennon's worst
recording session.

"I see that." Mr. Fetterman, who obviously could never have
done well enough on the MCATs to even consider a medical career, looked Jonathan up and down.

"I'm psychiatrically unable to work."

"That's what you put down here. And you are by profession...?"

"A physician."

"Yes." Fetterman nodded, confirming what he had read.
"You're a doctor, and you can't find anything to do."

"I'm psychiatrically unable to work; I have schizo-affective disorder with major depressive episodes and obsessive ideational content."

"That's a pretty professional-sounding diagnosis, Doctor," Fetterman said.

Trapped, Jonathan sagged in despair.

Fetterman said, "In order to receive assistance in the category you have requested, you must obtain a notarized affidavit from your physician."

"I am my physician. I'd be glad to write a statement on my letterhead and get it notarized."

"I'm a notary public," Fetterman one-upped with an insouciant wave. "But listen, are you telling me that as a licensed practitioner of medicine you're telling us that you are incapable of practicing medicine?"

"Yes."

"But by doing that you're practicing medicine, aren't you?"

Jonathan tried to look as genially civic-minded, as unshaken by the weight of social policy on his shoulders, as Fetterman himself. However, his legs wobbled and his stomach was miserable.

"Dr. Grove," Fetterman said with a weary grimace of goodfellowship, sweeping his hand over his hairless skull, "I don't know how well you keep up with current events, but doctors are needed in this world. I sympathize with the fact that you have personal troubles. I can believe that you yourself would benefit from consulting your own physician."

"I've been...," he tried to explain. "I've been to the hospital, to their clinics...." And I've learned that only I can heal myself, he thought. This persuasive-sounding sentence, which he was turning in his mind so as to make even finer, did not emerge from his mouth.

"Whatever," Mr. Fetterman said open-mindedly. "You're a young man in apparently good physical health and if you, as a licensed physician, think you don't need to see someone, who am I to disagree? What I'm saying is, Dr. Grove, there are many kinds of doctors that are needed. If you don't like being one kind, be another. Go to the jungle, be a doctor in the jungle. Be a doctor on a cruise ship, take a vacation at the same time. The prisons need doctors, the military needs doctors, oil pipelines and refugee camps and boxing commissions need doctors—do you follow my train of thought?"

"Yes. I've sometimes imagined—"

"Great. Keep imagining, and then put it into effect. That's my prescription," Fetterman added with a smirk. "Now, thank you for coming in." He stood up sharply, and gave Jonathan a firm but light handshake intended to instill confidence in some other kind of client.

That he lived in a world where *he* was permitted to practice medicine seemed to Jonathan the ultimate grotesquerie. From out of nowhere the sun had begun to shine. And who were these people walking toward him, beside him, with him? Heeding Fetterman with a vengeance, Jonathan turned them into patients.

"How would you rate the pain from one to ten?" he asked a wizened woman with a cane, who stopped in fright until he backed away.

"Any dizziness when you get out of bed?" he asked a wiry, short man unloading cartons from a moving van.

"I've seen a lot of that going around lately," he told the woman who had stopped against a traffic signal box to search through her address book for a missed appointment. "It's practically an epidemic."

The supreme healer does not merely trudge the path of his training; he invents a new specialty: the roving diagnostician, the inquiring practitioner. He has transcended the occidental categories of sick and well, of mind and body; the DSM-IV has turned to dust within him, to soil in which new diagnostic flowers will grow.

By the time he reached home he could hardly keep track of all the consultations he had done. "Did you go for a walk?" Lorna asked, turning from her phone console. He was prepared to shamble and evade by way of answer, but before he'd begun she was happily waving a computer printout. "I found it. Our home. Twelve acres of cleared land and forest abutting a trout stream in southern Missouri. Doctor's office is in the house, which comes with all the furnishings—he died of a heart attack last month, only sixty. I've talked to the realtor and a mortgage guy. It's a well-established practice, Jonathan, you wouldn't have to start from scratch, all his patients are just waiting for you to come in and take over. Can't you feel it right away, that this is the one we're meant to get, this is what we had to go through all the near-misses to get to?"

No, you can't go to Missouri, if you step on the sidewalk-crack of a state line you'll die. He shuffled to the frameless mattress in the floor in the corner, and fell into a recuperative trance.

All the rest of that dismal afternoon, as resentful clouds hulked and threatened across lower Manhattan, Jonathan felt his vital essence drain out of him. He could feel his surface skin cells slough off and blow away like windblown paper.

And what happened next must have been a memory, for everything was memory now, even while it was still happening. He stood at the window and opened it. He rubbed his cheek with the backs of his fingers. His cheek was smooth, and he was thinking that if he could force himself to stand motionless at that window until he felt the whiskers grow, he would be saved.

He used to stand at his parents' apartment window as a little child, high above West End Avenue, and think that if he jumped down and went splat, he wouldn't die but would become the same as all the other people he saw walking down below: a little bug-sized spot with arms and legs, happy to be walking down the street.

As he was thinking of that child, trying to call to that child—and trying to decide whether to call, "Jump!" or "Don't jump!"—Lorna slipped in under his elbow, between him and the open window. She kissed so strongly, he couldn't have pushed her away.

"We can do it if you want to," she dared him. She was unzipping her jeans. "But we have to do it together." She was unzipping his. "Locked together just like this. Docked like two spaceships. We can fly out the window together. We might land two seconds later, but for those two seconds we'll fly. Is that what you want to do? If you say so, I'll do it."

She half-sat on the sill and pulled him to her. She slipped onto him and held him back from his desire at the same time. There was the wide-open window and he couldn't get to it.

"No, you don't want to do that," she murmured to him, as if saying, *Take one teaspoon three times a day.* "I didn't think you really wanted to. We're going to start a new life in a new place. Trust me to make it good for you. You can be as crazy as you want, just as long as you're here to be it. I know all about this, I used to sit in the garage with my mama when she talked to Martians on the car radio. Stay inside the window and I'll take care of you. I can have all the contact with the outside world; you don't have to do anything you don't want, ever again. You don't have to see one single patient. I'll be your only patient. Just let me be your enabler."

He stretched his neck so he could see over her shoulder, out to the sky, out to the street. "Those two seconds would be worth everything else."

"We'll make our whole life those two seconds. It won't matter *when* we hit the ground. Sixty years from now, and it'll be those two seconds."

"I'm not just playing eccentric," he warned. "I don't do a little for fun and then go back. I don't stop ninety-nine percent of the way there. This is a journey to the center of the earth. There's no intermediate destination. All right? Do you understand me yet, can you give me your understanding, have you heard what you came to hear?"

And it came to him at the last instant: what if this—everything, this strip show, this woman, his medical career since age twenty-one—was not an actuality but a premonition? Maybe he was still a teenager and, in a flash of stress, had anticipated the wreck that his life would become if he followed this route. (Was he really back in 1979, taking a math test? Was he trying to ask a girl for a date?) A lucky warning to himself—good thing he was so foresightful. He would erase this entire disastrous possibility and choose a more auspicious path instead. There was still time.

He wept as usual in his orgasm, wept as the possible lives flooded out of him. He sagged heavily on her, testing how far backward into the window she would go, and she kept her feet planted.

"I hear," she said, with a hug that was stern and tough and grateful. "Do you hear, baby, that you found me? You found the person who'll hear whatever you say...."

But that, too, had to be trumped.

Jonathan, in the dark loft edged with pinkish street light, smiled down at Lorna as she slept on the futon mattress, and imagined the life of complete understanding, complete unembarrassment, that she saw for them. And he began to feel that the madstone in him had been expelled, and that in the morning they would optimistically discuss how to prepare for a move to an unknown state, a second-hand office. But he recognized that as part of his delusory system.

He couldn't burden someone like her with someone like him.

He spent several minutes in the bathroom, getting the big syringe and the rubber tubing, and reconstituting with tap water (which was all he needed for his purpose) the 500-milligram vial of high-potency dilaudid that he'd stolen when he still had hospital privileges. This was his emergency dose, the needle the parachutist pricks his finger with when captured in enemy territory, the ampule the spy bites open to avoid torture. Sitting on the corner of the futon, careful not to rock the mattress and wake her, he did himself up. Slowly, you had to press the plunger slowly. He lay down with his forehead touching hers and practiced breathing. In and out, slow, measured lungsful, with all the time in the world.

Then there was no longer any distance between New York and the Ozarks, between today and tomorrow, and although he was looking down on the loft from a vast height, seeing the woman asleep on the mattress from a hundred stories above, it could not really be said that there was up and down. Rather than space, there was a choral hum. Inhuman voices, never needing breath, shifted tones unnoticeably. Jonathan moved closer—although what that meant, he couldn't have said—and heard the song only the dying can sing: *I don't want to die.* He was singing too.

Lightning twitched his leg; the whole sky flooded white, with a thrill like endless falling. White light would fill the sky for as long as he could watch it. He could stay in it forever, falling in the same place. The choral hum was spreading into separate parts, like stars in an expanding universe. Jonathan was one of those stars, burning with terror and joy, which are, he now knew, the only states of existence.

Or he could go down a passageway to forgetting. Was the white light dissolving? And if so, did that mean he wanted it to? It seemed that as soon as you thought of its dissolving, it began to dissolve. Or had everything been this way from the beginning, so that a man, a woman, a building, a street, had existed only the way a dragon exists in a cloud shaped like a dragon?

He was alone among the sown, dispersing stars, and always had been. He looked at the world of man-woman-building-street as if it were inside him, as if his navel enclosed it. Yet he couldn't return to it. Did he envy it, did he pity it? The words, with their feelings, crumbled when he tried to touch them.

He saw people walking, people crying, people persisting and desisting and moaning and aching from the constant strain, the isometric presure of soul against flesh, of soul and flesh to fit into one space. Was he seeing this, or remembering it, or anticipating it? Was he in fact an unborn soul who had not yet done these things? Was he dissolving into flesh?

Don't worry, he told the man-woman-building-street world. Dissolution will not be the end of your existence. It will not even be the end of fear of dissolution.

But it will be the end of sadness. There could be no sadness amid pure terror and joy, and so there could be no Jonathan.

What would he become next? The question blew around him, a whirlwind in a vacuum, a foreknowledge of lives, and nausea overcame him like the feeling of having too many lovers. He didn't want to be flesh again. He didn't really believe that was happening. (The word *believe* crumbled as he tried to touch it. The word *happening* crumbled as he tried to touch it.) Being flesh is too much for a soul to bear. Just as a human being, permitted to live in only one era and dwell in only one land and work at only one task, feels confined and bound and kept from growing into his true shape, so the soul feels confined and bound and kept by being in flesh.

The woman: where would she go? What would become of her?

If he could have remembered which were the preferable answers, he would have wished them.

He stepped to a brink where all questions jumped into ecstasy.

Lorna, don't cry! You have no lover, but he loves you. (Waking up in the morning with her forehead touching a cold forehead. Seeing the empty syringe on the bed, the rubber tube kicked to the floor by a last leg-spasm.)

Lightning upon lightning, the fibers of himself flashed. The current lit him for as long as he could keep thinking about it. He had been sitting on a mattress beside a sleeping woman, but now he couldn't remember her name. He had been—but now he couldn't remember what he had been doing. He—but now he couldn't remember *he*.

Nonexistence folds upon itself to become existence: a dream that dreams itself. It was the next moment and billions of years later. Charged filaments frayed and raveled into free-floating packages of light. A rumor was coming true, though whose rumor? The rumor burned in every star, and if it came true, everything that went before would disappear. What was left was only The Thought that Thought Itself. That's what it all was. It had always been here. It could never be seen. It flung its net so far and stretched so thin that it broke and became solid. Over everything, it flung the shining net of dream.

Other Pleasure Boat Studio Books:

Orders

Pleasure Boat Studio fulfills orders placed by
telephone, fax, e-mail, or mail.
Response time is immediate.
Free shipping on pre-paid orders.
Send check, money order, Visa/Mastercard to:

Pleasure Boat Studio
8630 Wardwell Road
Bainbridge Island • WA 98110-1589 USA
Tel-Fax: 888.810.5308
E-mail: pleasboat@aol.com
URL: http://www.pbstudio.com
Terms and conditions:
standard to the trade and available upon request.
SAN: 299-0075

Pleasure Boat Studio
Books & Chapbooks are also distributed by:

Small Press Distribution
Tel 800.869.7553 • Fax 510.524.0852
Baker & Taylor
Tel 800.775.1100 • Fax 800.775.7480
Koen Pacific
Tel 206.575.7544 • Fax 206.575.7444
Partners/West
Tel 425.227.8486 • Fax 425.204.2448
Brodart
Tel 800.233.8467 • Fax 800.999.6799
Ingram
Tel 800.937.8000 • Fax 800.876.0186

from *Pleasure Boat Studio*
an essay written by Ouyang Xiu,
Song Dynasty poet, essayist, and scholar,
on the twelfth day of the twelfth month
in the *renwu* year (January 25, 1043)

*I have heard of men of antiquity who fled from the world to distant
rivers and lakes and refused to their dying day to return. They must
have found some source of pleasure there. If one is not anxious for
profit, even at the risk of danger, or is not convicted of a crime and
forced to embark; rather, if one has a favorable breeze and gentle seas
and is able to rest comfortably on a pillow and mat, sailing several
hundred miles in a single day, then is boat travel not enjoyable? Of
course, I have no time for such diversions. But since 'pleasure boat' is
the designation of boats used for such pastimes, I have now adopted it
as the name of my studio. Is there anything wrong with that?*

Translated by Ronald Egan
THE LITERARY WORKS OF OU-YANG HSIU
Cambridge University Press

About the Author

Richard Cohen was born and raised in the Bronx, New York. He graduated with a degree in anthropology from the University of Michigan, where he won the Hopwood Award for short fiction. He sold his first novel, *Domestic Tranquility,* the day he was scheduled to begin law school, so he immediately dropped out. Since then he has published two more novels (*Say You Want Me* and *Don't Mention the Moon*) as well as a book on the writing craft (*Writer's Mind: Crafting Fiction*). The father of two grown children, he lives in Austin, Texas, with his new family.